Strike the Match

MADISON MYERS

Copyright © 2025 by Madison Myers, Creativity Ink LLC

All rights reserved.

No part of this publication may be reproduced, distributed, or transmitted in any form or by any means, including photocopying, recording, or other electronic or mechanical methods, without the prior written permission of the publisher, except in the case of brief quotations embodied in critical reviews and certain other noncommercial uses permitted by copyright law. It is illegal to copy this book, post it to a website, or distribute it by any other means without permission.

Any references to historical events, real people, or real places are used fictitiously. Names, characters, and places are products of the author's imagination. Any resemblance to actual persons, living or dead, events or localities is entirely coincidental.

Front cover design by Ink and Laurel Designs

Proofreading by Juli Burgett

First printing edition 2025.

www.madisonmyersauthor.com

PLAYLIST

Love Somebody – Morgan Wallen
Trust Issues – Emei
Hey Lovely – Chance Peña
Project – Chase McDaniel
Sweetest Thing – Allman Brown
Shackles – Steven Rodriguez
You're Gonna Go Far – Noah Kahan
I'm With You – Vance Joy
Take It Slowly – Garrett Kato
willow – Taylor Swift
madly – Emily Vaughn, Joseph Tilley, we're ok!
Like You Mean It – Steven Rodriguez
Little Bit Better – Caleb Hearn, ROSIE
Lavender Haze – Taylor Swift
Small Town Boy – Dustin Lynch
Hold My Girl (Acoustic Version) – George Ezra
Hollow - Acoustic – Belle Mt.
Can't Help Falling in Love – Kacey Musgraves
ROOM FOR 2 – Benson Boone
Everywhere, Everything – Noah Kahan

PLAYLIST

colorblind – Mokita
I'll Be Around – Garrett Kato
Old Dirt Roads – Owen Riegling
Colour Me – Juke Ross
closest to heaven – Ella Langley
Home – Good Neighbours
Fall Into Me – Forest Blakk
Carry You Home – Alex Warren

*For the girls with dark senses of humor.
We deserve HEAs too.*

AUTHOR'S NOTE

There are some darker elements in this story, including a fair bit of focus on (mostly fictional but gory) true crime, as well as a dark past that gets uncovered. Please proceed with caution. It also contains explicit content.

While this book can be read as a standalone, there will be some spoilers for the first book in the series, so if you plan on reading *Rekindling the Flame*, I recommend you read it before starting this one. It is available on Kindle Unlimited and for purchase on Amazon and select retailers.

1
Weston

It kills me to say this, but this is the last blowjob I'll be getting for the foreseeable future.

And for a guy like me, that's a big fucking deal.

What's a guy like me? That's a guy who's never been able to find anyone who sparks so much as a twitch anywhere above the cock.

Someone who wishes he could be set—like my brother—with the girl he always knew he was meant for, his whole life laid out for him from a young age.

If only I could be so lucky.

Unfortunately, I'm broken.

In a stranger's apartment, halfway to coming down her throat, and it's doing nothing for me aside from the obvious. Not even the sight of her blonde hair spilled out over my thighs, or the hot noises she's making are making my blood pump any faster.

Nah, the only thing that makes my heart race is the thrill of a new chase, a new adventure. The boredom that creeps in and under my skin minutes after hooking up with someone new keeps me running, chasing the next new thing before my veins start to itch from the feeling of being captured.

Shit, the closest thing I've ever felt to what my brother Wyatt and his wife Rory have is a burrito that was so good I never wanted to let go of it.

It gave me food poisoning on the way out of my system. Fate couldn't even let me have *that* moment.

So my reputation as a heartbreaker in our small hometown might have been earned through an appetite for variety in the bedroom (the kind that's hard to satiate in a town of less than five thousand), but it's not my fault I don't get attached to my partners. I don't mislead them, it just happens. They catch feelings, and I don't. It's why I've spent much of my adult life on the open road, free from labels and judgement, the kind that my brother is full of.

And why is this my last blowie? Well, that's because this dumb fuck (still me) agreed to go *back* to said hometown for that very foreseeable future at his sister-in-law's request. And once I'm there, not only will there be a painfully limited selection of women, but my brother has made it all too clear I'm not to break a single heart during my stay. Which, if I were to read between the lines, meant keep it in my pants. I don't need another reason for him to hate me, to think of me as the fuckup little brother, so I plan to stick to his rules.

Basically, it all means I'm making the most of this moment, this mouth wrapped around my cock, this nameless woman bobbing on my lap, doing her best to suck more than half of me in and failing spectacularly.

I wrap my hand around the back of her head, threading my fingers through her honeyed hair to guide her down further—satisfaction rising in me at the way she moans as I take control—until I feel the back of her throat close around me.

That's more like it.

The feel of my release, hot against the soft insides of her mouth, scratches the itch, but only for a minute.

I've barely repaid the favor—gentleman that I am—kissed her cheek in farewell and made it back to my current abode all alone again before the itch of boredom is already seeping in and under my skin once again.

This is my fate. It's less of a curse, more of a burden. I know others out there have worse crosses to bear, but this is mine.

Never enough.

The need for more never sated.

Unfortunately, there's no *more* to be had where I'm headed.

A LONG DIRT road with only acres and acres of half-bare trees as my witness. If it weren't for my sister-in-law and her older sister at the other end of this path, I might be tempted to do something stupid when I get up there.

If I get up there.

The streaky light of early evening comes through the mix of pines and deciduous, their light green leaves just starting to bud and form, the first touches of spring well and truly blooming here in the Smoky Mountains.

Somehow I turned a five-hour drive into an all-day affair, I'm a bit later than maybe I should be, but I haven't been exactly chomping at the bit to come back to Smoky Heights, or the Heights, as the locals call it.

Being back for a few months doesn't make me a local. This isn't home.

I don't have a home anymore.

I go wherever I can find work when I need it. Wherever looks interesting.

Wyatt would, and probably has, called me flaky. I would say I'm just not tied down. Able to go where the wind takes me, just how I like it. Some fresh scent is on the air, I follow it.

All the trails out there I could be chasing, and somehow I let my sister-in-law Rory talk me into a several-month stint painting interiors of all the revamped and brand-new shops, homes, and businesses here in the Heights as part of their grand reopening of downtown.

Rory's the head of a whole project that's breathing new life into this place. She's pretty passionate about it, I guess that's how she won me over.

And if *she* can come back here and make a home here after what she (and my brother) went through, well, I guess I can't really complain about a short stint where I'll make a shitload of money and then be on my way again, can I?

Plus, some time with my first and only niece, I can't say no to that. She's probably the only thing I'm looking forward to at tonight's "family dinner."

Not much feels familial about it. A brother who can barely stand to hold a conversation with me. His first love, who I've hardly seen in almost fifteen years save a couple of short interactions and their wedding, plus her sister and their stepdad.

And me, the black sheep of the Grady family, at least in my brother's eyes. The one who never lived up to the bar Wyatt set but still tried.

If my mom were here, that would make all of this better, but she and my stepdad don't partake in this weekly tradition. I'll be seeing her in a few more days, but she's not here tonight to save me from this, beautiful buffer that she is between her boys.

When I pull up to the top of the hill and park in the gravel lot to the side of the modern cabin my brother built on the land our grandfather gifted him, it's no shock to my system that no welcome committee is waiting for me. In fact, I don't even see anyone around from here, so I take a second to check the rearview mirror and blow out a big breath at my reflection—the only thing that follows me everywhere I go.

Forest green eyes that blend in with the scenery around me. Evergreen, like my smile. Golden skin, from so many days in the sun, on a dirt bike or a four-wheeler, over the last thirty-something years. Dark blond hair, a little longer than my mother prefers it, but none of my partners have ever complained about the mop of carefree strands.

Smile at the ready, I'm good to go, I guess. It's all I have with me most days. My biggest weapon, my best defense, my sharpest offense. It can disarm damn near anyone.

Still don't spot the others, even when I get out of the car. The large windows, set in thick, modern black frames, let you see into most of the modest house from outdoors, but there's no sign of anyone in there. When my booted feet crunch over the gravel and around to the backyard (that's underselling its scope, trust me), I finally spot them.

My brother and his wife, in each other's arms at the back of the house, deep in conversation. A gruff look on his unshaven face, a warm expression on her much prettier one. She's whispering something to him, and he gives the smallest of nods in return, listening intently, paying no attention my way.

A few more steps and I spot the rest of the invitees at a rustic-looking picnic table on the far side of the house. Trudging across the lawn, I can't help the smile that breaks out on my face when I see my niece. She's gotta be the cutest baby I've ever seen. Pink, chubby cheeks, soft shock of light brown hair. Adorable as all hell in a bright silk dress, bouncing on her grandpa's lap, giggling as she reaches for her auntie sitting next to her.

"We're so happy you don't have your mama's original beak, aren't we, baby girl?" Lexi coos at the girl she's fawning over, who's gripping her aunt's fingers for all she's worth. "Yes, you're *much* prettier than she ever was, aren't you?" Alexis shakes her head, rubbing her nose against the baby's, wild hair shaking out around Lexi, as sweet giggles sound from the munchkin.

"Heard that," Rory's melodic voice snaps from where she's crossing the distance to the table, a sharp bite in it that still can't disguise a softness I'm not used to hearing from her just yet. Balancing a career, a marriage, and motherhood is working for her.

"I wasn't trying to hide the truth, you're a big girl, you can handle it," Lexi tosses back in her throatier tone, not breaking eye contact with her sister's mini-me.

"First of all, it was filler, okay, nothing surgical," Rory starts off, touching the bridge of her nose, but their stepdad cuts in to stop that from spiraling.

"Am I going to have to separate you girls?" the oldest one at the table pipes up—though still barely in his mid-fifties—in his amused, husky drawl.

Lexi looks up, amusement splayed across her sharp features, but it abandons her face, swapped out for something that might be surprise, brows buried in her hairline, when she takes in my form in front of her, not my brother's.

"West! No fucking way!"

"Fucking way," I confirm with a single nod.

She gives our niece a kiss on the cheek before pulling one thick leg out from underneath the table to remove herself from a straddle across the bench and gives me a swift but hearty hug.

Alexis doesn't bother with a trite insult, like "look what the cat drug in," or "never thought I'd see the day." She's usually a little more clever with her insults, but then again, she and I have never had beef, and therefore our exchanges tend to be a bit less tumultuous than those with her sister, or even my brother by extension. Count my blessings for that too. She's not one I'd want to tussle with on the regular. Some poor fucker's gonna have his hands full with her some year.

Her brown eyes, so similar to her sister's, bounce between my own and what I presume to be my brother's behind me, before the corner of her mouth pops up in a catty smirk. "Finally, the good-looking Grady is back in town."

"Don't tell me you're a closeted cougar, Lex?"

"Pfft," Alexis waves Aurora off. "Not the life for me, but *objectively* speaking, Weston is quite handsome, can we not admit that?"

"Please," Rory scoffs with zero delay, right next to me at this point. She leans in and gives me a giant hug, rubbing my back and scratching it briefly with those claws of hers before pulling back. "My husband is the hottest motherfucker in this town." Her cat-like eyes cut to me again. "No offense, Weston."

I pop a shoulder at her. "You're not hurting my ego, sis."

Her eyes run down me in a way that's assessing but not at all sexual—an unusual feeling for me—before she looks back at Wyatt. "I mean, Weston's not bad, but he's not *this*." Rory runs her arms over Wyatt's chest and shoulders, then down his arms, all the ink there, and I pretend not to notice him shiver underneath her touch. I *definitely* don't pay attention to the way his eyes darken and the promise in them when he glares at her in return.

"Ew," Lexi takes the word right out of my mouth. The disgust on her face is mostly comical but definitely rooted in the trauma of walking in on them a time too many in high school. "Maybe it's just because that one's been tainted by you from such a young age, but I dunno, I just think ever since, maybe twenty-five or so, Weston's really just been the closest thing to a Greek god the Heights has ever had. Puts you to shame, Grady Senior."

Lexi's got zero interest in me, she never has, but her riling up my brother is ten out of ten entertainment for me tonight.

"He's not my fucking son, he's less than four years younger than me for fuck's sake," my brother grumbles.

"Could've fooled me, old man," I tell him, punching his shoulder lightly as he lifts his chin in as much of a greeting as I'll get from him.

"If you're counting emotional maturity rather than number of times around the sun, maybe," he mutters.

Rory jabs an elbow into his ribs and he lets out a sharp exhale and narrows his gaze on her before rolling his eyes and gesturing to the table with a gruff, "Sit."

Wow. I'm blown away by the warm welcome.

A smile breaks out across my face anyway, because I guess I can be that guy that finds the silver lining in just about anything. And to break bread with my only sibling, the love of his life, and the baby that came out of their decades-long love that's probably *still* the talk of this town... hell, it's not a bad way to spend a Sunday night.

Rory grins at me, hand on my shoulder as I sit down next to Gramps, as we've taken to calling the Weiss girls' stepdad, and then she takes her daughter from him and lets me greet my niece thoroughly as she tells us all to dig in.

"Sorry it's not homemade," Rory offers with a small tilt of her head. "Actually, I'm *not* sorry, and you shouldn't be either. It's way fucking better for all of us this way. This is freshly frozen, straight from the boroughs, and warmed up locally. Enjoy."

We all laugh, but no one louder than her sister.

And it *is* good.

Maybe great even? The tasty meal, the volley of soft insults that fly across the table between girls that share half of the same

DNA, the undercurrent of warmth and familiarity in every exchange. The updates from Gramps on his recent travel overseas. Rory's intense, passionate spiels on the New Heights project she's heading to restore the businesses and breathe new life into the town as a whole. Even the chill in the air, the fresh scent that smells of new growth and fresh starts all around. It's all pretty damn great.

Until my brother opens his mouth.

"So, Wes—" Wyatt uses the nickname I loathe until his wife places another well-timed, not-at-all subtle jab to his side. He doesn't flinch, but he does elongate the syllable in a way that could almost be comical, and adds another consonant at the end. "—t."

His eyes—so like my own, when not much else between our appearance shares resemblance—shoot to his wife's and then back to mine.

"Welcome, uh, welcome back." The way he clears his throat, and the distinct lack of direction behind those words, tells me this isn't the speech he'd planned to give me. "Rory says you'll be here for a few months, huh?"

"I'd believe her," I say to him, eyes on her with a smile. She returns it, one hand rubbing Wyatt's back while he nestles their sleeping baby against his chest as Rory eats her dinner. "This is her master plan, after all."

"My master plan," she corrects me, "is to get you back for good." Not a bullshitter, my sister-in-law. She might be tough sometimes, but she's a straight shooter, I'll say that. "Or were you referring to New Heights, not the reunification of our family?"

I give her a bit of an awkward chuckle and shake my head. "We're going there on night one, huh?"

"My second-favorite Grady taught me that ugly truths are preferable to pretty lies."

Rory's stepfather lets out a hearty laugh at that, and the baby coos at the sound of it, still sound asleep on her dad.

"Second favorite?" Wyatt pulls back from her, offended.

Rory's eyes fall down to the precious sight in his arms pointedly, and his face relaxes, softening in a way it only does for those two girls. Her attention returns to me, face still lit with something unnameable.

"So, yeah, we're going there," Rory says. "All my cards on the table, I'll happily have you back for a few months. It works out a little too perfect to be able to hire you for all the interior painting at these properties being renovated, and I couldn't resist. But does a not-so-small part of me harbor hope that you'll fall back in love with the Heights like I did—" her eyes find Wyatt's again, "—and stay? Definitively."

Lexi holds her silver can of Diet Coke in the air. "Hear, hear!" she cheers.

"I'll toast to that." Gramps joins her with his brown bottle of beer.

Committing to a few months here was hard enough for me. Hard to go with the flow when you're confined to a tank. I like to leave my options open, not cage myself in. But I'd be lying to myself if I said something about that speech didn't tickle a foreign place inside of me. A feeling of longing for something that never has been, and doesn't seem destined to be, either.

I look back to my brother, the last one to hold his beer up, and he does, though with considerably less enthusiasm than everyone else at the table. When we all drink to it, Wyatt pipes up again.

"Seems a little far-fetched if you ask me."

Aaaand here it goes.

"What does?" Alexis takes the bait.

"That he'd be able to be here full-time without breaking the hearts of the rest of the single gals of our generation."

Lexi rolls her eyes exaggeratedly, but Rory's hand pauses on Wyatt's back, and I'd bet if I had x-ray vision, I'd see her claws digging into his shoulder.

"I'm a single girl in your generation, and I can promise you, I'll be just fine with your brother on the prowl here." Lexi shoots me a playful wink as she takes another bite to show me she's got me on this one.

"No, seriously," Wyatt continues. "Weston is incapable of hooking up with a girl without them tattooing his name on their ass, and then he leaves them. I don't know how he's supposed to go until the summer, much less beyond that, without giving in to some girl along the way and crushing her. This place is starting fresh, we don't need a river of tears flooding out downtown in his wake."

"He's a grown ass man," Rory chimes in. "He's not sixteen anymore, Wyatt."

"I remember having to talk to the two of you about your emotional recklessness not that long ago," her stepfather says thoughtfully, then looks back at the cabin directly behind him. "Seems like a lot of glass in your own house to be throwing stones, there, son."

Wyatt harrumphs, but at least he shuts up after that.

Maybe it's only visible in the daylight, but my smile seems to have sunk with the setting sun.

Why does this feel like an omen of my next few months trapped here? Committed to staying until downtown reopens this summer. Agreeing to weekly dinners with this lot. Constant jabs I can't duck from my brother, with the endless fear in the back of my mind that he's right.

That I'll never be able to assimilate into life in the Heights the way he always effortlessly has.

I'll never find the comfort, the belonging that he so clearly has.

I might not be the irresponsible shit I was as a teen, but Wyatt's not wrong to say I'm somewhat cursed on the subject of relationships. And Lord knows I'm not the best at the celibacy thing.

I either find a random hookup who can actually keep things casual, where it doesn't get back to Wyatt, or I might not survive this trip. My need for variety might kill me, or else my brother will.

2
Amelia

"Blood dripped from the trunk of the car, *drip, drip, drip,* alerting the officer that this man had *not* just been out for an evening drive, as he said." The familiar, low, cool, detached feminine voice is one I know better than my own at this point. I've certainly heard it more in recent times, at least.

"Check the trunk!" That's my voice. Higher-pitched, raspier, more out-of-practice. Very unladylike, but no one else is in the van with me to cast judgment. So I continue yelling at the podcast that's keeping me entertained on my drive to nowhere and everywhere. "Check the trunk, don't be an idiot!"

"Officer Jayce radioed for backup, but he didn't wait for help to arrive."

She's got me hanging onto her every syllable, my ass precariously balanced on the edge of my seat—literally. I can't have more than an inch of my tiny ass on the leather driver's seat.

"Of course no help is going to arrive, your partner is IN THE TRUNK." The palm of my hand smacks the steering wheel for emphasis on each word I yell, like the guy she's talking about from forty years ago can hear me. Luckily, the van doesn't swerve, it's probably used to my outbursts. Or maybe I'm just so slight that it takes nearly half my might to turn this damn wheel for real.

Some people yell at their TV while watching football. For me, it's true crime podcasts.

This one is my absolute favorite, *Vengeful Vixens*.

The basic bros have Joe Rogan. The true crime girlypops have VV.

The host, Jynx, is who I wanna be when I grow up. Think Lane Kim, if she had been the It girl instead of the outcast. Korean American with hair dyed almost platinum and the kind of unique style you have to be graced with from birth in order to pull off the way she does. Petite, like me, except she's gorgeous, effortlessly cool, and tells the juiciest, most riveting gory stories. There's a reason why she's nabbed the number one slot in true crime podcasts for four seasons straight. Ten million listeners an episode is impressive in any genre.

"As McNair got out of the vehicle, Officer Jayce saw what he was holding. A hunting knife, with a blade bigger than what most of your Hinge hookups have been working with. That's right, Vixens. *Five* whole inches of steel. He probably called it eight in his dating profile. The blade was jagged, for ripping flesh. And still dripping with fresh blood. Spoiler alert: It wasn't from a cute little deer."

My jaw hangs low enough I feel a breeze on my tongue, and I snap it shut before grabbing my Alani and taking a big swig.

A chill breaks across my upper body, even with my winter sweatshirt on. Technically, I guess we're out of winter, but driving north, just off the interstate now, fresh out of a long stint in Florida, this April spring air in the scenic Smoky Mountains is freezing to me. Or maybe it's just the way Jynx's voice rasps over the surface of my skin and beneath my bones that's giving me goosebumps. The would-be silence in her episode is filled with a soft but dramatic three-note riff that builds the tension in the tale to an almost painful level.

"OH MY GOD TELL US WHAT HAPPENED!"

Is it normal for people to think aloud? To converse with their streamed entertainment? Maybe not, but as someone who's spent the majority of the last eight years alone, it's become my normal.

Like my demand conjured the words from her lips into the microphone, through the cloud and out my Sprinter van's speakers, Jynx's sultry tone picks up again. "And as Jayce's eyes widen in realization, McNair's stare fills with determination. This cop is *not* going to be what stops the spree he's been planning for so long. McNair *lunges*. Jayce *dodges*."

Every word instills something in me.

Panic.

Hope.

Terror.

The need for *justice*.

The woman is a master. She should be an audiobook narrator.

Real talk: I'll listen to just about any true crime show, but no one does it like Jynx. She's got me shouting along like this is the Kentucky Derby.

"Screw your partner, get him for the dog's honor, Jayce! Tase him, tackle him, drop kick him in the *balls*, baby, let's go!"

"And as McNair pulls back his arm, the same knife that took so many other lives—including Jayce's partner's just an hour earlier—held high over his head, poised to take the final swipe and end yet another life on his mission from the devil himself, something glints on the blade. The sliver of metal that wasn't covered in his partner's blood lit up, reflected something star-bright, temporarily blinding both men."

A fresh round of chills breaks out across my arms, and I take another swig of my drink. This is the fucking life, I tell ya. The open road. Just me and Van Gogh. And Jynx for company.

The stunning scenery grabs my attention for just a flicker of a moment as I round a bend, and I soak it in. This view's not half bad. The bright green of the endless rolling forests that blanket the mountainsides. Peaks and valleys as far as the eye can see, in the final amethyst and rose hues of twilight. It's as gorgeous of an area as any to stay for a day or few.

I'm still a good fifty miles from the campsite I was planning on staying at for the night, but I've got at least a few more episodes downloaded. That should be more than enough to get me through these winding mountain roads after dusk.

"Jayce sprang forward, blindly attacking, knowing this was his one and only chance to break out of the psycho's hold and get free, but McNair wasn't having it. He pushes Jayce backward, hitting him with the butt of the knife as he does, and the officer gets knocked—" Jynx claps to emphasize the word, "—out." She claps again.

The thrill in her voice is contagious.

"It's game over for the second officer who tried to bring an end to the madman's spree. But then, the unthinkable happens. That glint on the blade? The reason for it comes barreling right at them. On this deserted highway, late at night, when no one else is around, comes a set of *headlights*."

The disbelief palpable in her words has me screaming. "No fucking way!"

"It wasn't the backup Jayce had called for. Of course it wasn't. The nearest other officers were still *miles* away. It was a regular old civilian. A *grandma*. McNair staggers back, tries to cover his eyes from the blinding light, but all the woman driving can see is a raving madman, holding a massive blade covered in blood, and an officer on the ground, unconscious."

"Channel Lightning McQueen. Gun it. Come on, lady, for the dog!"

"Of course she's heard of the Bladed Butcher, the whole I-70 corridor was on DEFCON levels of alertness for this mass murdering psychopath. So can you guess what happened next, Vixens?"

As I often try to, I channel someone much bigger than five foot nothing with my roar of, "GET HIM!"

"Officer Jayce stirred, regaining consciousness just as the Buick veered toward them. He rolled over, taking cover beneath the trunk of the killer's car, where the blood of his last victim still *drip, drip, dripped* onto the pavement below. And there, unknowingly beneath the body of his slain partner, Jayce watched as an eighty-four-year-old grandmother of nineteen sideswiped the most notorious serial killer of the decade, not just neutralizing the immediate threat, but putting him into a coma that lasted forty-seven hours."

The cheer that leaves the deepest part of my chest should be reserved for football games your own children are playing in. Professional ones. That come with gargantuan rings for winning. But that holler wasn't enough for me.

"That's right, you little punk ass bitch!"

"Believe it or not, when interviewed by law enforcement later, little old Mrs. Dixon confessed she'd gotten lost and shouldn't even have been on that road that night. Was it a wrong turn? Or did fate intervene in the name of vengeance?"

She gives a poignant pause before continuing.

"And two years later, when McNair was tried for no less than twenty-three capital felonies, old Mrs. Dixon was one of the key witnesses they called to the stand. She passed away just three days after his guilty verdict came through, but she made it long enough to see through her mission to bring him to justice.

Vengeance for his eleven human victims, and vengeance for Larry the dog."

For a moment, my thoughts get carried away without my permission. I imagine the rescue personnel that had to transport the killer that night. The medical team that had to care for him, keep him alive, despite their knowledge of who he was, what he'd done, the disdain they had for his actions and, more than likely, the rot that ran down to his very soul.

I wonder how the families and many loved ones of the victims felt, watching this killer be kept alive, at great expense to taxpayers like themselves, when their loved ones were no longer around to be offered that chance.

And for just a blip, I wonder if the killer himself had any family. Any who were left behind in his life to live with the horror, the realization that someone they thought they knew, maybe even cared for, was actually a monster, and the incredible hatred that would overtake them in the days and years to come at the slightest thought of him.

No one can say the victims of the crime and their families don't have the worst of it, but so many more than just them are affected by a tragedy like the Bladed Butcher. And in this case that spanned multiple episodes, consumed the last several hours of my conscious self and invaded the innermost corners of my thoughts, I can't even fathom the number of lives that were shattered by that scum who defies even my most creative insults.

It might get me worked up, but there's something about true crime that grips me. Heals me, in a way.

It's morbid, sure, but it keeps me in check. Gives me perspective and keeps me from thinking I'm the unluckiest fuck in the world.

Maybe I've had a shit hand dealt to me, maybe my life isn't everything I dreamed it would be, but there are others who have had it much, much worse.

Imagine being Jayce's partner.

The *spouse* of Jayce's partner. Not just losing your soulmate, but having to hear what the love of your life endured in their final hours and moments, and somehow go on to live another thirty or fifty years with that knowledge, that unspeakable loss in your everyday life.

In comparison, my life is pretty peachy.

I have a theory. I think most humans feel like their lives are pretty shit, but it could be worse. It doesn't matter if they've had a good upbringing or been through the bowels of hell. My theory is that our internal gauge—that meter of how much trauma one person can take—it expands as our human experience does.

Celebrities, criminals behind bars, trauma victims, and the lucky bastards who've never been through anything more scarring than losing a round of Monopoly at family game night or getting stood up at prom, we all have our reasons to gripe, to feel sad at times. Our outlooks are shaped by what we've been through so far.

Beyond that—while I'm soapboxing for a moment—I almost think until you've gone through something *truly* terrible, you might not realize how much there is to be thankful for, how much to appreciate in your everyday life. How sweet the sunshine on your face can be after so much darkness.

Me? I've got a lot to be thankful for.

"My name is Jynx, thanks for listening to my deep dives of the wildest murders of the eighties and nineties, you Vengeful Vixens. Season six might be coming to a close, but in season seven, get fucking ready. We're digging up some fresh dirt to quench your hunger, bitches. That's right, we're jumping forward, to the current millennium, with the inside scoop on stories you thought you knew, and some you've never heard of.

Get ready to dive into the grittiest, goriest details of killers who got what they deserved, like the—"

But I don't get to hear the rest of her closing monologue, because my van makes a noise I've never heard before.

Somewhere between a rattle and a clunk that drowns all other sound out for a moment.

Then the body of the van shakes, and a burning smell comes through my vents.

"—Slayer, and more. See you next time, Vixens, when we get more vengeance for victims who aren't here to tell their own stories."

"No, no, no!" I yell at my dashboard. "You couldn't have waited until I was at a campsite to eat shit?"

The van's check engine light mocks me in a steady orange glow. One I've gotten so used to seeing, I maybe, sort of, kinda forgot about it. It just became part of the scenery over time.

"We'll get it checked out in the next city," I told myself more times than I can count. "The next stop, when we have a fresh paycheck." I've said that to the dashboard so many times it must have stopped believing me.

But money's been tight, my checks are mostly spent before I even cash them out. I haven't been given as many hours as maybe I'd like. Those checks are a little thinner than I'd prefer. And now my engine seems to be done waiting for me to feel like getting it looked at.

Van Gogh slows to a crawl, and in a panic, I shut off the heater, but the burning smell lingers. Checking both mirrors and my digital rearview mirror on the windshield—*obviously* no one is around, I haven't seen another car in at least fifteen minutes, this could be the road McNair was taken down on for all I know—I gently depress the brake pedal and steer the van to a rolling stop on the shoulder of the road. If it can be considered that, what with the couple inches of margin separating me and my entire life from the side of a mountain beyond the flimsy metal on my right-hand side. I'm sure those crocus lilies pushing up through the dirt there will safeguard my fall if the van starts to slip.

My phone clicks, released from its holder near the dash and of course, of *freaking course*, I have no signal here. Because how else would this story go?

I might end up on *Vengeful Vixens* after all.

Do I turn off the van, grab my phone, and try to walk to signal?

Do I stay locked in the van, risk this burning smell getting a lot scarier, and try to fix my baby with the Care Bear Stare?

Do I just yeet myself over the side of the mountain?

Options, options.

It's as I'm debating recording a video for evidence (maybe Jynx would get to play it on her show someday if this goes badly), that a set of far-off headlights glint in my side mirror.

My reaction is automatic, I don't even think it through. In a split second, the van is off and I'm out the door, my phone in one hand, flashlight turned on, waving my arms like a lunatic begging to be slaughtered. But what other choice do I have?

All I can do is hope the person headed this way is part of the tiny percentile in this country who would 1) actually stop and 2) really help a girl in need, without trying anything shady, or worse.

The first part of that request is proven right when the red Ford pickup slows, headlights flashing at me in greeting as the driver pulls it off on the shoulder a ways back, and inches closer across the uneven ground.

I wave in possible thanks, possible future regret, before turning around to shut my flashlight off and start recording the encounter, just in case.

Speaking quickly, I give a ten-second recap as an intro to the video, then flip the phone around to take in the surrounding area.

As I film the mountainside, Van Gogh, the sprigs of early wildflowers starting to bloom along the shoulder—everything a detective or internet sleuths would need to figure out exactly where I am—I realize that this would be as beautiful of a place to die as any.

And wouldn't it just be cosmic karma if I met my end with some slasher right here and now?

The soft slam of a car door warns me that the other driver is out and headed my way, and I turn with the camera in hand to make sure to get them on (digital) film.

"Hey there," he hollers, arm up in greeting, a smile so charming on his tanned face I myself am feeling—alarmingly—rather disarmed.

Is this just because I missed my chance to get laid on the last few stops? Or is this man actually a walking Greek god out of some mythological fantasy?

I think it might be an age-old question, like, if no one was in the forest to hear, would a tree still make any noise when it fell? This one would be, if I were even somewhat recently sexually satisfied, would this man still be the most gorgeous human I'd ever seen? Or would my ovaries always skip a beat at his confident gait, the playful glint in his eyes, and that freshly mussed dark blond hair.

With my luck, he's a serial killer. Or worse, an early riser.

He walks closer, near enough now that I can see the striking green of his eyes in the light from my van as they bounce between my face, and the phone in my hand, clearly recording him.

"Name's Weston Grady," he says into the camera with another panty-melting smile. "You need some help, darlin'?"

3

Weston

The girl is the size of a pixie—a hot pixie—and her eyes narrow on me with shrewd calculation as I approach.

She's smart. Clever, to be filming me the way she is.

Clearly not from around here. It's not just the license plate that's tipping me off to that. I can feel it on her, even from back here. The aura of adventure. There's something familiar in it, kindred.

She's got enough street smarts to be wary of a tall man, significantly larger than she is, who's got her all alone on a dark road in the middle of nowhere. This is probably the start to a dozen horror movies.

But not in the Heights.

Not even starring two outsiders.

She clearly doesn't know that though, so it's my duty—in addition to being a good Samaritan stopping to help her—to disarm her and calm her worries a bit. Poor girl's probably having a rough fucking day if she's waving my ass down for help. She doesn't need to fear for her life while she's at it.

My ease, my readiness to be upfront about my identity, I

think it's helped smooth a couple of her feathers. Supposing she believes me, that is.

Her dark brown hair, barely past her chin, is full of attitude, just like her face. Wavy, choppy, not quite messy, but fierce all the same. Tiny features, absolutely adorable I'd go so far as to say, if I didn't think she'd stab me for the compliment, based on the way her face is screwed up as she takes me in. Perfectly straight button nose with a dainty metal ring through the septum. Oversized tan sweatshirt with the logo of a band I love on the front, New York Ave. It's probably a kid's size, but it hangs to the tops of her thighs, which are covered only in what looks like tight athletic shorts. Do my best not to be a creep and let my eyes linger beyond the obvious details, like her white sneakers and the stacked necklaces she's wearing.

It's her eyes, though, that intrigue me the most. Never seen another pair like 'em. Almost teal in color. A depth to them that is rarer than the shade itself. They call to me more than any other part of her, and that's saying something with how good the rest of her looks.

When I get close enough she doesn't have to shout, she responds to my offer of help with the most random three words.

"Van Gogh died."

Weird pickup line. Dropping hundred-and-fifty-year-old news on a stranger as an opening.

"I heard," I say dryly. "Someone beat you to giving me that news in, like, fourth grade."

She pops a hip at me and bites back a chuckle. Taps on her phone to stop the recording, I'm guessing, because then it gets tucked into those tight shorts of hers, and all her attention—all that attitude—is back on me.

"No, my van." She points one of her arms to the vehicle next to her. "Van Gogh. It died."

"Oh, yeah, that actually makes more sense." I nod, bobbing my head.

"You're not a serial killer, are you?" The girl—woman—doesn't ask it like a question she wants me to answer. She says it like it's a realization, confirmation of something she'd been weighing.

"If I am, I'm the worst one in history. Zero confirmed kills. Not even a single attempt. In fact, they're going to kick me out of the National Association of Serial Killers soon for just not getting the job done. Apparently, I'm an embarrassment. 'Bad for the brand.'" I give her air quotes.

"Oof," she says, not missing a beat. Her face pulls in a way that shouldn't look as good as it does. But then, full of interest, dry as the sawdust on the floor of my brother's auto shop, she asks, "Have you tried talking to your NASK union representative? There must be some form of recourse for you, this sounds unjust."

I give her a one-shouldered shrug and a long, defeated sigh. "They say I'm just not ambitious enough. Little do they know I was just there for the free buffet on the first day, and I only stayed this long for the benefits."

She puts on an affected, overly concerned tone. "Gosh, what are you going to do now? How will you make ends meet?"

"It's been rough," I say with a somber nod of my head. "Had to auction off two of my kids just so I could feed the other seven."

Her eyes make a run for my left hand—ring-free—and back up to my face, a sparkle in those unique-colored irises.

"Well, if you can help me get my van up and running again, I might be able to throw in a couple boxes of macaroni and cheese for your trouble. Afraid I don't have much more to offer when it comes to rugrats."

I give in to the pull, let my eyes rake down her frame for just a beat, before meeting that mysterious gaze once more. "Shame." It could be my imagination, or maybe it's the cool dusk air, but I could swear she shivers at the tone I use. "They could really use a new mom, since theirs left me for an ex-con. She told me, and I quote, 'at least he's got a record. What have you ever done?'"

Finally, *finally*, I get a giggle from the girl. She covers her mouth delicately with a few fingers and gives in for just a second before regaining her composure and looking back at me, straight-faced. I shouldn't be mesmerized by a stranger, a clearly morbid one at that.

What is this impulse I have to lighten her mood?

Why is it any of my business if she laughs or not?

Yet here I am, following her lead, this dark little angel with the morose sense of humor, determined to lighten her burden. Couldn't tell you what hers is, but I could tell you it's there. Undoubtedly.

"Maybe today is my lucky day," I tell her with a hopeful, boyish grin. "Maybe if I can fix your van, I can finally have an accomplishment to my name, and my family will be whole again."

"Who would I be to stand in the way of that?" the angel asks, a hand on her chest.

"Thank you for this opportunity," I tell her, flashing another smile. It pierces her cool exterior, I see it happen in real time.

This isn't one-sided. Seeing a visceral reaction like that in a woman I just met—hell, any woman—doesn't normally send a thrill running through my veins, but that sure just did.

My system must think a fresh scent is in the air for me to chase. It didn't get the memo that I'm here to help with rearranging her car's insides, not the beautiful girl's.

"Please, be my guest." She waves a hand in offer to the van behind her, and I step over toward it.

"So what's going on with this Van Gogh?" I ask.

"Everything was going fine, until we passed this other van on the road, and I dunno, I think he started to get jealous or something. Before I knew it, he cut off one of his own side mirrors and threw it at a prostitute we passed back in Florida, and now he's just a mess."

Now it's my turn to laugh. She's funny. Refreshingly so.

"And here I was hoping it was going to be as easy as a flat tire. If your van is having a mental health crisis, this might require a professional." One side of my mouth tips up at her and she grins back at me.

"I'm just kidding. Van Gogh is female, and she would *never* deface herself over another van. She doesn't get into other-van drama. She's got more self-esteem than that."

"The energy this world needs in these times," I say solemnly. "Maybe she could start a podcast and inspire more vehicles to feel good about themselves."

Her eyes widen before a grin splits her face. "Would you believe that she and I were *just* discussing her opportunities on the way here? I told her at her age, she's not going to land a TV gig without getting a new pair of headlights, but she's still got the presence for a podcast if she hustles. She's not getting any younger, you know."

My head falls back as my laugh splits the peaceful night air.

This is certainly somewhere I never saw my first evening back in Smoky Heights going. *Any* evening in the Heights going. I was already going to check out her van, but now I feel like I owe her more than that for the laughs and the best part of a half hour I'll probably get for the rest of my stay here.

"Well, why don't you tell me what's going on with her here, and I'll see if I can't help you get her back up and running and on your way. Is it a dead battery? Need a jump start? Forget to change your oil? How bad are we talking here?"

Her face pulls into a grimace. "Was I supposed to change the oil?"

"They say every three thousand miles, but it's a pyramid scheme. You're probably good for closer to ten, maybe even more on this girl right here if you gave her the good stuff. Don't tell me you've been driving her while she's thirsty?"

Her eyes narrow on me in a way that's somehow sardonic. "You really think I roam the country, living out of my van, and don't know to change the oil? Give me some credit."

I hold my hands up in innocence.

"Then tell me, darlin'. What are we dealing with?"

She opens the sliding door to the side of the van and steps inside, a clear invitation to follow her. I let out a loud whistle when I duck down and climb the couple of steps to get inside. "Damn. Van Gogh is *hot*."

She chuckles, nodding. "And she knows it."

Granted, I haven't been in many Sprinter vans that have been outfitted for the van life, but this shit is gorgeous. Natural wood finishes. A small living space, even an area I would refer to as a kitchen, lots of cabinets and hidden storage nooks, some sort of closed off tiny closet or room behind a door, and what is clearly her bed at the back of the van. I bet when you open the back doors, she's got the best view anyone's ever had from their bed.

"You live out of her?" I ask.

"Yep," she says, popping the *p*.

While I was taking in her setup, she climbed into the open space next to the driver's seat, and is now watching me from there, expectantly. Being what has to be well over a foot taller than her, it's not quite as comfortable for me to move about within the van as it clearly is for her, but I make it work, getting to the bucket seat she drives from, and plopping down in it.

"So, she, uh, how do I say this?"

The girl taps her chin with one finger thoughtfully, nose wiggling, and it's inexplicably cute. She's gotta be mid or late twenties—she's jaded enough to be older than that—but her features make her look on the lower end of her twenties.

"She shuddered? And then she didn't want to go forward anymore, and there was this terrible burning smell."

"Isn't that what stroke victims report?"

She levels her turquoise gaze at me and implores me wordlessly.

"Yeah, okay, that doesn't sound good," I admit. "Let's see what happens when I try to crank her up."

I press the power button without depressing the brake pedal to see if the battery is working, and sure enough, the dash lights up and the electronics start up too.

An orange light catches my eye, and I look at the owner of the van pointedly.

"Your check engine light is on."

"And aren't you going to check it?" she asks, somewhere between playful and hopeful.

"Let's try and start her up first and see what happens then."

I press the brake pedal and the on button once again, and what happens isn't good. That smell she warned me about hits, and I turn the thing off.

"Well, I hope it isn't a stroke, because if so, I'm having one too," I say dryly.

"Oh God," she moans, dropping her head into her hands. "This isn't good, is it?"

"Did you think it was?"

"I'm sort of an optimistic pessimist," she explains. "I knew it probably wasn't *great*, but I still hoped it wasn't *terrible*, if that makes sense."

The little shoulder shrug/head tilt combo she gives as she explains only further endears her to me. Am I under a spell?

Should I be checking the van for crystals and shit? I'm pretty sure this girl's got me wrapped around her finger and she's not even trying.

For all I know, she could have a boyfriend bigger than me behind that door back there, and he could be waiting to knock me over the head so they can take my debit card and enjoy all fourteen dollars on it. They should've caught me tomorrow, once I'm back to work and have some money again.

"All right," I relent. "Pop the hood for me and bring your phone as a flashlight."

A couple minutes of rummaging around under the pitifully short beam that her reach allowed and it's confirmed. The diagnosis isn't good, and it's out of my wheelhouse, at least on the side of the road.

A flat tire, I would've been your guy. Some extra coolant, or your belt slipped off, coulda been me. This? This is looking a lot more like something major, but I don't wanna be the one to give her *that* news.

I wipe my hands off as best I can on my pants, and she runs back inside to grab a hand towel for me and offers that instead. After getting as much off of my forearms and hands as seems possible without hot water and special soap, I let out a heavy sigh.

"Before we go any further, I feel like I've already been to second base, maybe third, with Van Gogh, and I still don't know what to call you. Call me old-fashioned, but where I come from, we learn a girl's name before we go elbow-deep under her hood."

The somber tension cracks, and she lets out a little laugh.

"Weston Grady, are you too proper to go any further without a meal or at least a movie?"

"All I need's a name, darlin'." Give her a little wink, and it's pretty dark out right now, but I think I see a flush in those cheeks of hers.

"A—" her eyes flash over my shoulder and I wonder if this is where her boyfriend clubs me over the head. I turn to check, but the coast is clear. Only Van Gogh is watching us. "Amelia."

"All right, Amelia. Not gonna lie to you. It's not something I can fix right here. She needs a professional."

Amelia's head drops back, and she lets out a little wail that's too comical to be truly pathetic.

"Just fucking perfect," she says. "My phone has no service, I'm in the middle of nowhere, and now I'm stuck."

"Hey now," I tell her. "You're not alone out here. I can call a tow truck."

Her eyes gleam softly at that. "Could you?"

"Yeah, of course. I'm not just gonna leave you out here. They'd revoke my country boy chivalry card. And my phone has service, so there's a little bit of luck."

"Ugh." She drops her head back again, short hair swaying as she does. "Thank you. You're a lot nicer than most people I've met."

"Hey, don't get any ideas now. I need that mac'n'cheese for the rugrats. This isn't philanthropic. It's transactional."

A tiny smirk pops out on that captivating face of hers, and she gives me a grateful smile. There's something soft about her looks, her energy, but there's sharpness there too. The mix intrigues me.

"Right," she says. "You get me a tow truck, and I'll make sure your nine kids get their mac'n'cheese."

"I'm down to seven, remember?" I correct her.

She nods solemnly. "That's right. The auction."

"Lucky for you, and my seven remaining kids, I know a guy who can help you. Let me get ahold of him."

She nods and puts her hands behind her, resting on her hips

in a way that makes her arms stick out to the side as she watches, and waits.

The phone rings, and rings, and rings.

"This is Wyatt. Don't leave a message."

I smile at Amelia, then turn around and glare at my phone.

"Don't do this to me now, you prick," I whisper, and then redial.

The same message greets my ears.

I call his wife, who answers on the second ring. "Hey West! You get into the house okay? Did the code work?"

"Actually, I need Wyatt. I ran across someone stranded on the road, their Sprinter van broke down. I can't get ahold of him."

"Can't you?" Why do those two words sound like a threat? I think she's speaking through bared teeth, and not at me.

"Wyatt, it's your *brother*." That word sounded a little dangerous for my liking. "He's been trying to call you apparently."

Some muffled noises on the other end of the line before I hear sounds that tell me the phone is passing hands. Maybe forced into a closed fist.

"Yeah?"

Here goes nothing. I screw my face up tight and hold my breath. "I need your help."

4
Amelia

The tow truck pulls off the single lane of the road and backs up until it's just in front of the van.

When the driver's side door opens and a man jumps down out of the tall cab, I'm caught bouncing my head between him and Weston.

It's not so much their physical characteristics, but something about this guy is similar to the one next to me. Stature more than mannerisms. Not sure I can even pinpoint what it is, but I can tell they're related.

Maybe it's the awkward tension between them.

Yep, that's the dead giveaway.

They're related.

Or they made eye contact during a devil's three-way and haven't figured out how to act around each other since. But nah, the dark-haired guy walking toward me now doesn't look like the sharing type.

I'm sticking with familial relations. Those can be all kinds of fucked up. Ask me how I'd know.

"Evenin'," he says, tipping the brim of his dark ballcap my

way, before heading over to Weston, who's waiting by the open hood.

The two of them duck under there, muttering between themselves, pointing at various parts and conferring before they both pop back out of it. They turn and walk back toward me, almost in tandem.

Weston, early thirties, golden skin and hair, in a white tee with khaki cargo pants and brown boots, those dark green eyes just like those of the man next to him. The other man is later thirties, with darkly tanned skin, dark hair and features, and scruff on his face that probably never goes away, shadowing his cut jawline above his Henley and Dickies. The band on his ring finger glints in the moonlight, which somehow makes him feel more foreboding rather than safer.

Everything about the new arrival says *hands off*, whereas everything about Weston says *stay awhile*. It's a dichotomy between them that I'd like to propose be more closely inspected, maybe a study could be conducted on. I'm certainly fascinated. For all their similarities, their differences jump out at me louder.

Warm and fuzzy versus cold and sharp.

Messy, precise.

Casual, uptight.

"I'm gonna have to take a better look at it in my shop, but it looks like your engine's done for," the tow truck driver says in a gruff, rather solemn voice.

My eyes flash to Weston's, much more comforting than the other pair. "Amelia, this is Wyatt," he says. "The local mechanic here in Smoky Heights."

Oh. Not just a tow truck driver then.

"And my brother," he tacks on after a second.

Double oh. Not just any mechanic-slash-tow truck driver either.

"He's still learning the basic human skill called manners,"

Weston says pointedly, with lighter delivery than most could pull off, but the levity doesn't stop the blow from hitting its intended target.

Wyatt makes a noncommittal sound from somewhere deep in his throat in response, and I nod back at him, giving him a tiny finger wave. "Total pleasure," I say with zero inflection, and without a pause, I ask, "What do you mean *done for*?"

"I mean if this were a hospital waiting room, I'd have brought Kleenex for you," he says dryly.

Weston scoffs a disbelieving laugh. "Jesus, man, can you cut her some slack?"

Wyatt turns his head to look at his brother and then looks back at me.

"I'll see if there's anything that can be done for it, but I've got a full garage right now. It might take me a couple days to get a good look at it."

"A couple days?" I shriek back.

"You're welcome to find someone else to take a look at it sooner," he retorts, managing an even drier tone than before.

"Great!" I leap on the optimism, which I'm guessing is rare for him. "Is there another shop nearby we can tow it to?"

"No." Flatter than my chest before the boob job, it's the only answer he gives.

I'd like to add another dichotomy to the list.

Polite, *jackass*.

Weston steps in front of his brother and blocks off my line of sight to the talkative, *super* helpful individual and takes over. When he jumps in, he makes an effort to be a lot more reassuring.

"Smoky Heights is a pretty small town. Only a few thousand residents. Wyatt's garage is kinda the only option." Weston shrugs, like he wishes it weren't so. "Were you headed somewhere urgent?"

My shoulders drop back, instantly slightly more relaxed for some reason.

"It's not that I'm headed anywhere urgent, really, it's just that I don't want to live out of his garage for a couple of days until we have an answer, and who knows how long it'll even take to fix after that, and—"

"Whoa, whoa, whoa." Wyatt steps out from behind Weston and barges into the conversation again. "You aren't living out of my garage. I don't even know you. I wouldn't even let *him* live out of my shop." He hikes a thumb in the direction of his brother. "Not a chance," he says with finality.

"My van *is* my house," I argue back. "What else am I supposed to do? Just trust that I can leave everything I own with the grumpiest person I've ever met and curl up beneath my failed hopes and dreams to stay warm on the side of the road? No thanks." I cross my arms and scowl at him, face pinched up.

"Good lord." It sounds more like *why me*. Wyatt blows out a heavy breath, head falling back to look at the sky.

"Okay, how about this," Weston chimes in. "We obviously don't want to leave you on the side of the road, even if this is a safe town, that wouldn't be very chivalrous of us, and the Grady men are at *least* considered that, aren't we?"

Weston sneaks a glance at his brother, who nods his head in a way that isn't very convincing, then mutters, "Yep, that's us. Just a couple of Southern fuckin' gentlemen."

My preferred brother keeps talking. "I'm open to other options, but here's what might be an idea. Wyatt takes your van to his shop and finds a way to fit in an assessment tomorrow, even if he has to stay a little late to do it."

Those dark green eyes flit away to the man with the matching pair once more.

"As for your living arrangements, I have a hunch his wife

can help find an opening for you, even this late on a Sunday night, somewhere safe for you to crash."

"You don't even have a hotel? Where the hell am I, the 1800s?"

Weston lets out a hoot of laughter and shakes his head. "We have an inn, but it's full right now with all the workers who are here to help with redoing the town. Rory's who found a place for me to stay while I'm here, she's kind of overseeing this whole project in town, and she's good at logistics and shit. I'll call her and see if she has any ideas."

When I nod back at him, he steps off to the side and gets back on the phone again.

A minute or so of awkward silence goes by, when finally Wyatt eyes Van Gogh wearily. "You're not going to get my shop raided for smuggling weed or something, are you?"

"You think I'm a hippie because I live in a van? Fantastic worldview you've got there. Incredible stereotyping skills. Does that come in handy as a mechanic? Alienating your clientele?"

"Awful defensive when I just wanna know my shop won't be harboring any illegal substances."

Narrow my eyes at the prick, I bite out, "I'm not a dealer, dude. I write code. Hardest thing I keep in my van is Alani, so unless there's a caffeine raid, your precious shop should be safe."

He ignores my dig. "What do you mean code? Like messages for pigeons to deliver?"

I snort derisively. "You're unreal."

"Thanks, my wife says the same." He gives me a cocky look that I might call a smirk if his face moved more than an eighth of an inch as he did it.

I mime typing on a keyboard. "Coding? Programming? You ever used a computer before, or are wrenches the most advanced technology you've touched?"

"I'm a simple guy," he says with a shrug.

"My god, you're insufferable," I bemoan.

This is who I'm trusting Van Gogh to?

"Good news!" Weston bursts in cheerfully, moving in between us once again. "She thinks the bed & breakfast might have something open, which is just off of Main Street near downtown, not five minutes away from his shop, where Van Gogh will be."

Not that I'm paying him any attention, but out of the corner of my eye I see Wyatt mouth "Van Gogh?" to himself, like the name offends him. Maybe he's more of a Monet fan.

I pop a brow at Weston. The man owes me nothing, yet he's going *this* far out of his way to help me? "You're really earning this mac'n'cheese, aren't you?"

He gives me a casual shrug in return. "What can I say? I'm a devoted father. Dedication costs nothing."

Something in my chest pinches, and I plaster a smile onto my face.

His phone lights up in his hand and so does his face as he checks the message. "All right, you're all set. She's got the B&B waiting for you. I can take you there after the van is squared away. Unless you rethought the side of the road."

He shoots me a wink as I shake my head, then looks back at his brother.

"All good, Wyatt?"

Wyatt gives him a single, wordless nod, and I stand by and watch as the two men get my baby loaded up onto the back of the tow truck and prepare to spend the first night apart since I got her, all those years ago, fresh out of my failed college experiment.

The grouchy mechanic was nice enough—if that's what you wanna call it—to let me pack my necessities before hoisting her up, so my laptop, chargers, toiletries, and tomorrow's outfit are now all I've got with me.

Not even my vibrator made the cut, and after all this tension, that might be a mistake. The universe is being cruel, knowing I could use a release with the stress today brought.

I'm used to living a minimalist lifestyle, but traveling *this* light is new for me. I won't be four steps away from my bed, my kitchen, my worktable, and a seat with two pedals that'll take me anywhere I wanna go at any given time of the day for once.

Hopefully I've gotten everything I need to work from wherever I'll be until Wyatt calls me with the news. We did at least agree that if nothing else, I'll come to the shop late tomorrow to see Van Gogh and refresh my bag.

As someone who only has a handful of outfits total, I'm not exactly prepared to pack for a long time away from my roving home. I'm going to need to find somewhere to do laundry here shortly, I was planning a whole refresh and reset at the next campsite.

Wyatt's reply to the plan was grumbled, but I'm going to pretend he said, "No problem, thanks for your business, ma'am, it's a pleasure being able to check on your precious van for you. Welcome to Smoky Heights, and I hope you have sweet dreams."

But as Weston drops me off at the adorable B&B and wishes me well ten minutes later, it's another fantasy my mind is entertaining.

My eyes drag over the tee clinging to his firm chest, those corded arms, and the black and gray tattoo of something mechanical on the back of one of them.

I find myself wondering if being here for a couple of days is too long to allow myself to see him again? If that's more time than the emotionless flings I prefer mandate, for my own wellbeing?

There's a reason I only do one-night stands.

And I already feel like this man knows too much about me,

like he sees deeper than I let others go, after an hour or two of nothing much more than joking around. Adding sex into that mix? Might only work if I'm on the road the next day.

Otherwise, I can already feel a tempting pull to let him further in. To get closer.

And I'll never be doing *that* again.

ALL RIGHT, this town is cute, I'll give it that much.

And no one else has been as much of a grumpy fucker as that tow truck driver either, and I've run into a surprising amount of people as I explored the quaint little downtown this morning.

I'm waiting for Sookie or maybe Luke himself to walk out of one of these buildings any minute now, this place is *that* damn charming.

The bed and breakfast was less than a five minute walk to the stretch of road they call downtown. It's just a couple of blocks once you cross under the big metal archway that says "Welcome to Downtown Smoky Heights."

It shouldn't be as endearing and welcoming as it is, with the variety of places I've seen, but somehow it's getting its claws deeper in me the longer I look around.

Adorable one and two-story brick buildings line both sides of the street, most under construction, several with banners hanging that say "Now Open." Wrought iron lampposts stand tall with colorful flower baskets hanging from them every so many feet along the walkways.

The sidewalks are also brick and look to have been there since the eighteen hundreds, if I had to guess. Not the sixteen hundreds of St. Augustine, or the seventeen hundreds of Baltimore, Boston, and the rest New England. I might not be a history buff, but I've seen enough of this country to get by on a pop quiz. When you're on the run for eight years, you end up seeing a lot. But I haven't been somewhere quite like this.

Planted on either side of Main Street are trees that cushion the sidewalk from the newly paved road. Different types of young trees appear to have been rehomed along the length of the street, and every third or fourth one is flowering a white delicate bud that almost reminds me of a cherry blossom. A grassy median separates the single lane of traffic designated for each direction, with more trees planted in the middle. Metal benches, merchandise displays, or bistro tables with chairs can be found outside of most open storefronts—those that aren't under construction—inviting the townsfolk to stop and stay a while.

I moseyed by and took my time inspecting several of the storefronts earlier this morning, perusing the local offerings and being besieged with well-wishes from strangers.

A salon, a hardware store, and a pharmacy all seemed to be bustling, while many more locations had plywood in the windows or scaffolding outside the perimeter as they're brought back to life.

Outside the hardware store at the edge of the downtown strip, a group of mostly middle-aged and older men sat on the benches, chatting. They stopped as I got close, all eyes falling on me. It should've made me uncomfortable, feeling like the center of attention, so much male gaze my way. But there was nothing creepy present, no weird vibes from any of them, something I've been highly attuned to for way too long now.

"Well, howdy there, miss," called the oldest of the group. "Been expecting you downtown. Welcome to Smoky Heights!"

I startled, stopping still and facing the small congregation, all watching me.

"Me?"

"You're the one who got stuck on the side of the road, aren't you?" another older man spoke up, gesturing with his arm toward the main road off in the distance.

Nodding, I grabbed my arm with the other and shifted my stance. "That's me. The unlucky one."

The man who spoke up next was the youngest of them all, handsome, probably not much older than me, with a dark mustache, and a navy blue t-shirt with the initials SHVFPD on it in white, above a fireman's cross. "Or maybe it was your lucky break to wind up on a detour here in the Heights." He winked, but it wasn't salacious, I think this guy is just the kind of optimist half of me could never live up to.

"You're in good hands with the Gradys," another man with a hook nose said from the far right of the bench.

"You trained him well, Gonzo," the second one told him.

When it hit me that the man with the nose was called Gonzo, I choked on my air rather than let the laugh come out and seem rude.

"Not just Wyatt, Ernie," the man called Gonzo replied. "The younger Grady is a good fellow too. And of course we all love Rory." He gestured up the street, like she was there.

Murmurs of agreement sounded from the entire group, and a bittersweet smile tugged at the corner of my mouth at the closeness evident between the residents in the town. I thought last night was a fluke, but I might have stepped into a vortex when I got out to wave Weston down. It looks like I've ended up somewhere people know their neighbors, and choose to interact with them rather than stay in their own bubbles, watching TV alone, or on their phones.

I'm still not entirely convinced I didn't walk into some version of *The Truman Show*.

"Are you boys giving this young lady a hard time?" A middle-aged Black woman asked, kind eyes crinkled in a knowing smile. She came up right beside me and crossed her arms, staring the men down.

"Ms. Snow," the youngest one with the mustache said as he stood up taller.

"I'm not your teacher anymore, Charlie, you can call me Wanda."

The man's cheeks heated, and he looked down at the ground, scuffing a boot. "Yes, ma'am."

She chuckled, turning to face me. "Do you need an excuse to get away from these old codgers and coots?"

"We were just welcoming her to town! And telling her the Grady boys will take care of her," another of the older men defended.

"Mmm," Wanda murmured. "Well, you welcomed her. Now it's my turn."

She linked her arm through mine and steered me up the street, away from the men, most of whom were protesting at our retreating forms.

When we were a storefront or two away, she unhooked our arms and spoke up again. "Sorry about that, but I didn't want you to get stuck there all day. Ernie would've kept you there until the bar opened, and too much excitement isn't good for Gonzo's heart. Most of them, like Samuel and Charlie, are harmless, but I thought I'd do you the favor."

A warm smile brushed my cheeks, and I didn't bother hiding it from her. "People here are, um, friendly."

"That's one word for it," she said, clucking her tongue. "Nosy, more like it."

As we wandered, one office caught my eye, New Heights Headquarters according to the sign in the window, but we walked right past it.

"Now I don't know how long you'll be here, but you need a woman's ear on somethin', you come find me or one of the others." Wanda pointed across the street, to the pharmacy at the far end of the downtown stretch, where a similar group was huddled around the bistro tables out front, made up of entirely women. One had blueish white curls I could see all the way from here. "We're never too far away," she said with a wink, and she headed away.

"Thank you, Wanda," I called after her.

Taking my bearings now that I could see more of the street, I let myself be pulled into the coffee shop, Foamy Heights, on the same block, but the opposite side of the street.

And it's made for a great temporary workstation all morning long, what with easy access to pastries (Made Local read the sign), a damn good London Fog, and Wi-Fi to give my hotspot a break as I cozied up at a corner table, slipped on my over-ear headphones and knocked out a few hours of code.

The large plate glass windows overlooking the center of downtown mean passersby wrapped in overcoats or hoodies dot my periphery as I work away on the current project I've been assigned.

As a freelance developer, my workload is sometimes lighter and sometimes a bit more full-on, depending on what the firm I contract with has available. I love the flexibility of what I do, but it's not always the most reliable when it comes to volume of work. Lately, it's been a little lighter than I wish it were, especially with Van Gogh on the fritz.

For the fortieth time today, a thought about my poor van hits me, and I remember why I'm sitting here, wondering about the status of Van Gogh instead of inside her at our next campsite. With those thoughts, the familiar tightening in my stomach comes back. The knots that drop lower and lower at the thought of what this will cost me.

One thing feels certain, it's more than my measly budget is prepared for.

When I wrap up for the day, I shoot a quick email to my contact at the firm, asking if there are any additional projects I could be an asset on in the near future.

Here's hoping they've got a little something more for me to get my van up and running again, so I can do what I've been doing for close to a decade: Keep moving.

A tinny, robotic sound plays in my headphones that alerts me the email has been sent, and I stare at the screen in front of me. The empty inbox in my encrypted email—one that's generally favored by international hackers due to being virtually untraceable and anonymous—might as well have crickets chirping while tumbleweeds roll through the desert for all the correspondence I have. It's a reminder of the loneliness my life entails.

Ignoring the pinch in my chest, the sting that always accompanies my regret, I start a new email.

Hi,

Me again. I am on the move once more. It's not so warm where I am now. Makes me wonder how chilly you must be right about now. Good thing is, spring is already springing! I hope you send me a picture when your tulips start to bloom. What colors will you have this year?

Had a slight hiccup but should be on the go again in no time. Will tell you more about it later.

I'd love to hear what you've been up to!

Sorry again we couldn't be together on your favorite day. Maybe this is the year we can meet somewhere? Let's start dreaming. Where would you want to go?

Look out for a postcard from me before long.

Miss you always. Love you longer.

A

I've heard spring allergies in the South can be a real bitch. Once I put away my laptop, toss my recycling, hit the restroom, and step outside into the nippy early evening air on Main Street, I chalk it up to some henceforth unknown allergies that have me wiping my eyes as I head back toward the B&B.

Eyes still glistening, I don't make it more than a couple of doors down—the hammering and whirring noises of construction having died down for the day—when a tall brunette woman across the street waves me down.

"Amelia!" she hollers, bouncing a baby in one arm, waving somehow both frantically and elegantly with the other. Once she has my attention, she returns to finishing locking the door on the New Heights Headquarters behind her, then hustles over to me. I've never seen someone move so quickly in a pencil skirt and heels, much less while holding a cooing infant, but she's giving anomaly vibes all around. Definitely doesn't look like most of the local women I've run into so far, I'll say that much.

"Rory Weiss-Grady," she introduces once she's close enough. "Head of the New Heights committee. Wyatt's wife, Weston's sister-in-law. I'm the one who—"

"Got me the place to stay," I finish her sentence as she nods, a warm smile on her oval face.

"Right. Are you headed to the garage?"

I pull out my phone to check the time and see a missed call from an area code I don't recognize.

Rory's eyes follow my motion. "My husband tried to call you," she says, not apologizing for snooping on my phone screen. I have a feeling she makes sure to notice more than most. "He had a look at your van today. He's got a grasp on your options and is ready for you."

Well, that doesn't sound promising. Even the optimist in me is hiding from the outcome when she puts it like that.

"Right." Not sure what to say now. I rock forward on the

balls of my feet, trying not to shiver in my athletic shorts that leave most of my legs exposed to the breeze. Just because I'm short doesn't mean there's not plenty of skin to still freeze. I bury my hands in the long sleeves of my sweatshirt and nod up at the gorgeous woman who would still tower over me even if she weren't in heels.

"I'm headed there now, he's got a late night ahead of him, just thought I'd offer you a ride if you'd like one. Save you from this breeze as the sun starts to sink."

The baby in her arms reaches for something, leaning out of her mom's arms and giggling. Rory kisses her on the side of her head, indulgent, and then looks back at me expectantly.

I practically trip over my tongue accepting her offer. "Yeah, that'd be great, thank you."

"This way," she says briskly, and marches off toward a parking lot nestled behind the row of buildings I hadn't even noticed on my first walkthrough of downtown. The air of authority around her is mesmerizing and I follow, entranced by this woman after just a few words. She has more confidence and swagger than the women I've been exposed to in my life.

That intensity stirring behind her brown eyes makes everything I've done to appear bigger and stronger feel almost childlike in comparison.

I bet no one considers *her* fragile or delicate, or in need of defending.

I think she's my new hero.

5
Weston

It's an excuse. A shallow one at that. I know it. He'll probably know it. I just hope he doesn't call me out on it.

Gravel crunches beneath my work boots with each step I take toward Gonzo's Garage. Its namesake is nowhere in sight when I approach though.

Just my warm, welcoming older brother.

Like a mug of warm apple cider.

Warm apple cider vinegar maybe.

I'd call out in greeting, but it'd be no use. He's decked out in his gear, coveralls and a welding hood, shade down as he finishes working on a body panel.

My eyes roam the place while he finishes what he's doing rather than risk startling him with a jump scare and getting treated like the Tin Man.

Large, open space, cleaner than I remember it being. Three bays, doors wide open, in the front of the garage, one with the Oldsmobile that seems to be missing a body panel, another with an ancient Mercury Sable, and the third with a Sprinter van that shouldn't make my stomach leap up into the space reserved for my heart. Only one four-wheeled ride is supposed to do that, and it's my own.

Behind the cars in the front of the shop, an assortment of small and large vehicles fill the rest of the space, up to the back bay doors, currently closed. One wall appears reserved for workbenches and every tool a mechanic might ever need, plus a restroom and a small office that's probably in complete disarray if Gonzo uses it. The other wall has a sink, an eye wash station, and a first aid kit, with more equipment for more specialized jobs, like his welding cart, plus a washer and dryer for shop rags, and some cabinets. There's an assortment of chairs that I think Gonzo considers a waiting room along the wall too.

Scanning the ATVs, RZRs, motorbikes, and cars they've got stored in here, I'm starting to think he wasn't just being a dick when he said it might take a few days to get to Amelia's diagnosis and estimate. This place is *packed*.

And in the back corner, near a large boombox that's probably almost as old as I am, I spy a dirty tarp slung across a familiar shape.

Bingo. My excuse for being here.

The sizzling and hissing of the welding stops, and I turn to see my brother emerge from behind the shade as he pushes it back up and removes the hood entirely.

"Gonzo lets you play with the big boy equipment now, huh?"

He doesn't even crack a smile or try to jab me back. "It's just me here now. Gonzo's all but retired these days. Had a heart attack."

Oof. Buzzkill much?

He must see the look on my face because he softens those words—which is shocking enough on its own. "It was a minor one, but it made him reevaluate his priorities. Old lady has him on a health regimen that doesn't include shoveling honey buns and Moon Pies while hitting his head on shit in the garage."

"Well, fuck." What else is there to say?

Changing the subject in a flash, my brother is getting better at conversation than I remember him being. "You seen Mom yet?"

"Nah, but we're catching up this week."

His mouth flattens into an even tighter line somehow. "Good." He sniffs. "She'll be happy."

Wyatt unzips then steps out of the coveralls, down to his usual—a dark Henley and a pair of charcoal Dickies. The grease and engine soot blend right in. I look down at my cargo pants and white tee. The shirt is fairly clean, I buy a new pack practically every week. But the pants are covered in swipes of at least a dozen different paint colors.

Now that I'm seeing just how messed up this pair is, I might be *slightly* regretting not changing into something clean before dashing over here, but I didn't want to miss her.

Today was my first day on the job, and yeah, sure, maybe I got a little bit of a late start, but it also took longer than I expected to finish the rooms I was working on today, and I didn't have time to change first. But I'm here now and going to see it through, dirty pants be damned.

I had to know if last night was a fluke. If that instant attraction, that deep draw I felt toward her was just the full moon, or if my mind was playing tricks on me, knowing I'll be sentenced to months of celibacy. Surely she wasn't as hot as my libido has been telling me she was. Delicate features that scream innocence, with something lurking under the surface that tells me she's anything but. And that sense of humor of hers, dark, but adorable at the same time... A blend all her own, Amelia hasn't left my mind since I dropped her off last night.

On the side of the road when a girl is stranded and you're

her only hope isn't exactly the time to make a move, as much as I might have wanted to. Plus, Amelia's the kind of girl that seems like she'd run in a heartbeat if you pushed her the wrong way. Too shrewd to fall for a random pickup line. Asking for her number while I was her only recourse on a dark, deserted road would've probably spooked her and cost me a nut shot, if not worse.

But also, what would getting her number even do for me? If Wyatt fixes her engine in a day and she's gone, what am I going to do? Write her sonnets and poems over text about how perfect her tits looked underneath that sweatshirt she was wearing? Send her dick pics like every other schmuck online (even if mine is worth looking at)? No thanks.

That girl's a rolling stone if I've ever seen one, outside of the mirror. A day of stewing on it told me my only chance to see her again was gonna be right here, right now.

If Wyatt is gonna get her back on the road, I might as well shoot my shot with her before she's gone, get my one night of happiness for the rest of my damn stay in town and have the memory of that night to hold me over until I'm out of here.

My brother stares at me, a question that he doesn't bother to ask in his eyes. *What are you doing here?*

I thrust an arm out to point at my baby in the corner. "Came to see the Charger."

Wyatt's brow and quasi-beard twitch in a way that's unusual.

Emotion on his face is what's unusual.

Unease? Discomfort? Not sure, but also don't care.

"You sure you're not here to spy on a five-foot nothing spitfire?"

Pretending he didn't just see right through me, call me out like that, I ignore the remark, heading over toward the dusty tarp, his weighted footfalls following me. In one swift motion, I yank the material that's kept my baby safe for years and pull it away.

Dust and particles fly everywhere, but it doesn't matter. I'm reunited at long last with my only real belonging of value. My grandfather's legacy he left to me. It might not be the hectares and hectares of family land my brother got, but it's a hell of a consolation prize.

The 1970 Dodge Charger in Go Mango Orange with black racing stripes.

Might get half-hard just looking at her, if my brother weren't standing here ruining this moment for me and her both.

My boots crunch slowly over the sawdust-coated cement floor as I walk my way around the car, taking her in. I'd run my fingers along the side as I go, but I don't want to disrespect her like that. She's not some trashy, cheap ride to feel up, ride hard, and put up wet, abuse and turn into a rental car. She's worthy of *worship* and reverence.

Small vehicles might be what I'm best at—they might be what you'd call a passion, if I were to have one. Not that I've done it much since leaving town, but motorbikes, ATVs, dirt bikes, the shit I grew up working on with my brother was the only job that ever had a piece of my soul. But this timeless beauty in front of me holds a special place in my heart.

She's stunning.

Sleek, with curves in all the right places.

She might be a bit older than me, but I know how to treat her right and keep her happy.

Sure, she needs a little work, but don't we all?

And damn if she isn't still as gorgeous as ever, paint a little more pumpkin pie than vibrant mango these days, but that's nothing we can't fix.

I bet she's missed me as much as I've missed her all this time. This might've been just a handy cover story to pop on by, but seeing this beast of a machine in front of my own eyes again, it's reminded me what it felt like to drive her, feel her roar to life beneath me as we hugged the pavement of the curvy mountain roads, going faster than sensible when it was too dark to see beyond the light of the moon. Fuck, I might actually get under that hood and make her purr again before I leave town.

I mean, look at her. Sexy, perfect body with—what the fuck is that? On the trunk?

The sound of tires rolling over gravel is in some distant corner of my awareness, but that's not important right now. *What* is on my trunk?

Wyatt steps away, toward the arriving vehicle, but he's got a little more acceleration in his gait than usual. Instead of a casual amble, it's hurried. Another chalk mark in the *weird behavior* column in the mental tab.

I hear his wife's voice and the coos of a baby and am going to assume his eagerness is just wanting to see them after spending the whole day apart.

I'm too busy rubbing a gentle finger over the finish of my car's trunk, caressing the mark, trying to see if it'll come off, if there's texture to it, if we're dealing with a—gasp!—scratch, or what on earth is going on, to pay them any more attention.

But when minutes pass, my nose practically pressed to the paint, and he hasn't come back, my patience has worn as thin as this mark right here. "GRADY!" my voice booms, deeper than usual.

"Talking to yourself?" Rory's melodic voice teases me, but I can hear her heels tip-tapping and click-clacking as she approaches.

"Talking to your husband," I reply, deadpan. Never thought I'd say it, but this isn't the time for humor. "Get over here, Wyatt Andrew!"

"You're not Mom, asshat. You can't middle name me." Lucky for him, his voice sounds from right next to me.

"I'm about to call you a lot worse than your God-given name. What the fuck is this on my trunk?"

My eyes finally part with the scuff-skid hybrid—as I'm refusing to believe it could actually be a scratch—and I meet his gaze. Something cocky shines back at me.

"Looks like a scuff to me."

"You'd better hope it's just a scuff. I left her in pristine condition, so what is this from?" My eyes narrow on his, but Rory's cheeks flushing distract me for a second. She quickly looks down at the baby in her arms and nuzzles her, nose-to-nose, rather than look at me.

Wyatt decides to take the bull by the horns. "That's from my wife's heels." The way he owns those words, the pride in them, it creates a drop in my stomach that might be considered envy. Longing, just to even know what that's like.

"Why were you *walking* on my trunk?" I stare her down, arms crossed, but she keeps talking to the baby, not the pissed off brother-in-law in front of her.

Wyatt's smirk turns unbearable. "She wasn't walking."

His meaning hits in an instant.

"Aw, dude, gross! Come on, bro."

Rory blushes, cheeks turning a shade of pink I've never seen on her before, and she drops her head further, burying herself in the adorable rolls of their child instead of looking me in the eye.

"Tell me that baby wasn't conceived on my fucking *car*."

Wyatt's eyes narrow on me, like he doesn't love the tone I'm using when it comes to his precious girls. "Of course not. Your car was just the background to the hottes—"

"NO!" I cut him off, not letting him finish the word, much less the sentence I don't want to know the ending of.

I don't need nightmares when I look at my pride and joy.

"Not cool, man. Not. Fucking. Cool."

I shake my head at both of them, as stern as I probably have the ability to be if we're not throwing fists, and I realize Rory's shoulders are shaking. She's laughing at all of this?

The disrespect. Not even to me, because my brother has never respected me. But at least to the car. He's a mechanic, oil runs in our family blood. He knows better. That's like when a rock star smashes a guitar. Nothing cool about it, you just look like a prick, trashing a creation you proclaim to love.

"Fucking fix it. I'm going to get her up and running again, starting tomorrow. And you're going to not just buff that shit out, you're going to make her body *sparkle*."

"Well, now you're just making Van Gogh jealous," comes a higher pitched voice that I wasn't expecting. That little rasp in it rakes its nails across my skin, leaving goosebumps in its wake.

I flinch, jumping and turning around to face her. Was I so absorbed in my car that I missed her arrival? Luckily, I collect myself quickly.

"Aww, no need to be jealous, darlin'. She can get the full treatment too. Just as soon as Wyatt's done with mine." I shoot her a wink and hope she can't see my veins throbbing, pulsing beneath my skin, from the electricity racing through them right now.

Nope, yesterday definitely wasn't a fluke. This girl is even hotter than I remember.

Short, toned legs on display beneath those tight little shorts, most of her upper body hidden beneath the same NYA sweatshirt as last night, but she's got makeup on today.

Her hair is styled a little more carefully. Messy waves that frame her thin face and dust her shoulders. Bone structure that any woman would kill for. Something tells me that's not filler in those full lips, those plump cheeks. She's naturally both soft and sharp, all at the same time.

I want to draw her close, even though I have the feeling she'd claw to keep her distance. She'd be worth the scars of any battle it took to win her time.

Speaking of making our vehicles jealous, my car should be *green* with envy over the thoughts I'm having about this girl right now. My Charger is used to being the sole object of my affections.

Lust is a mistress I'm familiar with.

Love? Never met her.

But lust, I've been pretty much exclusive with her since I was a teen.

This? What lights me up when I look at Amelia? It's a potent hit of that shit that doesn't come around often.

If Wyatt weren't here, if I weren't under his *rules* for my stay in the Heights, if she and I were anywhere else, I'd be taking my chance, exploring this live wire of a connection between us, see if her senses are telling her that my body was made for hers too.

It's the tiny changes in her appearance that tell me I'm not alone in this. Things I've been attuned to notice in the fairer sex since high school. Her pupils expanding, nostrils flaring ever so slightly. Chest rising with a sharp inhale, cheeks and lips just slightly flushed. If I could see her thighs beneath that hoodie, they'd probably be flexing just a bit. As it is, I can see her cross one white sneakered foot in front of the other, one arm stretched across her abdomen, holding her other elbow.

I can tell when a woman is attracted to me with a blindfold on. And I have, by the way.

This one? Definitely into me.

Not like I can make a move on her right here and now, with this audience. I'm the Lothario who stomps on hearts, according to my only sibling.

Doesn't matter that I'm always up front with them. I

promise them a good time and nothing more. When they get it in their heads that we could be more, that's when it goes south.

And that's why I'm a one-and-done, and that's it.

I sure would like to get just that once with her though.

Maybe once my brother is done going over her van, I can get my chance to get her alone.

"We can go over this later, Weston. I need to go over Amelia's van with her."

I nod my head, bowing slightly in acceptance, and let them head back toward the open bay doors. I follow behind because it would be weird to stay in the corner all alone, not because I'm trying to insert myself in her business.

My niece reaches for her father as they walk, making grabby hands and noises of distress until he takes her from Rory. The change in him is instantaneous, becoming a softer version of the guy that I grew up with, someone I don't entirely recognize.

I catch Amelia watching too. Her face melts as she watches their interactions, the purity of the love between a father and daughter. She doesn't strike me as the overly sentimental type, but I could swear I see a tear close to dripping from one of those gorgeous ocean eyes. She turns around, both hands going up to her face, and I'm distracted by the noise of my niece starting to cry.

"No, no tears, baby girl. You're staying right here. Just need you to go to Mama for a minute." Wyatt's version of a baby voice isn't going to get him a YouTube channel for kids anytime soon, but his daughter seems to love it.

"Come here, little love," Rory soothes her, but she's inconsolable, reaching back for her father, wailing. Her little screams hurt my chest, and I step in.

"Wanna come see Uncle West?" I hold my hands out to her, and she stops screaming. Her little cherub cheeks, all pink from her sobs, they pull up in a toothless grin, and I swoop in to take her from her mom's arms. "Come here, munchkin. Let's do a lesson on why motocross is cooler than street racing."

Wyatt rolls his eyes at me and Rory snorts a laugh, but we all know it'll be plenty of time before I'm getting this little rascal into any trouble on anything more than her chubby legs.

My brother steps over to the office for a moment and comes back with a box of tissues. For a moment I wonder if he's watching Amelia as closely as I am, but her eyes are dry now. He yanks one tissue out and waves it in the air like a white flag. Then he extends one arm, offering her the square box.

"I'm afraid I've got some bad news for you," he says, so solemn I realize this is his version of humor.

"Is this the hospital waiting room then?" Amelia asks, catching on immediately.

Wyatt nods a couple of times, and she takes a deep breath, seeming to center herself. "All right then. Lay it on me."

"It's not just your engine. It's your transmission too."

Her face falls, cracking like an egg, and I watch as the shock of it runs down her face.

"Both?" she practically squeaks the word.

Rory's eyes bounce between her husband and the girl I shouldn't be so fascinated by, nearly as invested in this exchange as I am.

"Why don't you start by telling me the van's history," Wyatt suggests, leaning back on the hood of the vehicle behind him.

Amelia shifts her weight between her legs, grabs onto one elbow, and speaks. "She's a 2005, but I got her about eight years ago. She'd been through a lot by then, almost two hundred thousand miles on her dash, but she was all I could afford. She'd been an airport shuttle for a chain hotel out west, and they ran her hard from what I heard. I gutted her and outfitted her for the van life, and I know she looks pretty good for her age, but that's just because I gave her a facelift. Her guts are still original."

Amelia wraps one fist in the material of her sleeve that hangs past her free hand before she continues.

"I've taken her around the country slowly, tried not to wear her down too fast, but I've still put another two hundred or so on her since then."

Wyatt lets out a low whistle. "Then I say you're damn lucky. This thing should've died on you a long time ago."

Guilt flashes across her features before she answers him. "My check engine light has been on...a while." She says the last bit delicately, face alight with a refreshing kind of self-deprecating humor. That buzz inside me gets stronger, and I resist the urge to step into her personal space, busying myself by bouncing my niece in my arms.

"If it makes you feel any better, there's not really anything you could've done to save her life," Wyatt tells her. "Even humans who live to be a hundred can be taken out by a damn cold. You never know what's going to be the kiss of death."

Rory flinches so slightly I bet Amelia didn't even notice, but Wyatt keeps talking, though one hand does move to his wife's back.

"We've all only got so much in us. But I'd say you got a hundred and twenty human years out of this one here, and to count your blessings."

Amelia takes another deep breath in and then nods, that hand now rubbing up and down her arm. "So are you saying it's time for a funeral?"

Wyatt's mouth turns down, and he shakes his head. "Nah, not unless you want it to be. There are options." He taps the printout in his hand.

Amelia's gaze drifts over the paper, stepping closer to take it in, and her eyes widen. "Walk me through what I'm looking at here before I have a heart attack at twenty-seven and you're found liable for my death *and* Van Gogh's."

"I think our insurance policy covers death by shock from estimates," Rory says, straight-faced. "As long as you don't have any gold diggers in your family who'll come after us for our last few bucks, we should be fine," she jokes.

But Amelia's laugh in response isn't real, like the ones I earned from her last night were. It's forced, like she doesn't want to bring attention to whatever it is she's mentally sprinting past there.

Lucky for her, Wyatt's never dragged out a conversation in his life. "We can rebuild with OEM parts, or do an aftermarket build. Getting parts straight from the manufacturer is that top number."

"The arm and two legs," Amelia tosses out, deadpan.

"Still cheaper than a new van with all the bells and whistles yours has," he points out.

"Barely," she mumbles.

"The second number is if we get aftermarket parts and rebuild the engine and transmission cheaper. I checked my suppliers, and I couldn't find any new or even decent used engines that'll work for your van, so we'd have to source the parts individually and then put it together here."

Amelia takes just a second to grapple with the bad news before standing up straighter and nodding her head again. Is it wrong that it intrigues me? That I'm dying to know what she's been through that she's so quick to accept the worst-case scenario and go right into moving forward, rather than mourning what she's lost?

"And that price, how would that be charged?" she asks, all

business. I think Rory might even be impressed, which is saying something.

"This right here," Wyatt taps something on the paper, "is the deposit. It's the cost of the materials we'd have to order for the job. The rest is labor, which would be due on completion, you're looking at about three, maybe four weeks until that would be due."

"Three weeks?" Her brows raise, but she seems like she's already accepted this change in her course of fate.

"The parts will take at least a week to get here, and then it's gonna be another week or two to get the engine rebuilt, installed, and ready for ya. Maybe three, with all the work we have backing up right now." His eyes move pointedly around the shop. Not sure if she catches it, but that was Wyatt for "be thankful I fit you in today."

"And my alternatives are...?" she trails off the question, waiting for Wyatt to fill in the rest.

"Sell her to someone who wants to put the work in. Scrap her for parts, but that's a shame considering the condition the rest of her is in. You've kept her up well." Wyatt shrugs a shoulder. "Or tow her to another shop, fifty or a hundred miles away —though the nearest one I'd recommend is about two hundred miles or so—and see if they'll lie to you and sell you something cheaper that'll get you just far enough away from them before you break down again."

"Have you considered writing self-help books?" Amelia asks with surprising grit for someone who's a good foot shorter and close to a hundred pounds lighter than the man she's staring down. "If so, I wanna throw a title in the suggestion box."

Wyatt huffs out some sort of amused breath, and she takes it as encouragement.

"Life on the Sunny Side."

Rory bursts out laughing, causing the baby in my arms to

giggle too. I don't blame either of them. Sure as hell can't help the smile breaking out across my face either.

Something tells me life is gonna be a lot brighter with her in the Heights for the next few weeks. Even if I have to wait to shoot my shot with her.

6

Amelia

"Listen, I'm not a forensic psychiatrist. All I'm saying is that I don't think we're doing the world any favors by naming the worst possible human beings these names that sound desirable to psychopaths. If we'd gone with 'The Tiny Peened Rapist with ED' I think the Golden State Killer might've stopped right in his damn tracks before any murders were committed. Maybe he wouldn't have wanted to risk another victim embarrassing him by talking about his tiny fucking button mushroom below the belt. But instead, the media glorified him with some name that gives him a sense of accomplishment. He doesn't deserve that. No murderer should be memorialized on a pedestal or cast in bronze."

Jynx's husky voice would've been ideal for a career in a smoky burlesque lounge, warming up the crowd, introducing the cast. Her face, body, and effortless charisma could've made her a star on the center of that stage, if you ask me. But she chose to pursue telling the stories of survivors, shining light on some of the most gruesome parts of society in an effort to enlighten and empower a generation against becoming victims.

The way her throaty tone floats through my Sprinter van,

filling the small space—even as it's immobilized outside the only auto shop in Smoky Heights—sets an entire mood on its own, and I'm thankful she chose this route instead of any others.

"And I'm just saying, Vixens, if they were publicly *shamed* instead of awarded these fucked up names that almost *celebrate* their derangements, maybe fewer psychopaths would have aspirations of getting their own name. If they thought their legacy might be 'The Cuck Who Had a Foot Fetish' rather than the Eerie Eradicator, maybe they wouldn't be so quick to transition from experimenting on roadkill to killing human beings."

"Hear fucking hear!" I shout back to Jynx, like she can hear me all the way through the vortex of time and space, from Smoky Heights to NYC, now to the years ago when this was recorded.

I started listening to *Vengeful Vixens* when an episode from season four shot her to the number one podcast in the country, and then I just kept listening straight through, so now I'm circling back to season one, catching up on all of her earlier episodes I've missed out on till now, while I wait for her new season to come out. I can't believe I was living my life, traveling the country with Van Gogh, for *years* without knowing she existed. She is an icon.

I mean, she's really got a point. Why *do* these horrific acts of unnecessary violence get awarded names that inspire fear in the population, and give the most vile among us hard-ons for their own claim to fame?

The Beast of Chicago, Jack the Ripper, the Bladed Butcher. The Santa Slayer. A shudder rips through me. These men, their horrid acts, don't deserve recognition.

The survivors are the ones we should be celebrating.

As Jynx starts to read off ads from sponsors of the show, I turn in my van, hands on my hips, a breeze on my bare tits.

It's been a few days that I've been back home in Van Gogh.

After I accepted the estimate from Wyatt, he graciously agreed to move the van out into his parking lot where he said I could stay, up until he needed to actually swap out the engine and he'll need the van back.

It's been enough time that I've gotten my bearings in this little town. Not long enough for the pull toward Weston to chill the heck out and flush itself out of my system.

With the way he's overtaken my thoughts since I landed in this small town, it might take getting laid by a rock star—maybe Josh, the singer of my favorite band, New York Ave (or even better, a sandwich with him and the bassist, Blondie)—and leaving town for my next fresh start for that to happen.

But damn, is it good to be back home. There's not much that makes me feel safe, but this small van, these walls that have traveled coast to coast with me, they've done it.

In my private world, where I'm stashed with everything I need and I never stay in one place long, I'm able to maintain the boundaries and secrecy I need to feel safe.

Got to run out to do my laundry today, a cute little laundromat downtown called Smoky Suds, which is a little confusing because I'm pretty sure the bar I passed on my way had the same exact name. I asked Rory, who was the one who dropped me off on her lunch break and picked me up again at the end of the day, and she just laughed and said it's being addressed.

Now I'm stuck with my least favorite part of laundry, the part where I have to fold it and put it back away in the drawers beneath my bed in the back of the van. Crawling around under there creeps me out. Which is probably why I'm mostly just staring at the piles of folded crop tees, athletic shorts, skimpy underwear, and the one sweatshirt I own.

Listening to true crime podcasts helps pass the time, keep my mind entertained while I confront the worst task of first world human existence. Washing it isn't that bad. Drying it isn't that bad. But putting it away? Yeesh. When you only have a small capsule wardrobe and have to do laundry more than most, I'm going to go out on a limb and say you grow to hate it even quicker. Or maybe that's just one of my many personality deficiencies speaking.

Today is one of those days where throwing myself in the dryer on a steam cycle sounds better than dealing with this pile staring back at me. But, hey, that's just my pessimist half talking. I can buck up, knock this out, and get back to my favorite hobby. Watching Weston work on his car like a creeper who hasn't gotten laid in way too long. There's some inspiration for me.

Thanks to analysis paralysis, I still haven't decided *which* crop tee to wear tonight, hence the slight breeze on my nips.

At least I can still live in my van, even if I can't drive her. The battery packs still work just fine, and Wyatt's been kind enough to let me plug in as needed and even refill my water tanks from his shop. He's a gruff sorta guy, maybe not as much of a dick as I originally thought. Nice where it counts, I guess.

Not like the *other* Grady, who's nice in *all* the ways and then some. I fight a chill in the room, but my nipples still perk up anyway.

I swear, this set of tits was worth every penny just for the nipples that are always looking up. They might actually be where I get my optimism from.

Sure, it started off as a way to not look so slight, so delicate, give me a little more shape and curve and feel a little bit fiercer, but they've come to be one of my favorite parts of myself. That, and the other embellishment I gave them.

My laptop chimes with the familiar electronic beep of an incoming email, and I pause the podcast just as Jynx comes back from the ad break to check it. Hopefully it's my damn employer coming back with the increase in workload I asked for so I have a way to cover the repairs Van Gogh needs.

It was all I could do not to vomit on the spot when Wyatt showed me that estimate. Had to use my years of stone-faced composure that keeps strangers—the only type of people I get to have in my life—at bay and nod, like he isn't asking for ten times my monthly disposable income to get Van Gogh moving again.

This is why we keep savings, I hear the loving voice of my mother in my head, teaching me a life lesson in my early teen years when our only car broke down and we had to sacrifice a few meals to pay the bill, so she could still get to work at the diner and sneak some food out of the kitchen for the two of us at the end of each shift so we didn't have to go *completely* without that month.

"I tried, Mom." I say the words out loud, as my thoughts so often are.

There just hasn't been enough work for a while to add to savings *and* send money back home. Plus, I had to dip into my sad little savings a few too many times when I had to stay at a campground because some snobby tourist called the cops to complain about my van being parked out at the beach. Or one of the big chain stores where they don't allow overnight vehicles anymore.

Or that time my signal cut out and I couldn't find my way to the stop I had planned when a road was washed out, so I pulled over in a neighborhood for the night and someone called in a complaint. I download the maps for my routes ahead of time these days but can't go back and change the past.

If I could, I'd go a lot further back than not finding a better place to park that night. Draining my measly savings account is far from the worst thing to happen to me.

I plop down on the bed, breasts bouncing with the rest of me as I do, laptop on my thighs to check it out.

It's not more work.

It's something better. It might not pay in money, but it warms my insides in ways material things—even food—can't. Reminds me why I stay strong, of my purpose, why I survived as long as I have, and why sharing anything I can do without from my pay is worth it, even when it means struggling in times like this.

> *Hello my sweet angel,*
>
> *It's so good to hear from you. Thank you for writing!*
> *I tried to email you last week, but silly me, I used your last address by mistake. I tried to find this one, but I think it disappeared from my inbox or something. You know me and technology.*
>
> *What's this about a hiccup? Are you okay? Are you safe? Let me know if I can help in some way.*
>
> *I planted pinks, yellows, and red tulips this year. Should be another month or so before they're blooming, but of course I'll send you pictures.*
>
> *Not much new here. Yes, it's chilly. I've got to stay bundled up not just on the way to and from work, but sometimes even in the diner. Jeff likes to say keeping it a few degrees colder in the cafe makes people spend more money, but I think it's more than a few degrees, and it just keeps the staff shivering. He's probably losing more in dropped plates and orders that have to be remade because our fingers have gone numb than people can possibly be spending. I know heat is expensive, but surely customers would pay a few cents more to be comfortable while they eat?*
>
> *Anyway, don't mind me, I'm just happy the snowy season is all but gone. That last storm, I was pretty sure we were going to get snow inside the cafe there for a minute!*

Haha! But don't worry, Minnesota will be sunny and beautiful again in no time, and my poor fingers are already nearly thawed.

I can't wait to hear about your latest adventures and where you are now or what you're up to! Looking forward to my next postcard.

Meeting up with you for New Year's would mean the world to me, sweetheart. But only if it's safe for you. But as long as we're dreaming, if we could go anywhere, I'd say let's meet in Hawaii. Or maybe Norway. Anywhere we could spend time together would be heaven for me, even McDonald's.

Miss you always. Love you longer.

Mom

My chest pinches, my heart constricting tight, and I have to squeeze my eyes shut to stop the stinging in them from turning into more.

A familiar sort of rage courses through me for just a moment, hatred for the men in my life who put us in this position, followed by a desolate resignation that this is the status quo now. My mom, stuck where she is, kept in place by her past, with no hope for her future. And me, on the run, doing my best to hide from that same past, while never allowing anyone new in because history has proven that isn't an option for me.

This is as good as it gets for someone with karma like mine. When countless lives are ruined because of you, you can't expect a life of rainbows and butterflies in return.

I get to find my escape in the open road, a new place to explore, or a new body to find release with. Except there won't be any of those for me, at least not for the next few weeks.

Well, there is *one* body that's been on my mind lately, and speak of the devil... I know curiosity killed the cat, but what's so great about life anyway if I can't indulge in what makes it worthwhile when given the chance?

He's been at the shop most nights, working on that hot rod of his, and my plans for tonight include sneaking a peek to get my daily dose of eye candy and spank bank fodder.

Setting my laptop to the side where it's safe and I can reply to her later, when I'm in a better mood, I army crawl to the back window and pull the covering up just enough for an eyeball to see through it. The bay doors are open, but I can't make out any shapes moving around inside. Either Wyatt is still here, working out of sight in his office, or Weston is in the back, beneath the hood of that car he's obsessed with.

I'd be lying if I said I hadn't been keeping an eye on him when I can these past few nights. Finding excuses to set up a folding chair outside my door "to get some sun" (even after dark, when there's only one kind of Vitamin D available) and watch his muscles flex as he toils in the beam of the work lights set up in the garage. Or working outside so I can get a bit of fresh air (mostly motor oil and gas fumes), computer on my lap as I work a hell of a lot slower than usual, distracted by the view, and the occasional flirty lines thrown my way.

Hey, if there's one thing I've learned through my hardships, it's that you've gotta take pleasure where you can find it, in the simplest of things. Like admiring the male form in all its glory when you're presented with the chance.

With a sigh of acceptance—looks like my plans tonight include nothing but laundry after all—I press play on the podcast and resume my heated exchange with the host who can't hear me.

"Going through your suggestions on social media, thank you, Vixens, for chipping in with your ideas of better names for real-life villains, here we go. The Flaccid, Tiny Penised Pervert. FTPP. That one's got a nice ring to it."

I cheer, like it's a live audience show, as the suggestions get even more ridiculous. Laughing through her tears, Jynx tries to sober up again before wrapping up the segment. "Stop empowering horrible men, that's all I'm saying. I hope the FBI is listening."

Biting the bullet, I drop down to my knees and crawl underneath the bed, pulling out the drawer from the very back of my storage space so I can put my lesser worn clothes back into it. It's like a sound vacuum down there, like an interactive exhibit I saw at a museum as a child, with my father, back in better times, if you can call it that. Nothing but blackness, not even the sound of my podcast makes it through. It's freaky being *that* alone with just my thoughts and demons, and I back out rapidly, jumping back up and rejoining the conversation.

"I bet the FBI *is* listening," I murmur in response to the last thing I heard from her to my empty van. "I hope they're taking notes too. Might be able to save some lives."

"So what do you say, Vixens? Are we going to put up with more of this?"

"NO!" I shout, unbridled passion in my voice.

The door to my van slides open and I turn around, shrieking in surprise, only to see a very shocked Weston there, staring at my chest, rapt, jaw dropped, chin practically to his collarbone.

That fifty-degree air is mighty chilly on my bare skin, even if the way he's taking me in will keep me warm for *many* nights to come. The draft from the open door caresses my skin almost as strongly as his gaze does, the heat in his stare warring with the chill, and my flesh erupts in goosebumps. After a few seconds that feel like hours, I regain my senses about the same instant he does.

"Fuck!" He slams his hands over both eyes, like he didn't

just gawk at my half-naked form long enough to be able to commission an accurate police sketch in perfect detail of every freckle on my upper body.

Let's put it another way. If my body ever needs to be identified, Weston would probably recognize my tits before my face at the coroner's office.

"Well don't just stand there!" I huff, covering my freezing skin with my palms and turning my back on him. "Come in and close the door."

He huffs out some sort of confused sound, but I hear the heavy footfalls and feel the van rock with the motion before the side door slides and latches closed.

"Are you okay?" he asks, still sounding stunned.

I grab a shirt from one of the piles on the bed at random and yank it on over my head, letting it fall into place, the cut-off edge ending just below the bottoms of my breasts.

"Clearly."

I shut the podcast off, leaving the van quietly humming with electricity, nothing but the awkward silence and raging hormones in the air now.

Turning around to face him again, I cross my arms over my chest and stare at him, brows raised in self-defense mode. I don't get a chance to form questions or accusations, because he lets out a sound like a growl before I can speak, shock still all over his face.

"You have your nipple pierced." There's no judgment in the statement. Surprise, yes. But mostly, it's just awe, appreciation, and wonder.

"Did you win some sort of award on observation as a Boy Scout?"

He shakes his head back and forth slowly, tongue dragging over his lower lip as he keeps those heated eyes focused on my face, with some effort. "Naw, darlin'. That's a skill I've been saving just for you. One of many. Should we do some cramming so I can pass the pop quiz later?"

His eyes drag down my face, jaw, and neck with a palpable pressure on my skin, awakening my nerve endings as he goes.

I drop my hands instinctively, putting them on the backs of my hips as he takes in the sight of me in this shirt. How little of me it covers, and what he can still see through it.

"Hottest tits I ever fuckin saw. Hands down."

"I'll add it to my award collection," I deadpan, pointing to a shelf behind me like it's full of trophies and plaques of my many achievements, not every measly thing I own, stowed for travel.

Weston still stands in the space in front of my door, hand to his jaw, still seemingly mesmerized.

"Did you break in just to drool at me? You're going to leave a puddle if you keep staring."

I'm past the point of worrying for my physical safety around this guy. My mental fortifications might need some work around him, he makes me want things that aren't safe for me, but physically I know I'm in no danger with him.

Call it experience, or a woman's intuition, maybe it's my Pisces gifts, or the males I was around in my younger years. Whatever you want to chalk it up to, I can sense when a guy has danger below the surface, and in my few encounters with this man, I can already tell you that he ain't it.

Could I see him throwing down with an asshole who overstepped some boundaries once or twice? Sure. But he's not one of these guys with anger issues seething beneath the surface, waiting for someone to take them out on.

So whatever he came here for tonight, it was wholesome enough. I'm not getting creeper vibes from him.

Quite the opposite.

I wish he'd be a little *less* respectful of me with all that fire in his eyes. I'd like to see how it burns when he sets it free.

That yearning is back, boiling my blood and making my cells sing with something unfamiliar. A desire so strong I can only blame the fact that I missed my chance to hook up in the last few cities I stopped over in. I'm overdue for human contact, the exchange of pleasure, and my body is demanding I pay, with interest.

"I didn't break in," he finally answers, forcing his eyes back onto mine. "I knocked, but you didn't answer, and then I heard you yelling 'NO!' and thought maybe you needed help."

Did I yell that? It's possible. I have a lot of conversations with myself, or the podcasts I listen to. But right now my memory is failing me, the way his eyes burned for me etched permanently into my brain, the only thing it wants to focus on. But I need him to know I'm just fine without his help.

"For the record, it's never safe to open a random woman's door without her permission. Especially mine."

A small voice in my head wonders why I didn't lock it. Why I didn't feel the constant pressure I'm used to putting on myself to protect myself at all hours of the day, no matter how harmless my environment appears. What part of me felt safe here, outside of this garage, in this small town?

"Noted." He nods once, dark blond hair flopping with the movement. "So you were, just...talking to Van Gogh? I thought that whole talking to your van thing was just a joke."

"Oh no, it's very serious. She and I discuss everything."

His mouth twitches, amusement leaking through his expression, but I have a point to make here.

"I don't need protecting. You're lucky I didn't mace you."

"Your tits did the trick," he says, with another dip of his head. "I was frozen in place, my eyes are *still* burning with that picture. Hell, you could've knocked me over with an exhale, I wasn't going anywhere. All yours to do with what you'd like, darlin'. Shit, you could mace me now if you want, it'd still be worth it."

I roll my eyes and let out a flutter of a sigh, trying not to smile at how thick he's laying it on. "Been a while since you've seen a pair that weren't on your phone, huh?"

His dark green eyes twinkle with mischief before he answers me. "Nah, just never seen a pair that gorgeous, that's all. Forgive my manners, I wasn't expecting that welcome. I just stopped by because my brother needed me to check something on a part real quick. But now..." His voice trails off, those eyes lingering on my face, drawing me deeper into his every word. "I feel like I have this unfair advantage in that I've seen what you're working with, but you haven't seen mine."

I'm not sure if eyes can really bulge, the way they do in cartoons, but I think mine make a concerted effort at it, and I'm surprised to feel my cheeks heat at the implication. My voice is steady, however, when I retaliate.

"Calm down, Boy Scout. No need to whip out your python just so you can call us even. They're boobs. I'll be fine living with the knowledge you've seen them. I've been through worse."

Weston puts a hand on his chest, and I try not to notice the way the tendons flex in his forearm and hand as he does. "But I don't think *I* can live with the disparity of having been gifted that vision from the titty gods and not repaying you in some way. It feels like the universe is out of balance."

"If you wanna make a contribution to the hidden folder in my Photos app, at least do me the honor of good lighting."

His mouth tilts up in a filthy smirk, and his lips might as well be pressed against my skin for the ways I can feel that look.

"You want a keepsake, darlin', say the word and we can get this photo shoot started."

My hand flies to my chest as a laugh bubbles out of me. "You're really sure of yourself, aren't you, Boy Scout?"

"You seem to know what you're working with." Those glittering eyes flash down to my chest, barely covered, before he shrugs one shoulder. "I know my strengths too."

"And here I thought your arms and that pretty face were what you had to offer."

"Hell, darlin', you ain't seen anything yet." His teeth catch the corner of his lip in another delicious smirk and dammit if my thighs don't clench in response. The man has such a wholesome way about him, but then those filthy undertones come out, and my head just spins in his presence. It's an unfair combination, really.

"All right, Boy Scout. Show me what you're working with. But I gotta warn you, if nothing is pierced, I *will* be disappointed, and the universe will still be misaligned."

One palm grabs the hem of his shirt and fists in the material.

My eyes are glued to it, and I know this moment should be comical, this should be ridiculous, it started as a joke and I should be laughing at him, but somehow the air has become so thin in the van that all humor has evaporated with my sense of self preservation.

My curiosity has got the best of me now, or maybe that's just my libido that's calling the shots.

Mouth dry, lips parted, I watch a bit too intently as he grips the material of his white tee and begins to pull it up, slowly, like I'm going to tip him if he does it right.

Full disclosure, I don't think there's a wrong way this man can do something right now, unless he stops.

In fact, there's a good chance this preview is going to turn into a full feature film. One where Van Gogh sees things she's never seen before. Me, on my back on this mattress, legs split like a hung jury, this man in between them, making the van rock harder than NYA when they play a sold out show.

His other hand travels down his abdomen, over his shirt,

until the tips of his fingers meet the start of his pants. Weston slips a thumb beneath the waistband and pulls down, away from the shirt that's slinking up, up, up too slowly for me to possibly see enough.

"Tell me when to stop," he says in a low voice.

My eyes find his, defiant in my silence, and then crawl down his body as slowly as his did on mine. The way he soaked in my bare skin shamelessly, I pay it forward, doubled. I watch as his left hand brings that shirt higher, revealing inch by inch of tanned, toned skin covering more abs than I can count as my breath whooshes out of me.

Is he for real? Who does he think he is, a fitness influencer? Nobody *needs* that many abs.

Why does he bother painting when he could sell shots of his muscles and never have to do a day of physical labor again? Better yet, maybe he could offer body shots off of that stomach?

One hand pulls down further on his pants, and a dangerous dusting of soft hair makes my lips part with a gasp of a breath I'm praying he couldn't hear. I might as well have moaned "fuck me."

This would be a good time to wipe my mouth in case any drool is getting out, but I'm too distracted. That hand with the shirt finally, finally clears his stomach, showing me his defined pecs—not a piercing in sight, and I'm almost glad. It would've been a desecration of his creator's will to do *anything* other than worship that chest with my own body.

The muscles beneath the golden skin that force my eyes to follow the hard lines down, down, across his chiseled abs, those indentations at his hips, to the rest of him he's so clearly willing to show me.

"Are we even?" His voice has dropped dangerously low, to a timbre that makes me shiver as it scrapes across my skin. "I saw your chest, you saw mine. Or would you like to have the upper hand here?"

My eyes are locked on his right hand, the way it's dragging the waistband further down than I thought he'd go.

"It's your call, darlin'." He pulls my eyes back up to his, but my mouth is too dry to speak up.

This is a game of chicken where there are no losers if he just doesn't stop the show.

I won't call him on his bluff if he doesn't call me on mine.

Proving how well he intuits me already, Weston takes the hint, hears the silent plea—maybe he smells the change in my chemical makeup, the way I'm ready for him, all bets are off, fuck my normal rules, I'll bend them all to appease this growing need that blazes to life inside me every time I'm around him.

With his shirt held high, there's nothing blocking my view from his entire lower abdomen, as he pulls the pants lower, lower, until I can see the base of *much* more than I showed him.

The stem of what would surely be the best ride of my life, given the chance.

My stomach drops into my core, thighs tightening, inner muscles clenching at the thickness I see there, the hint of what continues far, far below what I can see, if that girth is any indication of the length.

Is it my time to leave town yet?

Do I even need to wait for my last night?

This pull between us is intoxicating, a heavy presence in the van that makes the air thick as we stare one another down. I'm so desperate to explore it, I can probably talk myself into giving in now, instead of waiting until my van and I are ready to keep moving.

A visceral memory as a keepsake of this adorable town, the kind people in it, and the hottest man I've ever seen seems like a worthwhile compromise to my ordinarily stringent rules.

Besides, I've avoided emotional attachment all this time. It should be no problem to keep my heart out of this equation, just like with all the other one-night stands, even if I am stuck here for another few weeks after the hookup.

Hooking up with him would surely be worth any awkwardness that lingered after the orgasms have faded.

My imagination runs wild with what Weston looks like beneath the remaining clothes, what he looks like hard and ready. How he'd look as he's *entering* me, and that's when my knees start to buckle.

I drop backward onto the bed, not entirely a conscious move, but fuck it. I'm ready to break some of my rules and take it there. Finish what his hands and both our eyes have started.

But the knock at the door might as well be the wet rag tossed over the budding flame. Or maybe an entire bucket of cool water, judging from the look on Weston's face as he drops his shirt and yanks his pants back up in less than a blink when he hears Wyatt's voice on the other side.

"Amelia, are you in there?"

The roar of the flame between us turns into a sizzle and douses out completely with a lackluster hiss.

7
Weston

"I'm here!" Amelia's voice is even higher than usual when she calls out quickly to Wyatt, deceptively innocent. Now that I've seen those tits she's sporting, I feel pretty damn confident there's nothing innocent about this girl.

She's got the face of a doll, the humor of a mortician, and the tits of an angel. In short, my dream girl.

Somehow I didn't see the nipple ring coming.

That's a sight that'll be hard to get out of my head anytime soon, but if anything could kill my growing boner, it's the sound of my brother's voice crashing this party.

Did I come here tonight to flirt? No.

Did I mean to start something that I'm not supposed to finish? Also no.

I came here to do him a favor, that's it. But I wasn't about to leave her feeling awkward about that snafu of an entrance. Not in my nature to make a woman uncomfortable or leave her without a smile on her face. Had to turn that around before I could get back to business as usual.

Though now that I recall the text exchange with my brother, I'm thinking he wanted an answer immediately, and I may have left my phone in my truck when I got here and headed straight over to her. It's highly possible he's been buzzing me the whole time I've been in here, wondering if the boundaries he set apply to girls who are only *visiting* the town, not locals. He must've zipped back to the garage to get the answer himself rather than wait for me.

"Give me a second!" she hollers to an answering grunt.

No matter how you paint this picture, he's not going to see this as something virtuous, or me succeeding at the task he gave me if he opens this door and finds the two of us in here alone, still breathing heavy from the aftermath of the *almost* that just occurred.

"Hide," she whispers in a hiss through her teeth, accurately interpreting that deer in the headlights look on my face as *he can't find me here*.

"I'm taller than your van is long, how am I supposed to do that?" I whisper back at her in a panic.

"You are not, just get in my bed."

"All you had to do was ask." I can't resist the line.

She points her narrowed eyes at me, finger inches from my nose. "You want him to find you here?"

I shake my head quickly, and her face goes from stone to something softer. "Get in the corner and shut the fuck up for once in your life."

"Says the woman who apparently talks to herself. You're still going to need to come clean on that to me, by the way."

Her palm claps down over my mouth, trying to silence my hushed whispers, and I obey, falling quiet under the feel of her velvet soft skin and the flurry of images it calls to mind.

Amelia grabs a sweatshirt from next to me on the bed and quickly dons it before opening the door wide enough for her slim body to be visible to Wyatt on the other side.

"Hey, sorry to intrude. Weston's not in there, is he?"

My stomach dips in a way that's a lot less of a flirty *let's do this, darlin'* and a lot more *stay six feet back in case of projectile vomiting.*

"The blond mythological sex god also known as your brother? Yeah, we fucked all day and I just cut him loose."

Incredulous laughter almost bursts out of me at her gall, but I can practically hear my brother's disapproving glare. Not sure there's a brand of humor that's for him, but that *definitely* wasn't it.

"He said he'd come by to check on a part for me." The next line is grumbled so low I'm surprised I can even make it out. "Should've known better than to ask him to do something that was important." The heavy sigh that follows weighs me down where I lay crouched down out of sight, an extra hundred pounds of disappointment on my shoulders.

"Maybe he got caught up working on his car or something?" She offers an alternative to him thinking the worst of me, because she doesn't realize yet that Wyatt will always jump to the worst-case option when it comes to me and my responsibility.

Amelia's so casual, so quick on her feet, I bet he has no clue she's lying to his face. The practice it must take to master that skill, to be so smooth, so effortless as you're pulling the wool over someone's eyes. I'm not sure if I revere her or fear her as I watch.

There's quiet for a moment, where I imagine my brother looking down the lot, eyeing my truck parked near the shop, the bay doors wide open, trying to spot where I might be hiding, what I might be doing that's more important than what he asked for my help with. More likely he's assuming I just forgot entirely.

"Anyway," his gruff voice goes on. "Supplier's out of one of the parts we ordered, and I just needed to double check if the substitute they offered will work. Okay if I drop under your hood for a sec?"

"Sure, I'll pop it."

The door latches shut and I stay hidden as she climbs into the driver's seat, releases the hood and waits for him to finish what he's doing. The *thunk* that rocks the whole van not a minute later tells me he's got what he needed. She smiles out her window, waving at him as he drives off in his dark blue pickup. If I had the love of my life to get home to, I'd probably fly out of work every day too. The pressure on my chest turns into a knot in my stomach that's all too similar to the food poisoning that burrito gave me, and I do my best to ignore it.

Amelia stands and walks back to me. "Sorry I distracted you from your *very important* task." She gets all stuffy for a second, impersonating Wyatt, and it draws one side of my mouth up.

"Don't be. Seeing your tits has been the highlight of my entire trip back so far, darlin'. Much better than looking under Van Gogh's hood again."

"Don't let her hear that. She's insecure about the way gravity is affecting her pipes."

That gets a chuckle out of me, but this pattern of hers, deflecting with humor, it's familiar in a way that means I know what's beneath it. She chooses to laugh, to make others laugh, instead of retreat into the loneliness I recognize in her, and that earns her even more respect from me. Just furthers my need to get to peek behind her curtain and see what else makes her tick.

"Probably none of my business, darlin', but should I be asking how you're so good at bullshitting?"

"You're right, Boy Scout. None of your business." Her blueish green eyes harden into armor, determined to keep me out, watching me laying on her bed, propped on my elbows as I wait for more. After a moment, something in them warms, just a little. It's a visible change, her irises going from steely to a state like liquid metal before she opens up.

"But you've done me more than your fair share of solids."

Her hands rest on her low back once more, arms out to her sides, and I try not to get distracted by her chest popping out.

"So I'll just say it comes with the territory of being on the move. People get nosy."

She gives me a pointed look and I shoot an unapologetic grin at her.

"They wanna know more than I wanna share."

One shoulder shrugs softly, and it takes some concentration to not stare at the way her tits move beneath that sweatshirt as she does, now that I can visualize them in perfect clarity, but her words have me captivated right now.

"Had to get good at keeping people out. It's a lot easier if they don't realize you're doing it."

How matter of fact she is on the subject could be depressing if I let it, but I'm a fellow disciple of the *Make the Most Outta Life* handbook she seems to have taken a few pages out of.

I opt for applying that life philosophy right about now.

"Wanna get shitfaced?"

"Are you trying to get me drunk and into my own bed?" she asks playfully.

"Aw, I won't make the first move when a woman is drunk," I tell her.

"When will you make it?" The flint in her voice rolls down my spine, urging me to move in.

Suck in a breath through my teeth because with the knowledge of how insanely perfect her tits are, that look on her face that's begging for trouble, and this energy that pulses between us I haven't been able to tune out since that first night I met her, this isn't the answer I wanna give her.

"'Fraid I'm not going to make one."

Disappointment drips down her face, pulls into this little pout of a frown that shouldn't look so good, and I can't let that stay there. It'd be a crime to ruin a perfect face like hers with something as needless as unhappiness.

"Not because I don't want to."

Her face screws up in confusion, but she waits for more.

"It's complicated."

"Oh God, tell me you don't have a partner. Did I flash a taken man?"

Amelia's palms clap to her face, covering her eyes and forehead as she spins around to give me her back, and actually this might be the first time I've gotten a good look at her ass, with no shirt in the way of my view. It's pulled up with the motion of her arms right now, and that might make *me* an ass for noticing when she's clearly distressed, but I can't help but take in that perfect little round bottom that would look so damn good sliding down on me, reverse cowgirl—shit, my libido is going to get me in trouble again.

My brother might be right about me.

I can't even have a conversation with this girl without planning all the ways I want to wreck her body.

Amelia continues muttering to herself, "Oh God, oh God, oh God," pulling me out of my dirty thoughts and onto her spiral. *Do I have a partner?*

"No, God, no," I assure her. "I don't do relationships. I'm not that guy."

"Thank fuck," she breathes out, turning on one foot just as quickly to face me once more.

Not the usual reaction. Usually I get a pout, with soft eyes that say *I can change him*. Should I be hurt that she doesn't want more?

"Not that you don't deserve someone," she hurries to clarify.

Not that you don't deserve someone.

If my eyes could sting, they would. No one's ever put it like that. Considered it might be something I *want*. Something I've longed for. Something I've never found, and all but given up on.

But this girl. This borderline stranger chose *those* words for me over any others.

She hurries to continue, "I'm just not a commitment girl myself."

I believe those words about as much as I'd believe them about myself, but sure, I'll play along.

"If I had crossed the line with somebody else's...whatever, I would've had to shank myself. Girl code and all that."

"No need to shank anyone tonight."

I soothe her with my usual humorous thread through every word. It dies out though when I try to expand on my sorry excuse for an explanation.

"It's complicated because of...family dynamics." I choose the words carefully, but she still nods like she gets it. "Not because I don't want you."

"Your brother."

"What are you, a detective? That why you're so obsessed with true crime? It would explain that dark sense of humor of yours."

She scoffs, shuffling her feet and rolling her eyes. "Your brother's clearly got something going on where you're concerned."

Sharp. Winds me for just a second, actually. Most don't seem to think twice about the comments Wyatt makes about me.

My tongue runs across my lower lip as I consider how to respond. How much is too much to tell someone you just met, especially when said person is relying on that same brother's business to get back to her normal life.

"We've...had some differences over the years. He doesn't

appreciate the way I run my life, especially not where women are concerned. Wyatt made it pretty clear when I came back that I'm not to start anything with any of the local girls and I'm not here to stir shit up with him."

I know Amelia sees the depth behind my words, but bless her for keeping it light. "I'm not a local girl," she says with a devilish quirk of her lips.

"Somehow I don't think he'd see it that way."

She sits down next to me on the bed and places a small hand on my knee, right overtop the dried paint on my pants, not seeming to care about the mess there, despite the pristine environment in her own van.

"I know I don't know either of you for shit, but can I just say something?"

"Anything, darlin'." It's barely more than an exhale, she's got me captivated with those eyes, that sweet face, and everything sinister it's hiding. "Whatever you've got to say, hit me."

"Sometimes the people who've known us the longest are the people who can't drop their own opinions about us that hold us back. We all grow with time, and sometimes it's hard for them to see who we *are* and not who we were. At some point, you're going to have to move forward and live your life the way that's right for you, with or without his permission. It's not his life, Weston. It's yours. And you seem perfectly capable of living it to me."

Was that delivery supposed to punch me in the chest? So soft-spoken, so earnest, she slid right past those guards I usually keep up and socked me in something vital. I'm still reassessing my insides, trying to gauge if they're all there when she opens that sweet mouth again.

"Oh, and for his sake, I hope he catches up and realizes what kind of man he has for a brother when you do."

She's too kind. Genuinely too kind. I reject it.

"How can you say that? You don't even know me."

Amelia pulls her hand back and uses it to run through her chin-length hair. "Maybe I don't know how you take your coffee, or how old you were when you lost your virginity, or why you left town, but I know that in just a few encounters you've proven yourself to be one of the nicest people I've ever met."

My mouth opens to shoot her down, but she stares me down and keeps talking, making sure I'm hearing her every word.

"You pulled over and tried to help me when no one else ever has. Most people call the cops on me when they see my van. Then, when you couldn't fix it yourself, you called in not one, but two favors to get me taken care of, and personally escorted me to somewhere safe to stay yourself.

"I've seen you several times since then too, Weston. And you might have this whole front on for others, but I notice the way you're always keeping everyone around you laughing, whether it was making me feel comfortable on an abandoned highway, or your niece when she was crying for her dad, and I'd be willing to bet you even do it with the other locals you come across while you're painting your way across town.

"You put everyone around you first, you make it your *job* to lighten their loads, and you brighten up every room you walk into. That's what I know about you after just a few days, Boy Scout. And you can't even say you did it all to get in my pants, because you admitted you're not going to. So, yeah, your sourpuss brother should be fucking proud to have you around. I would be."

I'd kiss her if I could. Lean right in and capture her mouth with mine, nibble on her lower lip before my tongue swooped in and made her melt, the way she just did for me. No one's ever made me feel *seen* so simply, so wholly. I want to repay the favor the only way I know how.

Without thought, I lean forward, body gravitating toward

hers like we're opposing poles, drawn together in a way that isn't a choice, it's a need.

Her eyes widen the tiniest amount, brows raising, lips parting just enough to bring me back down to reality.

I use the momentum of the motion to stand, pretend that's all I was doing anyway, like I'm not having to force myself away from her against every instinct, and I brush a hand through my loose hair with a chuckle that I hope she doesn't hear the nervousness in.

"How about those beers?" I ask. "I know where there's a stash."

Tilt my head toward the garage with a smirk that should cover all the rest that's raging inside me right now.

"Fuck me up, Grady," she says with a dangerous look of her own.

ONE SIX-PACK in and we've laughed about everything from the resurgence of mullets and wondering if rat tails are next, to the ridiculousness of the societal expectations for humankind as a whole. The surface level, the dark, we've dipped down past the polite and into the layers of deep conversation normally reserved for only your closest counterparts, or fights with strangers on the internet.

Something I'm realizing that makes us kindred is that neither of us has anyone to call close. And that might be what makes tonight such an easy escape for both of us.

Or maybe that's just the beer. Amazingly, she's kept up with me on the alcohol intake, despite our substantial size difference.

The intense attraction between us—instantaneous and immediate, like the striking of a match that only burns hotter the longer it goes unchecked, the closer it gets to your fingers, the more intense the flame—it's not just the physical draw that sucks me into her gravity.

The more she shares—whether it's as silly as her views on Crocs being considered acceptable footwear (only post 2020, when the cultural landscape shifted toward embracing the comfortable, in her words), or on deeper topics, like her heartfelt (if tipsy) spiel on the bleak, hopeless state of the world if the division of humanity continues—the more I find myself glued to her, needing to hear whatever comes next.

I wait for the boredom, that itch under my skin to chase the next hit of intrigue, but it doesn't come.

Not by nightfall, not by midnight, not by three a.m., when the rain is tapping on the roof above our heads. I'm not sure what spell she's got me under, but I don't want out of it.

I hope sunrise doesn't break it.

Eventually, she's given me the short version of her time on the road. How she's been living the van life since she dropped out of college freshman year. The way she's spent at least two weeks in forty-six different states so far, and her plans to finish out the contiguous US this year (just Rhode Island and Maine left). Her method of staying interested in life on the road, by making a Pinterest board called "Shit to Do" she adds places to go and things to see. Once she's done them, they go to a board titled "Been There, Seen That."

We scroll through both boards, sharing stories of our individual adventures, picture by picture. I find a number of my own bucket list items on her "Been There, Seen That" board, and I interrogate her relentlessly on the national parks of the west, like Glacier National Park, Mount Rainier, and Yellowstone, where I've yet to go.

On her "Shit to Do," I share tidbits of my travels on several stops she has flagged for her future quests.

"It's just not worth it. Overrated," I tell her, pointing to images of fire poi from Mallory Square in Key West.

"You're just saying that because you couldn't get any of them to sleep with you." She laughs into the soft, earth-toned comforter, face first on the bed, just like I am.

"Guilty," I grin wickedly at her. "But only because all the fire dancers I saw that night were married, and that's a line I won't cross."

"Eh, that's fine," she says with a dismissing wave of her hand. "I've seen enough of Florida anyway. Spent the last half a year traveling all over the state. I'm ready for some new scenery for a while. Something that isn't flat and covered in swamp."

I'm shocked to hear her favorite stop so far was a ski town out west. I'll admit, the pictures of it on her Pinterest might have grabbed my eye. Amelia said she would've loved to have stayed, but it was too rich for her blood for anything more than a quick stop. "You heard of it?" she asks me.

"What's it called?"

"Rocky Heights."

"Like Smoky Heights, but in the Rockies?"

"Yeah."

I laugh. "That feels a little derivative, don't you think?"

She giggles without holding back. Not sure if it's the alcohol, or the same warm comfort I feel deep in my gut after hours of intimate conversation, but I'm loving the ease I'm seeing out of her. "I dunno, it's a pretty old town. A lot of history there. For all you know, they were named first. And it was pretty charming too. You guys might have some competition on your hands."

I get back to the pictures on her phone. "You've got the synchronous fireflies on here?" I ask her, hovering my thumb over the stunning image on her Pinterest board that looks like it's an illustration from a fairy tale, not an actual photograph.

Likely taken just miles from where we both are right now, in the heart of the Smoky Mountains.

"Yes!" Her face lights up with more than just the buzz, eyes aglow. "What is it, April now? When do those start?"

"Usually late May or early June," I tell her. "But you can always come back, right?"

Something I've become more and more sure of throughout the night—like there was any question about it until now—is this girl doesn't stay in one area long enough to grow any moss on that rolling stone of hers.

She tilts her head back and forth, considering. "Maybe. Depends where I go after this, I guess. The whole engine dying thing has kind of changed my travel plans. I'd love to check off Maine and Rhode Island this summer, so I might have to shoot up there next."

I whip out my phone to look up the ticket system for the synchronous fireflies. "Bad news is the lottery is almost impossible to win."

"Were you banking on winning the jackpot so you didn't have to turn to Only Fans if you ever want to retire from painting?"

"First of all, we both know I could make a *killing* if I chose to go that route and offer up the goods," I say, head tilted toward her. "But I like to keep viewing rights exclusive. One-night only, one at a time." The grin that splits my face sends her laughing into the mattress again.

"But I was talking about the lottery to see the synchronous fireflies. It's super hard to get a parking ticket. Most people try for years before they get it, and some never get the chance to go."

Her face falls, and I hate myself for doing that to it, so I quickly backtrack.

"But maybe we can both enter it this year and double our

chances. You know, if you can make it back here before they're gone for the season."

She nods, but it's not with the same gusto she had before, and I reach out to tuck some of her hair back behind an ear, keep it out of the way of my view of that face. Her perfect little nose, soft cheeks and eyes, with those cheekbones and jawline that give her a fierceness that suits her perfectly.

"Fuck the fireflies," I tell her seriously. "We'll find some better shit you can do this year. Maybe there's a synchronous lobster dance in Maine or something you can catch."

That giggle that I'm pretty sure only comes out when she's drunk is back, and I bite down on a smile at being the one to put it there.

Amelia pushes up onto all fours, then rocks back into a sitting position, and her gaze turns heavy as it drags over my features, taking her time getting her fill.

Her sweatshirt is long gone, back to just that little tee with nothing underneath. My eyes aren't doing so good at following my directions, 'cause they keep roaming down, wandering back to her chest, wondering if her nipples are as excited to see me as I'd be to see them again.

I sit up, mirroring her, and she puffs out a little breath. I'd take a second to be impressed I can sit straight up on this bed and not hit my head on the roof of the van if I wasn't so preoccupied by that look in her eyes. The molten heat pouring out of them.

"Amelia?" Her name is question enough. She knows what I'm asking.

"Weston." It's not a question. It's what she wants.

"You're drunk," I remind her gently.

"So are you," she bats right back. "But you should know, for the record, I wouldn't have stopped you earlier. And I wasn't drunk then."

"For the record, my offer from before is still on the table. When you're sober, that is. You wanna see the rest, it's only fair."

"But you're not going to fuck me?" Her voice drips with the tease of her words, and my cock strains against the tight material of my boxer briefs at that word, from those plush lips.

"You got any toys around?" I ask, instead of answering her.

She sucks her lower lip into her mouth and nods, eyes soft on mine.

"Where?"

Amelia rolls off of the bed and lands on the floor with a thunk. She crouches down beneath the bed for a moment and returns, a little mint plastic clamshell in hand. Almost the same hue I'll be using on the walls of the pizza place when I get to them on the schedule.

She climbs back up onto the mattress and places the case next to her on the light comforter, watching me with a kind of focus I could revel in, if I was free to do as I please where she's concerned.

But after talking all night, I know now that she, too, prefers one-night stands, for reasons of her own. If there could be some fun between us, it's gonna have to be at the end of her stay here, when no attachment could be formed, and no older brother could condemn me for it.

So I'll be strong for both of us until then.

But if she's up for one hell of a mind-bending night before she's gone... I'll give her something to remember. Shit, I've got weeks to plan it out.

"Before you leave town, Amelia," I promise her.

Her throat bobs with a swallow I need to feel for myself, but now isn't the time.

"Your last night here, it belongs to me, darlin'."

That delicate mouth parts, her breath hitching as she moves

her head in a small nod, lying back down, eyes never leaving mine.

Standing, I lean forward, into her personal space, and grab the plastic case. My lips find her ear, and I hear her suck in a sharp breath from the proximity, the electricity sparking between us at such a close range.

My hand finds hers, and I place the toy in her grasp.

"For tonight, use this on yourself and think of me while you do," I whisper into her ear.

And then, with all the strength I possess, I leave, stepping into the early morning light of the sunrise, and heading back to my temporary home, where nothing but my hand—and thoughts of a beautiful girl with short dark hair, perfect tits, and multiple piercings—is waiting for me.

8
Amelia

I hope this van is ready soon. Because if I don't get on the road and find someone to cure this raging appetite of sexual destruction with, I'm liable to corner Weston Grady and try to change his mind on waiting until my last night by pleading a case with *lots* of physical evidence.

Begging for sex really isn't my vibe, though, and if his brother is his holdup, I'm not about to get in between him and Oscar the Grouch.

Seriously, if this garage were going to be named after any Sesame Street character, that one sure seems pretty spot-on if you ask me.

"Parts are in," less fuzzy, grumpier Oscar says to me, plopping a bag of small metal pieces down on the workbench beside him.

One step closer to being back on the road.

That thought should make me happy. So why do my insides feel chilled and hollow?

I give him all the enthusiasm I can muster in a lackluster little cheer, arms over my head, pulling my crop top dangerously high, but this man couldn't be less interested in anyone that isn't a tall bombshell in killer heels who goes by Rory, and he doesn't even notice when I tug my shirt back down for modesty's sake.

"So now?" I prompt him.

"Now we gotta get the tranny and the engine rebuilt, in between all this other *shit*." Wyatt waves an arm around the garage, which somehow has even more vehicles in it than it did when mine arrived.

Labor costs for rebuilding a transmission *and* an engine. Just what I wanted to think about. Yay for me.

Regulating my voice to the approximate moisture level of sandpaper, I say, "Don't give me too much hope now. Might give me a reason to live, and we wouldn't want that."

His eyes—so similar in color to Weston's, so different in sentiment—float toward the ceiling, as close as he probably gets to rolling them.

"Hand over the razor blades, Wednesday Shortcake. Today's not your day. Not on my watch."

"Did you call me Wednesday Shortcake?"

"You're half depressing, half irritatingly sunny. Could call you Strawberry Addams instead, I guess."

That's what I get for trying to find the bright side after the trauma I've been through. An amateur diagnosis of manic-depressive and suicidal by a mechanic with the emotional range of a carburetor. Hasn't he ever heard of dark humor? *It's called coping, asshole.*

"Or you could just call me Amelia?"

"Heeeeeey!" Weston's upbeat voice booms through the garage, scattering Wyatt and I from an incredibly uncomfortable conversation. The only kind he and I have shared this past week and a half. Seriously struggling to see how these two men are related, but then again...look who I'm related to.

"Did you miss me?" he calls out, and I look up, hoping the surprise isn't all over my face.

This man has proven he can see through even my most reliable masks, which is more than a little unsettling, but I didn't expect to be called out like that. Like he knows he's the bright spot in my day, these little glimpses I get of him in the evenings, when he's working on his car and I'm finding excuses to hang around in the shop. My cheeks are probably heating from him calling me out so brazenly.

"Couldn't sleep without you," Wyatt responds, zero rise or fall in his pitch, which actually catches me off guard and I laugh. Like, a full belly laugh.

The shocked look on Weston's face only makes it funnier, and soon even the hard line that is Wyatt's mouth tilts up at one corner, which from my estimation means he's basically pissing himself.

"I was talking to my car, but that's good to know." Weston's eyes glow with the exchange—I'm guessing it's one of the lightest they've had in recent memory—and I try to ignore the pang of desire that pulls low in my abdomen when I watch him light up.

Like I wasn't already wanton enough before I got to Smoky Heights, unfulfilled for too many hormonal cycles on end, this man had to do and say the things he did in my van the other night. Leave me a mess on the bed, more puddle than woman by the time the door shut behind him, counting down to my last night in town.

And I have to say, I think my vibrator is just about sick of me after these last few days. It's about ready to go on strike if it has to keep me close to satisfied for two more damn weeks.

I don't think that thing was built for the kind of extreme demand I've been putting it through lately. Like taking a Prius off-roading.

Not sure tonight is going to have any other forecast in store for it, though, with how edible this man looks as he slides into the garage, tanned, golden, muscular forearms on display beneath that staple white tee of his, and those cargo pants. This pair looks clean, maybe they're new even, but I don't mind when he's a little dirty. It suits him. Like he's a man willing to get the job done, even if it leaves a mess behind.

Even his tan work boots add to his appeal. Walking the walk, not just talking the talk.

When he turns around, I get a peek of the tattoo that slips out of his right sleeve. Some mechanical parts, an assortment of cogs, on the back of his triceps. It just adds to the masculine appeal of him. Hell, if he was in front of me right now, I'd probably lean right in and take a whiff, no better than an animal, uncouth and needy, filling my lungs with that manly, woodsy scent that's all Weston.

I have to fight the urge to cross my legs, squeeze my thighs and count down until I'm alone with my favorite little substitute again.

I'm better than this, right? Is my life so unfulfilling that I can't even bear to be alone for this short time? Surely I can go a few months without a hookup?

Even if it feels like this is some celibacy challenge from the gods, and Adonis himself is the final boss I have to battle to reach the other side, where nirvana awaits.

I'm not sure it'd be worth it, honestly.

I think I'd take a night with Weston Grady over nirvana.

Weston and Wyatt dive into shop talk, going back and forth about something or other about a repair on a Mercury Sable (I didn't know those were still in circulation) as I try to keep my mask in place while I reassure myself.

My plans are back on track. With the parts in, we're just a couple weeks away from me being able to hit the road and find my next home port for a few days at a time, as usual.

Knowing that Weston and I will both give in as a parting gift to one another, before I leave town—well and truly not a local girl by any stretch of the definition—fair game (by both of our standards) for one, no-holds-barred night together.

Something tells me if I spend the night with Weston, the next unlucky fellow who gets to bed me will have impossibly large boots to fill. But, hey, at least I'll have scratched that itch.

It'll give me something to think about next time my partner of the evening isn't exactly everything I wish he were, and I need some help to get over the finish line.

A gruff voice breaks through my daydreams. "Well, I got a daughter to get home to, and a wife who deserves one hell of a night from me."

"What's the occasion?" Weston asks.

Wyatt's scruffy jaw twitches with the hint of a smile. "Eh, today's a day that ends in Y. Don't burn the place down, yeah, West?" He double taps the workbench with one open palm, and he heads off.

"Drink some electrolytes! I know you're getting old, but it'll help with the stamina!" Weston shouts after his brother.

Wyatt keeps striding toward his truck, one middle finger held high over his head as his only response, no shortage of swagger in his step.

These brothers do *not* have a confidence problem.

Weston turns back to me, traces of laughter still on his golden face as he takes me in. The chiseled jaw. Green eyes. Those laugh lines, and don't get me started on the cheekbones. It's all too much, I'm just a girl.

"Parts came in, huh?" he asks.

"That's the word around town," I confirm with a nod, still a little breathless from the sight of him.

"Hot gossip for this place," he says with way too much gravitas. "I think news had spread to downtown by the time I left the flower shop. Ernie was telling everyone who would listen down by the hardware store. It's probably all over the Heights Facebook group, and honestly, I wouldn't be surprised if the paparazzi came looking for you to get a piece of the story."

"You're ridiculous."

"When you become a local celebrity, will you sign one of the paparazzi photos for me before you go?"

The tilt of his plush mouth, the dimple that breaks out when he grins like that, the glint in his eye, they're all so fucking dangerous. Worse than most predators, because he could trap me where others have failed. That charm of his is more lethal than weapons.

"Afraid I have some bad news for you on that front," I say with a sigh.

"Yeah, what's that?"

"I might have to charge an awful lot for that photo. Enough to help me cover the cost of the repairs."

He catches on immediately. "Boss not giving you extra work?" I filled him in on that situation the other night when we discussed damn near every topic under the moon and stars that didn't involve my life before Van Gogh.

"He's barely giving me work, period," I respond, arms flapping at my sides in distress. "If anything, since I asked for a bigger workload, I'm pretty sure he's cutting back on what he gives me. At this rate, I can barely afford my normal expenses, much less that huge bill Wyatt will be demanding payment on in a couple weeks."

His mouth pulls to one side, but his eyes stay on me, deep in thought.

"Have you talked to Rory?"

"Plenty."

"About work?"

"Does she need help with a coding project?"

He shakes his head. "Doubt it, but she does run the grant

program. There's loads of places hiring, maybe she could hook you up with a job somewhere here? She might try to pitch you on staying longer, taking a grant payout to settle down here or something like that, but just pretend it's a timeshare seminar you have to sit through to get the cheap tickets to Disney World. Smile and nod, then walk away at the end with what you came for. That's what I did."

Take a normal job? Have regular hours, with a real, live, in-person boss, and somewhere I have to show up every day?

Forget the fact I'd rather peel my own fingernails off than submit my ID willingly to a stranger to have them dig around into my identity. A nine-to-five would mean—excuse me while I gag—waking up early enough to be somewhere by nine. It's literally in the title.

I rarely wake before the sun is winding down for the day. Maybe it's all the darkness hiding within me, but I tend to do my best work at night.

He must read the look on my face and discern the answer without the need for words, because he puts his hand to his chin and keeps thinking.

"Okay, what if..." Weston lets the mystery build as he steps around the car that's separating us and walks closer. I find myself turning to face him as he moves, like a daisy staying in the rays of his light.

"What if you spit out whatever idea you had?" I ask with a little more sass than I'm really feeling, because a girl can't give away all her secrets, or look too soft, the way I probably do when I'm under his spell.

"Easy, darlin'. I'm gettin' there."

He settles in, ass against the door of the muscle car behind him, thick arms crossed over his broad chest, and stares me down as rain starts to pour outside the open bays at the entrance of the garage, filling the shop with the fresh scent.

"What if I talk to Wyatt about helping out on your rebuild. I'm already here at night working on my car anyway. Might as well do a good deed and work on yours. The Charger has been waiting all these years for me, it can hang tight a little longer."

My jaw practically unhinges. "You would do that?"

He lifts a shoulder casually. "I'm sure I'd need his help on some of it, his oversight probably on most of it. But I'd come cheaper than Wyatt. Free ninety-nine for my labor, if he agrees to it. And he's got so much to do anyway, he'd probably welcome the load off his plate."

I'm nodding vigorously before I've even thought it over, the ends of my hair bouncing across my shoulders with the movement. "That would be *amazing*, Weston. Seriously."

"I'd need you to realize I'm not exactly in my element with this. It's been a while since I've done a project like this, and you'll have to bear with me if it takes a little longer than he would."

"Are you seriously offering to do my repairs for free, but telling me I'd have to be just a little bit patient for them?" I make the motion for *little* with my forefinger and thumb.

"I can't promise there won't be any charge, but it should cut down significantly on Wyatt's labor charges, sure."

This man defies all logic, all I've come to know about what to expect from men. His offer is so insanely kind, but he owes me nothing and keeps doing me favors. It's too much. I refuse to be a charity case any more than I already have been.

"Weston, you can't. I'm not your problem to solve."

"I can't what? Be nice? Be a good neighbor? I can tell that wherever you came from, whatever history you have that I don't know about... I know it left you jaded and sure that the world is full of dicks. And it is, but that's not all there is out there. Especially around here. People in Smoky Heights look out for one another. Help each other. Yeah, sure, they snoop and overstep, and they talk—God, do they talk—but this isn't some ulterior motive from me. I like working on motors. I like you. I don't mind helping you get back on your feet."

His lips tilt up in that wholesome way of his that makes me certain he's one of a kind. His kindness, sincerity, the way he gives himself wherever it will help out, even if that's just a smile, he's too good for this world. Too good for my tainted self.

Weston keeps talking, his low voice rumbling in a way that warms something low in my belly as he goes in for the kill shot. "It's okay to say yes when you need help sometimes, darlin'. Doesn't make you weak."

My mouth opens and closes a few times, not sure how to even respond to that. I've been alone since I became an adult. Help is a foreign concept to me. Being seen as weak or incapable of handling my own shit is something I never want to live through again.

Breathing out through my nose, words slip out of my mouth before my brain gets to filter them. "You have to let me repay you somehow. I'm not a charity case."

That didn't sound as appreciative as it could've, if we're nitpicking, but it doesn't seem to bother him. Those green eyes of his, like fresh grass after the last frost, damn near sparkle as they watch me.

"I'd be open to some sort of barter system," he throws out playfully.

"Barter?" I echo. "What the heck do I have that you could want?"

His eyes move rapidly across the shop, intentionally away from me, and I realize that's a stupid question. There's something he desperately wants from me. Same thing I want from him. But he's not asking for me to pay him with sex.

Lifting a shoulder again, he says, "You could help me paint if you're not busy with programming."

"Like, tell you true crime stories while you work to keep you entertained?"

"More like you paint *with* me, so we get the jobs done faster and I can come here and work on your van."

"Yeah, listen, I'm really not much of a painter. I might be good with detail-oriented work on a keyboard, but having to cut in ceilings and baseboards sounds like literal torture to me."

"Says the one who listens to gruesome podcasts detailing *actual* torture. Is that what Binx talks about? Victims who were made to paint trim before their systems just quit and they flatlined from the sheer horror of it all?"

"Binx?" I can barely say the word through my uncontrollable laughter.

"Isn't that her name?"

"She's not a cat from a 90s Halloween movie. Her name is Jynx."

"Same fucking difference."

"It is not!"

He leans in closer to me, ass still resting against the car, but face now directly in front of mine.

"That is the *exact* same, and there is no way you're being serious right now. You know that's the same, right?"

I place my palm against his face, dig my fingers into his cheeks and forehead, and shove him back with a laugh.

"Rule number one if you want me to paint with you, is you don't disrespect Jynx."

He stands straight, holding one hand up like a damn Boy Scout. "I solemnly swear to respect the sanctity of the high holiness of true crime podcasts, all that is gory, her royal highness, Jynx."

"That's a start," I say, nose in the air.

"What are the other terms of the barter?" he asks, brows raised in amusement.

"You do all the trim, all the cutting in, and all I do is the rolly thing on the big surfaces." I make the motion, like I have a roller in my hand.

"This might not actually go any faster then," Weston groans.

"Those are my terms, take it or leave it," I say, arms extended out to my side.

"And here I thought I was doing you a favor," he grumbles, lips still twitched upward.

"May this be a valuable life lesson for you. Being a good person comes with a heavy cost."

"Is this the only cost then? Doing the shittiest parts of the job to be graced with your presence while I do it?"

I wiggle my head side to side, weighing over the final term I'd like to barter.

"There is *one* more thing," I say delicately.

"Here we go," he says, with absolutely no acidity, like he's gearing up for a joyride. I half expect him to rub his hands together, but he must have more self-discipline than Wyatt seems to think, and he holds himself back.

I let out a sigh, laying it on thick as I tilt my head to one side. "I do think it would be a *slightly* unfair working environment considering every day I show up on the job, you'll know exactly what I have going on beneath this," I gesture to my shirt. "And I'll still be wondering what's going on under that." My head inclines toward his body with meaning.

He gets a knowing glint in his eyes and nods at me, faux seriousness in the motion.

"That would be a drastically unfair advantage, I agree."

Nodding, I fold my arms over my chest expectantly and wait.

"Any special requests?" he asks me.

"I don't need rose petals and candlelight, if that's what you mean. It's just, since you offered the other night... I can't stop wondering. Put me out of my misery, West."

His lips twitch, but he tries to stay deadpan. "I just didn't know if you'd rather see him... ready to go, shall we say?"

"Sure, if the offer's on the table. It'll be a lot easier to get off to the thought when I can picture him hard, rather than dangling in elephant trunk mode."

Weston huffs a laugh, shaking his head. "Not holding back, are you, darlin'?"

"What, like you're not thinking of my tits every night?"

His lips tilt up in a devilish grin. Caught him.

"I'm just leveling the playing field. Filling up my spank bank to match yours. So how does this work?" I ask. "Is this just an on-demand thing, we just place the order, wait a few minutes, and he'll be good to go?"

"It won't take a few minutes," he says, eyes zeroing in on my body. "Shit, I have to work *not* to be hard around you, Amelia."

I didn't think there was a breeze today, but a chill sweeps my body like there was, and I feel my nipples perk up to attention beneath the phantom touch. His eyes don't miss it, heating at the visual, and I watch his hands drift to the front of his pants.

"Matter of fact, he's good to go."

Fixated, my eyes don't move from his hands on his fly, even if my tongue might have a mind of its own as it sweeps my lower lip eagerly.

"And to clarify, after this, we have a deal, right darlin'?"

"Yep," I promise. "After this, I'm all yours."

Those words ring out through the shop, and I hear how it sounded.

"For painting. While you're fixing my van, I mean." Never mind that it feels like he's already sneaked into a place within me no one else has managed to find in a long, long time.

This might be the worst idea I've ever had—aside from the

reason my life turned out this way in the first place. To keep pushing the boundaries when it comes to flirting with this man. To follow his lead and then take it two steps farther.

We both might be masters of the good time, not a long time mentality, but letting this crush fester and evolve into anything more than just that while we still have weeks to spend together, counting down until we can both get our fill can't be a recipe for anything good.

But when his pants are finally unzipped and his hand slides in the front of his dark underwear and comes back out with the largest handful I've ever seen, I've forgotten any and all reasons why this wasn't the best damn idea I've ever had.

Long, thick, and throbbing with a magnetism all its own, I'm pretty sure Weston Grady's cock just became my newest obsession.

And when he tucks it away with nothing but a cocky, boyish wink in my direction, he knows it.

My last night in town can't come soon enough.

TRANSFIXED. I've become one-track minded ever since that glimpse that was more than I expected, yet nowhere near enough. My poor vibrator has *no* hope of living up to the fantasies going on in my head after last night.

"Yeah, just like that," Weston praises me. "Keep going until it's soaked, darlin', mmhmm."

My core clenches and flutters.

"You might have to use your hand, pump your fist over it and make sure it's really coated before you begin. Just put on some protection first."

My head turns to the right until I'm staring him down. "You do realize what that sounds like, don't you?"

"Like I'm teaching you to paint with a roller?"

"Sure. That's all it sounds like."

Fitting a glove over my hand, I rub the paint into the fuzzy roller like Weston instructed.

"Fuck, you're a natural," he croons.

Now he's just playing mean. Good thing I know how to hit below the belt too.

"Yeah?"

I moan far too sensually for what the task at hand calls for, bringing the roller up to the first wall and pressing it against the flat surface. The sound of moistness and friction ricochets throughout the empty suite.

"Like that?" My tone is straight out of a porno from the seventies, completely overdone just to prove my point. "Or should I go... *harder*?"

I begin rolling the brush, the wet noises it's making lewd when paired with the exchange we just shared, the sex dripping from my voice.

Weston stares at me, eyes hard as I keep the show going.

"Mmmm, it's soaked. Are you watching it drip?"

I make an exaggerated noise of pleasure, one I've never actually made in bed before, because no woman *really* sounds like that when she's enjoying herself.

"Sorry to interrupt," comes an amused, throaty voice, and I freeze in place, roller to the wall, eyes on Weston, pleading for him to save me. "Didn't mean to stop what you were doing, just passing through, don't mind me."

"Hey Lex," Weston says easily, waving at the woman walking through the empty business we're painting that is *clearly* not, in fact, empty.

"Hey West," she calls back just as casually.

"Have you met Amelia yet?"

"The pleasure is all mine," the woman says, laughter building in her throat.

I give in, placing the roller back in the paint tray and turning to face her, wiping my hands on my shorts with a nervous laugh. "That's funny," I tell her. "Because of the noises, and the... yeah."

Weston crosses his arms over his chest and watches me, practically giddy in his silence, watching me dig my way out of this one.

"This, uh, this could be pretty awkward," I try again. "But would you believe me if I said he started it?"

The woman—at least ten years older, a half a foot taller, and a few dozen pounds heavier than me, with wild brunette hair framing her face and the kind of innate self-confidence I envy—watches on with a sparkle in her eye.

"Yeah, that wouldn't surprise me. Shit-stirrer that he is."

My heartbeat lowers from my throat back down toward my chest, and the pounding softens to a less deafening roar in my ears.

"Amelia." I give her a little wave.

"Alexis." She gives me a nod with her chin in return.

"This is Rory's older sister," Weston explains.

I grab the open can of Alani on the floor by my feet and throw back a swig for courage.

"He's my little sister's husband's little brother," she says back.

"A vivid family tree," I reply, still feeling like she walked in on something she shouldn't have and unable to shake the embarrassment.

"Damn, the air's so thick in here you could cut it with a machete."

"I don't think that's a saying, Lex," West says, smiling at her.

"I dunno what kind of pent-up tension the two of you have going that I clearly stepped into, but I'm not gonna run and tattle about your little porn-off to Wyatt, if that's what you're worried about. He doesn't scare me, and honestly, we could use another chick with balls in the Heights. More power to ya." She holds a fist up, careful not to spill her Diet Coke in the other hand.

A slight smile makes its way onto my face once more, and I steal a glance at Weston before giving the newcomer my attention again.

Her guttural voice is so sure of herself, I want to take notes when she speaks again. "I just wanted to introduce myself. Rory told me you're gonna be in town for a bit longer, and I thought I'd take the chance to invite you out for a girl's night. If the Gradys have been your only company since arriving, you're probably overdue for some normal company."

A toothy grin and a wink tell me it's all in good fun, and she pulls an awkward smile out of me too.

"My best friend Gracie is the hairstylist at the salon just there," she points out the plate glass windows to another storefront across the street, "and I work at the grocery store just up the road. We try to go out at least once a week, and sometimes I even get Rory to go with us too. You're welcome to come with us Friday night, if you'd like."

She pops her gum and takes a sip from the can to give me a second to respond, but I'm speechless. It doesn't phase her.

"Not to put you on the spot. Just tell West to text me if you want a ride, I'll come grab ya."

Stunned, I stare at her for a moment too long to be a normal reaction, until Weston speaks up for me. "Thanks for stopping by, Alexis. It was a real...pleasure." His words are still laced with humor, and it's clear he'll be laughing in my face about this all afternoon.

"Thanks," I remember to say a bit too late.

"Hope you two...have fun," she says with an exaggerated wink, and leaves us to it.

It's weird that I'm in shock, unable to form a sentence like a twenty-something woman should be able to do. I know it is.

It's just that I don't know what to do with myself, or how to respond like a socialized human being.

I think that's the closest thing to a friend I've made since the day my life ended when I was twelve.

"OKAY, if Weston doesn't fuck you soon, I think I will." Lexi's gravelly voice is naturally sultry enough that I almost think she's being serious, but then her grin comes out and I realize she's not into me, she's just complimenting me in her own way.

Her warm brown eyes travel over my outfit—the one pair of jeans I have to my name, the ass-kicking combat boots I couldn't live without, and one of my staple crop tops, my messy waves and bangs, the extra eyeliner I put on tonight—and I feel like the Amelia I wish I were when I see the approval in her gaze. Like she recognizes the fire inside of me that I try so hard to keep alight, and it burns brighter by her side.

So it seems my nerves were unnecessary. There's something easy about Lexi, there's no pretenses with her. Her best friend Gracie is exactly what I'd imagine a sweet Southern woman to be. And being around the two of them, somehow I don't overthink my response. I just let it fly.

Biting down on my lower lip, my eyes rove over Lexi's body right back. Curves hugged in denim, hair wild and curly, the girl is a stunner, and I let my eyes tell her so.

But then I sigh, and my mouth says, "Sorry, but you just don't have his dick, and that's *really* high on my list."

Lexi guffaws, doubling over in a laugh that bisects the crowd around us. So uninhibited, I crave the lack of restraint she shows. It's not even a thought for her, I'd bet. Keeping parts of herself tucked away and hidden. Not letting others see anything beyond the surface so carefully curated.

And for tonight? I think I can do just that.

A night off, just one evening to enjoy where I am rather than remind myself not to get too attached. It's a novelty to me, to be spending a night with other women. Anyone else, period, who I haven't picked up in a bar for forty-five minutes of something you could almost call fun.

Though the bar we're at tonight, Smoky Suds, looks like a hell of a place to find someone if I were just drifting through. Southern men packed in from barnwood wall to barnwood wall, TVs mounted up high, country music playing overhead, and a pool table and some dart boards on the far end of the single room that makes this place up.

I wonder if Weston would be here, if he weren't busy working on my van. If he'd be at the square bar in the center of the room, flirting with a tall blonde who looks like the perfect match, the Barbie to his Ken.

Even though it has no right to, an acidic streak of jealousy shoots through my stomach and up into my throat. The taste needs to be washed away, and I forge a path through the growing crowd straight to the probably once-shiny wooden counter at the bar. It's worn down, patchy in places now, like it's seen better days. Haven't we all?

Standing, waiting to be noticed, the counter barely up to my tits, Lexi and Gracie catch up with me in a couple of strides. Perks of being tall women, I guess.

"You can't just leave it at that." Lexi's jaw is set, eyes fierce.

"You're going to have to tell us everything. I have to know if the rumors are true," Gracie gushes. "I'm not saying I regret marrying the first man I ever slept with, but a girl does wonder what's behind the other tent flaps in this town, if you know what I mean."

My head tilts to the side and Lexi's mouth flies open immediately.

"Gracie, that wasn't even the slightest bit subtle. Just say it. You want to know about Weston's dick. Yeah, babe, we all do. No need to be shy about it. I think Amelia is the only one who wants to know more than you do at this point."

Gracie blushes, giggling into her shoulder, and I think she really is struggling to meet either of us in the eye. Surprising, with how forward and unapologetically open her best friend is, for her to be so coy on the topic. She gathers her strength before speaking again. "It's just... I mean, everyone knows someone who's slept with him, and he's practically an urban legend at this point. He doesn't even feel like a local anymore, he's more like some fabled great lay of years past."

I snort a laugh, but she keeps going.

"It's been so long since he lived here, I think the tales only grew with time."

Lexi nods her head, agreeing. "Yeah, that's valid. From the stories I've heard, he's either the size of a baseball bat, or he can pick one up with it, like it's an elephant trunk. With the swagger that man walked back into town with, I'm not even sure I doubt either one of those at this point."

Hell, with the glimpse I had the other night, I can understand the rumors. Laughter spews from my mouth until Lexi puts a hand on my shoulder, face tight with concern, and I sober.

"Have you heard of oiling the downstairs?"

"Erm, no?"

"It's something Rory told me *way* too much about when she was pregnant. A massage her husband gave her to get ready for childbirth." She uses air quotes on *massage*. "Ew. Like I wanted to know. But I think you need to start prepping for Weston now."

Gracie leans closer, eyes soft with concern, and she nods her head sympathetically.

"Look at you, you're just a teeny little thing, aren't you? If what I've heard around the bonfire over the years is even a quarter true, he's gonna split you in half."

"Like an axe to a log." Lexi nods sagely.

My eyes stretch wide—I guess that's called foreshadowing for what the rest of me will be doing in two more weeks—at the X-rated images these women are putting in my head.

"You get those videos too?" Gracie turns to Lexi.

"Do I ever! The things I would do to a strapped, six five tattooed man..." She growls, low in her throat, and a grizzled man next to us turns to look at her.

The girls pay him no attention, continuing to giggle about inked up lumberjacks until I interrupt them, needing to speak up, to defend Weston's honor somehow. The visual they painted won't leave me alone.

"I mean, it's not as *long* as a baseball bat..." My voice trails off, and Lexi grips my shoulders with both hands, jarring me as she turns me to face her.

"Are you holding out on us? We've been here ten minutes, if you're telling me you've already fucked him and we haven't heard, I'm gonna have to revoke the town citizenship card of half this place. Nobody, and I mean *nobody* in this town can keep a secret that well."

"Shh!" Gracie is far from discreet—really it's more of a shout than a whispered hush—but Lexi lowers her voice instantly.

"I'm gonna need more than that, Big Momma."

My lips peel into a smile. "Big Momma?"

"You're one big, bad bitch hiding in that lil pipsqueak of a package."

The laugh tears out of me, surprising even myself with how readily it spills past my lips and into the heavy, hoppy air of the bar.

She winks at me. "You don't have me fooled, girl. I see you." Lexi bumps into me with her hip and—not being braced for it—the movement slides me over into Gracie, who catches me gently and lets me catch my balance again.

"Quit changing the subject," Gracie whines.

"Can you stop depriving us of the tea now?" Lexi asks, eyes flaring with mischief. "Just put us out of our misery. How good is he?"

The thought of that sneak peek I got of what Weston's packin', it makes me lick my lips, and I probably look thirsty for more than just the drink we're still waiting to order.

Both women whine in unison, groaning, and Lexi even throws her head back.

"Oh, oh that's not fair!"

"That face you just made!" Gracie squeaks.

"Let me just order," I beg, ready for something that burns on the way down. "Then we can find a table somewhere no one else is listening and I'll answer two questions."

Gracie's face lights up and Lexi's brows raise.

"Might have to go a few towns over to find somewhere no one is listening, but it'll be worth it."

Gracie leans into Lexi, eyes glowing. "What should we ask?"

"Only two questions," I tell them, finger held high, but it doesn't block my smirk.

"Big Momma has spoken," Lexi jeers, nudging Gracie with

her elbow before wrapping an arm around each of our shoulders. "We'd better choose wisely."

"Ladies." The low voice that utters the single word in lieu of a full sentence grips all three of our attention with those two syllables.

Turning, I face the bar to see one of the most intense looking men I've ever laid eyes on.

Black hair—short on the sides, longer on top—eyes like coal, and an air about him that sends a chill through me, I'm not prepared for his gaze to burn when it lands on me.

Perhaps if I hadn't met Weston, I'd have returned the look. But this man isn't even on my radar tonight. Nope, the only blip on my navigation system is the blond, sun-kissed guy back at the garage, greased up and working over my van, like the lucky bitch she is.

As attractive as the bartender is, it only makes me wish I was with Weston tonight instead. The man has broken my libido. Like I said, my last night in Smoky Heights can't come soon enough.

9
Weston

It was actual relief on my brother's face when I proposed taking over most of the labor on Amelia's van. His workload is starting to overwhelm him, with the influx in population we've had recently and Gonzo not being around.

It'd probably help if a few of the old-timers traded in their rides for something newer, but good luck getting people around here to part with their prides and joys.

Like me.

Have I burned the rubber on my baby in a decade or more? No, but I dare you to try to take her from me.

So who am I to blame Old Lady Dix if she wants to keep her Bessie around for another round of the automotive equivalent of a knee replacement or seven? Even if it does make my brother's life a little more difficult.

The first day on Amelia's van, Wyatt and I removed the engine block together and he assigned a section of the garage to me for the project. He checks in with me on it daily, offering oversight, direction, and a second opinion when I need one, but is glad to not have to do the bulk of the time-intensive labor on it.

It's a good thing I got in some time with my mom my first week in town, because my schedule isn't as comfortably loose as I prefer it right about now. She was so excited to have me back in the Heights, but texts are gonna have to be enough for a little while.

All week long I've picked Amelia up late morning (both of our preferred starting time), when we go tackle the day's painting at whichever shop is closest to opening. Then, when we've made good progress for the day, we return to Gonzo's Garage, where she brings her laptop over with a foldout chair and I get to work on her engine.

Wyatt is nearby, at least until closing time, so we don't tend to get into the kind of dangerous territory our flirting likes to drift into when we're alone. But it's comfortable, and it's become routine.

So tonight, when she asked me to text Lexi to come get her for girl's night, this hopeful look on her face that told me this meant something to her, I couldn't object. Sure, it doesn't feel the same, toiling away on the rebuild without her talking to herself on the sidelines—cutest habit ever, by the way—but I'm not complaining.

Being alone is good, it's what I'm used to. I work well on my own.

So why do my eyes keep flicking to the side, toward the open bays where her short, toned legs are usually in my periphery, bouncing as she sits in a fold-out chair, while I sweat over her engine to the soundtrack of her gushing about this or that.

She's not there. Of course she isn't there. She's down at Suds with the girls. And half of the guys in this town. Including Dallas, the bartender, and the most eligible bachelor in the Heights, last I knew. Pretty sure that hasn't changed.

One of my eyes twitches at the thought of them hitting it off. Him catching wind of the new arrival with his own eyes for the first time. Her, intrigued by the darkness that swallows that guy whole. The two of them finding a dim corner of the bar.

The back of one wrist—since both hands are filthy—slaps to my eye, effectively stopping the twitch, but possibly blinding myself permanently in the act. A fair trade.

I distract myself by focusing *extra* hard on assembling these pistons, the assembly lube thick and sticky on my hands as I test each component to make sure it's working as it should.

Eventually—definitely long enough for a bathroom hookup or three if I were keeping track of time, which I'm totally not—headlights bounce through the gravel lot and into the shop, the sound of tires rolling across the loose rocks echoing through the garage. I make my way to the sink on the cement block wall and use about a pound of that orange, gritty soap to wash my hands as I hear car doors opening and raucous giggling roll in.

I try not to think they're laughing about something as stupid as, oh, I don't know, Amelia getting bent over the pool table by the bartender, and make my way over to them, keeping my pace even, like it's not taking all my effort to hold myself back from sprinting to the car.

Amelia is *clearly* inebriated, which makes me wonder how much she's had to drink, because I've seen her pound beers with no issue.

She's also clearly having the time of her damn life, which calms my revved up insides instantly, and returns my usual, easy smile back to my face. And it's for real.

Lexi is doubled over in laughter, legs crossed to keep from peeing, if I had to guess, as she helps Amelia out of the car while they scream-laugh together. Neither of them look up as I approach, engrossed in whatever new inside joke is between them that has them hardly able to take breaths between their howls.

After a couple minutes of unintelligible speech that they

somehow seem to understand between the two of them, I finally clear my throat loudly.

Lexi, clearly not shitfaced like the girl I'm here for, looks up at me quickly, sobering from her laughing fit and shooting me a knowing smirk. Amelia takes a fraction of a second longer to gather her bearings and bring her bleary gaze to mine, a blithe grin stretched across her small mouth.

"There he is!" she shouts, pointing at me. Except her whole body points with her, and she starts to tip over. Lexi, who has an arm around her, catches her easily, but I take the chance to rush forward anyway and stabilize her with both hands on her slim shoulders.

"You been lookin' for me, darlin'?" I ask her, lips curved up with the thought that my eyes weren't the only ones seeking the other out tonight.

"Talkin' about you," she says with a slur. Her eyes slide down my body until they come to rest on my groin. "Your giant fucking cock."

Oh, boy.

My eyes widen and fly to Lexi, who looks amused, and (thankfully) like she doesn't give a fuck at the same time. My sister-in-law's sibling can be cool. It's mine that can't.

I turn my gaze back to Amelia. "I'd love to hear what you had to say about it, maybe you could tell me over coffee tomorrow?"

"I'll tell you now," she drawls, and she's so damn cute my mouth pulls up at one side. "I said it was beautiful. Massive."

"And I said maybe I finally understand why all the girls fall in love with you," Lexi adds, a crooked grin on her face.

Bite back a bigger smirk at that.

"No wonder Wyatt has to threaten you to keep it in your pants. One look and she's obsessed."

My stomach falls. She's not obsessed. She's just drunk. And maybe a little horny. Hell, who here isn't?

"I'm not obsessed. I'm fascinated. There's a difference. And you would be too if you'd seen it," Amelia says, her nose an inch from Alexis's face.

"This again," Lexi says, but she's laughing. "You, my sister, even my best friend's husband. I'm surrounded by people who are obsessed with Grady cock. Is this payback from the universe for something I did?"

Amelia gasps. "You believe in cosmic karma too? I knew I liked you."

"Okay, darlin'. Let's get you to bed, yeah?"

Amelia's eyes practically zoom in on me. "You gonna take me to bed, Boy Scout?"

My cock doesn't have the filter on it my brain does, it doesn't consider the fact that she's drunk, off limits while she's staying in town, and that Wyatt's sister-in-law is standing right next to her. He practically jumps at the suggestion, all for doing just that.

"I'm going to *put* you to bed, there's a big difference there. Jesus Christ, you're gonna get me in trouble, Amelia."

"He's such a Boy Scout!" She jabs a thumb at me.

Lexi waves dismissively. "I already told you, I'm not gonna tattle to your brother. What do I care if two consenting adults have a little fun?"

My eyes narrow in on her.

"Oh, relax. Live a little, West. I'm not saying break her heart, but don't be so scared to enjoy yourself while you're here. He doesn't own you."

"Hear fucking hear!" Amelia calls out, fist raised in the air in enthusiasm. "Life's short. Have a little fun." She waves one arm, gesturing up and down at her body. "I'm little, and I'm fun. Have me!"

Lexi laughs at her before speaking. "Plus, she told me about your dick way before she was shitfaced, so I know it's not the alcohol talking."

Amelia shakes her head from side to side in big motions. "Not the alcohol. Maybe a little the alcohol. But not *just* the alcohol." She's speaking a lot slower than she normally does, with a slur I've never heard before.

"Okay, Big Momma," Lexi tells her, spinning Amelia to face me. "I'm going to put you in some good hands now. I want you to text me in the morning and reassure me you survived the night, and I can bring you some painkillers if you need them then."

"We exchanged numbers," Amelia tries to whisper it to me, but everyone within fifty feet heard.

I try not to be jealous that Lexi got this girl's number, and after these couple of weeks I still haven't. Though, if I had access to her around the clock, I'd probably get us both in trouble, fast. Last thing I need is to be able to tell her the filthy thoughts running through my mind as I'm falling asleep each night.

"We're officially friends now," Amelia shout-whispers to me.

"Night, new bestie!" Lexi calls, grinning at the two of us, then patting me on the shoulder as she heads back around to her driver's side and leaves Amelia with me.

"Let's get you to bed," I say to Amelia, one arm under hers, leaned down to support her tiny body with mine.

"Finally! I thought it wasn't gonna happen for ages but fuck waiting. Let's do this."

I tilt my head back for a quick second, ask the Lord what I did to deserve this kind of temptation, this unfair treatment, and regain my resolve.

"What did I tell you the other night?"

She has to pause for longer than usual to think back in this state. "You're not going to make the first move on me while I'm drunk?"

"Exactly."

We're about a quarter of the way to her van now, making slow progress through the gravel lot.

"For the record, I think waiting is bullshit. It's no one else's business but ours."

I hum, wishing that were true. "Sadly, I know someone who would disagree."

"What stick does your brother have up his ass?"

"Wish I knew, angel."

She gasps, stopping in her tracks and pulling back from me enough so that she can stare up at my face. "Why did you call me that?"

"Angel? It's the first thing you reminded me of when I saw you pulled over that night. A dark, morbid little angel with that sense of humor of yours. And, ya know, those tits are heavenly."

Her eyes shine a little brighter beneath the exterior lights of the garage, but she doesn't say anything else. Just turns and starts walking toward the van again.

"Good to know you want me," she huffs. "You're not just pushing me off."

Is she feeling rejected? This is a little more hot and cold than I've seen from her so far, which I can blame on Dallas for overserving her, but I doubt she's the kind of woman who gets turned down often. She needs to know that my waiting has nothing to do with her.

"Aw, darlin'. If it isn't clear to you, I've wanted you since the moment I laid eyes on you. I just think this plan we have of it happening on your last night is the smartest thing for both of us. We both have our reasons."

"Ugh," she practically squeals the word. I can't tell if it's excitement, frustration, or some blend of emotions I can't decipher. And then I catch a faint whisper that I'm not sure she realizes she said aloud. "Two more weeks."

My fly feels abnormally tight at the thought, and I remind myself I'm being chivalrous here. Putting her to bed, as much as I might want to join her in it.

I shut the van door behind us and look around as she turns on the lights. It's a gorgeous setup she's got in here. The finishes look bespoke and damn near brand new, even though I know she's had this thing for nearly a decade at this point. She upkeeps it well.

Is it weird for me to say that's hot? A woman that takes care of her vehicle is a turn on for me. Let's not talk about the state of her engine by the time I found her on the highway, but the fact that she's kept this van going as well as she has for as long as she has, it's impressive.

She plops backward, falling onto the bed, arms out in a full starfish.

"What do we have to do to get you ready for bed?"

"Please just let me sleep off the shame of being rejected by you yet again. Hopefully when I wake up, I don't remember this. I think I deserve that little bit of grace from the universe, don't you?"

"I have never, and—for the record—would never reject you. There is no shame here, darlin'. But let's go ahead and get you set up for sleep. What do you need to do?"

"Shower," she mumbles the word into her shoulder.

"Can you... can you do that here?"

Her arm flops up to point at the mystery door along the side of the van and then falls back down again. I open it up, peer in, and see a wet room complete with a small toilet, a handheld shower wand above it, and a sink in the opposite corner of the tiny room.

I turn on the knob for the water and she jumps out of bed,

reanimated instantly at the sound, and damn near runs into me in her haste.

"'Scuse me. Gotta get in, not much water."

She grabs a towel from some hidden cabinet behind me and shuts herself in the wet room.

Committed to making sure she gets to bed safely, I wander the van, waiting for her, inspecting what I can without invading her privacy by opening drawers or doors.

Several moments later, the water stops, there are more noises from behind the door, and then it cracks open. One tiny, dark-haired enigma of a girl steps out, wet hair down past her chin, nothing but a tan towel wrapped around her body, a few droplets of water still dripping from the ends of her hair onto her bony shoulders.

She looks up at me almost shyly, then squeezes past me to get back to her bed. Amelia pulls the covers back and faces me. "Turn around," she says quietly, and I do without question.

I hear a soft swish, and the unmistakable sounds of her climbing into bed before there's a soft, "'Kay."

When I turn around again, she's nestled beneath the covers, towel on the floor at the edge of the bed.

"You good to go to sleep now?" I ask her, and she nods sleepily, eyes still on me.

"Can I tell you something before you go?" she asks softly.

"Sure."

"I can't stop thinking about it."

Her eyes haze over as they fall down my body and land on my package, and her meaning becomes clear as the midday sky above the Smokies.

"I want to ride it. Just once."

If I could bite my knuckle, I would, but I need to keep it together. At least while she can still see me.

"I want that too," I tell her, the simplest confession of my own.

The fantasies my mind has been racing with starring this woman don't start or stop with her riding my cock, but that's certainly going to be the main attraction in tonight's prime time feature when I'm behind a locked door.

"You still got your toy handy?" I ask her.

Her hand dives beneath the pillow her head is on, and she pulls the case out and waves it in the air. "It's never far away these days," she says softly, and that's my cue.

"You know what to do. Sweet dreams," I tell her, trying not to smirk.

"They'll be dirty," she promises.

"RORY, you missed a good one Friday night." Lexi's throaty voice is laced with humor as she watches her sister for a reaction across the picnic table out back at the Grady cabin.

"I had the time of my life here with Miss Front Tooth," Rory responds, jiggling the knee her baby is sitting on and making her giggle. "Let me tell you, it was a *blast* for everyone."

"A fucking hoot," Wyatt agrees sarcastically.

"Show us that tooth, missy," her grandfather coos from beside me. It's hard not to get caught up in the cuteness of these gruff bastards fawning over the sweet little addition to the Grady family, but if you'd told me a few years back these two fuckers would end up like this, dad and grandpa, I wouldn't have believed you.

Lexi, from my other side, reaches out across the table like she's going to lift her lip. "Show us that tooth! Come on!"

Our niece giggles, revealing the hint of her lower front

incisor in that gummy smile, and everyone at the table cheers, even her dad. Rory pumps the baby's arms up and down, like she's celebrating, too, and she giggles even harder.

I try not to focus on the jealousy that surges inside me at the gooey look Wyatt shares with Aurora.

"Well, while I'm sure you were living it up with the teething situation—my literal worst nightmare, by the way—I recruited a new participant into girls' night," Lexi continues in her gives-no-fucks drawl.

"You know how I despise cliffhangers, Alexis," Rory intones.

"All right, buzzkill. It was Amelia. And you should know she's a fucking riot."

I feel Lexi's brown eyes slide onto me, the side of my face hot under her stare, but I keep eating my Gray's Papaya hot dogs flown in from New York like they're talking about nothing more than the weather.

If my heart is beating just a little bit faster, a touch louder than usual, no one else seems to notice.

"Yeah?" Rory takes a swig of her papaya drink and puts it down gently on the table before looking back at her sister. "How so?"

This is it, I think. *This is where Lexi throws me under the bus and my short-lived peace with Wyatt explodes into cinders and ash.*

Instead, Lexi just shrugs and takes a sip of her own drink. "She's feisty. Our speed. A weirdo, but a funny one. Little bit twisted and dark when you least expect it."

"Huh," Rory replies. "What did you guys get up to?"

Wyatt takes his daughter back from his wife's lap and begins entertaining her, bringing his scruffy face close to hers, cooing and making ridiculous noises at her that make her happy.

It's hard to be jealous when I saw the man he was for more than a decade without Rory in his life. I don't begrudge him his happiness. He fucking deserves it. But why is he the only one who gets to find that?

Lexi's voice brings me out of my head and back into the conversation at hand. "We went to Suds. Played some pool."

Wyatt smirks at his wife and she makes a face at him I wish I hadn't seen. Her stepfather, or Gramps as we call him now, huffs and looks off to the side.

"She can really handle her bourbon," Lex continues.

"Bourbon?" Wyatt asks, a touch of respect in his voice.

"Yep. Even Dallas seemed impressed. He hooked her up with a bunch of shots on the house."

Lexi looks at the man at the other end of the bench from her and sucks in a breath through her teeth. "Pretend you didn't hear me say that, eh, Gramps?"

Me? My ears are ringing. Dallas? Took a liking to her?

"I can see that," Wyatt muses after a second of considering it. "They've both got that dark something going for them, don't they?" He looks at his wife for confirmation. "I'm not much of a romantic, but I think they'd be cute," he says, and my stomach drops onto the wooden bench where my ass is.

"Sure, you're not much of a romantic," Gramps says, looking pointedly at the house behind us all.

"Hmm," Rory says, breezing past her stepfather's comment and replying to her husband. "I'm not sure. Might be one of those too much of a good thing kind of situations. Sure she's cute and adorably morbid on her own, but put her with someone who's also dark and maybe that takes over. I don't know, I vote she should be with whoever she wants, but I picture her with someone...lighter. Who balances her out. But that's just me."

I could swear it's not just Lexi's eyes on me now, I feel Rory's, too, but I couldn't tell you because I've never been so interested in a hot dog with sauerkraut in my damn life.

"Her engine's going all right," Wyatt pipes up.

"Yeah," I grunt in agreement.

"Probably be done next week," Wyatt continues, like he doesn't realize those words are carving holes in my insides.

Or maybe he's doing it on purpose?

I look up to meet his green gaze and there's nothing malicious there. In fact, I think this is something like pride he's looking at me with. Brotherly respect.

Probably the closest thing I could hope for to friendship with him at this point in our lives. It's enough to warm some of the shadowy parts in me, the two of us, getting along like this. Mom will want video evidence.

Rory looks between us, a rare smile beaming on her face.

"Should be," I grunt out, nodding at Wyatt.

Next week already? Not sure if I want to drag it out so she's stuck here, or get it over with so I can finally put my imagination to use.

"Damn, y'all tryin' to run her out of town already or what?" Lexi jokes.

"Just running a business here, Alexis," Wyatt retorts. "Something you might get to know about someday." He eyes her meaningfully and she screeches, glaring at her sister.

"What the fuck Aurora?"

"Like my husband wasn't going to hear?"

"What happened to attorney client privilege?"

"I'm not your attorney, idiot."

"Then what are you doing in that fancy office of yours downtown?"

"Running a committee."

"You're a lawyer!"

"You never paid me to be *your* lawyer."

"Oh, fuck off, you knew that was in confidence!"

"Please, feel free to find the clause that says sisterly confidence holds up in a court of law. I'll wait here." Rory couldn't be dryer if her throat was a desert.

"Oh, so we're sharing sisterly secrets, is that it?" Lexi's voice gets dangerously passionate and Rory's hackles go up.

"Don't start a war with me you can't win," Rory threatens.

"Hey, Wyatt," Lexi taunts.

"What are you doing?" Rory's voice is dangerously low.

"Did Rory ever tell you about that guy in New York who—"

Lexi doesn't get to finish because Rory launches herself around the table and tackles her sister to cover her mouth.

"Take it back!" Lexi roars when she breaks free of Rory's grip.

"Fine! You can have attorney client privilege!" Rory concedes.

The three men at the table, myself included, and the baby watch on, the closest thing we'll get to the kind of entertainment normally reserved for college football here in the Heights.

I bet if I turned my head from the show in front of me and looked at the chicken coop, all the girls would be lined up watching, too, even Henrietta the Eighth who's notoriously fussy and choosy about who she reveals herself around.

"Fine," Lexi says, head held high.

"Sucker," Rory mutters as she heads back to her seat.

"What did you just call me?"

"Nothing."

"Oh, okay. Well then, why don't we talk about the—"

"Oh, for crying out loud!" Rory backpedals, but it's too late. Lexi's eyes are locked on Wyatt's.

"—man who used to make her sandwiches at the bodega!" Lexi declares triumphantly, and Rory huffs out loudly, stomping a foot and glaring her down with narrowed eyes.

"You're such a bitch!"

"Takes one to know one!" Lexi retorts.

"You know, if you ever get in a relationship, I'm going to remember this moment. Payback is an even bigger twat than you are sometimes," Rory tells her.

"Sandwich man?" Wyatt asks in a dangerously low voice.

"There's nothing to know," Rory insists, reclaiming her seat next to him and putting a hand on his thigh for reassurance. "He was just really good with his meat," she says calmly, with a little shrug.

My brother's eye twitches.

It feels like poetic justice for all the shit he's given me since my return.

And for that reason—*maybe* just the tiniest bit also because of the progress we've made while working together this past week—my third family dinner in the Heights is the best one I've had so far.

10

Amelia

I should've changed my email sooner.

I've been distracted, with Van Gogh, with this little crush of mine, this fixation. The new routine here, it lulled me into a false sense of security. I lost track of time, whittling away the days painting new businesses, watching Weston work on my engine at night, and programming in between, with occasional texts from Lexi to distract me. It's been two and a half weeks of that routine already, and it's flown by.

Normally I change my email addresses every month, at most. It's probably been six weeks or more that I've had this one.

The tinny robotic sound that came through was just like every other, the ones that alert me to emails from my mom, from my co-workers, or the occasional message offering to enlarge my penis size.

Hope filled me at the notification. Maybe Mom's tulips have bloomed and I'll get to see this year's bed.

It gives me a sense of home whenever I see the colorful buds, no matter where in the world I am, the soft petals take me right back to a different time. I can feel the safety I used to know before everything went to shit. Smell the hotdish in the oven, hear the music blasting from my brother's bedroom down the hall. My mom's whistling as she makes taking care of her family look like something she's lucky to be able to do.

After seeing the subject line of this email, though, that sound will now send my body into fight or flight.

The way my blood chilled, icing through my veins in slow motion as the horror spread through my system, cell by cell. My stomach turned to liquid and slid through my middle, pooling somewhere around my coccyx. The mental turmoil that went into overdrive at the realization he found me.

I force myself to take a deep breath and read the words, not just stare at the subject line.

I'd rather freak out obsessively over the actuality than the mystery of this thing.

Re: You think your clever

Angel (or whatever your calling yourself these days),

You can keep running but I'm always rite behind you.
All you have to do is give me the money and I'll leave you alone.

I won't stop until your life is ruined, like you ruined dad's & mine.

I'm done playing games. Give me the rest of the money or I expose you and put you into the public eye. I bet America would love to know where you are now.

You are the reason for all our lives being ruined, but you can make it rite and go live out the rest of your days as a nobody, just like what you want. It doesn't have to be like this. Just give me the money and I'll leave your miserable ass alone.

What is it you and Mom always say? Miss you always?

I'm on your tail. Soon, I won't miss you at all.

Your loving brother

It takes minutes for my fingers to stop shaking. For my breaths to come back from the jagged things they were and fall back under my control, some semblance of a rhythmic pattern to them once more. To be able to run a check on the sender and find the IP address the email was sent from.

Someone smarter who was trying to extort their sister over email might try to hide their IP address, use a proxy through some third-party system, make it look like it's coming from Sweden, or anywhere you *aren't*.

My brother? Let's just say he didn't get the brains in the family.

Within minutes of my fingers operating as normal again, I have the results.

Minnesota.

Still back home.

My breath falls out of me in a long *whoosh*.

He still has nothing on me. No clue where I am.

It means he's still back home, pressuring Mom, ruining her life, but she won't crack.

I never tell her where I am not because I don't trust her, I don't want her to know, I don't *miss* her so much it makes it hard to breathe every fucking day. I keep my location hidden from her so my brother can't hold it over her head. So he has nothing he can do to her, nothing he can get from her, to make her feel she has to comply with him and his shitty demands any more than she already is.

Mom has no money, we both know that.

She didn't want the payout, wouldn't take a cent of it. Even dad would've wanted it to go to me, according to her. That's why she made sure just as soon as I turned eighteen the trust was accessible by me and only me. And that Randall didn't find out about it for so long.

By the time he did, I was long gone.

He's always been a real piece of shit, but when he has something to gain? He knows no boundaries. Randall will stop at nothing to step on my neck, crush me as he tries to raise himself up the ladder of the shitty world he calls his life.

At this point, it wouldn't even matter to him that I don't have a penny left of all we have left of our father.

He's spent so long being single-minded, this one focus to pour all of his vile self into, that he wouldn't stop just because of the silly truth that I don't have the money he's after.

No.

Mom has tried to reason with him time and again over the years, and he hasn't listened.

My brother feels wronged by not getting a cut, and maybe if he hadn't been a junkie since high school he would've gotten half, but he alienated our parents all by his damn self and wants to blame me for it.

Now? He's after humiliation. Making sure I can't escape the past I've spent so long running from, distancing myself from.

Not only that, he refuses to believe the money is gone. It's what keeps him motivated to go on, the thought of some windfall that means he'd never have to work again in order to get his next fix. I shudder to think about what he might do if he realized there's nothing left.

Without a doubt, he'd try to ruin me for it.

I was lucky enough to get a full scholarship to college, but that only lasted a semester. A few glorious months away from home, a new name, a new identity, a new life untainted by the past. Until I made the mistake of trusting my first and only boyfriend. Revealing my history to him, for it to become all he saw in me.

Within days, I was a pariah. The place that had become my escape became my place of torment. Impossible to ignore the judgmental looks. Not to hear the whispers loud enough I couldn't miss 'em everywhere I went. It became no different than the town I fled as soon as I'd graduated.

Mom was right. She said anywhere we went, it would be the same. Even if we could've afforded to up and move somewhere else, the truth would've followed us there. The stigma.

So, I did what I had to do to survive. I used the money to build out Van Gogh while I studied code online. It took a few months to start earning my own living from that, and then I donated the rest, and I hit the road. I've never looked back since. Not as Angel. Not as Avery. Not as Amelia. Or any of the half a dozen names that came in between.

I haven't stopped running for eight years. In all that time, he's only gotten close two times.

Early on, I didn't mix up which postcards I sent to Mom when. He rifled through her mail, pilfering my correspondence with her, and he retraced my steps. Back then I didn't zigzag my route either. I've gotten unpredictable with my stops now. When I was nineteen, I didn't think to do anything other than keep driving down the interstate. Now, I'll surprise even myself with where my stops take me. Random keeps me safe.

The first and only time he almost caught me in person was the night my modus operandi changed. I was heading up the PCH, crashing in parking lots on beaches and living the best part of van dweller life, stopping every hundred miles or so, a few days at a time, sending a postcard from each stop. Until Randall was waiting at the dive bar in a little town north of Monterey.

We locked eyes from across the room and I ran. Screamed

fire, pushed open the emergency exit, triggered the alarm, and the restaurant emptied out in a mass exodus of mostly drunken patrons that made for a hell of an obstacle course for my brother.

I took off east, changing course often, and didn't sleep for 48 hours, until I was in South Dakota. At least I got to see Mount Rushmore.

The second time he got closer than I'd like was three years later, when he started going through Mom's email. That's when he started sending me threatening emails, but I knew he had nothing to go off of after I had implemented the safety protocol. There's no way he can track me down the way my life is set up now.

Unless he's a *lot* smarter than he's ever let on, he won't find me if I stick to the plan. It's kept me safe all these years since.

That second time was when I swapped to a more secure email platform. One that hackers choose for a reason. And I started changing my email address regularly, for extra good measure, and I haven't heard from him since.

Even Mom has no clue what email address I'll write from next. She usually deletes my emails after responding to me, and I keep a stack of postcards, shuffled like a deck of cards, and send her one every now and again.

It's worked all this time, up until now.

I got sloppy. Comfortable, for the first time since I've been on the road, staying as far away from my brother and our past as possible.

A sigh of relief flows through my nostrils and into the air around me when it sinks in that he truly has nothing. He got my email from Mom, he tried to push me around again, and that's it. I'll change my email, and we're back to the same old that's kept me safe from him, and the memory of our father, for all this time.

It doesn't stop the pall of gloom from rolling in and taking root over me.

I'm two days from being back on the road, just two damn days. Can't I enjoy the rest of my time here in Smoky Heights?

It's surprisingly high on my list of favorite places I've visited, considering how extensive my travel history really is. I'd hate to have the tail end of this stay ruined by the taint of my brother.

After taking a screenshot of his email, all necessary sender information and tracking data I could obtain, I purge the email account and set up a new one, immediately alerting my supervisor to the new form of contact. He probably thinks it's a little weird, but he's never asked questions, and for that, I'm thankful.

Fresh starts are what I do best.

This is just the beginning of my next one. I need to look on the bright side and treat it as such. Not let my pessimistic half win.

Hell, if I was in the habit of listening to that voice, I'd have yeeted myself over a cliff years ago.

A knock on my van door breaks me out of my focused state and I secure my laptop.

"Come in," I say in as normal of a voice as I can. I might have an edge in that area—so many years of practice—but I feel like I do a pretty good job of even fooling myself with that one.

My van rocks as one heavy foot comes in, then another.

"Hey, darlin'. We're ready for Van Gogh now, if I can steal her from you."

Weston has clearly just showered, clean shaven, golden hair and tanned skin popping with that fresh white tee stretched across his muscular chest and biceps. It reminds me of the beauty there can be in fresh starts.

Some things I have to look forward to on my last night, tomorrow.

I give him a smile, a real smile he's earned, and nod my head at him. "Yeah, you're good to take her. I gotta warn you though, she's the least valuable Van Gogh on the planet. You might be wasting your efforts here."

The burning look he gives me—in lieu of cracking another joke like we normally would—tells me I'm not the only one with their mind on tomorrow night. When he speaks, his voice is low, the timbre raspier than usual. "She's worth more to me than any painting, Amelia. I'll take good care of her."

Taking one last glance around the space I've called home my entire adult life, I grab the bag with everything I'll need for the night and turn her over into the care of the Grady brothers one last time.

They're going to start the installation on the transmission tonight, but since they're squeezing this in after hours Wyatt has warned me that he's going to need tomorrow night for the engine, so she won't be ready to drive until sometime tomorrow evening.

That leaves me homeless for the night, except for one benevolent gentleman. A Boy Scout, if you will.

The brothers move my van, my whole world, into the shop for the rest of her stay here, and I watch them work together, grumbling and laughing as they take out whatever's left of the old parts inside Van Gogh and place the new ones in.

And I get it. Over the course of the evening, I see how important this is to Weston. This relationship with his brother, why he wouldn't want to jeopardize this bond that I've seen grow in the past couple of weeks. Even if I was willing to abandon my reasoning in the name of one steamy night together, he wasn't, and after watching them all this time, I get it.

The rare twitch of the lips that passes for a smile from Wyatt, the looks of respect and pride as he checks over Weston's work. I'm guessing it's a tenuous sort of peace that's new for both of them.

I might not understand why Weston being happy would trigger Wyatt, or why Weston is okay with putting himself on hold for someone else, but I do see the beauty in what he's going for here.

If making things right with my family was an option, I'd probably suffer through a lot to make it happen too. But there isn't a happily ever after for my family, not even a family reunion is possible at this point.

The Grady brothers get to a point they're happy with for tonight and assure me it shouldn't be as long of a wait when they wrap it tomorrow.

By ten p.m. Weston is giving me the very abbreviated tour of his current home. A small Craftsman he's renting with one bedroom and one bathroom, it's barely bigger than my van. Okay, that's an exaggeration, but the tour takes about as long. There's the kitchen, there's the living room, there's the bedroom, there's the bathroom. I get it.

The problem comes when he tries to insist I take the bed while he takes the sorry excuse for a couch.

I drop down onto it to test it out, and a metal spring nearly gives me an enema.

"Not to yuck your yum or anything, but how are you going to sleep on this without getting a prostate exam? You weigh, like, twice as much as me and it's already breaching fifth base with me."

Weston gives me a look that reaches every single nerve cell all the way down to my toes before answering. "We've got one more night to last, darlin'. I can put up with just about anything tonight knowing I'll be in your bed tomorrow."

That wink he follows it up with should be illegal.

"I mean, if this is what you're into, if you want a romantic night alone with the couch, let's just pick a safe word now and I'll say no more. All you've gotta say is *polar bear* and I'll take the hint."

"Is that your safe word?" The way his lips pull up and curve into a smile promises to give me a reason to use it.

"No, mine is *I've got mace*," I joke.

Weston pulls a tight grimace and shakes his head. "Yeah, you're gonna have to give me some clear boundaries before we start tomorrow. I'm not risking some Vixen-worthy move below the belt because I pulled on your hair when you only wanted me to stroke it."

Only one word of that diatribe stands out to me.

"Vixen?" My eyes light up, finding his. "You listened to *Vengeful Vixens?*"

He pops a shoulder up casually, almost carelessly. "I had to hear it for myself after all your talk about it."

"And?" I practically shriek the word.

"Getting vengeance for those victims who aren't here to tell their own stories," he says in a scary accurate impression of Jynx's husky voice as he nails the delivery on the show's tagline. "No, it's pretty solid actually."

"I knew it!" That was definitely more of a shriek, and I jump up off the couch and hug him excitedly. It's a testament to his character that he doesn't let that be weird, that he doesn't pull back or shrink away from me.

For two people who are used to staying detached, that was a *wee* bit personal. But he runs with it, holding me close with one arm and rubbing my back with the other for just a moment, releasing me as I pull back and pretend I didn't just memorize the way his body felt against mine.

The firm abs beneath his shirt that absorbed the impact of my body running into his.

Those strong arms that held me for a too-short moment that will keep me embarrassingly toasty for the rest of the night.

His throat works as he swallows, and I think of a way to move past that awkward moment, spitting out the first thing I think of.

"Can I use your shower?"

His eyes flutter shut, jaw clenching with a tic for the briefest second before he collects himself. "Of course, darlin'. Right this way."

He gets me set up with everything I might need, my bag with my clothes and toiletries, and I take my time getting ready for bed. Relishing in the unlimited hot water his house has, that I can stand under the spray that could melt flesh for a quarter of an hour, maybe even longer if I dared. Trying not to inhale the steam and wonder if I can smell him in it. His body wash on the small, built-in bench, tempts me to pick it up and take a whiff. But I'm not a total creeper psycho, whatever my DNA, and I pass on the chance.

Instead, I force myself to shut the water off before he asks if I'm drowning myself, like a good little house guest, dry myself off, do my nighttime routine and ready myself for bed.

Does that include an extra thorough cleaning of all my most personal areas? Some shaving? Possibly, what are you, a journalist?

When I emerge back into the hallway I don't see Weston, so I let myself into the bedroom and sort out my belongings, putting away toiletries I don't need anymore.

I would simply refuse to sleep in here, but we had a pretty thorough back-and-forth about it on the way here, and I can tell I'm not going to change his mind on the matter. The man is a Southern gentleman to his own detriment. He outright refuses to sleep in the bed while I'm relegated to the sofa. But I'm not about to let him sleep on the couch and let that thing round the bases with him while I have his bed all to myself.

That would certainly throw the universe out of balance yet again, and I'm not about it.

I didn't *plan* on wearing a small pair of panties—or a thin, stretchy bralette that traces every secret my chest holds—to bed out of any scheme to seduce him or ruin our plan when we're not even twenty-four hours away from victory. I didn't even know I'd be staying in his bed when I packed my bag.

And maybe I'm not from the South, but you know, in the Midwest, we tend to be decent people, too, and I just can't let this literal golden retriever of a man throw his back out on that janky couch and ruin my chances of a real, live rodeo experience tomorrow night.

So really, I'm being selfish, if you wanna look at it that way.

He can do this as a favor to *me*. I'm looking out for my own interests with this move. He doesn't have to trade in his gentleman card by taking me up on this offer, because there's nothing uncouth about it on his part. What would be rude is turning me down.

"Boy Scout, I hope you know I'm not going to bed without you," I call loud enough to travel down the hall to wherever he's hiding out.

"Then I guess you're in for a long night," he drawls from the doorway, and I try not to startle at his sudden appearance. His minty fresh breath and that smell that's uniquely him—the one that's come to make my knees buckle at the hint of the woody fragrance with a strong masculine undertone—reach me from several feet away and I steel myself.

Weston looks like he's trying to keep his balance when he spots me. Spies what I'm wearing. His grip tightens on the doorjamb, knuckles turning white as his eyes slowly move their way down my body, skimming over the clear outline of my breasts, my flat stomach, my thighs and the small triangle of nude material in between them. It might as well be his tongue for the way my body reacts to it.

"I won't complain about a long night," I tell him with a heavy-lidded look that betrays my impatience. "Just don't make it a lonely night."

"Darlin', you'll be the death of me. That face. Those tits. That body. I won't survive a night in a bed with you where I can't touch you."

"Then touch me," I offer.

"So eager, angel, when the wait is only going to make it that much sweeter."

I let out a loud sigh and turn my back on him, walking to the bed and pulling back the covers. If he watches my ass as I walk away, that's his prerogative. His scent overwhelms me as the sheets fold back, that blend of maybe cedar, and something else I can't place, it invades my senses. It melts my insides, and I'm lucky my knees don't give out. To be wrapped in his scent, the fabric that's touched every inch of him, I hope it's enough to hold me over for one last sleep.

When I climb in the bed, perch myself up on some pillows and pull the covers up to my stomach, I find Weston watching with a fixated stare that gives away just how he feels about waiting one more damn night.

He looks like the last tether on his restraint is about to snap.

Good. Mine snapped a week ago. It's time for his to catch up.

I pat the empty side of the bed on my left and wait expectantly.

He sucks in a breath through his teeth and turns his head to one side.

"You're really testing my resolve here, darlin'."

"I can keep my hands to myself if you can." I think.

"That's the problem. I'm not sure I can."

"What if I promise not to let you touch anything you're not supposed to?"

He shakes his head, running his free hand through that messy blond hair, the strands falling dangerously over his forehead, begging for feminine fingers to explore them.

His other hand, still on the doorframe, grips it harder, and I worry the wood will split if he keeps it up.

"You've got a lot of faith in my self-restraint."

"I have a lot of faith in you, period."

He blows out a big breath and those green irises find me from the corners of his eyes and he studies me for a second.

For just a sliver in time, I let the weight, the burden I carry with me every day, show through. I take down my walls, barriers, and masks, and I let him see the heaviness I can never escape. The one that was triggered this afternoon by the email from my brother.

I stop trying to hide my load, and instead I let him see my desperation to *not* feel it all for once.

"Honestly?" I ask him.

He nods.

"I've had a really shitty day, and I don't want to be alone tonight. We don't have to do anything. Just lay with me?"

His eyes shutter, and his resolve to stay away melts in front of my eyes.

"If you said that to start, I would've brought tea and snacks and we could be watching some true crime documentary right now. Give me a sec." He turns to leave the room, but I call out to him.

"I don't need any of that, Weston. Just be with me?"

His hand drops from the doorframe and he's by the bed in an instant, pulling back the covers from the other side of the mattress, soft eyes on mine.

"I'm just warning you that I'm not responsible for anything my little explorer does tonight."

"Your little explorer?" I question.

Weston uses both hands to gesture between his legs and my mouth twitches, a smile trying to take over and erase the traces of the frown.

"I'll keep him under control. But he has a mind of his own sometimes. I can't lie, he thinks of you a lot, and he might not understand that having you in my bed doesn't mean what he thinks it means."

I giggle, the solemnity of the moment broken that fast, and I know this was the right choice tonight. Carrying a load like mine can be so isolating, so heavy on my own. But sharing it with him, even just by keeping me company? Suddenly it doesn't feel like so much.

"Close those gorgeous eyes, darlin'."

"Got a surprise for me?" I ask, with a taunt in my voice.

"You've already gotten an eyeful of my surprise, but might as well not rub it in your face tonight."

"I wouldn't complain if you did," I tease.

"Mmhmm," he says in a low voice. "Eyes to yourself for just a bit longer. Then all of you can have your fill. If I see your eyes wandering tonight, I might not be able to stop myself from giving them something worth watching."

My stomach flutters, desire dipping down south. I place my hands over my eyes and listen to the sounds of him stripping down. The shedding of a shirt. A zipper, the rush of pants falling to the ground, and the noise of him stepping out of them.

Finally, as if he's dragging this out just to tease me, to ratchet my need up from a nine point five out of ten to an eleven, I hear the flick of a switch and seconds later feel the bed shift under his weight.

I cheat, just a little, and let my hands fall away before he releases me from the command, just in time to see him yank on the sheets, pulling them up and over his body. That glimpse of my new obsession, even still in his dark green boxer briefs, before it's hidden beneath the navy comforter...it does things to me. Things that turn my blood hot—the air on my skin freezing in contrast—and make my nipples pebble. My panties damp.

The moonlight streaking in through the crack in the curtains on his window is enough light for him to notice the change in me, and for me to watch his eyes darken in response.

"Fuck me. I'm gonna have to sleep facing the wall, aren't I?" There's nothing bitter in his voice, just tortured resignation.

"I thought all this anticipation was your idea?" I taunt.

"Yeah, well, much more of it and we might have a problem on our hands."

"My hands can handle it," I promise.

Weston yanks a pillow out from beneath his head and slams it down over his face, muffling an exaggerated groan. He pulls it off his face and looks over at me.

"Why? Why did we agree to this last night bullshit again?"

I slide down the mattress until my body is flush against it, on my left side so I'm facing him, one hand supporting my head as I concentrate on taking in his features. His strong cheekbones and square jaw. That sharp nose and forehead that the ancient poets would've written sonnets about.

Me? Best I can do is trace the shape with the tips of my fingers, vowing to memorialize him in my mind like he is right now. Selfless, gorgeous, and without judgment.

Though, if he knew who I really was, that might be different.

But for my own sake, I'm going to enjoy the rest of my time in the Heights as Amelia Marsh. And Amelia Marsh has no reason to be judged, to fear this closeness that we're pretending isn't blooming with every interaction between us.

So I allow myself this moment of weakness. Where my feather light touches across his face—those hewn features I'm tracing, imprinting on my soul with every touch—they dust goosebumps across his flesh.

I relish in the power of it, the rush it sends through my bloodstream to see the way he's affected by the simplest of connections between us. Let myself imagine it could be more.

Just while we're here, in the dark, I can dream that it's not just the physical attraction that's moving him, reducing him to this shivering vessel of need.

That *I* could be what he needs. This beautiful, selfless man who makes the world around him so much brighter just by existing.

That my darkness doesn't dampen his light, my taint can't corrode his bronze shine.

The hunger in me ramps up, desire coursing through my cells, liquifying me and pooling in my center.

He sucks in a sharp breath through parted lips, whether it's the way my fingers caress his forehead, the lazy fall of his golden strands across it, or the look in my eyes.

Fuck, maybe he can scent the change in my pheromones, my chemical makeup that's radiating my lust to him on a base level that defies words but has existed for millennia. It's what's propagated society and civilization all this time. This ancient, primal signal between the hunter and the hunted. Right now, I'm not sure which of us is which.

Weston grabs my hand and stops it from continuing its exploration, down his jaw and beyond, where it would've loved to have gone.

"Amelia."

No one has ever said my name like that. None of my names. Like he needs me.

Like I'm what's tethering him to this plane.

Like I'm killing him with every touch.

"Weston."

It's a breath, it's a request, it's permission.

"You're making it really fucking hard not to touch you right now," he whispers, face inches from my own.

"Don't touch me," I say soft as velvet.

He stares at me, trying to follow.

"You don't want me to touch you?"

"I want you to touch yourself," I whisper back.

His eyelids slam shut, his throat bobs, and his entire face strains. The comforter shifts beneath us, but neither of us have moved. Realization sinks in, and my face flushes.

"Fuck," he says, and follows it with a groan.

"Isn't that what you do when you get home every night? Touch yourself, knowing that I'm in my bed doing the same?"

"Aw, darlin'. You're going to kill me with that mouth of yours. It looks so innocent, but it's pure fucking filth, isn't it? Just like the rest of you."

"It's just speaking the truth." At least right now.

"You think of me fucking my fist?" he asks, eyes alight with a kind of intensity I've never seen in another pair in all my life. There's nothing malicious, or sick about this kind of need. It's pure, it's reciprocated. It's something I can fall into.

"No," I tell him truthfully.

His brow comes down just a touch, closer to his eyes, not wavering from mine.

"I think of you fucking me."

"Goddamn," he breathes out, rolling over to face me completely.

"Show me," I whisper.

"What do you want to see?"

"What I do to you."

"I'll show you exactly what you do to me, angel."

My stomach flips at the use of my real name. What no one else has called me in almost a decade. From him, it doesn't hold those connotations though. From him it feels like something holy.

I wait, holding my breath, lower lip between my teeth as I watch. Weston pulls the covers back, revealing his cut abs, all six of them, and the waistband of his underwear, taut against his lean frame.

My nipples tighten, my core flutters, and desire floods me at the sight of his masculine form. No part of me isn't ready for this man.

Weston launches the bedspread the rest of the way off his body, and it lands at the foot of the bed in a whoosh of air. His cock juts up, fighting against the constraints of his boxer briefs, which have the challenging task of holding all of him in. I don't know if my pussy could do the job, but I'm volunteering here and now to try, if he's accepting applications.

"I'll give you the live demonstration tomorrow," he says huskily. "Make sure you know *exactly* what you to do to me. Feel it from the inside, all the way from your throat to your toes."

I let out a hum that might be embarrassing if I didn't stand behind it a hundred percent.

"But for now, I'll show you just how hard you get me, Amelia."

I sit up, such an attentive pupil, here to remember every detail of tonight.

Weston reaches down and peels his underwear off, removing them entirely before laying back once more so I can take him in, entirely naked for the first time.

My breath leaves me, as does any shred of inhibition, as I take in the sight of the most beautiful man I've ever seen, laid before me like a feast for my eyes. I wish it were an interactive exhibit, but I can make do just fine with this view for now.

His cock is massive, entirely erect, and the veins look damn near angry, the head almost purple from the rush of blood.

I want to taste it. To feel the smoothness of him, the hardness as he notches that fat head into my center and pushes in. I'm not sure if I can stretch wide enough to take him, being as slight as I am. It might break me, but it'd be a worthy end to a life I hardly deserve in the first place.

"Is that what you wanted to see, darlin'?" His voice is gravel and carefully coiled restraint, like a bobcat ready to strike given the signal, at the first twitch of his prey.

Power, muscle, golden perfection, all ready and waiting.

I nod at him, tongue tracing my lower lip more out of the wish it were tracing something else than some conscious attempt to lure him in.

"I haven't stopped thinking about it," I admit, breath caught in my throat.

"I haven't stopped thinking about your tits either," he says. "That fucking ring through your nipple. I want to bite it. Tug on it with my teeth and see what happens."

My body responds like he did just that. Nipples firm, pussy soaked, and clit pulsing. He's not the only one about to burst here. I moan at the thought, the picture he's painted, and I want him to paint something else for me. My face, my chest, my stomach. The thought turns me on in ways I can't explain, and I need it.

"Show me what you do when you think of me," I urge him, shifting so I'm kneeling, resting back with my ass on my heels, legs spread just enough for him to see, maybe even to smell what he's doing to me.

"You want me to jerk off?"

I nod again, subtle movements of my head, eyes homed in on the view in front of me.

"Can... Can I watch you?" I manage to get the question out with only a small blush.

"Oh, fuck. Hell yeah you can," he says with the kind of enthusiasm reserved for people with clean hearts and good souls. It's a kind I haven't felt myself in far too long.

His nostrils flare as he rotates, positions himself up until he's on his knees in front of me, towering over me as he moves one hand to grip himself.

It's the perfect view.

Those cut lines on his hips jut down, dragging my eyes straight to the main attraction, like they'd have any trouble finding it on their own. There's no missing this man, that cock that could be the mold that pleases the masses. But for twenty-four hours, it's for me alone. I'm not going to waste a moment that I have him—*it*—to myself.

"What do you normally do?" The question is so soft I worry he won't hear it, but he answers immediately.

"First," he says, flexing his fingers around his shaft, "I slick my hand down my shaft, imagining you're in front of me."

"Like this?" I ask him, bouncing in place just once, just enough that my tits jiggle and his eyes drag down to my spread thighs.

"Fuck, you're better than perfect. Yeah, angel, like that."

"Then what?"

"Then I pull on it, squeeze it as I stroke it upward."

My mouth can't decide what to do. It dries out, then fills back up with saliva, desperate to get involved in the action somehow. My pussy has no such confusions. It knows *exactly* how to prepare for its eventual master. Those inner walls flex and flutter at the sight, his narration of this religious experience for me. My underwear feel hot, uncomfortably wet, and I want them gone. They're in the way. But I practice restraint.

Right now, I'm here to watch, not to play.

I'll have my turn.

Weston's hand pumps at a slow pace, his strong, sure grip moving up and down the length of his thick shaft.

My breaths mold to his movements, every inhale mirroring his downstroke, my exhales matching his upstrokes.

It feels like even our blood is flowing in the same rhythm. Like we're so connected right now that watching him come might push me over the edge.

I break eye contact with the one-eyed monster and look up at that godlike face to see him staring at me, not watching the show he's putting on for me like I expected. It takes my breath away, stutters my heart for a second with the intensity I see there.

"My imagination hasn't done this justice," he says through staggered breaths. "I'm not talented enough to picture you looking this perfect. Like you'd do anything for a taste."

I sway my head from one side to the other. "No touching, remember?" I remind him. "I'm being a good girl. That's what you like, right?"

He screws his eyes shut and I watch in fascination as a bead of sweat starts to roll down one temple. Those biceps of his bulge as his strokes get firmer, stronger as he works himself harder to show me what I want to see.

"God dammit, Amelia, you're so fucking sexy it's unreal."

"What do you think about when you do this normally?" I ask him.

"Your tits," he says, without hesitation.

"These tits?" I ask him, bringing my hands over my thighs, up my stomach, and resting them on my favorite investment I've ever made. My skin lights up beneath the featherlight touch of my own fingers, so used to coming alive in the pleasure I have to offer myself.

"God, fuck, yes, those," he says through clenched teeth. His neck is strained, tendons flaring and jaw pulled tight. It allows me to picture exactly what he'll look like if I ever let him get on top of me, forced to brace his weight to not crush me, hold himself back to not wreck me. Our foot-plus size difference could be an obstacle for someone less motivated, but I have a feeling he'll be determined to make it work.

I slip my fingers beneath the hem of the thin bralette and pull it up, up, up, just as slowly as he teased me with his shirt the first night he saw my chest, and I focus on his breathing, how labored it is, the curses he's biting out as he continues fucking his fist with a kind of passion no man has treated me to before.

The full bottoms of my heavy C cups are revealed to him. The cool air hitting them is one tell, but his hot gaze is far more palpable to my sensitive skin.

I continue peeling the fabric up and over my breasts, until my nipples are free, and he curses the loudest one yet.

Looking down, I see my nipple ring winking at him in the rays of moonlight from my right breast, and I watch his gaze narrow on that spot as his hand doesn't stop, never stops moving, while his other buries itself in his hair, needing purchase somewhere and not being able to touch me. His fingertips dig into the roots, press into his scalp, and I wish it were my own.

My top comes all the way off, and the sound he makes will live in my memory for the rest of my days. Vulnerable, needy, and so fucking earnest.

"You don't have to imagine tonight," I tell him, letting the bralette fly off of my fingers, giving him full viewing rights. My hands run back down my taut stomach, my thin frame not having much in the way of curves, but he seems to be enjoying it just *fine* based off of the groans, the unforgettable show I'm getting.

"Best fucking tits I've ever seen," he tells me again, just like the first time.

"They could be better," I say, looking down at them and then back up.

"Bullshit," he spits, cock starting to leak from the tip. But he bites anyway. "How?"

Voice soft, breathy, my natural rasp taking center stage, I say, "They could be painted in your cum."

He swears, and I watch as his balls tighten, that precum getting thick and stringy as his hand continues jerking that length that I wish I had the honor of handling for myself right now.

"That what you want?" He's running out of breath. Out of words. Out of sanity.

I nod at him, leaning forward to get closer to him.

"Holy shit," he mutters, cursing over and over again as he loses control, the pleasure taking over.

I smile at him, a demure look that only hints at the rest of my plans for him, and I let that smile do my talking for me. Wordlessly, I broadcast all those daydreams of our one night together to him, my imagination running wild, and something tells me it all hits him loud and fucking clear.

"Hope those tits are ready," he grunts out.

Holding steady, I press my chest out just enough to show him how much I want this. How I've come to the thought of being covered in his time and again. My stomach, my chest, my face. I want it all, and I want it everywhere.

With a final series of strong strokes, abs clenched, sweat dripping down the carved muscles from his pecs all the way down to his cock, I watch in fascination, fixation, as this man comes with his entire body, maybe even part of his soul breaks free as he releases. He holds nothing back.

A groan gives way as his cock jumps, balls jerking, and the head erupts, spewing his thick, hot, sticky release all over my chest. Like a Pollock, there's no pattern or predictability to it. It just scatters, spraying my sternum and both breasts, dripping down in rivulets across my nipples.

I shouldn't be so willing to admit the feelings that evokes in me. Being worthy of being covered in this part of him. This wholesome man, so much better than I deserve, who gives himself so freely, came to the thought of me. The *sight* of me, on my knees for him. Not even my touch, just the concept of it was enough to make him explode.

It's the hottest thing I've ever seen, and the first time I've tried something like this. But the thought hasn't left me alone for weeks and I had to know what it would be like.

This is a level of turned on I've never been before, and it's all because of *him*.

His strokes slow, arm pumping less and less, and finally pauses entirely, squeezing the last drops of his release from the tip of his dick. I watch on, eager to lap up every memory tonight has to offer.

When Weston removes his hand from his cock, leaving it to its own devices, still bobbing at attention, red and exhausted, he reaches out with his thumb and forefinger and takes hold of my nipple ring, careful not to touch my skin.

"I'm not touching you," he points out. He's just touching the metal, and this might be the best loophole of all time. The way my core clenches you'd think he was inside me.

Weston's fingers grip the stainless steel hoop and twist it, turning it so that the metal runs through my body. The cum all over the piercing goes into my body, and I moan at the visual.

"But at least my cum is inside you."

If my piercing were fresh, that could present a *host* of problems. But I've had it for years and years now, and I have absolutely no issue with that filthy little maneuver he just pulled.

Quite the opposite.

Considering, on a cellular level, his cum had already probably dripped inside the piercing, it doesn't really make a difference logically. But *watching* him push the metal, covered in his release, through the hole in my nipple, watching it spread and the metal slip through it with ease, like it were lube... It's the dirtiest thing I've ever done.

My face, or maybe that little moan I make in response, must give away how much I liked that, and he grins at me, a wicked tilt of his lips that hints at a filthy secret we now share.

Still on my knees, I let myself fall straight back, ass landing on my feet and back flat on the bed.

My knees are shoulder-width apart, my barely concealed pussy on full display for him. Cum-covered chest there for him to appreciate his handiwork on as well.

"Now, it's your turn to watch," I tell him.

11
Weston

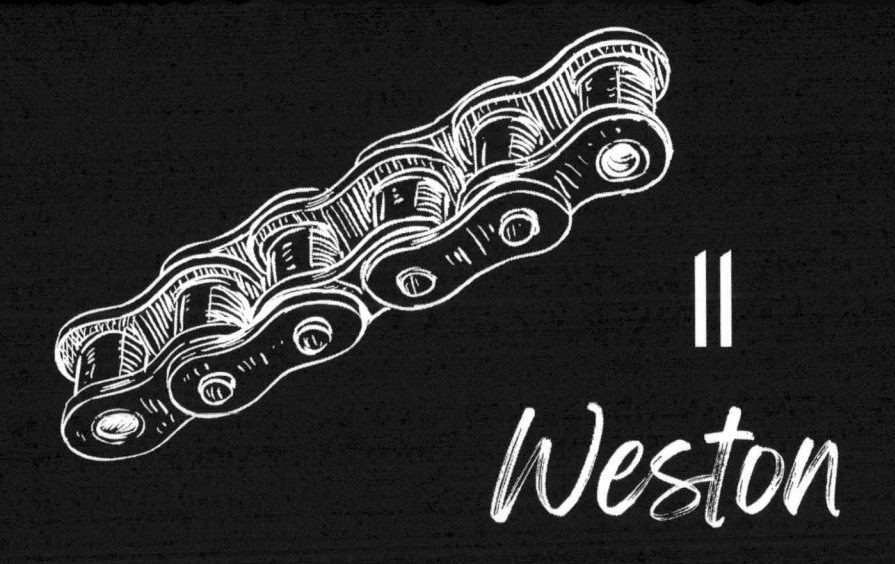

I want to do a lot more than watch.

I want to change her life, skin to skin.

Brand her on a molecular level. Flesh, tongue, teeth, fingers, cock. I want to use every part of me to make her feel good.

This gorgeous girl who's too perfect for words. I'll use my body to show her what she's worth. What she should hold out her heart for.

Make her back bow, her legs shake, until she's crying out. For more, for less, until she screams that it's too much.

I won't stop until I'm satisfied she's had enough.

This whole waiting game we've played might be dangerous. Because it's built up a thirst, a raging appetite that will be damn near impossible to quench in just one night.

I'll do my fucking best to try though.

But that's still hours away.

Right now? I'll happily watch, like the good boy I am. Not touching anything I'm not supposed to, because I *can* follow the rules, despite popular opinion about me. In fact, this girl in my bed might be about the only one who believes the best in me, and I'm going to prove her right.

"Please," I croon. "Show me what I've been missing out on, darlin'."

Amelia shifts on the bed beneath me, stretched out on her back, legs tucked under her, thighs spread just enough for me to watch anything she wants to show me. Her tits are a worthwhile distraction, covered in my cum as she lays there, and if I were allowed to touch her I'd run my fingers through it, trace designs on her skin with the marks of my release that was all for her.

"Burn it into my memory, angel. Make sure every time I get in this bed, I remember you coming in it."

She makes the sexiest noise my ears have been graced with and slips her right hand down the plane of her stomach, those short black nails like beacons for my eyes to follow their progress.

They don't stop at the top of her underwear, but slide over the top of it, over her mound, the outline of her lips, before spreading them to brush her clit in a tease that brings a groan to her lips, and also to mine.

"You gonna let me see what you're doin' to that beautiful pussy? Or am I going to have to keep imagining how perfect it looks underneath there?"

Her eyelids drop lower, watching me from beneath them when she speaks. "You're awful impatient for someone who's spent the last several weeks teasing me and dragging out every single taste I've been given." Her voice is thick with desire, lower pitched than usual, with a husk to it that hardens my cock all over again.

From how turned on she is—all the signs are there, pink cheeks, puffy lips, stiff nipples, blown out pupils, I bet she's perfectly soaked between her thighs from that heady scent I'm getting—I wouldn't be surprised if she came quick.

I can say I sure as fuck plan to make the first one fast tomorrow, get it out of the way so the real fun can begin. Where we take our time, me exploring, her lavishing in that state of bliss that has her floating between planes, not sure what's real and what's a dream anymore. On the brink of insanity from the pleasure that won't quit, pushing her farther than she thought she could go. I've had weeks to study, to prep for this, and I'm more than ready.

But something tells me she won't want to make tonight too easy on me. She needs this escape. Needs the distraction a partner for one night can provide. The temporary reality that can be woven between two people getting lost in one another's physical selves.

Hell, even I could use a night of forgetting the insecurities that haunt me doggedly in my waking hours. How I'll never be enough, the fact that I'm a disappointment to everyone in my life. Shit, this reprieve is good for both of us. Remind us that there are others out there who see worth, who see value in us as we are.

And this girl has a lot of value to me.

I might not know why she's on the run, why she thinks she wouldn't be able to form connections, grow roots, stay in one place and bloom, but I see how special she is.

She says *I'm* the one who brightens everything around me, but I see something kindred in her.

So distanced from everyone else, for whatever reasons of her own, I recognize the lonely soul inside. And I hope, if just for a couple of nights, I can make her feel seen, felt, and appreciated. That's a gift I can leave her with, something she can take with her when she's off to wherever is next.

And maybe, just maybe, it's a seed I can plant that'll take root in her and, over time, convince her she's worth everything she wants and more. That there's someone out there she can let in and share all of herself with. The way I wish for too.

So I'm not exaggerating when I say she has me wrapped

around her finger. The finger I'm watching drag over her pussy so softly, so slowly, it's like she's trying to be my undoing.

My breaths come out ragged, heavier than they should for someone who's just kneeling, watching. Her chest rises and falls in time with mine, that gorgeous face of hers drawn tight, focusing on the pleasure she's bringing herself, and I take it in. The sight of her, soaking with her need, wet with my cum, writhing on her back, fingers on herself, right where I wish my mouth could be.

"You're so fucking perfect, angel," I whisper roughly.

Her eyes squeeze tight at that, face looking pained for a second, before she opens them again.

"Don't say that."

"Sorry, but I'm not a liar," I tell her, eyes focused between her thighs, where her fingers are starting to slip beneath the edge of fabric keeping this final mystery from me.

One delicate finger slides beneath the material and pulls it to the side, finally allowing me to see what's overtaken my fantasies, my waking dreams.

Soft. Pink. Glistening. Worthy of a thousand more dreams and then some.

"Perfect," I growl.

She moans, releasing the fabric, letting it stay to one side of her pussy, leaving it on display for me.

"I knew the rest of you would be just as gorgeous, but this?" I blow out a shaky breath, and I know she can hear what I can't find the words for. I settle for, "Fuck, darlin'."

Unable to help myself, I dive down between her legs and press my face as close as I can without touching her skin, following the rules we set for tonight. Inhaling deeply, I let her scent fill my nostrils, mouth watering at the musky, feminine scent that I can *taste* from here. Hands quivering with the need to feel her for myself, I pop back up to my knees before I break my word.

I need to know what it feels like to be wrapped in her warmth, how tight she is, how hot and wet. What she tastes like when she comes. From my current vantage point, I can finally visualize what it would look like to sink two fingers into her, the sight of her stretching around me as I prep her to take more.

My cock stands at attention, ready for duty, but this isn't about him right now.

"Let me see," I tell her softly.

"You wanna see what you do to me?" she asks, an offer to flip the table.

"God, yes."

Amelia takes her two middle fingers and runs them from the top of her slit, down over her clit, and through all the wetness waiting for her there as she nears her center. I watch as her fingers part the folds, working their way right down her middle, and dip into that honeypot that's waiting there.

It's all I can do to stay put as her fingers disappear, knuckle by knuckle, and I watch her body twitch and buck under the intrusion. She pulls out until her hand is free again, and she holds it up for my inspection.

Soaked, damn near dripping in all that nectar. Saliva pools in my mouth, wishing I could take her fingers into my mouth and test it for myself, get a mouthful of her taste, but I stay still.

"I've had to fuck my toy so many times since that first night I'm surprised it hasn't died yet," she admits, watching my gaze darken on hers.

That fucking toy. I've never been so jealous of silicone in my life. Getting to do the job I wish I could've every night. Several times a night, I'd bet.

I know exactly which one she means too. May have spent an insane number of hours scouring through websites until I found the exact one so I could order it for myself and see exactly what she likes. All part of my prep for tomorrow.

"There's no toy here tonight, Amelia. You're gonna have to show me how gorgeous you are when you come with just your fingers."

She nods, her head moving in place against the comforter that will never look the same after tonight.

Her hand, those soaking wet fingers, drop down to her pussy once more and she uses the pads of her two middle fingers to start to rub her clit. The impulse I have to drop down with her, to lean in and lick her fingers clean, suck that swollen clit like her favorite toy does until she's drenching my face instead of my bedspread, it's tough to master control over my base desires right now, but I should get points for effort here.

It's as I'm watching her tease both of us with those slow movements, those dragging touches that pull at her puffy skin and make my cock twitch with need that I realize the rules of the game.

We promised not to touch anything we weren't supposed to.

I grasped the metal through her nipple, not her breasts themselves, however much I was dying to.

I might not be able to shove my fingers inside of her tight heat, but her hand is fair fucking game for me to touch freely.

That's a part of her I've felt before and have no qualms about touching right now.

"Keep showing me what you like to do to yourself, angel," I coax her, bringing one hand down to cover hers.

She gasps, sucking in a sharp breath at the contact of my skin on hers as she brings herself close to orgasm beneath my touch.

I let my fingers mold to hers as she presses, lightly at first, then harder, rubbing herself just how she likes it. I memorize the motion, the pressure she uses, the rhythm of it as her breath stutters, her eyelids flutter shut, and her breaths come in pants.

Her free hand grips the bedsheet and I want to see it do more. "What's that other hand gonna do?" I ask her.

Amelia's fiery teal gaze locks on mine, burning me from the inside out, as she releases the comforter with that hand and instead brings it up to caress her breast. She trails those fingertips over the skin, running through the glaze of cum there and dragging it with her fingers as they move over her sensitive skin.

I let out a hoarse moan, my brain struggles to take it all in, the way her body writhes on the bed, how her fingers of one hand move beneath mine, stroking and toying with her clit, while I watch her other hand pull my cum up to her nipple and start to tweak it, pulling on it hard enough that I can feel it in my own body.

It's a visceral response, watching what she does to herself, covered in the mess I left on her. My balls tighten, precum leaks out of my tip, and I ignore it all to focus on her. How to make the most out of this night for this stunning woman who's brought so much into my world. I want to rock hers.

I press down on the fingers beneath mine, that barrier between her pussy and my hand that's keeping this from broaching inappropriate territory.

Okay, who am I kidding. There's nothing appropriate about her finger fucking herself beneath my hand, but at least I can say *I* didn't fuck her while she was still in town, not with my fingers or any other part of me.

Her eyes widen and her lips part when she feels me take control of the movements. Harder, then softer. Faster, then in a circle. I use her fingers like they were a toy I could get her off with, pressing in, easing up, and moving quickly, fast enough to feel like vibrations against her skin.

Those gorgeous eyes close, rolling back in her head, and I

move my hand down, urging hers to come with it. She obeys, fingers trailing lower, taking my hint.

"Put them in, darlin'."

Like the perfect woman of my dreams she continues to prove she is, she does. An A+ student, this one.

Her two fingers slide into her opening and get sucked in by the grip of her pussy. I bite down on my lip hard enough to leave marks as I feel it happen.

I start to pulse my hand on top of her fingers, pressing them in and feeling her muscles pull them further, before releasing. A growl escapes me at the sensation of it.

My other hand comes up, hooks around her thumb and pulls it up so it touches her clit.

"Keep fucking yourself," I order her.

The first hand stays on her fingers, feeling her pump in and out, searching for that spot on her front wall that I wish I could touch for myself, while my other hand bounces on her thumb in the rhythm that had her so close to the edge before.

"Oh God." She moans the words with a vibrato to her voice that's not normally there. Amelia throws her head back, neck pulled tight, shoulders back as she allows herself to fall into the pleasure we're giving her together.

The plunge of her fingers, the pulse of attention to her clit. It builds into a crescendo and I watch it happen in real time. The way her other hand keeps plucking at her nipple, smearing my slick cum over it as she pinches and pulls, the way I'd be doing if I was allowed to right now. How her whole body tenses, and I see her start to shake beneath me.

"Oh God," she says again, but the words are louder. A cry of warning. A plea for help, how to deal with the onslaught that's building in her system, but one isn't coming. I'm going to throw her so far over the edge she won't find the bottom for ages, free falling until she crashes.

My left hand presses her fingers in deeper, harder, slick with her wetness, taking over the rhythm there as my other hand works her clit in ways that will force her over the precipice. Leave her floating for endless seconds of torturous bliss, in a preview of what tomorrow night will look like.

"Weston," she cries out my name, eyes screwed shut as I continue controlling her fingers and her thumb, making her make herself come for me.

Gruff, throat tight, I say, "Let me watch you, darlin'. It's my turn now."

My eyes laser focus on her nipple between her thumb and forefinger, then realign on the beautiful mess between her thighs, both of my hands and one of hers there, slipping and sliding over the surface of her skin, demanding she give in to what's between us.

I'm sure she'd love to be kicking her legs, strangling me with them, wrapping them around me as she convulses and shakes, but she's laying on them. They're trapped, tucked beneath her, and there's nothing she can do other than take exactly what my hands are giving her.

She thrashes, head tossing from side to side as she lets out a little scream that I'll be replaying for a *long* time to come, as her orgasm hits her full force. Her pussy must be clenching down on those fingers *so* damn hard, and I watch the show, softening my ministrations on her clit but not stopping. Her gasps tell the story and I ride out the rhythm of her orgasm, pressing and controlling her fingers to milk every possible moment of this release for her.

I imagine what her fingers get to feel right now, those hot, wet walls clamping down, keeping them in place while her muscles clench in a sensual cadence, fluttering against her own skin.

If only my fingers could be so lucky.

Her eyes blink back open, disbelief all over her face as she pulls her left hand back and withdraws her right from beneath my touch as well.

"Like I said," I growl, "absolutely fucking *perfect*."

One foot touching the floor, I step back from the bed, allowing her to unfold and untangle herself at her own pace.

Her cheeks are heated, the flush running down her chest in splotches that show me how thorough of a job we did wrecking her without even letting me touch her properly tonight.

She lets out something like a whimper as she rights herself, legs coming back out slowly, probably numb and tingly after what we just put them through.

"Hang tight for a sec," I tell her, finger in the air. "I'm gonna grab something to clean up with."

Finger in front of my face, I notice it's still slick with what made it from her hand to mine, and I take my chance.

Eyes on hers, I bring my fingers to my mouth and lick, not wasting a drop of her juices.

Subtle but musky, there's something in her taste, in her scent, that calls to me. Like I could lick at her all night and never have enough. It pulls a groan from somewhere deep in my throat.

"I hope you're ready for tomorrow," I tell her, voice husky with lust. "Once I start feasting on you, I might never stop."

"Is that a promise, Boy Scout?" she asks, lips drawing up in a teasing smirk, even as she's all soft and mussed after her orgasm.

"No, darlin'. That's a warning," I tell her with a wicked grin.

I'm back in moments with a large towel, wet and warm, boxer briefs back on to try to contain my perma-boner (patent pending, thanks to having seen Amelia naked and coming in my bed, under my hands), and I climb back onto the mattress to clean her up.

One last look at my handiwork before I do has me smiling wistfully.

"My new favorite piece of art," I drawl. "You're fucking priceless, darlin'. This is going to be on display in my mental art gallery forever."

She smiles, shaking her head in some kind of wonder, and lays there as I wipe up her chest and body. It takes most of the towel to do the job, with how hard she made me come and what a mess we made after that, but eventually I get her cleaned up.

I pull the covers up and over her tiny body and bend down to give her a kiss on the forehead.

"Are you tucking me in?" she asks, surprised.

I give her a wink in the dimming moonlight and say, "I'm making sure you sleep tight, because tomorrow you're not getting *any* rest."

12
Amelia

My last day in Smoky Heights is a beautiful one.

It's like the universe knew I deserved a pretty sendoff from this place that brought me the brightest few weeks of my travels and it pulled some strings.

The skies turned from grays to light blues, the birds are out, and I would say spring is fully, finally here. The last vestiges of cold weather have disappeared and this early May day is straight out of a travel guide.

Vibrant yellow and orange blooms in the grass, white and pink blooms on the trees, and a mild breeze that feels comfortable instead of chilly for once.

I spent the earlier part of the afternoon working from Foamy Heights in my favorite nook in the front corner to hide away in while I fall into the programming language I sometimes seem to know better than English.

But before the day is over, I wanted to wish this place farewell. I've strolled through downtown, stopping into several of the newly opened stores (several of which I even helped paint, which feels like a special kind of accomplishment now that I see how cute they've all become), and tried to get my fill of this place.

The one and two-story brick buildings that line either side of Main Street have a kind of character that comes with time, tradition, and heart. Plate glass window fronts with seasonal displays. Spring flowers on the table and stuffed bunnies in the chairs of the dining set in the window of the antique shop. Fake hands with pastel nails on show in the window of Mane on Main, the combo hair and nail salon where Gracie works. A springtime special, apricot Danish, available for a limited time in the bakery display at Foamy Heights. I treated myself to one this morning, a small splurge, and nearly groaned when I took a bite.

Even the post office has a stuffed bunny on the counter, dressed as a mail carrier, a basket of floral stamps in hand.

I hand over the postcard to the postal worker and it takes my fingers just a second to let it go. The postcards (already chosen at random) never get sent until I leave town, another precaution, in case Randall ever learns to read postmarks after watching a string of spy movies or something.

My fingers seem to know I don't *really* want to leave, and they hang on for a beat too long. Even if it's what I know I have to do. Keep moving. Stay safe. Don't let my past catch up with me.

It doesn't mean that being here this past month, making *friends*—first with Weston (my stomach flutters), then with Lexi and her friend Gracie, and even to an extent Wyatt and Rory—didn't warm a part of my frozen soul that I didn't think could ever be thawed.

I force my fingers to let go of the postcard and force myself to let go of the idea of staying here any longer. It's time to go wherever the wind might want to take me next. And who knows? Maybe I can come back, break my own rule and visit this place for a second time? Maybe see those fireflies after all?

The man behind the counter smiles at me as he takes the memento for my mom fully from my grip, eyes kind as he nods and wishes me a good afternoon. I think he actually means it.

That first night, when Weston stopped to help me, I thought he was a fluke. Either a serial killer, or a fluke to be so nice. But spending almost four whole weeks here, I see it now. This town is *full* of nice people. It wasn't just that first day I walked through town either. Every time I'm out and about, strangers smile, say hi, introduce themselves, welcome me here, and maybe press me for a bit of harmless gossip about my stay.

I bid the graying Black man with the kind eyes at the post office farewell and head back out again, coming out at the far end of Main, giving myself the chance to walk back down the entire strip of downtown for a final time.

Turning left out of the door instead of taking the crosswalk over to the drugstore at the other side, I head south. The first door I pass on my left is the bar, Smoky Suds. It's a rustic, wooden door that looks almost like a barn door. Seeing it reminds me of the girl's night I went to with Lexi and Gracie.

The bartender who served me *very* well that night, Dallas. Dark hair, dark eyes, darkness pouring out of him everywhere. My stomach does a little flip at the memory of him, the way his gaze consumed me.

But not in the way my stomach erupts for Weston. This flip was a warning. Not to go near this one. Not in a dangerous way, not my instincts that have been in overdrive since I was a preteen working to keep me out of the way of men who would wish me harm. More like a yellow caution sign that reads Too Much for You.

I don't need to be choked or spanked to get off. As much as I dream of being able to give up just a little bit of control over my own body to someone else for the first time, the vibe from that bartender is something I don't think I'll ever be ready for.

No, those reactions are *completely* different from the feelings that overtake me when I think of Weston. The way my stomach swoops, my insides melt. It's been hard to stay focused today when he changed my DNA last night.

My face heats as I recall exactly what transpired between us just hours ago. The way I was able to provoke him into that little show and tell. Watching him bring himself to ruin, then feeling his hands on mine as I did the same to myself.

Saying goodbye to Weston this morning, knowing what would happen next time we saw one another... My cells have been vibrating all day in anticipation. The way his hair fell over his forehead, his dark green eyes glinted at me from beneath the blond strands, and the filthy smirk laced with promise as he told me to drink plenty of water throughout the day, the vision of him has haunted me ever since.

I can feel how pink my cheeks are as my body reacts to the memories, and I hope I don't run into anyone I know while looking this guilty.

But of course, just across the street at the first storefront on this side of downtown, sits a gaggle of women who I can hear clucking their tongues and cackling from here. I raise a hand, waving at them, and several of them nod and wave back.

"You be good, Amelia," Wanda calls out.

"Is her van ready?" I hear the blue-haired lady, Mrs. Dixon, ask the other women at the table. "Did Wyatt Grady forget about Ole Bessie? My poor Bessie has been there since before *she* got to town."

Bessie? That sounds like a cow's name. *Is he a vet on the side?*

The women continue chattering, and with a final fond smile I turn away and continue taking in the rest of the street.

The newly opened pizza shop just next to the pharmacy, Smoky Slice, has a teal neon Open sign in the window, drawing locals into the recently renovated building. I can imagine the faint buzz of the sign, the one I'd hear if I were on the other side of the street in front of the storefront. Light aqua paint on the walls that I can see from here, the work site where Weston dabbed some paint on my nose not two weeks ago, telling me I looked damn good in that color. The way he looked at me as he said it told me he wanted to see me in *just* that paint.

Two doors down, on that same side of the street, a Coming Soon sign hangs on the glass double doors. It's one of the biggest retail spaces on the block, apparently it used to be the old diner once upon a time. We painted the walls in there a soft pink, so pale it's barely more than white. In the back, where the kitchen area is, is where Weston made me laugh so hard I nearly peed while he did an impression of his brother with an entire log up his ass.

On my left I pass open storefront after open storefront, before passing the newly opened general store (walls a shade of white with pewter undertones—the place where I entertained Weston the entire day by recapping some of Jynx's best episodes), the laundromat I've had to frequent in my time here (aka the second building on this block called Smoky Suds, and one I didn't have to paint), the brand new bakery and patisserie that just had its grand opening this week, Smoky Sweets (most of the walls painted in thick, Parisian black and white stripes, where Lexi and I first met that first day I was painting with West), and I find myself across from the salon, gazing across the street at it.

Eyes on the storefronts opposite me, I don't hear the chime of the bell of the one opening right next to me.

A much larger, softer body bumps into mine, sending me

toppling backward until strong hands grab my arms to steady me.

I look up into dark brown eyes, a thin nose set between them, dusted with freckles, and wild, tumbling curls of cocoa and hazel spilling all over her face and shoulders.

"Lexi," I greet her.

"Big Momma!" she calls back, a grin splitting her face. That name can't help but remind both of us about our girl's night out and I give her a big smile back.

Lexi is the first person who has texted me, just for fun, ever. I might have to change my number again soon as part of my protocol, but a part of me is trying to figure out if I can text her from the next one or if it's too risky. The optimistic half of me says it's worth it for the lightness in my heart every time I'm with this woman.

Rory's voice, mid-argument with some poor sucker who must've tried to test her, floats out to me through the open door before it closes shut with a little bounce.

I was so focused on taking in the town, the other side of the street, the gardening that's going in on both the east and west sides of the street, the people sat on the benches that line the edge of the sidewalk—and, okay, fine, maybe memories that involve a certain golden-haired, bronze-skinned semblance of an ancient god—I didn't realize I'd already made it to the New Heights Headquarters.

"Don't tell me you're really leaving?" she asks, a big, oversized pout on that plush mouth of hers as her hands drop back down to her sides with a slapping noise.

"Soon as my baby's up and running, probably in the morning," I say, more sadly than I meant to.

"At least tell me you're coming back to visit," she presses.

A shrug of one shoulder will have to do. I don't even have it in me to banter with her, to crack a joke, because for the first time since I left my mom all alone in that hellhole of horrible memories, I feel like I'm going to miss someone when I drive away. Lexi, with her fiery insults, fierce comebacks, and infectious, uninhibited laugh, has become one of my favorite parts of this town.

These Weiss women, they make me feel bigger, badder, just by being in their orbit. I like who I am around them. I don't feel fragile or delicate or in need of defending. I feel like a badass, just because these women are badass, and they lift me up where others might look down.

"If I'm ever in your neck of the woods again," I relent.

"You don't have to break down next time, I promise Weston will bend over backward for you even if you're not a damsel in distress."

My face heats at the implication in her tone, and she gives me a knowing smirk.

"Have you bent over forward for him yet?" Lexi adds with an even dirtier look, and my face flames. I look around, frantic, wondering who might have heard her, if somehow Wyatt, or one of the town gossips who's even worse than him, like Ernie or Mrs. Dixon, will show up.

She keeps her earthen eyes locked on mine, pushing me for an answer until I crack.

"No," I hiss, trying to remain discreet. "Not yet at least." A smile cracks out on my own face, and she howls, head thrown back, zero fucks given. What must it be like to be her. To have nothing to hide, no reason to not let yourself all out.

"So you're not going to tell me why you're positively *glowing* then?" she presses, still grinning.

"My God, are you a tarot reader or something?"

"Nah, babe. Just really good at telling when someone's finally gotten some action." She thumbs in the direction of her sister, through the glass door next to us, and I laugh. "That one and her man used to be about twenty times more miserable, if you can imagine it." Lexi gives an exaggerated, comical shudder and screws up her face in disgust. "I got better than I wish I were at picking up on the clues. And you, my dear friend? You have *grade A dick* written all over you."

I want to make a joke about the way his grade A dick *literally* wrote all over me last night, but as is my custom when traveling through pitstops, I keep my mouth shut.

Lexi channels her best Elijah Wood. "Keep your secrets, then," she says. "But text me about them later, will ya?"

Something in my heart smarts at the thought of having someone to text after I leave town. Wondering what it might be like to not change my SIM card and get a new number in a few more weeks just because it's my routine. But to pretend I'm normal, and I have the same number for years on end, people to stay in touch with.

For an insane second, I must have some sort of personality transplant, or maybe my Danish was spiked, because I have this impulse to open up to her. To tell her who I am, my past and what's had me running for so long. That maybe she won't judge me for it the way everyone else who's ever known has before, that maybe I'd be safe here with these kind people. But I'm smarter than that.

I curl my fingers in a small wave at her, and she knows this is goodbye.

Someone else comes out of the New Heights building as Lexi and I are hugging, and I hear Rory's voice tumble out of the door. "You'd better be coming in here next, Amelia!"

Rory's stepdad, a silver fox with graying hair and a smooth jawline nods in greeting to me as he passes, the door shutting behind him as he heads down the street, in the direction of the bar.

Lex gives me a quick peck on the top of the head and starts

to walk away, long denim skirt swishing with her curves as she does. "Until next time, Big Momma," she calls out, and I have to turn and head into the office before I embarrass myself further. If public tears enter the equation I might have to change my name *again*.

And dammit, I'm kind of attached to Amelia Marsh now.

It's not fierce like some of the first names I chose. Avery Flint was one I was particularly fond of and stuck with for a couple of years before changing it again. It sounded strong to me, sharp. Like someone assholes wouldn't fuck with. Eventually I just wanted to blend in rather than scare people off, and by the time I settled on Amelia Marsh, well, I just think it suits me at this point.

And if I can confess one more thing, I'm so tired of changing everything about me all the damn time. Just being myself suddenly has an appeal it never really has before.

The glass door shuts behind me, just short of a slam, and I adjust to the new environment. I can see Rory at her desk in the far corner, a wizened older man sitting at one of the chairs in front of her, bickering away like crazy, so I busy myself taking a thorough peek since I've yet to visit this place.

One of the smaller properties on the downtown stretch of Main, the New Heights Headquarters is chic and minimalist, decorated in shades of gray with stark black accents. A few chairs and a modern coffee table in the front of the office serve as a sitting area.

In the window display is a to-scale model of what the future Downtown Smoky Heights will look like, made out of foam. Every single location on the model is a vibrant, lively business, none are empty or abandoned. Trees bloom along both edges of the sidewalks, beautiful maples with their leaves changing colors, fir trees, white dogwoods in full bloom, like they were when I first arrived here, and another tree with bushy pink flowers I'm not familiar with.

There are even little adorable miniature people in this diorama. Two parents swinging a child between them outside of Smoky Scoops on their way for ice cream.

Someone picking up a coffee from a to-go window built into the exterior of Foamy Heights.

A man buying flowers from a florist stand while several women sit nearby on benches, smiles on their faces. In front of every storefront, every shop, there is life.

Her vision for this town is stunning. I can see it's come a long way toward this already, even in my short time here. I have no doubt she will bring this whole strip to life before she calls this project done.

"I just don't see why *I* have to be the one to change my business name!" the old man in the back argues with Rory.

He's a brave soul for that. I wouldn't want to go up against her.

"Are you going to make me repeat myself again?" she asks him, drolly.

"It makes more sense for a laundromat to be called Smoky Suds than a bar! He could be Heights Hops! What am I going to be? Smoky Bubbles? Heights Hampers? That just sounds stupid, Rory."

"Well, Tom, you don't *have* to include the town name in your business name."

"Everyone else downtown has! Why shouldn't I get to?"

Rory lets out an exasperated sigh, her head falling forward into her hands, elbows on the desk while her fingers massage her temples. "For the last time, unless you want to go back to 1976 and beat Duke's dad to naming your business Smoky Suds, your application isn't going to be approved. The discussion is over. Pick another name. Call it Smoky Skid Marks for all I care. But until you pick a unique name, I can't help you get your forms through the grant commission."

The older man grumbles all the way to the door, forms to fix in hand, and Rory's attention can finally come to me.

"Amelia!" She holds her arms out, standing, like she's actually happy to see me.

Lexi's younger sister is in a white top that can only be referred to as a blouse, so much sleeker than my cut off crop tee or anything else in my drawers in the van. Her slim skirt is something like a leather pencil skirt, black in color, that's beyond flattering. She's wearing heeled black boots that go past her calves and all in all I think I can see why Wyatt did everything he did to win her back, from the stories Weston's told me while painting. Not that looks are everything. But she's not just looks. She's brilliant, fierce, the whole package. I'd probably never get over her either.

My eyes finally make it to her desk, and really, what's over it. The focal piece of the entire office actually. A massive black and white print, at least six or seven feet wide, of an older lady being arrested, bending over as she gets into a sheriff's car, a look on her face like she's a mob boss from the heyday of the 20s and this is just another day for her. An odd choice in art for a lawyer's office, I have to say, but it's intriguing. There's something in the woman's eyes that sparks something in me. I can see why she was drawn to the piece.

Crossing the twenty feet or so to get to Rory's desk, I nod with my chin to the print. "What's with the mugshot?"

She grins and there's something feral in it. "That? Is the inspiration behind New Heights."

"Getting arrested?" I ask, deadpan.

"Living life to the fullest," she says simply, whisking me into the vacated chair in front of her desk as she sits down behind it. "Not waiting to grab life by the balls. And taking our town back from the pricks who stole it from us in the first place."

"And dealing with *Grumpy Old Men* casting rejects is living life to the fullest, or is that grabbing life by the balls?"

"Tom?" Rory scoffs. "He's harmless. Just a Tuesday morning for me. My *favorite* part of this project is seeing all the new life that comes into the Heights after it was dying off for too long." Her brown eyes sparkle at me as she says it, and I catch her drift.

Holding up my hands in front of me, I protest. "Oh, no, no, no. You're not roping me into staying here, no matter how scary you are."

"You think I'm scary?"

She pouts, clawed fingers tapping on the desk in a slow rhythm. My eyes are drawn to them and I notice her current manicure seems to be spring inspired, a soft pink with white detail that makes me think of Easter and fresh tulips.

My stomach clenches as those thoughts evoke memories of my mom, and I refocus on the woman in front of me.

"Well, yeah, you're pretty..." I fish for a less insensitive word. "Intense."

"I like to think of it as passionate," she says, chin in the air.

"Okay, well, your passion comes out as dragon fire sometimes," I tell her, and she laughs loudly.

"And that's why I get paid the big bucks, babe."

I want her to teach me her ways.

She's an icon, this woman.

"So," she says, placing her elbows on the desktop and lacing her fingers, leaning forward with interest. "How much do you know about New Heights?"

Damn, she doesn't even give me an out. "West has told me a little about it," I hedge. "You run a fund to help rebuild the town, right?"

She nods, elegant brunette ponytail bouncing behind her with the motion. "That's correct. But what you might not know is that we have grants available to people moving to the town."

I can't stop my eyebrows from shooting up. I *try*, but they don't listen to me.

Her cat got the canary smirk tells me she knows she got me too with that one. It's me, I'm the canary.

"We have several types of grants available, and I would be remiss to not at least inform you of your options on them before you flash us those taillights and move onto wherever is next. Think of me as a recruiter for the town at this point, poaching talent that will help us grow and blossom for decades and generations to come."

I think I'm stunned speechless. Maybe it's by her aura, maybe it's by this vivid picture of the future she's painting for me. One where I have a home. A gorgeous small town, nestled in the scenic mountains, full of people who have been kind to me, with nothing but good memories here.

A fever dream must be what shows me Weston and me walking down that street out there, swinging a child between our arms, on our way to get ice cream. Something I've never been crazy enough to consider after the betrayal of my own father, but Rory's started a movie in my mind I have no control over.

Whatever the cause of my temporary insanity, all I do is nod at her in permission to go on.

She smiles demurely and does. "We have one available grant for young professionals moving to the city to open a business within the community here. There's another that helps offset moving and resettling costs for those who plan to work within the Smoky Heights community."

I try not to let my face fall, it doesn't seem to be listening to me today, but silly me somehow got my hopes up and let myself dream for just a second there. Weston already talked to me about getting a job in town, and that doesn't interest me any more than opening my own business here would. No, thank you. Even if I were trying to turn over a new leaf, I don't need to bring *that* much attention to myself, thank you very much. I've gotten enough stares just walking down the street. If I were to work at the new diner, for instance, as an outsider? I feel like I'd become a zoo exhibit, faces pressed to the glass to get a look at me.

"There is also another," Rory continues, and I swear my ear physically perks up, like a dog's, "where a stipend is granted to young professionals who move to this town who already have remote work."

"What? Why would they do that?"

"We're far from the first to offer it. In towns where populations are declining, sometimes they approve a special fund to lure new residents in, so to speak, who are either already parents, or of childbearing age, and offer them either land or money with the promise to stay in that town for a certain amount of time. Beyond just bringing new life to the community, it can also help stimulate the local economy. Someone like yourself, a digital nomad with a reliable work history, could be a great candidate for it."

"So you're...giving away money? Or land? For new residents to move here? Whether they already have a job or want to get one here?"

Rory nods decisively. "That's correct. In our case, it's money. Or even more money if they plan to open a business here. And we also can help with housing too."

If I could stammer, I would. I've never been in shock from *good* news before.

And as if I could like this woman, or her family, any more, she reads it on my face and doesn't push me.

"I'm not going to force you to make any decisions, Amelia. I just wanted you to know that you always have a home in Smoky Heights if you want one. And New Heights can help with the transition to make it a little easier on you if you ever want to take us up on it. You wouldn't even have to decide yet, you could just do an application and make up your mind once the approval is back."

The door tinkles with the arrival of another townsperson who must need her help.

"Be right with you," she calls, then turns back to me. "Just do me a favor and scan this QR code before you go. It's the link to our site and the application forms. Then I'll let you go if you promise me you'll think it over."

And though I try every trick I've ever had to use to stay focused on the next town, the next step on the path to safety, I can't get this picture she painted out of my mind. A future where I'm brave enough to stay in one place. To fight for what I want. To build a life, with connections, and friends, even a partner. Where I run into people I know on the street and it's not looks of pity, or horror, or whispers behind hands, but smiles I get instead.

I never knew how much I could want for myself until I came to Smoky Heights, and I'm not sure I can forgive these people for that.

13
Weston

Wyatt ducks his whole upper body beneath the hood, getting his face right up and in there as his arm slips between parts to finish threading the last of the bolts. The concentration on his face means he's not watching me give Amelia *the eyes*. Reminding her of what's coming next. Her. Then her again, her again, and eventually, both of us.

I doubt she's forgotten. It's been tough for me to think of anything *but* tonight, unless of course, I've been thinking about *last* night. And last night isn't what I should be thinking about when I'm close enough to my fucking brother for him to feel my stiffy if it decided to poke its head up.

So I force my eyes back onto the engine, the rebuild and install that's being given the final QC by the boss of this garage. Yeah, it might've taken me a lot longer than Wyatt to do the work needed on her engine and transmission, but he only had to spend a few hours in total to oversee the whole thing, and that saved Amelia a ton of money. I'm not complaining about all the extra time I got with her either. Painting building after building during the day, her sitting out to work on her laptop while I worked on her parts at night.

I make plenty of money to get by when I accept jobs, not like I couldn't part with half of it to give her for her time, and it was good to do something fun with my hands—something I used to love—in my off time.

Not like I could do my usual routine of barhopping and breaking backs while I'm under adult supervision from my brother anyway. Or that I'd even want to when there's only one woman both my heads are thinking about lately.

Hell, I'll almost *miss* this project when she drives outta here shortly.

I'll definitely miss her company when I show up to paint alone for the first time in a while on Monday morning. Hopefully this weekend resets me, recalibrates me back to my original factory settings. The way I was fine to be alone a month ago, before I met her. My curse is something I know how to deal with.

"All right," Wyatt says, pulling himself free of the mechanical maze he managed to fold himself into.

Abruptly, my eyes turn from heated to neutral. From on her, to on the engine. And I feel her gaze cool and retract as well. Where her eyes were glued to my chest, my arms, my back, they're now large, innocent, and on my brother as he wipes his hands and prepares to speak.

"Not bad, West," he tells me.

Why does that feel like an accomplishment coming from him?

And why did it take until I'm thirty-three to get those simple words?

"Should be good to go. I think she's ready for a spin," Wyatt says.

I let him do the honors, stepping back and watching from beside Amelia as he starts up Van Gogh. The garage doesn't explode, so I'm thinking we're off to a good start and I might even get invited to Thanksgiving this year if nothing goes majorly wrong on this test drive.

We both watch the taillights light up and take off out of the open bay door, and it feels like a punch in the gut when I realize that the next time I see those bad boys turn red, it'll be the last time I see that van, or the girl who lives in it.

It's been nice having something of a partner as I work. Companionship without judgment is rare for me, and I'm pretty sure it has been for her too.

"You did it," Amelia breathes out, turning to face me. Her nose wiggles, the small septum ring that goes through it twitching with the motion. "You got us up and running again." Her voice is softer than usual, but I can't read it for once. "For a while there I wasn't sure we'd get out of Smoky Heights. Seemed like Van Gogh was dead, and I was stuck."

Is that hint of sadness at a future where her van was dead and she was confined to one place? Or is it possibly at the thought of leaving?

Now I'm just getting hopeful. Knowing one night with her won't be enough, but I'm gonna have to do everything in my power for both of us to get our fill before the sun comes up and she's just a silhouette on the horizon.

"Thank you." The words are so soft, I'm not even sure what they're in reference to at this point. For helping on the van? For the company, letting her feel like a normal twenty-something woman for a few weeks instead of a stranger to everyone she meets? For the night we already had that will fuel my fantasies for months, maybe even years? Or the one that's yet to come that will hopefully convince her to come back once in a while for a repeat?

"Of course," I tell her with a lift of one shoulder.

"You've done me so many favors already, and now..." The

way her voice trails off, was that supposed to imply that tonight is another *favor*?

Placing one finger under her chin, I bring her teal gaze back to mine, no matter how interesting she seems to find the floor right about now.

"And now *what*?" I ask softly, hint of danger peeking through at that inference in her tone, like anything about what's coming next is a favor, not because my veins will fucking explode if I don't finally get to have her.

Favor is a dirty fucking word compared to the need I have for this woman. There's nothing charitable about it.

"Choose your words well, Amelia. They'd better not disparage this. Us. You." My free hand motions between our two bodies, hers so much shorter than mine.

When my meaning hits her, her entire demeanor changes. Her eyes light up with mischief and the corner of her lip folds between her teeth as she bites down on it, chin still in my grasp. From shy and self-deprecating to sexy and playful all in a flash. I want all the sides this gorgeous girl has to show me.

"Now..." she draws out the word, reworking her sentence, "I'm going to show you how much I appreciate you," she says with a devilish smirk that matches those dirty little secrets of hers.

The ring through the nipple, those perfect tits I'll never get over, so unexpectedly filthy beneath that angelic exterior. The way she gets off, so unapologetic, so needy. I haven't stopped dreaming up all the ways I can give her what she needs.

At this point, my plans for her should require a permit.

"You're mine to appreciate, darlin'," I tell her, and I watch desire course through her, melting down through her body and pooling somewhere low in her middle. I can't wait to taste that desire later.

Vaguely, I consider whisking her away to the dark office

along the side wall, or perhaps one of Wyatt's vehicles around here, a little payback of my own for those marks on my Charger. But the sound of Van Gogh's arrival interrupts those thoughts and reminds me that I want seclusion when I finally get to have all of her.

Seclusion and one other thing.

The entire fucking night.

I could imagine a world where I've had her enough times that a quickie would suffice. A strong imagination I was blessed with, because five or ten minutes wouldn't even begin to scratch the surface of what I need from her right now.

My hand drops away faster than a car backfiring and the two of us separate instantly, turning to face the open bay door, the thick silver chains that control the garage doors hanging vertically along the concrete block walls, framing either side of the middle bay.

Van Gogh comes to a stop on the gravel just outside the garage and my brother hops out of the front seat and down to the ground. In his trademark dark Henley with the sleeves pushed up to the elbows, engine tattoo on display on his forearm, he runs a hand through his nearly black hair and gives a small tilt of his head. That's about as much enthusiasm as we'll get out of Wyatt, unless his wife or daughter are involved.

"She's all good?" It's nearly a squeal from Amelia.

Wyatt nods his head once. "Yep."

I watch in a flurry of motion, some strange mix of slow-mo and fast forward that doesn't feel real, as Amelia gets her keys from Wyatt, pays the final invoice (a thankful smile my way when she sees the reduced total), and he waves goodbye to her. Like she's just another customer, like the town will continue to go on just fine without her in our midst.

Part of me wonders if when my time here is done, if I could follow Van Gogh. Hit the road and find work town to town, following adventures wherever they go, as long as it's her I get to curl up with at night.

But that's insane. It may have been a month of getting close to her—strangely close for two people who were so recently strangers—but we haven't even hooked up yet, for crying out loud.

Besides, I have jobs I've committed to here through the rest of spring. And she's clearly in solo mode, in a one player game.

What is with me? Am I the one catching feelings for once?

That's ridiculous, right? This is just what weeks of anticipation looks like instead of instant gratification like I'm used to. It's all culminated in a thrumming, uncontrollable desire.

Best not to let my mind wander on things that could never be beyond that.

I know all too well that the familiar itch of boredom will creep under my skin as soon as the fascination with her wears off. Probably about an hour after I'm out of her bed. It always does.

But first, I have a different itch to scratch. One particular to a petite woman with a fierceness that pulses just beneath her skin, pulling me to her, and I'm ready for her to unleash it all on me tonight.

I head to my truck as Wyatt closes up the garage, probably eager to stop working extended hours and get home to his girls. Amelia thanks the both of us, like this is goodbye, but I jump in the cab of my pickup before I hear the words come out of her mouth. I'm not ready for them.

Waving before pulling out of the gravel lot like it's any other regular old night, I play it cool for the last of our audience—like I'm not leading her somewhere private to get her all to myself before she's really gone.

I lay a path for her to follow to an overlook point that's always empty. A gorgeous grassy field of wildflowers with the perfect view of the nearest ridges of the Smokies, where she can park her van for the night and no one will bother us. Hell, no one will even pass us, much less notice us.

Practicing patience, something my brother thinks I don't have a drop of in my blood, I wait by my truck door, one leg bent, foot flat on the door, as she backs Van Gogh up and lines up with my truck in the perfect spot to be able to open the back doors of the van and watch the sunrise come up from behind the peaks, right from her bed. Like camping, but better because she's got A/C, power, and all the creature comforts of a portable home.

Once she's got herself situated just how she wants, the van's engine turns off, but the low hum of the house batteries that power her residence stay on. Painfully slow seconds later, the side door slides open.

In a throwback I didn't know I needed, Amelia is standing in the doorway, topless. The dark, star-studded night sky as the backdrop to my latest fantasy, this woman stands there, hands on the edge of the door, backlit by the dim under-cabinet lighting, casting a nearly white glow around her perfect form.

Her wavy brown hair tickles her shoulders, feathery bangs framing her delicate face, ring through her nose, all making her look like that sweet, dark angel I've become so enamored with.

But as my gaze travels down her slim form, catching on her chest, the metal in it glinting at me in the low light, her flat stomach, and the gorgeous pussy I know is hidden beneath her short shorts, it's the devilish side of her that I want to get to know right now.

"Fuck, darlin'." One hand drops down to readjust my boys, my cock that's getting a little too excited this early in the game. "You look absolutely edible."

"So come have a taste." Amelia raises one shoulder in a way that moves her breasts, too, and it's impossible not to trace their motion with my eyes. "One night only, it's all you can eat, Boy Scout."

She doesn't have to ask me twice. The only thing covering her delicious frame from my eyes, or the rest of me, is a tiny pair of hot pink athletic shorts that barely come down past her ass. I'll have them gone in a blink.

My hands come out of my pockets as I push myself off the truck door and stalk toward her. She backs up with each step I take, not in fear, but to draw me closer. This might've been the trap she set for me all along, and I'm the prey who's going to walk willingly into it.

One foot onto the stairs and the van rocks with my weight as I step into her home. It's not the only rocking it'll be doing tonight. The door slides shut on the rollers with a simple tug, and we both watch it latch shut, the lock clicking into place with one touch of a button on the fob in her hand, before I hook the secondary lock into place. She places the remote on the counter, then rests her hands on the edge of the butcher block surface behind her, arms bent as she watches my approach.

I tear my shirt off, grabbing hold of the back collar and ripping it right off my body, letting the white cotton fall to the floor in the front of the van, near the driver's seat. Then, I pounce. Springing forward, I close the distance between us in one final motion that has her gasping when it happens so suddenly. But it's her web, I'm just the lucky fucker who got caught.

Smile on my face, I grab hold of her hips and pull her up onto my waist. Her legs wrap around me instinctively, knees gripping the bare skin on my back to hold herself upright. My hands stay on her ass, just to be sure. Safety first, and all that shit you're taught when you're working on motors and moving parts from a young age.

My eyes, though, they're on her face. The way her teal eyes

are alight with wonder and need, like twin pools of some exotic sea, private, warm, and inviting, and something so fucking special you never thought it'd make it off your bucket list.

"There's so much I want to do with you." She says the words quietly, more like a thought that was breathed aloud than something meant for my ears.

"I know exactly where I'm starting with you," I tell her, not a trace of doubt in any bone in my body.

Taking the few steps to reach her bed, I lean forward to drop her backward, and she lets go, falling, arms splayed, and bouncing there. Watching the whole way, my eyes trail down to her breasts that are too perky and full to be natural, but I wouldn't ask for them to be any other way. Like the little nose ring and the nipple ring, everything she adds to her body suits her perfectly, like she was always meant to look this way.

Wasting no time, I slip the tips of my fingers beneath her waistband and pull the bottoms right off of her, leaving her naked, fully on display for me, sprawled out on her bed. Small noises come from Amelia as I relish the moment, sparing a second to just take her in.

I'm not sure if what I'm doing would be considered grunting, growling, or maybe it's more of a purr, like a wildcat who knows they're about to enjoy their meal they've worked so hard for.

Dropping to my knees, I slide my arms under her thighs and hips, pulling her forward, exactly where I need her. She slides easily, tiny thing that she is. But she hums as I move her, her body slipping over the light comforter as I pull her to the edge.

This is where my preparation kicks in. All of my research these past nights, learning exactly what she likes.

It's not that I wouldn't like to take my time, enjoy every inch of her, get acquainted with all the secrets her body is hiding along the way. It's purely because I only get one night with her and, fuck, do I have a lot planned, that I dive right in, with no other foreplay. Only because I don't have the luxury of time.

"You have no idea how badly I need this," is the only warning she gets.

My face crashes down against the cradle of her thighs, and I latch straight onto her clit. Lips suctioning, tongue flicking over the engorged bud, I'm ready for her instant reaction. My arms band tight around her hips and thighs as her back bows, her entire upper body coming off the bed as I suck on her clit.

She squirms, she damn near screams, she pulls back, but she doesn't get away from me as my mouth works her just like that little mint colored toy she's so fond of does.

Every motion she makes brings her tighter into my hold on her, closer to my mouth, my grip on her more sure the more she wriggles and bucks from the intensity. Gasping, her hips jerk, legs twitch, but Amelia can't shake me as I continue pulsing and sucking on her, doing my best to liquify her entire body as I work her over.

I can feel her pussy flooding near my chin, dripping with how turned on she is, and she's making these incomprehensible noises, almost in distress, whimpering like she needs help. But then she does this thing with her breathing, this staggered, sexy scale of a cry that tells me it's not a complaint. That it might be out of her control, it might be overwhelming, an onslaught of pleasure she wasn't expecting, she wasn't prepared for, maybe even more than she thought she wanted, but she's very definitely going to enjoy what's happening to her right now.

I'll help make sure of that.

The thing is, we're both so wound up, so fucking hot for each other, I know she's going to come so fucking fast this first time. I'd rather get that done and out of the way so I can have some fun with the next few.

So I keep her in position, arms locked around her so she

can't wriggle free. My mouth might as well be glued to her, for all her whimpers and attempts at bucking and moving her hips, my face hasn't moved even a fraction of an inch.

Precision. Constancy. Unrelenting pleasure as I move my lips and tongue to emulate that clit sucker she's been using for so long while thinking of me. I'll give her something new to think of while she's using it next time.

It's fast, so fast, I've barely registered the sweet taste of her and stored it away for my own purposes when her legs start shaking. More than her legs, her hips, her entire midsection is practically vibrating with the approach of her orgasm as her whole body hums.

"Weston," she calls my name, some sort of pleading, panting mess, and it's never sounded so hot before.

My eyes flick up to hers, across the flat plane of her stomach, those incredible tits, I catch her eyes watching me, and my cock thickens even more at the look on her face. Disbelief, incredulity, rapture.

It's *me* that's making her look like that.

If my mouth weren't so busy blowing her fucking mind, I'd use it in other ways to help push her over the edge.

I'd tell her, *You look so fucking good on my tongue, darlin'.*

I could tongue fuck you all day just to hear those noises.

You taste as good as you look, angel.

A dozen other lines running through my head that would have her coming for me.

But my mouth *is* busy right now, so I let it do what it does best. I amp up the suction, matching one of the strongest levels on that toy I've been studying in my lonely nights.

Amelia's jaw drops just a bit, eyes rounding, brows low and heavy, mouth forming an O as her pussy starts to give me one of its own. She watches as long as she can, and it's the hottest thing I've ever seen, the way she's looking at me like she can't believe what's happening while I'm getting my first taste of her, her chest heaving, legs shaking as she struggles to take it.

The pleasure overtakes her entire system and it's the purest thing. There's nothing demure about it. She gives in fully, turning herself over to the sensations wracking her body as her eyes slam shut and she throws her head back, convulsing, riding out the waves as the release hits her.

She calls out again and again, more noises than words, and I follow the rhythm of her body, the way she leads me through touch alone, and I give her what she needs, relishing in the ripples, the aftershocks of pleasure I can sense rolling through her body right now, from her entire midsection, deep in her pussy, all the way down to her toes against my back.

It's addicting.

It's nowhere near enough.

Forcing myself to pull back, I slowly lower the pressure I'm using until the suction is entirely gone, and it's just my tongue caressing her softly, lapping at her bud as the occasional twitch makes her hips jerk against me, while she murmurs incoherently somewhere from the mattress above me.

Slowly, I move my head to the side, trailing kisses across her soft pussy and over to her thigh, continuing to taste her while she comes down, groaning in a puddle that used to be Amelia on the bed.

I don't give her that long to recover though. I can't.

Time is what we don't have enough of tonight.

My lips keep moving, roving, until they've found their way to her center and I can taste what I earned. Tongue lapping, I hold back a groan at the concentrated taste of her. Mostly I keep the noise in just so I don't miss any of the sounds *she's* making.

I watch as her head flops from side to side, still overwhelmed by her release, and now the feel of me soaking every drop of it up.

"Fuck, Weston. You're killing me. I thought you were gonna suck my soul out for a minute there."

A dark chuckle, so unlike my usual, spills out from between her legs. "There's still time," I tell her.

My tongue plunges in deep, finding new ways to taste her, feel her, and this time I can't hold the groan in. She's so small, so tight, so fucking hot, the width of my tongue can barely probe her. My cock doesn't stand a chance, but this is something I'm not going to quit on. We'll find a way to make it work.

Amelia moans, noises of complaint, a grumble about it being *her turn*, but I'm nowhere near done with my turn yet. As I eat out her core, ignoring her protests, one of my hands slides out from under her leg and I use the thumb to start teasing her clit by pressing on it through one side of her pussy. Not direct contact, but enough pressure to stimulate it just the same.

She jolts, whimpering my name, but my finger keeps working her clit, while my tongue fucks her the way I can't wait to shortly. Well, maybe *later* is a safer word. I'm not in any fucking rush right where I'm at.

As patient as I'm capable of being, I give her a couple minutes to finish winding down from the last orgasm before my tongue slides up from her opening and finds her clit again. Her entire body shivers, but I'm delicate enough this time that she doesn't pull back or try to get away.

This time it's slow, savoring the feel of her soft skin beneath my mouth. Her taste that invades my entire being. That musky, feminine flavor—only enhanced by her scent overpowering me, something fruity, like coconut, something spicy—might never leave my memory.

I drag this one out, being slow and deliberate with every swipe, every stroke of my tongue as I find what else she likes.

When one spot in particular seems to drive her crazy, I play with it. Lick it, nibble at it, pull back just enough that she soaks my mouth in her need for more.

Amelia leans over, propping herself up on an elbow to watch closer as I make a hobby out of having my cake and eating it too.

Pulling my mouth back, I unwrap my other hand from her body and bring my fingers to her entrance, both of us watching intently.

Amelia curses breathily as I put just the tip of one finger in her pussy, feeling it grip me instantly.

"Jesus," she gasps.

"I'm the one fucking you, first with my tongue, now my fingers, and next, my cock. Mine is the only name you should be thanking tonight."

Her eyes heat, flaming with a raw kind of desire that lights my insides up.

I push that finger in just a bit further, up to the first knuckle, not even an inch in. She lets out a little moan at the tease, and her warm heat is so inviting, I push in farther, unable to stop myself from finding out what she feels like.

She leans forward, watching almost as closely as I am as my finger pushes all the way into her. The noise it makes is obscene. Filthy. Delicious.

And this time, it's *my* name she calls out, eyes fluttering shut at the feel of me inside of her.

When I pull back out of her, I add another finger in and plunge back into her, painfully slow. I feel her inner walls clamp down on me as I do, so tight they only just let me in.

"You're so fucking tight," I tell her. "You can barely take my fingers. Gonna take some work to get you ready for me."

Amelia drops her upper body back onto the bed with a huff of impatience, hands in her short hair as she lets out a noise of frustration.

"Don't worry, angel. It'll be fun," I promise, and turn my attention back to her pussy.

Sliding the same two fingers in, I use the thumb to press on her clit as my fingers ride her front wall, exploring, searching.

A sharp inhale from the girl on the bed and a change in texture beneath my hand tell me I've found just what I'm looking for. I play with that spot, stroking, pressing, working it when I find the rhythm and pattern that takes her breath away.

Leaning forward, my mouth gravitates back to her clit, and my tongue takes its time playing with its new favorite toy.

My hand, mouth, and fingers work in tandem. One in her pussy, the other roving up her body until it finds her nipple ring and starts toying with it, too, tugging, teasing, tweaking. She gasps softly, urging me on.

I draw it out, not shoving her over the edge this time, but letting the pleasure build slowly, rising within her until it spills out and over, almost gentle in comparison to the harsh abruptness of that first one that ripped through her like lightning.

Her sweet noises, the way she curses, whispers my name in increasingly needy tones as I let the crescendo build gradually until she finally peaks and it bubbles over into long moments of pleasure, it's going to stick with me.

I pretend it's her pussy, this physical chemistry between us, that's what I'm going to miss most. Not the girl who's the reason for the sting in my chest when I imagine her pulling out of here for good, just hours from now.

14

Amelia

The first orgasm made me see stars. Electric, like I was lit up from within, a thousand volts straight to my nerve endings.

The second one felt like I was floating among the stars. Soft, gentle, so fucking deeply satisfying, my poor vibrator is never going to do it for me again.

The third and fourth? Let's just say I can barely breathe, much less form coherent thoughts after them.

"How many times do you make yourself come most nights?" Weston asked me, voice thick and gruff with lust, as his fingers were plunging inside of me, both of us watching.

"Used to be one," I told him, throat tight.

"And now?" he asked.

"At least three or four," I told him honestly.

He grunted, accepting my answer, and I think he took it as a challenge. To outperform my rechargeable friend.

It would have only taken one orgasm for that. Any one of the four he's given me so far would've hit that mark, but that first one blew any toy—or other man, for that matter—completely out of the water. I don't know what the hell possessed him, what took over the body of the Weston I thought I was coming to know, and turned him into this feral, starving creature with a Hoover for a mouth.

That's not a complaint, for the record. Just, still spinning, trying to find the new center of gravity after he completely shook me to the core, upending everything I thought I knew about lust, sex, and my own needs, and left me here, shivering, somehow still craving more.

I watch him now, lying next to me in my bed, so tall that his legs hang off the short edge of the mattress. In nothing but dark red boxer briefs, his package is doing its best to set itself free—strangled by the tight, stretchy fabric beneath the elastic waistband—reaching for me, just inches out of his jurisdiction.

Weston has a smile on his face, as usual, but this one is content. Almost bliss. The urgency he used in eating me out within seconds of stepping into my van doesn't shine through on that golden face, those dark green eyes, bright despite the dim light.

Now he almost looks like the visual representation of the feeling I have when I move things from my "Shit to Do" Pinterest board over to my "Been There, Seen That" board. Pleased. Accomplished. Relishing in the moment, though I know he's far from done for the night.

One of his strong hands comes out to cup my face, then he pushes it back into my hair, running his fingers through the short, dyed dark strands and fingering them thoughtfully as he lets me catch my breath from number four. Or maybe still from number one.

"Even better than I imagined," he says quietly, lips so close to mine as we stare at one another's faces, lying on our sides.

"You haven't even fucked me yet," I remind him.

"I meant your taste." Weston's eyes glint in the low light. "Fucking delicious."

Amazingly, his stomach picks this moment, after those

words, to rumble so loudly it shatters the mood entirely. Laughter breaks out between us, and I hunch forward, head on his hard, bare chest, body shaking as I give in to the fits of giggles.

"Doesn't seem like that's enough for you to live on," I finally say when I can compose myself, fingers wiping away tears from my eyes.

"I may have skipped dinner so I could get your van done faster and get you to myself," he admits.

His face is more prideful than sheepish at the admission, and it's so fucking cute I reach up to kiss his cheek. Something I can't remember doing with a single partner since freshman year.

"Can't have you passing out on me before I get to see what the big deal is with that package of yours," I kid.

I doubt he'll be able to pick up a baseball bat with it, but I'm pretty sure he has some tricks up his sleeve. Or pant leg, more like. There's a lot more to this man than the stories that go around the grapevine in this town, but I'd be lying if I said I wasn't curious to see for myself how much of those whisperings are true.

Pushing myself back up onto all fours, I back off of the bed to find something to whip up for us. Van life means a condensed life, minimalistic to the extreme, per most people's standards. It's something I've gotten used to after all these years. Sure, there might be moments I wish my pantry could hold more than one grocery bag worth of stuff, or that I could have a full-size fridge and freezer instead of mini ones so a grocery trip could last me a whole week instead of just a couple days. And don't get me started on my dreams for an actual closet. But I've made it work for this long, now I can show off some of my skills.

"Pop those doors open," I tell Weston, gesturing to the back of the van with a nod of my chin. "Don't wanna cook with them closed."

"You're cooking for me?" His smile turns into a grin, and he scampers over the mattress to open the back doors.

"For us," I correct. My stomach decided it was time for a concert, harmonizing with his, apparently.

A gentle breeze filters in through the open doors, and though it's dark out, between the light from the moon and the muted glow of the infinite stars, I can just make out the outline of the ridge of the Smokies that I'm backed up to.

Ducking down to my knees, I raid the fridge, then the pull-out pantry, as the pan and air fryer both preheat, until I have everything I need. It wasn't like I was much of a cook when I hit the road at nineteen—I'd been subsisting on cafeteria food, living the bare-bones dorm life on a scholarship—but I've learned to fend for myself out here.

Pinterest has been invaluable, but over the years my mom has also helped me with some recipe ideas that can be whipped together with one pan, one burner, and an air fryer. This is one of my favorites, my take on something she used to make for our family when I was young.

I heat up some frozen vegetables in the pan, then add the meat and sauté it all together. Weston watches, fascinated, as I pour the mixture into a glass dish, top it off with all the good stuff, then finish it with a layer of frozen tater tots, and pop it in the front of the air fryer.

It takes just a few minutes to clean up the mess from cooking and put everything back where it goes, and while I work Weston chatters. He asks questions about van life, about what I'm making (a Minnesota classic, the tater tot hotdish), what I normally eat as a nomad (it's not usually glamorous, but I try to sneak some fresh food in wherever possible because Alani and veggie straws can only keep me going for so long), and more.

Hands on my naked hips, I turn to face him, and his eyes rove every inch of me as I do. "What about you?" I ask.

"What about me?" It's casual, offhand. Designed to look like there's nothing to see here, so that the other person won't press further. I recognize the tone well.

"What are you going to tell me about *your* life, Weston Grady?"

"What's there even to tell?"

He manages to shrug a shoulder while laying back on the mattress, stretched out long ways this time, where he just barely fits with his knees bent, but at least his calves aren't hanging off the edge like this. "You know all the important stuff by now," he says. "Name's Weston, I paint houses when I need work. Screw around when I don't. I'm pretty much an open book, darlin'. Life's simple, it's good."

Some sort of grunt comes out of me, disbelief, maybe even accusation.

"Give me something you've never told me," I demand. "Never told anyone," I say quickly, correcting my request.

That tongue of his goes into his bottom lip as he stares at me, weighing whether or not to give me something worthwhile. Eventually, he nods. "The reason I left the Heights in the first place is because my brother makes me feel like shit for being who I am. I'm not responsible enough for him because I didn't fall in love as a teenager and have my life laid out ahead of me by the time I graduated like he did, so I guess I'm useless to him."

Not much of that is news to me, based on things Weston's already shared with me and the interactions between the brothers I've caught over the past month, but I'd be willing to bet half my storage space in the van that he's never voiced this to anyone else before, so I nod and encourage him to go on.

Weston's arms animate his point as he speaks. "He's held it against me for probably fifteen years now, but what really sucks about it all is he doesn't realize that I *wish* I could be him. That my life would be so much easier if I were just a copy of him. I wasn't programmed the same way he was. And it's what's driven a wedge between us our whole lives."

That part catches me off guard. I stop scrubbing and look over at him, meeting his gaze, deeper than it usually is.

"What do you mean?"

Wyatt should be so lucky to have a bit of Weston in him, not the other way around.

"I'm the funny one in the family, he's the useful one," Weston says with a shrug. The words could be heavy, they could tank the vibe, but somehow, they don't. Just feels like he's laying part of himself bare for me, not looking for pity. "He didn't appreciate that about me, thought I should be a harder worker, fuck around a lot less, shit like that."

"You're a really hard worker," I say, shaking my head at that assessment. "I saw you; I worked with you for weeks. Painting, and also while you fixed my engine. You're not lazy, or useless, or whatever other insinuations were in there." I flourish my hand in the air, circling and waving at all the bullshit in the ether of his brother's words. "And fuck him for making you feel less about yourself. You deserve just as much good as he does. More, I'd say, if he's been this big of an asshole your whole lives."

"Thanks," he says, dropping his head down and giving me a sad chuckle.

He turns to laughter even when he's feeling low, and it's so familiar, something I find myself doing on the regular—my own darkness, my only constant companion—it makes me like him that much more.

"I think he has this concept of me as some goofy fuckup of a kid who can't keep his dick in his pants, when he's always known what he's wanted. Gone after it."

"First of all, I'd say you're a little *too* good at keeping your dick in your pants," I crack, and he smiles, some of that inherent lightness right back in him, like it never went out. "But he and Rory have been together a long time, huh?" I ask, back to cleaning up in the sink. He's told me bits and pieces about their history, stories of growing up together, whenever it's come up as we painted together, but I haven't heard the entire story.

"They got together in high school. Were together for ages, up until she left town. But she's been back and they've been together again for, shit, probably almost two years now. She was it for him though. From the moment they got together his path was clear as the river, right in front of his eyes. That never happened for me, I guess. My future wasn't here the way his was. Dunno where it was really."

Circling back to how he started this little sharing session, I ask, "Did you *want* to leave town?"

He shrugs again, rolling over on his side to sit up. "Nah, not really. The Heights isn't a bad place to live. 'Specially now with what Rory's doing to it. But it was easier to get out than have the thing you hate most about yourself used against you like a weapon, ya know?"

Do I fucking ever.

"I really do. And for the record, I think you need to set your brother straight. He can live his own life however he wants, but he has no right to try to control yours, or to *stop* you from being your own self."

My own words punch me in the gut with the hypocrisy in them, and I hope he doesn't notice that I rush past it.

"I meant it when I said your brother was lucky to have you. And I mean it even more now after everything I've seen since then."

Weston takes a deep breath, arms on his knees. "Your turn," he says, rising to his feet. His head nearly brushes the ceiling when he's barefoot like this. If he were in his work boots, he'd have to duck down.

I decide to give him something honest about me in return. "I haven't seen my mom in a really long time. She's my favorite person in the world, but I can't go back to where we're from, and she can't meet me on the road. It's...complicated."

He can't possibly understand, I know that was cryptic, but it's as honest as I've been with anyone outside of my own head since I left college and tried to turn over a new leaf. But like the wonderful fucking person he is, he doesn't press me for more. He's never pressed me for more than I give him, which is why this friendship has worked out so far. As usual, Weston accepts what I tell him, and then he miraculously keeps the mood light, despite our somber confessions to one another.

"So what you're making us now, that from your mom?"

"Yeah," I smile. "It's a classic back where I'm from. There are a million variations on the recipe, but this is the one that tastes like home to me."

"I think home has a new taste for me after tonight," he says, a little swagger in his smirk as he eyes my body.

A flutter of a thrill shoots down into my core, and I try to stay focused on getting the kitchen reset. It doesn't take that long, but I learned in my first week on the road that putting things where they belong right when you're done using them is the *only* way to make life work in a living space as compact as this. Nothing gets put off until later. You never know when you're going to hit the road next, and the last thing Van Gogh or I need is a hot plate or a pan of leftovers flying through the living area, splattering onto the cabinetry, or worse.

By the time the dinner prep is cleaned up, all the cookware has been stowed once again, and the counters are completely empty (minus the air fryer), and wiped down, Weston is seated on the edge of the bed, and the conversation has turned *personal*.

"What about a fantasy? Anything we can check off tonight?"

Weston's brows bounce playfully with my question. "Tonight *is* a fantasy for me, are you kidding?"

My face heats at the raw honesty in his tone, and the flush spreads down to my chest when he keeps talking.

"Getting to taste that perfect pussy, touch those designer tits. Breaking you in and being able to finally fuck you is everything I've been dreaming of, angel. It's all one big, giant check for me." He grips his dick through his underwear on the last line, and I laugh against my own will because really, that was just ridiculous.

How I still want to ride him senseless after some of the shit that leaves his mouth can only be explained by magic. That must be his superpower. Being completely over the top half the time, and still totally doable. More than doable. He lights my nerves on fire in an instant with a single look, and that mouth of his is just fuel for the flames.

Weston's tone drops into a lower range and he asks, "How about your fantasies, darlin'? What can I do for you?"

Anything.

Everything.

All of the things, and some new ones I haven't thought of yet.

But I don't say that.

Truthfully, there's a *lot* I'd love to do that I haven't been brave enough to do with a one-night stand.

Maybe I could be with Weston?

"I still wanna ride it," I remind him of that truth that slipped out of my tipsy mouth weeks ago. "But I have other fantasies too."

The images I conjure when it's late at night, just me and my B.O.B. flash through my mind's eye. A man—who used to be faceless, just a ripped abdomen and arms with a blurry face, who's since been replaced by a golden man with an endless tan, deep green eyes, and laugh lines on a face I could never forget—overtop of me for once. Broad shoulders taking up my view, hips pinning me in place as one of his arms holds my hands over my head, and I'm forced to take what he has to give.

A vision I've never given into in real life, where I've never trusted a partner to be in control, much less to dominate. It's been so damn long since I trusted a man. It would be nice, in some instances, to know what that's like. Like fulfilling fantasies, for starters.

He watches my eyes cloud over in the daydream, a hungry look in his own.

"Yeah?"

I shake my head, tucking my head into my shoulder. "Let's start with getting to ride an authentic Southern gentleman first. That's one pin I'd like to move to my "Been There, Seen That" board tonight. Finally." I grumble the last word, more of a complaint, and he chuckles.

"I'll give you your money's worth," he promises. "And I'm happy to help you tick off any other items on your list while you're here." Head down, his eyes flick up to meet mine from beneath heavy lids. "Or next time you're in town."

He offers it so simply, like I'm someone who could come back to visit. Like I'm not bound to keep on the road, never hitting the same place twice. His confidence in me, this simple belief he holds that I could be this version of that girl, it reminds me of everything Rory told me today. Of Lexi's parting words. And a yearning fills me that's more than just sexual. It's one that's achingly familiar, but deeper than I've known it before.

The need for connection. For a home, even if it's just a little while. One where I wouldn't be an outcast.

It's a future so close I can practically taste it, if only I let myself give in to the daydream of a life that will never be mine.

"You know, Rory cornered me today," I tell him.

His brows dart up. "Is this part of your fantasy? Because I could be into this, I just need to imagine someone *not* my sister-in-law."

"No," I laugh, shoving his shoulder from where I stand between his legs at the side of the bed. "She wanted to give me that pitch you warned me about."

"Oh," he says, nodding like he knows where this is going.

"Yeah. Turns out, there's some pretty cool incentives to stick around in this town."

He nods again before speaking. "It's not a bad place to slow down for a bit," he says carefully, casually. "If… one wanted to stop moving for a breather."

It's my turn to nod.

The timer on the air fryer dings at us, and I jump back, further away from him. His eyes don't even fall to my bare breasts as I do. They're still locked on mine.

It only takes a minute to get the dish out of the air fryer and serve the meal up on the one plate I own. The plate is steaming, overflowing with one of my favorite recipes, and I hand it to Weston as I climb up to join him sitting on the bed.

"Sorry I don't have more plates and forks. We'll have to share."

"No problem for me, darlin'. And might I just say, that was pretty damn impressive that you didn't burn yourself even once while you made all this." He looks pointedly at my nude form, blessedly free from oil splatters.

I laugh. "Well, as you've probably figured out by now, I'm not huge on clothes unless I have to, like if I'm leaving the van or something." My head swivels to the open doors behind us, the mountain range silhouetted in the night sky. "You're sure no one can see us here, right?" I reconfirm.

He shakes his head, eyes dancing. "Not a chance I'd share this view with anyone." His eyes aren't on the mountains.

Weston takes the first bite, not even blowing on it, just piling a huge mouthful in, a smile breaking out on his face when it hits him.

"It's nothing fancy," I tell him, while his mouth is busy chewing, to get him off the hook of the mandatory compliments.

He hands me the fork to let me take a bite and does these huge, exaggerated motions with his mouth so he can swallow the hot, colossal bite faster. Like everything between our sizes, my forkful is a lot smaller than his, but it's full of flavor, nostalgia, and times that were good.

"Are you kidding? It's delicious, Amelia. Ever since the diner closed here there's been shit for options. You've got the flapjack house for breakfast, or something fried at Suds to soak up a little of the beer. And instant ramen can only last me so long. This is the first homemade *anything* I've had in an embarrassing amount of time."

My insides warm from more than just the hotdish.

We keep talking while eating, about harmless things, funny stories, whatever comes to mind. It's a sort of ease between us I haven't had with a one-night stand before. An hour ago he was making me hear colors and see ancient deities, and now we're talking about our demons, scratching the surface of that deep-baked trauma we all carry with us, and making each other laugh all within minutes of one another, no lingering weirdness as we hop from topic to topic.

We drag the meal out for far too long, talking for ages, until what has to be the early morning hours. It's only fitting that the blaze between us returns to a full burn as soon as the meal is finally done, and like a good Boy Scout, Weston has cleaned the plate and fork and put them away for me while I use the restroom and make sure I'm ready for what's next.

When I emerge, he sneaks in behind me, asking to borrow some toothpaste before closing the door, and I hear the toilet flush, the water run, and then he's back in the bedroom portion of Van Gogh, somewhere around her haunches.

"So about this ride," he says with a taunting smirk as he walks out of my wet room, completely naked, cock thickening at our matching outfits. "What exactly are you planning for me, darlin'?"

And just like that, I'm wet, everywhere. My thighs are slick, my mouth waters, and I want him in every way I can have him.

I let my eyes feast first, roaming over his strong chest, to his lean, cut abdomen, those muscled arms, and the tanned, corded forearms that lead my wandering gaze down to the lines at his hips that showcase the absolute beast that's clearly awoken.

In fact, I think it's looking at me, its one eye is definitely trying to grab mine.

Challenge accepted.

"I want you to lie on your back and hold on tight, Boy Scout."

"Fuck," he breathes, but he damn near jogs past me, launching himself onto the bed and sprawling on his back.

Weston pats his lap, dick erect and so inviting, and I put a knee up on the mattress, ready to crawl to him for a night he'll never forget.

"I was gonna say fuck me up, Grady, but I think you might actually break me with that kraken between your legs."

"Wait!" It's practically a shout from his lips, panic in his green eyes, and I reel back.

"I wasn't looking for an out. I'll heal."

"No," he breathes out heavily. "Just, need a wrapper."

Putting my foot back on the ground, I stare at him. "Tell me you brought some. I don't have any in Thor size."

"I did, I did, in my pocket." He thrusts an arm out, pointing to his pants crumpled on the ground.

I bend down to grab his wallet, when I consider how big his girth is compared to the rubbers I'm used to seeing. No way a normal one would fit around him, right?

"Where do you get your condoms, a tent store?"

Weston laughs, a rich, deep sound that fills the van and the crisp night air outside of it too.

"Seriously, you could probably use a fucking tarp to cover that thing and go camping under it," I mutter, digging through his pants. His chuckle scrapes my nipples deliciously, and I pop back up, expensive-looking wallet in hand.

"Nah, not in there, darlin'. Side pocket."

I put his designer wallet back and find that one of the side pockets of his cargo pants feels bulkier than the other. Opening the flap, an accordion of condoms pops out, an entire strip of massive rubbers falls to the floor.

"Such a Boy Scout," I tease, holding up the length of them by one end. "So prepared."

"Not taking any chances at missing a single round with you, darlin'."

I toss the foils onto the bed and he rips one off and tears the top, peeling the protection out. My eyes follow every single roll of the material as he slides it over and down his thick cock, and I gulp at the sight of his fist following the latex.

"I could barely take two of your fingers. How the hell do we think this is going to work, anyway?"

West holds up his two fingers next to his dick, and my throat bobs at the way his cock dwarfs them. I'm *so* screwed.

"Slowly," he says with a filthy smirk. "Now hop on."

He doesn't have to tell me twice. I jump up and scuttle

across the bed, throwing one leg over his midsection to straddle him, watching his gaze heat at the show, and then I'm backing down onto him.

As soon as I feel the pressure of his thick head at my entrance, my eyes shut and he groans.

Knees spread as wide as I can, I lower myself onto him just a fraction of an inch, feeling the stretch already. A whimper escapes me, his eyes flame as he feels my tightness around his crown.

"Holy fuck." It sounds like a prayer coming from his lips.

I can't wait to see what else he says, what he looks like when I'm the one making him come. This man, thoughts of our night together have consumed me so completely for weeks now it's probably bordering on unhealthy, but I don't care. I want to make the most of every single moment we have tonight.

Weston's fingers dig into my hips sharply, like it's taking restraint not to slam his hips up into me, and it steels me to push myself, lowering down a bit more, until I'm so full of him I feel stuck.

I bounce in place for a few beats but can barely move with him lodged inside me like this.

"You're gonna have to let me in," he says, eyes on where we're joined. "You can do it, angel. Open up for me."

I look down and realize I've got nothing but the head inside me.

"Shit, you're huge," I groan. "Maybe you should use your fingers on me again and stretch me out some more."

I roll my hips over him, but it doesn't get me much further. Weston's face is pulled tight and he looks strained for the first time since I've known him.

"Breathe with me, darlin'," he tells me through clenched teeth, and I do. In, and out, in, and out. I watch his chest rise and fall, and match his breaths.

That gets us another inch, at most.

I gasp at the intrusion, the progress, the *feel* of him, so thick, so hard inside of me. My walls are squeezing him. It's not a choice; it's a visceral response.

"Back up," he mutters, tapping my ass with one hand gently.

I pull up, feeling the delicious slide of our bodies as I rise off of him, and try to sink down again with more weight behind it this time.

My eyes flutter, rolling back in my head as the feel of him registers deep in my cells. I can't help the noises I'm making, trying to take him, nails digging into his chest as I push my hips, grinding on him, his cock slipping in just a bit at a time.

His eyes are pressed shut tight, lip between his teeth, like he's in pain.

"Are you okay?" I ask him.

Weston's eyes, dark green with flecks of gold, shoot open, landing on mine, full of emotion.

"No, I'm not okay. Tightest pussy I've ever had and you're gonna kill me with these noises, those tits in my face as you're trying to take me. I'm gonna blow before I'm balls deep, and I'll never forgive myself for ruining this. Ever."

A laugh falls out of me at his face, the anger at the situation apparent all over it.

"You think it's funny?"

His hips jerk upward, enough to push himself just a bit further, to sting in a way I'll feel for days, and I let out a loud moan, all the humor instantly gone. My head falls back, hair swinging, and my hands go to his thighs behind me to brace myself as my back arches.

"Jesus, Amelia, you're gonna make me come if you keep doing that."

I've told him before not to threaten me with a good time.

Keeping my back arched, head thrown, I pivot my hips,

rolling them over his cock, and letting my body take what it needs from him. Up, then back down, up, and down, hitting all the right spots as I go.

"Fuck," he grunts out, and his fingers dig in even tighter.

I change up my movements, putting more weight onto his thighs and swapping to a quick, shallow bounce, mostly on the head of his cock.

I'm never quiet in my own home, and that doesn't change just because Weston is here with me. Moans and noises of pleasure coat the walls of my van as I let myself explore his body with my own, at the pace that I want to.

"Fuck, you should see you right now," he grits out.

"Paint me a picture," I beg him, head still tilted back, unable to keep my eyes open at the feel of the invasion of his thickness, knowing that I'm not even halfway to taking him yet. It's taking all my concentration to survive this.

"Bright pink cunt, stretched out, dripping on my cock as you bounce there, perfect fucking tits matching every stroke."

I let the groan building in my chest escape. "You feel so good," I tell him.

"I almost feel bad for you," he says, panting.

"Because I won't be able to walk for a week?"

"Because you'll never get to feel perfection. You'll never know what it's like to be squeezed by this cunt of yours. Best thing on earth, Amelia. Never felt anything like it."

At that, I swivel my head to look at him once more. He brings a hand up from my side to grab one whole breast in his palm. I look down, watching my flesh mold to his fingers, the imprints of his fingertips leaving white marks around his strong grip. Past his arm, I see the rest of the show.

I watch his sheathed cock, larger than even the fake ones I've used over the years, struggle to open me up wide enough for him. It's obscene. The sight turns me on more than it should, and I feel a fresh flood of desire course through my system.

"That's it, darlin'," he tells me, fingers squeezing my breast. "Watch this pussy stretch for me." His other hand comes down to my front and we both watch as he swipes a finger through the mess I'm leaving on his dick and then he brings it up to my clit, playing with me.

The noise I make, the reaction of my body, tells him everything he needs to know about what that's doing to me. I feel my body let more of him in, the sharp pinch giving way to a burn that's satisfying, it feels like I've earned his cock.

"Ah, Jesus." Weston curses. "How are you this tight? You a fucking virgin, angel? Am I the first to take this pussy?"

I shake my head at him while I go back to bouncing softly, willing my body to stretch faster, hands on the roof of the van to steady me. "It's been a while though." His breaths are strained, like he's having to focus not to fuck this up. "And you're definitely the biggest I've ever had," I add on. That throws his breathing off.

"Fuck this," he says, and his hands are back on my waist, pulling me up, up, and off of him.

"What?" I ask.

Is he stopping?

"It'll fit," I plead with him. "Just give it some more time."

"You wanna be on top, right?" he asks.

I nod, appreciating that he isn't making me tell him that I can't be on the bottom. That my trust issues won't let me be in the moment if we try it that way.

"Then we're going to have to get creative."

Hovering over him, I watch as he leans forward, sucking my pierced nipple into his mouth, pulling on it with that magical suction of his. I wrap my arms around his head, holding him to me, running my fingers through his hair, urging him on.

"Shit, West," I moan. "I think you could make me come just from that."

"Another time," he gets the words out around my nipple before taking the piercing between his teeth and tugging on it.

A little scream comes out, but it's not a protest. Shock, maybe, definitely surprise at the move, but clearly I fucking liked it because my lower abdomen heats, pussy flooding newly.

One of his hands comes down to check on me, fingers entering me with ease, stretching, pushing in and out in a way that makes lewd noises.

"If we didn't need all of this, I'd be licking up every drop, I just want you to know that," Weston murmurs against the skin of my other breast, giving it its fair turn of play.

"Should I just blow you?" I ask him. Van Gogh might as well be a lemonade stand after all the lemons life has been handing me since I was a preteen. "We could sixty-nine?"

Weston pulls back from my chest, eyes on mine again. "I'm getting inside this cunt tonight," he promises. "You can sit on my face after. We'll go for number eight while you get ate." That filthy smirk graces his gorgeous face again. "Right now, I'm fucking you, and giving you five through seven. Hope you're ready to keep counting."

A little whimper of disbelief parts my lips, and he speaks again.

"I'm not sayin' it'll be easy, darlin'. But I'm sayin' we'll make it work."

Still watching me, heavy-lidded, sinful green eyes on mine, Weston puts one of his hands in front of his face and spits.

Again.

And again.

I blush just at the sound of it, but the visual is enough to send me over the edge.

Lips quirked up at one side, palm full of saliva, he slaps it to my pussy, shoving the wetness inside of me with his fingers, and my knees buckle on contact.

The sting of his palm is instantly quelled by the pressure of his fingers, and the delicious heat that warms my insides at the sheer dirtiness of that move. The onslaught of need I feel, the way I won't be whole until he's inside of me, it overwhelms me in ways I've never known. The smirk on his face tells me he knows what that did to me, eyes glinting dangerously as he watches my reactions.

"Now sit on my cock, Amelia. All of it."

Whimpering, I sit back down, lowering myself onto him, and I feel the give as my walls expand, stretching, molding to the shape of him as he infiltrates every iota of space I have to offer him, claiming it as his own.

We both groan as the rest of him finds its way home and he bottoms out, skin to skin past the base of the condom.

He spews a string of curses, as my entire world shifts to adjust to the feel of him, a chill erupting over my entire body, nipples peaking.

"Start moving," he orders me, and his hands grip my ass cheeks and lift me up, bouncing me there.

The feel of his hands owning me like that, while his cock invades me, the tips of his fingers slipping back into my crack with every jostle of my body on his, it sends me over the edge. It's so much. There's so *much* of him, it touches all of me. Every single spot that feels good and some new ones I didn't know I was into. I can't stop the spiral of pleasure, even if I wanted to.

"Fuck yeah," he whispers, breaths heavy and labored as he lifts me up and down again, my legs failing me at this point. "You coming on my cock, been dreaming of this since we met. Let me feel it."

My eyes flutter shut, the last image they see is his arms straining, jaw clenched, pecs and abs taut as he does the work for both of us, messy dark blond hair spilling over his forehead, tickling that gorgeous face of his. That's what I picture as I fall, pleasure cresting and bursting, waves of it lapping against my nerves and receding out, as he keeps me moving, up then down over his hard length.

When I come back to consciousness, regain use of my limbs, his eyes are darker than I've ever seen them.

"Jesus Christ, that was so fucking hot. What number was that?"

"Five," I whisper, hardly able to form words.

"Damn right," he says. "Two to go."

His hips start pumping, pulling his hands back a bit, letting me regain control of my rhythm, and he matches me stroke for stroke. The slap of our skin, the press of him against my clit every time I sink down, it's like a bonus for all my hard work. Encouragement to not let my legs give out, but to keep going and let myself get turned inside out all over again.

My last three hookups combined didn't make me come this many times. Not even once have I come as hard with another partner as I have so many times already with Weston, the way it's a violent storm, crashing against my cells, raking my nerve endings until they're nothing but puddles.

Is this the universe giving me what I'm long overdue for? Or is this like a bear who's about to hibernate for the long season ahead, stocking up while I can before I go so long without once more?

Either way, I'm not going to miss a single chance to get my fill of this man. And it doesn't take long before another release is brewing, my nerves tingling with impending pleasure.

Weston watches greedily, so aware of what's going on with me that he knows as soon as I'm close. One hand pinches my nipple, the other plays with my clit, and I hum, louder and louder, back to the open doors, the mountains behind me and the cool air tickling my skin as I ride him, coming apart from the inside out as he melts my fucking insides with a kind of mind-bending pleasure I never knew I was missing out on.

I always thought porn stars were faking it, but if any of those guys fuck like Weston, I can actually understand the way most of those women react. The faces they make, the way they scream, how they can't get enough.

I've never been that girl before tonight, but I'm surprising myself with my enthusiasm here. My insatiable appetite, able to not just come during intercourse, but over and over again. I'm normally kicking the guy out the door after a single hard-earned O, done for the night, ready to get back on the road, happy to be alone with Van Gogh and my vibrator and onto the next adventure.

This? This is a feeling I could get addicted to.

My movements slow as I come down from the sixth high so far of the very long night, and I'm nowhere near done yet.

"How many times are you going to come for me?" I ask him, a teasing smile on my face. Any bite I might have is probably long gone, I can feel my eyes are bleary, hazy from bliss, my cheeks rosy, my nipples permanently pebbled at this point, and somehow my pussy is still hanging in there, still here for the ride. She's a trooper.

"As many as you tell me to," he says, hands on my hips, tongue on his lower lip.

"Such a good boy," I tease him, watch his eyes glow when I do. "I want your first one of the night next. But I want to ride you reverse when you come."

"You can ride me any way you want to," he spits out. "If you circle back to the Heights, you can use my lap as your personal saddle next time."

"I thought that was your face?"

"That too. My dick. My mouth. Fuck, they're all yours, darlin'. Take them."

He must be close to coming, because now he's just spitting nonsense. He'd probably give me his wallet and everything in it if I asked him right now.

We work in tandem to spin me around, resituating me so I'm facing the view outdoors, the faintest light in the sky highlighting some of the furthest peaks on the horizon.

I lean forward, arms outstretched, hands on his thighs as I find my pace like this.

"Goddamn, this view." His voice is strained, and it comes in between his breathy pants.

"It's stunning," I agree, moving slowly over him as I coax my pussy not to give out on me just yet. She can have a break when Weston Grady isn't beneath me. Until then...

Voice tight, Weston says, "You ever get tired of running, Amelia, Smoky Heights is here. *I'm* here."

Before I can complain about that feeling like more than we agreed to, he gives me even more. A thumb, or the tip of one, in my back entrance. I gasp, jumping at the intrusion, and lean further forward, which presses my clit into his balls with every move.

And that's how we both come, who knows how long later. Eyes on the horizon, the faint sounds of nature welcoming a fresh start with a new day, a new dawn, as the gray skies turn to orange, yellow, and eventually blue, Weston invading all my senses, the only thing I can feel, all around me as I take in the sights and sounds. The experience of this time with him, from the rays of sunlight, to the chirping of the birds, and the spring air caressing my bare chest. It's all *him*.

It feels like my first real sunrise after a years-long darkness, a nearly eternal period of night in my life.

Neither of us goes to sleep, we don't want tonight to end.

He keeps his promise. And he doesn't stop at eight. In fact, we get through half the strip he brought. I'm going to need an IV drip, an elephant's dose of ibuprofen, and an ice pack on my seat when I hit the road, but it'll be worth it.

Though it's a lot more than the orgasms this man gives me that are going to be hard to drive away from. It's all of him, the way he shares himself so freely with me that makes me want to stay.

Maybe it's just the optimist in me, but from this vantage point, Smoky Heights looks like it has an awfully temptingly bright future.

And when I finally, finally watch him drive away beneath the glaring sun in the late morning, taillights on his pickup glowing white and red against the horizon, I don't like the way the thought of never seeing him again feels one bit.

15

Weston

The low din of chatter, beer bottles clinking several lanes away, along with the racket of bowling balls rolling and crashing against pins, sending them clattering to the maple and pine floors of the lanes, it makes for a good cover for conversation with my brother. Nosy ears won't pick much up in this place. And make no mistake, residents of Smoky Heights can be *nosy*.

In fact, with the sounds of the records playing from the DJ booth in the corner—currently Lynyrd Skynyrd—the noise level at Pins + Needles actually makes it so we don't even have to talk if we don't want to.

I know that's Wyatt's preferred mode.

Me? I've got a few things to say after a certain short, pierced little goddess inspired me last night. Just gotta figure out how to get the words out.

I didn't have it in me to watch Amelia drive away one more time, so I left her to get some rest before she hit the road and I went back to my rental place sometime late this morning. Thank God I was able to fall asleep after I got there. Lord knows I used up enough energy last night, I wouldn't have any left for this talk tonight if I hadn't slept the damn day away.

Beer for breakfast might not be the way of the champions, but it's not such a far stretch for some of the locals around here, and tonight, I'm one of them.

"Bottoms up," I tell my brother, clinking my brown bottle of brew against his.

Now that my nights are free again, no more engine rebuilds taking up my spare time, I've got time for things like brotherly bonding.

Apparently, that's high on his list, because here we are on my first free evening.

My guess is it's high on *Rory's* list and he doesn't want to be on her shit list.

Either way, this is our Saturday night now.

Probably better we have a little brotherly bonding *before* we schedule any family game nights with our mom and stepdad. It might break her heart to watch us go at it the way we normally do, given two minutes in the same room. But we've made progress this past month, and tonight might help too.

With a tight mouth Wyatt tips his bottle to his lips and I follow suit.

The alcohol gives me something else in my stomach to focus on, rather than the knot of the knowledge Amelia's probably long gone by now. The unexpected tug of emotion in my gut at missing her, instead of the usual itch to move on by now. I need a distraction from the unfamiliar sensation. It'll probably just take another few hours, maybe a night, to disappear and the same old itch to return.

Though, now that I think about it, I haven't exactly noticed feeling the itch in recent weeks. I was so caught up in wanting her, rather than the instant gratification I'm used to, maybe it'll take a second for the usual boredom to return.

Or maybe I just don't want to think about how she might

never be out of my system and I'll be stuck with the need for more of her forever.

We're four frames in on this brotherly game of bowling, and so far haven't discussed anything other than the spare I got in the second, or the strike he got in the third. Wyatt's lips tilted up in a very uncharacteristic smile when he saw the X flash on the screen above, and, shit, I guess he likes bowling more than I realized.

It's cool this place reopened. It was a staple hangout in our youths, but I heard it was shut down for a while, foreclosed on by the same bank that had jacked up the rates and fucked over most of the residents and businesses of the Heights and tanked our local economy. Rory's worked hard to get this place, and a bunch of others, reopened, better than before.

"Looks good," I tell my brother, eyeing the restored bowling alley.

What used to be wood-paneled walls are now covered in a rustic reclaimed wood, with the alley's logo burned into the far wall, several feet wide, as a focal point.

This is one place I didn't have to paint hardly anything in, mostly just the back offices. The rest is done in that old barn wood, kinda like the bar is.

"She did good," he says, and that scruffy face of his can't hide the way the corner of his mouth tilts up, the way it only does for her.

Apparently, ever since its grand reopening last month, it's been pretty packed out, especially on Saturday nights like these. The people of our town have somewhere to go, soon to be lots of places to go. Hell, word on the street is we'll even have somewhere to eat soon. A regular ole mini New York City, that's what Rory is turning us into. Spoiled for options.

All right, maybe that's a little heavy-handed on the sunny

optimism, even for me. But the town is definitely waking up, turning into somewhere with something for just about everyone.

Standing by the ball return, I wait for my green and white marbled bowling ball to come back to me, after Wyatt just sunk his plain, boring black one down the right-hand side of the lane, only hitting four pins and cursing the shot.

With a series of rolling clunks, it appears in the mouth of the machine, and I grab it and decide to throw with my eyes closed.

"Look, Ma!" I yell to my brother. "No eyes!"

My arm pulls back and swings through, releasing the ball on muscle memory, and I open my eyes to watch it knock down the entire middle section of the pins. Seven and ten are holding on, teetering, and I cheer them on.

"Go down! Down, bitches!"

The universe loves me, and they topple with my encouragement. Or it could've been the other pins, still spinning on the ground, that knocked them over. Either way, I'll take it.

I turn around with a grin and a wink, and my brother is scoffing.

"You did not just do that with your eyes closed," he refutes.

"Are you calling me a liar or a cheater?" I put up fisticuffs, bouncing in place, laughing at the exchange.

Wyatt does something like an eye roll and blows out a heavy breath.

"You're an absolute idiot. I'm still convinced the stork dropped you off when Mom was out at the store or something. There's no way we're closely related."

I bump him with my shoulder. "I know. It makes no sense. If we were, you'd be so much more handsome and radiant."

Wyatt shoves me away from his personal space, but there isn't heat behind it. It's his version of playful.

I drop back into the shitty plastic bench seats that line the lane (they couldn't have upgraded those to something nicer?

Plush couches, maybe?) and pick my beer back up, nursing it with a sigh.

My brother doesn't get up to bowl his turn. Instead, he stays there, ass planted on the bench behind the input for the scoreboard, watching me, beer dangling from his grip.

"How's life, West?" It's an uncharacteristic question for him, with genuine interest behind it.

I give him the answer I always give everyone, usually our mother. "It's good. Things are good." The automatic response leaves my mouth without thought, despite the twinge of longing in me for something more. A driving purpose in life, someone who makes everything else in this world make sense. Something that anchors me, gives me a reason to stop floating on by, existing in the moment and really *live*.

But that longing has been there since I hit puberty, since I saw my brother find his purpose in Rory. If the universe really loved me, wouldn't it have led me to her by now? My person?

By twenty-one, I doubted she was in the Heights.

By my mid-twenties, I doubted any part of my future was in the Heights, that there even was someone for me at all, and I hit the road to stop the constant reminders of it.

Sure, my brother was a miserable fuck while his girl was gone, but at least he knew what it was like to love someone as much as he did.

I spent those years wondering if I was just broken, incapable of a serious feeling toward another human being.

Eventually, I just steered into the skid and kept it casual with everyone, never expecting sparks to fly or for deeper feelings to emerge. Harder to be disappointed that way every time they don't come.

Now, here we are, thirty-three and only just having my first brush with anyone who makes me feel anything above the cock. And now she's gone too.

"Good?" Wyatt reiterates it like a question, like he doesn't fucking believe me. His green eyes pierce mine, the one thing that's so similar between us, and I avert my gaze.

This isn't the talk I want to have with him. My issues are *my* issues. I don't put my shit on other people. I make other people laugh, I keep things light. That's my role in life.

So I force a smile to crack back out on my face before I answer him.

"Yeah, man. Felt good to get elbow-deep in grease again."

That's not a lie. I've missed working on engines. Even if I prefer smaller ones than a Sprinter van. And now that pinch in my chest is back.

"You did good on that shit, you know that?"

"Thanks, bro."

"Y'know," he starts, leaning back, legs outstretched. "Gonzo's accepting that he's not really coming back. He's talked to Rory about putting a contract together to sell the garage to me."

"No shit?"

He nods his head once. "Looks like it's happening. Anyway, you know how me and Rory go to New York every few months?"

My turn to nod.

"Well, our next trip is coming up soon, and this'll be the first time without Gonzo at the shop. I was wondering if you might wanna hold the fort down while I'm gone? It'll only be a few weekdays. But we've been so busy lately, it would be kinda dick to screw people over by just leaving their vehicles there, untouched, while I'm off with my wife."

My chest hollows, then refills with more emotion than it had before. "You trust me to handle the garage?"

"I'm desperate, but not desperate enough to ask you if I didn't trust you'd do a good job." A smirk peeks out of his scruff, and I think he means it. "I saw your work on the van. Plus, Google or ChatGPT will be able to give you better advice than Gonzo ever gave me way back when, and it's not like I won't have my phone on me if you fuck something up."

This is my chance, I think. *This is my opening.*

As much as it feels like an honor to have some form of respect and trust from him like this, I need to clear the air before I can accept in good conscience.

"I know you're probably booked with work," he says. "I hope it's not too much of a pain in the ass to reschedule some shit for a few days."

"It'll be fine," I tell him, waving the beer-less hand. "But..."

Wyatt's dark gaze sharpens on mine. He grunts, and it's basically a *yeah?*

"Well, I just wanna make sure you know that I'm not the same irresponsible schmuck I was when we were kids."

Another grunt, but it's more of an agreement. Looks like I'm still fluent in caveman after all the years I lived with this one.

"I know you'll probably always have on the older brother goggles when you look at me, probably a highlight reel of all my dumbest fuckups," I go on, trying to keep it light, my signature move. Wyatt's face cracks a little, probably remembering some of my more impressive fuckups.

This is as heavy as I've probably gotten with anyone as far back as I can remember, save those couple of deep dives with Amelia. It's like working on an electric car instead of a fuel-guzzler. Unfamiliar territory for me, but I try.

"But I'm thirty-three, man. I need to know you're not still seeing me like who I was at sixteen or twenty or whatever. I'm not the same kid I was then."

He nods, taking a sip of his beer, before standing and placing the bottle on the counter there. Wyatt holds out a hand for me, and I take it, rising up to join him, and falling into a handshake and a bro hug with him. He claps my back, I clap his, and it feels like a new leaf for us.

For a second, I think Amelia would be proud.

Then I realize she wouldn't *be* anything, because she's gone. She's not a part of my life to even have an opinion on the happenings in it. Don't love the way that feels.

The rest of the game whizzes by, me doing my best to ignore the hollow pang in my gut with occasional jokes and laughter ringing out above the sounds of the ball rolling down the lane, knocking down pins. He beats me by seven, so we play another round, where I beat him by nine. We're mid the tiebreaker game when he brings up family dinner tomorrow night.

"I was thinking, now that it's getting warmer we could grill out some steaks tomorrow. I'm gonna borrow a grill from Duke. I could swing by and grab you on my way to get it, you can help me get it in the truck and home and all that?"

And, shit, call me Wyatt, because everything my brother said just went in one ear and out the other at the sight before me. I grunt some sort of acknowledgement to him, and he keeps talking, but I don't hear a word he's saying.

The doors to Pins + Needles opened around the time my brother's mouth did, and the women that came in took *all* of my attention as he was jabbering away there.

Must be girls' night in Smoky Heights, not just the guys' night out, because three women strut toward us, and I can't take my eyes off of them. One in particular.

And here I thought my stomach might not ever float again.

Rory leads the pack, a wrap dress clinging to her willowy frame as she saunters down the walkway in her heels, arms up and waving. Next to her is Lexi, thicker than her sister in tight jeans and a low-cut top. The third, much shorter and slighter than the other two, is wearing white sneakers, tight athletic shorts, and a pastel tee cut off above her navel.

My Adam's apple lodges somewhere near my chest as I take in her face, let myself believe my eyes.

It really is *her*.

Amelia is in the Heights.

Wyatt notices me staring, or maybe he just feels the presence of his wife in the room, some sort of sixth sense he's a lucky fucker to have, and he turns to face the approaching women, all with giant smiles on their faces.

"What's this?" Wyatt beats me to the question as soon as they're in range.

"No reason you get to have all the fun!" Rory taps Wyatt on the nose, leaning in for a kiss. I ignore his hand roaming down her dress and grabbing a fistful of her ass. She pulls back to continue addressing us. "We're here to celebrate the newest future resident of Smoky Heights. Guess who filled out her grant paperwork today?"

Lexi cheers loudly, leaning back, hands cupped around her mouth as she hoots and hollers, while Rory gestures to Amelia, who's looking brighter than I've ever seen her. Cheeks pink, eyes sharp, there's a glow about her that seems surreal.

My stomach abruptly stops floating and drops down toward my balls as it all sinks in.

Amelia stayed.

She applied for a grant.

She is *staying* in Smoky Heights.

I want to swoop right in, lift her off her feet, swing her around and kiss her in front of everyone. I want her to know what this means to me. For them to know what *she* means to me. That last night wasn't enough, and I don't know what this is between us, but I want to keep finding out. Together.

Fuck, I wanna scoop her up and head to the back of the alley, somewhere private where I can show her how she hasn't left my mind since I left her this morning. The new ideas I've had for her in that time.

I save it all. Try to show her with just my eyes and a normal smile, the kind I toss out to everyone around me on the daily, and hope she can read into it. That she knows that I know what a big deal this is for her. That I'll do everything in my power to make sure she doesn't regret it.

Instead, I give her a hug, just like I do to Lexi, and Rory, in greeting. Bending a good foot down so I can reach her, I pull her in for a quick embrace.

"Congrats," I tell her, because it's all I can say in front of everyone else. I let the way my arms wrap around her, how tight I told her, try to do my talking for me. "I'm so damn glad you're here," I whisper into her ear.

Lexi starts talking to Wyatt loudly behind us, telling a story about how annoying Rory was with the paperwork, and damn if it doesn't feel like she's buying us a few seconds of privacy.

Jumping on it, I take the chance to soak in the moment, just for a sec—the feel of her shoulder-length waves as they brush my face, the scent of her filling my airways, coconut and something spicier, her tiny frame pressed against mine. My cock twitches, hardening against her leg, and I feel her intake of breath when she notices. Absorbing every detail of her in my arms, I lock it into my memory as the sisters start to go at each other's throats, as per usual.

"Says the woman who's *still* wearing skinny jeans!" I hear Rory clap back at whatever insult Lexi threw her way.

"Hey!" Lexi retorts. "This is a good look for me. I've been wearing it since high school!"

"Exactly," Rory says, and I can practically hear her eye roll. "It's been out of style for *years* at this point, Lex. Get with the times. Stop clinging to the millennial safety blankets of side parts and skinny jeans. Flick through Pinterest instead of flicking the bean for once. Your wardrobe will thank you, and maybe your sex life will too."

The sisters start bickering worse than before, but that's about as much of a distraction as I can count on for the moment, so I force myself to release Amelia.

Pulling back, I give her body a once-over, and finish with a dirty look that's just for her. Delicate features, perfect little upturned nose with the understated hoop through it, blue-green eyes glowing, she looks absolutely perfect.

"Good to see you back," I say, casual as any other day, loud enough for the others to hear, with a filthy undertone I hope no one else is paying enough attention to notice.

"Something about the Heights," she says, crossing one leg over the other and lifting a slim shoulder. "I just keep sticking around this place. Didn't feel right to leave yet."

This addiction she started in me, last night was never gonna be enough. I dunno what it'll take to get her out of my system, but I'm happy we have the time to do it.

16

Amelia

My back crashes to the wall, jiggling the stock artwork that whoever rents this place out must've picked out. It's certainly not the style of the man who's currently sucking my tongue. The wall bounces with the abrupt motion and I feel it all the way to my core, which makes me groan straight into his mouth.

Weston's body crushes mine to the drywall, my legs wrapped around his waist and his hands splayed across my ass, supporting my weight as we devour one another's faces.

We definitely didn't do *this* last night. It's so intimate, so deeply personal, the way he's consuming me with his mouth, like there isn't enough of me to go around.

Hands roaming, I work to get his shirt off without breaking contact between my pelvis and his abs. It's not working out for me, but I'm inspired.

Grinding on his belt buckle, I time my movements to let me peel the button down from beneath my legs and pull it up.

Why is this the one time he's not wearing a white tee shirt?

Once it's freed from my thighs, at least I can unbutton it without stopping our make-out session.

His talented tongue sweeps into my mouth again, sending

chills down my spine and making me grip him tighter, using my legs for leverage. A growl rumbles across my tongue, and I nearly come on the spot. In return I whimper, which drives him crazier.

His hands leave my ass, trusting his hips and the wall to hold me up as he uses both hands to grip my face, cupping my jaw, fingertips on the back of my skull as I work frantically to undo the buttons, one by one. I'm close to ripping the damn thing off at this point, and he chuckles against my lips at the exasperation brought on by my raw need.

"So impatient, darlin'."

Weston nips at my swollen lower lip and I nip right back, capturing his lip in my teeth and biting down enough to show him I'm not playing.

"Not the time to be a Boy Scout, Weston. Fuck me like you mean it."

His eyes darken in an instant, and that playful demeanor melts into a kind of skillful predator I don't want to imagine how he perfected over his life without me. I'm feeling a little possessive at the moment.

"Those are the magic words, angel. Tell me why you stayed and I'll give you whatever you want."

"Because I wanted to," I gasp around drugging kisses.

"Why?" he presses.

"I like it here," I divert.

His lips close on my jaw, then move over to my chin as he works his mouth down my neck, using his tongue to tease me as he wants to along the way.

My shirt gets pulled up to my shoulders where he pins it in place with one forearm, mouth still roaming my bare skin.

"Why?" he asks again before closing his lips over my pierced nipple through the bralette and tugging on the metal.

That gets a loud moan out of me, head thrown back against

the wall, core pressed as close as I can get to him on that shiny belt buckle he wore over his jeans tonight.

"Last night wasn't enough," I admit, breathless.

"Fuck no it wasn't." His teeth come out to play with my nipple, bringing new noises out of me, and then he licks it all better, straight through the fabric.

"Tell me what you want."

He's out of breath, as needy as I am, but he holds my hips with his hands until I drop my legs, then he falls to his knees, leaving me floating against the wall, pinned by his grip.

Weston presses his face between my legs, nipping at my pussy through the thin material of my stretchy shorts, and I think I might've broken him last night, or maybe it was by coming back. Whatever the cause, he's absolutely unhinged right now, feral compared to the composed, laid-back, golden retriever of a man I've spent so much time with these past weeks.

He swings my legs over his bare shoulders, face pressed into me, waiting for my answer.

I want to be brave enough to go after what I want.

A home.

Friends.

Family.

Him.

"All of you," I tell him the short answer, and that does it.

He growls, ferocious and gravelly, before lifting me from the wall, supporting me with his arms behind my body, my legs over his shoulders as I squeal the entire way to his bed. He drops me down, letting me fall several feet under his watchful stare.

The man must be a pro, because in what seems like a flash, he's naked and so am I.

In another breath, he's pushing inside of me, from the top, and I don't stop him. On the contrary, I urge him on, short black nails in his back, lips to his ear, mewling, begging him to take me, to give me more.

I want all of what he has to give me.

And I think I finally trust someone enough to let myself take what they have to offer.

As long as his name is Weston Grady.

SOFT FINGERS TRAIL through my hair, playing with the strands as I wake, face nestled in a hard, bare, masculine chest that smells familiar. Something woody, spicy, and safe that stirs memories of feeling cherished, even worshipped.

"Mmm," I murmur, opening my eyes to take in the man beneath me.

His other hand traces over my arm, stretched lazily across his upper body.

"Mornin', darlin'," he says in a sleepy voice that might even be hotter than his normal one.

"Time is it?" I ask, bleary-eyed.

"Late," he says with a quiet chuckle.

We stayed up most of the night again, making the most of my return to Smoky Heights. When the girls and guys night at the bowling alley *finally* ended, I went to my van, acting like I was going to spend the night in Van Gogh, and when the others had left Weston grabbed me and whisked me to his place in his pickup, covering our tracks. Our hands wandered the entire way home, and we barely made it in the door without him inside of me. We didn't waste a minute of the night after that.

Not too keen on wasting any time today either. It's Sunday, meaning neither of us have work until tomorrow and we have the whole day to ourselves.

Weston lifts his shoulders off the bed so he can kiss the top of my head, and I snuggle further into his body. Settling back in, I feel something solid poke my arm, and some parts of me wake up faster than others. A low burn pulls in my belly, and I shift my hips closer to him.

My left hand trails down his abdomen to greet my visitor. West sucks in a breath when I grasp his thick cock, and a smile pulls my lips up at one side.

"I couldn't leave without getting to suck you off," I tell him sleepily.

"You can't leave after that, either," he teases. "If that's all that's keeping you here, I'm going to have to hold out on you, darlin'."

"Mmm, no fair," I say in my soft morning voice.

I can barely open my eyes, but I manage to bring my head further down his stomach until the head of his cock is at my lips.

My tongue darts out, teasing the slit, and I feel him jolt beneath my touch.

"You drive a hard bargain, Miss Marsh," he says, throat thick, words strained.

Waking up faster now, I give him a giggle as I roll over onto all fours, facing him, tongue out and ready.

"God," he breathes out, eyes heated, looking like a deity himself, muscular body on full display on the navy sheets, giant cock standing erect. "You couldn't look better."

That earns him a dirty smile before I take a long lick on the underside of the sensitive head, and his eyes shut. "I take that back. Only way you could look better is with my cock inside you."

Using my tongue, I wet my lips and open my mouth to take him in. It's true, he's enormous, but it's also true that I'm tiny. I'm not sure whether to blame his giant dick or my small mouth, but it only takes a couple of attempts for me to realize this isn't going to work the way I'd hoped.

"That's okay," he tells me, leaning forward to run the backs of his fingers along my cheek. "You don't have to."

"I want to," I tell him. "Let me keep trying."

Sitting back he puts an extra pillow under his head to get a better angle on watching the performance, and it makes him look even hotter. Like I'm the one worth watching, not him looking like a Norse god.

"Can't decide which way to have you face, what's the better view here, darlin'. Watching that sweet mouth try to fit my cock in it, or looking at you dripping for me while you suck the cum right out of my tip."

My eyes flutter shut at that visual, as my pussy does just that at his dirty words. Bending further down, I waggle my ass in the air and his pupils blow out, looking between it and my face a few times before settling on my face for good.

"I'll just have to lick you up after you're done sucking me dry, I guess."

My nipples peak and I rub my thighs together, trying to relieve some of the need that's building in me already at his never-ending stream of filth. The delicious, aching soreness that's acted as a constant reminder for two days now isn't even enough to keep me from wanting more from him when he looks and talks like *that*.

"Do me a favor," he says, face pulled tight. "Leave your legs spread the whole time. Let the cool air hit that pretty pussy and remind you who every drop is for."

I bite back the words that want to taunt him right back, the groan building deep in me, and I channel my efforts into sucking him off.

Head has never been my strong suit, whether it's the disadvantage of my size, my history of predominantly one-night stands where I never got too adventurous with any one partner, or maybe it's just not my gift in life, but I'm giving it all I've fucking got for this man.

Tongue out, I trace the underside of his cock, from the base, pressing in where it joins his ball sac, and lick a path all the way up to the tip. He hisses out a breath and I flick my eyes up to watch his reaction.

Still using my tongue, I lick all the way around his head, getting it nice and wet, and then my lips press to it, doing everything I can to slip it in, suck it down. I usually get lockjaw after a couple minutes, but I've never had *this* particular issue before. This is about to get embarrassing.

"'S all good, angel. Just take what you can, you're doing so good," he tells me, tone gentle. It hardens a moment later, when he says, "Shit, I could come just from you breathing on my dick, I don't need to fuck your face to get off. Just play with it."

Those words unlock a freedom in me to experiment in a way I've never felt safe to with anyone before him.

Play, I do.

Lips trailing his length, I kiss the entire thing, up, down, anywhere that calls to me. I make excellent use of my tongue, dragging the tip of it around his girth, drawing a design, then tracing his veins as we both watch.

Precum bubbles from the opening at his head and I lick it up instantly.

Eventually I've sucked my way around the whole thing enough times that I want to taste the cum of his I've earned, and my hands come out to play too.

Thighs still spread—breeze teasing me just like he wanted—leaning forward on my elbows, I use both hands to grip him, jerk him off, and get the rhythm going that my mouth wishes it could be delivering on right now.

The stream of grunts, curses, and encouragements he's kept

up this whole time turn more strained, and I notice a tendon in his neck popping out as he struggles to keep his eyes open.

"Gonna come if you keep that up," he tells me.

Part of me wants to keep playing longer, to ease up on this grip, this rhythm, and drag this moment out for both of us. But the knowledge that I can just do this to him again in a few minutes makes the decision for me.

Not that I've had that many repeat hook-ups, but I've never met a guy with a refractory period as quick as Weston's. My mind races with ideas for the rest of our day together, and my smile ticks up, thoughts probably written all over my face.

I lock my grip, jerking him at a furious pace that jiggles my chest with every motion of my arms, loving that he's watching what I'm doing to him so closely.

"You wet?" he asks me.

"Soaked."

"Get ready to scream," he grunts out, teeth clenched. "Gonna eat you out all night after this."

I *tsk* him, shaking my head slowly from side to side, and press my lips to his cock again, sucking him wherever I can.

"Tonight's my turn," I say against his purpling flesh, loud enough he can hear me up there, which earns me a fierce curse.

"Unless you want a facial, back up," he warns me, just in time.

I sit up on my folded legs, thighs still spread, arms still working him, and watch as he erupts. His cock spurts with his release, and at the first shot I lean down, suctioning my lips over the head and sucking the cum out as he explodes into my mouth.

Weston's hips jerk when my mouth makes contact and he curses. The salty release coats my tongue and I swallow it down with every rope he gives me.

"Fuck, Amelia," I hear him muttering, cursing, worshipping

my name over and over again, and I don't stop until his dick is done, totally spent.

Pulling back, I sit up and look up at him, a cocky smirk on my face.

His eyes soak in my appearance, my swollen lips, pebbled nipples, thighs spread wide, pussy on display for him—practically dripping, just like he asked for.

"You're so fucking perfect, angel." His voice is incredulous, face earnest.

Before two nights ago I would've said his words were too much. I tried to stop him last time he told me that. But now, somehow, the praise slips under my skin, warming me in a way I never expected, and I smile instead.

"Best head of my damn life and you didn't even get me past your lips."

I just tap his thigh impatiently. "Let's go, Boy Scout. Pitch me another tent, that was just the first round. You're the one keeping count this time while I get to play."

Amazingly, his cock twitches, thickening again as I watch. Incredibly, my mouth waters at the sight, like I didn't just swallow down a load and a half from this huge man.

And even more insane is the door we hear opening, a male voice calling, "Weston!" as footsteps head down toward the bedroom.

"You ready?" comes the familiar timbre.

Squealing, I dive for the top of the bed, leaping up and under the covers, pulling them to my chin as Weston only has time to shove a pillow over his lap, shouting to the intruder, "No, man, gimme a sec!"

But his brother must not register the words because Wyatt steps into the doorway, taking in the very guilty sight in front of him.

"What the fuck!"

"Come on, bro!"

The two men yell at the same time, and I just let out a squeak of despair.

Wyatt slaps his hands to his eyes, turning his back on the two of us, and storms down the hall.

"Gimme a sec, Wyatt!"

Weston scrambles out of bed and into some sweats, jogging into the hall. At the doorway he looks back at me, apology in his eyes, and holds a finger up.

"Let me fix this," he pleads. "Stay here."

I've never needed a knight in shining sweatpants and I don't need one now either.

What *would* be great is if the Grady men learned to knock though.

I follow behind him, rapidly dressing in the first clothes I can find. A tee of his that hangs to my mid thighs, and my shorts, just to be safe. I don't need to scar Wyatt any further than he's already been damaged by this moment.

As I rush after them, I hear their argument from the bedroom.

"You're not the same fuckup, isn't that what you said?" Wyatt's voice is angrier than he has a right to be.

"Hey!" That bite is new for Weston. "This isn't like that. She's not some random hookup for me."

"I can't believe you!" Wyatt hisses. "Rory is working her ass off, trying to get her to stay in town, and you can't even wait a day to get her in your bed, doing your damn best to run her right back out of here."

"That's not fair! I can explain, man."

Wyatt doesn't give Weston time to respond, his scathing attack just keeps going. "What? You asked Santa for some pussy for Christmas and he delivered four months late?"

My blood chills at the words and my temper takes hold of me.

"Excuse the fuck out of you!" I say, barging into the kitchen, where the two men are facing off. "You have no right to put your nose in his fucking business like this. And you have even less right to put it in mine."

Puffing up my chest, bringing myself up to all of my five feet tall, I hold my hand in Wyatt's face and he dodges it with a swerve of annoyance.

"Your face has clearly been in *his* business," Wyatt spits out, eyes on my swollen mouth.

Shame that the only time my lips look like anything is after a BJ. As useless as having to go to the beach to get beach hair. The puffy pout is a dead giveaway, and while it's none of his damn business, there's no denying his accusation either.

"My face can do what the hell it wants," I retort.

"My brother and I had plans now," Wyatt seethes, face close to mine. "Seems you were distracting him from our family dinner, and what pisses off my wife, pisses me off tenfold. So this *is* my family's business, I'm afraid."

"Don't you fucking talk to her like that!" Weston is in front of me, protective stance and all, roaring at his brother.

"I don't need you to defend me!" I shout right back at Weston.

"Fuck this," Wyatt says, shaking his head. "Don't bother coming. I'll get the grill by myself. You just have fun, like you always do. Don't worry about a thing. You never fucking do."

Wyatt turns his back and stomps off, but Weston calls out after him.

"Why do you need my help with the grill?"

"I don't, asshole, I was trying to spend time with you. My mistake."

The door slams, shaking the house, and Weston shouts, "Fuck!"

He spins around, hands knotted in his messy, thoroughly sexed golden hair.

"He's such a prick!" Weston yells.

"So are you!" I tell him.

"Me? What the fuck did I do? I was standing up for you!"

"Yeah, well, don't! I don't need you defending my honor. I can take care of myself, Weston."

The mask of anger falls from his face, replaced with concern as he steps closer to me.

"Hey now, I know you can."

He reaches out an arm for me, and I duck it, pissed.

"Talk to me, Amelia. What's going on?"

Taking a few calming breaths, I reevaluate my environment. Count the knives on the block on the counter. Realize there is no danger here. Weston isn't my dad.

As much as that encounter annoyed me, I'm okay. We're all okay.

But the worst part of that little blowup is the memories I work so hard to outrun have caught up to me. Triggered by their words, the anger in their voices, and Weston's stupid need to defend me, the worst days of my life float in front of my eyes once more.

Flashing lights, sirens. Headlines that I couldn't escape. Whispers, jeers, and taunts.

Questions pound my mind, the kind that kept me up for years, that I do my best not to think about these days.

Is someone's entire existence reduced to their worst hour? The final moments of someone's life?

I can't help but think the human experience is more nuanced than that.

No part of me excuses any part of what my dad did. No part of me apologizes for the things he's done. But sometimes I miss the good times we had before he ruined everything. And while I'll never stop loathing him for the last hours of his life, a part of me can't stop hating myself for still loving who he was before that day.

How can a good person miss a monster?

The conflicts physically churn in my stomach, making me nauseous.

It's just a small part of why I try to *never* revisit the past.

Which, thanks to the two Grady brothers, is now swallowing me whole.

I head to Weston's cabinet, grabbing a glass and filling it with water from the filtered pitcher next to the sink, then taking several gulps, practicing my breathing as I do.

It'll take me a while to calm down, but in a day or two, I'll be normal again. Back to pretending my past isn't the specter over my shoulder no matter how fast or far I run. It's not like I haven't been going through this for fifteen years now.

I just need Weston not to fight my battles for me again.

After a moment of deep breaths I turn back to face him.

"I have a thing with men trying to defend me," I admit. "I don't want to get into it, okay? Just please don't do that again. I'm not some delicate little flower that will get crushed without you. I'm strong and hard to fucking kill. I don't need the macho bullshit."

His gaze steadies on my eyes, tries to read me for everything I'm not saying, and he nods. Weston opens his arms and I fold myself into them, nuzzling into his chest as he wraps his strong arms around me.

"You got it, darlin'. I'll be here if you need me though, okay?"

I nod against his chest, not having the strength to argue that point.

I won't need him. I haven't needed anyone but myself in all these years.

17
Weston

If the past week and a half is anything to go off of, my brother is somewhere on the pissed-off scale between *no longer welcome at family dinners* to *disinvited from my niece's future graduation*.

According to the text I got last night, Wyatt's not *quite* mad enough at me not to let me cover the shop for him while he's gone.

Ticked off enough not to talk to me for a whole nine days, sure, but seems like his seasonal trips to the Big Apple for his wife are so important even his fuckup of a brother can't derail them.

Guess I have seventeen or so years to get back into his mid-graces in time for the little one's high school graduation then. It's a tall order, based on the icy silence I've been blessed with ever since he walked in on the aftermath of the best blowie I've ever gotten in my life.

Though, I will say, one bonus of all of this is that Amelia and I can just be *together*.

No bullshit, no hiding it.

Wyatt's the only one who cared in the first place, his weird little obsession with keeping my dick dry, as Amelia puts it. And we haven't had any more hiccups like that night, with Wyatt out of the picture. No more arguments between her and I either, just good times.

I was a little worried about how worked up she'd gotten after Wyatt walked in on us, but she's back to normal and doesn't want to talk about it, so I guess that's that.

The best part is she's been able to come over a *lot*. Her flexible work schedule and me busting through my painting projects has been working in our favor lately.

The Heights isn't quite *done* done, but it's getting there. Soft opening of downtown is in just over a month. Grand opening with the whole shindig's not until August, but everything should be open and operating as normal long before then. Most of the buildings downtown are fully ready at this point, and a bunch are already open to the public.

Which means my work here will be done before long.

With the amount of jobs I got given while here, shit, I could coast for close to a year, probably more, before needing to go find another gig.

Though, if Amelia is staying... I might have a reason to hang around for a while too.

The thought bolsters me, and I exhale a heavy breath as my boots disrupt the gravel with every step toward Gonzo's Garage. Or whatever it'll be called once the sale goes through.

Rory's SUV is already backed up to the open bay at the far left of the garage, surrounded by flowering trees at the end of the lot. This May weather is so balmy I can't even see steam coming from the exhaust pipe anymore. Summer isn't far off at this rate.

The blooms on the sides of the road, the lawns, and across the town have gone through several color cycles since I've been here. White, then soft pink, yellow, some blues and purples, and now brighter pink is starting to dominate the landscapes.

The crepe myrtle trees that border the lot here will be budding soon, white, purple, and hot pink flowers that grace the leaves all summer long, even when it's as muggy as the devil's ass crack. Amelia's been so excited by the constantly changing landscape of spring in the Smokies, I can't wait for her to see those when their time comes in summer. I think they're even one of the trees planted along the sidewalks downtown.

"There he is!" Rory welcomes my approach in a shirt with a big bow tied on it and some pants that look awful fancy for travel, along with her usual—a pair of heels.

My brother—if I'm allowed to still call him that—grumbles something unintelligible and Rory digs her elbow in his side. He must have a permanent bruise there at this point.

"We gotta hit the road, can we make this fast, gentlemen?" Rory asks, looking at her husband pointedly.

He grunts, and I nod. But then it hits me. "Wait a damn minute. Y'all are driving to New York? Not flying?"

"Yes," she says calmly.

"It's like a ten hour drive," I point out.

"Twelve-ish now that we've got the little one. Used to make it in ten though." She shoots Wyatt a smirk that he returns.

"Why the hell aren't you just flying?"

"Well, we go to stock up on necessities and the airlines max you out at two checked bags."

"Each, Rory. Two bags *each*. Plus a carry-on."

Rory shrugs her slim shoulders, somehow still looking elegant as she does. "Exactly. We'd never fit everything if we flew."

My brother shakes his head softly, then kisses the top of hers, hearts in his dark eyes, and opens the passenger side door for his wife. He's so fucking gone for her it's ridiculous.

"You're sweet, but you're still not getting any," she tells him under her breath, and I don't wanna know, so I jump on the chance to change the subject.

"By necessities, you mean...?" I let the question trail off.

"Shopping. Clothes, shoes, dry goods, you know. The stuff I can only get in Manhattan."

How the hell they fit all that in their cozy little home, I'll never understand. Her closet must be a vortex through space and time to fit as much as I'm sure she buys every few months.

As Wyatt herds her to the open door, helping her in, I poke my head in the back seat to say goodbye to my niece. "I'll miss you, little munchkin," I coo to her. Missing family dinner these past two Sunday nights meant not getting much time with her, and I'm surprised at how much she's changed in just a couple of weeks and how much I've missed her little toothy smiles and chubby cheeks.

When Wyatt is busy closing Rory's door with a grunt and heading back toward the garage, I get my wallet out and hand my sister-in-law a few large bills. "Bring me back something worthwhile, yeah?"

She laughs. "You already miss the finer things, too, huh?"

I haven't spent much time in New York, but I have been in a decently big city much of the last ten years or so. There's a lot the Heights has to offer, but dammit, sometimes I miss that life too. Convenience. Luxury. Change of pace. I guess she's worked out how to get the best of both worlds.

"You know it," I tell her and pull myself back out of the bench seat with one final air kiss to my niece.

Turning back to the garage, I find my brother waiting by the office door.

It takes almost no time at all for Wyatt to explain the vehicles he needs me to work on in his absence, run me through the paperwork on the desk, and fit in a record number of scowls at me along the way.

"Don't burn the place down," he tells me, back turned, strolling away to the dark SUV he got his wife when she decided to stay in the Heights once and for all.

"Your faith in me is reassuring," I call out to his back.

Wyatt turns around, scruffy face pulled tight. "And don't call me. I'll be trying to fix things with my wife because she's mad at me over this bullshit with you and won't touch me. You've managed to ruin my relationship by your mere presence, which is a new accomplishment, even for you."

My brother has held me accountable for damn near every issue in his life, starting from when we were kids. If I had to guess, I'd say it was our parents' divorce that started him on this road, and my teen years only helped confirm his biases against me. But he certainly didn't get any kinder once Rory left him.

I'll admit I've made some mistakes along the way, but I try to own up to 'em when I do. This shit with his wife is his own doing, and he can shove it.

"We're blaming me for that too? You sure it's not just because you're a dick?" I offer, only a tiny bit joking.

He flips me off and heads to the driver's side.

"You still owe me fixing my trunk, asshole!" I'm kinda proud that's all I called him.

The car dips as he gets in, and then they're gone.

Sighing, I head into the office and re-review the paperwork he showed me. I think I got the gist of it, but there's a lot of fucking vehicles, all at different stages of their repairs.

I don't think I give him enough credit for keeping so many things going at once, this is almost impressive for a guy who can barely string ten words together.

Two of the vehicles here are some of my favorite kinds to work on. An ATV and a dirt bike. The side by side is having an issue with its alternator, and the dirt bike needs a new crankshaft. I make a plan to start on those first, because they seem like the most fun. I'm not sure that's how Wyatt runs his business—there was some buzzing in my ears about first in, first out and priority sequences—but while I'm here, that's my plan.

My mind drifts back to my brother and a heavy sigh sags my shoulders. From Rory's texts every other day, checking on me and Amelia, offering her support, I know she is happy for us. But I can't decide if I'm relieved that Rory is on my side of this blowup with Wyatt, or if I don't want her getting involved in our spat.

They've been through enough together, getting him to sort their shit out was probably enough drama for them. She doesn't need to insert herself into our family issues.

Though at the thought, I'm vaguely tempted to call my mom in for backup. She *always* takes my side, but that's one surefire way to really piss my brother off. It riles him up, the way I always get the benefit of the doubt and he never does.

But what can I say? I'm the baby. I make her smile every time I visit, and he just huffs and puffs. Who wants to hug the big bad wolf when you've got a golden retriever right there?

Speaking of, I really should make more of an effort to see my mom while I'm in town, however long that's gonna be. I've barely squeezed in a few dinners with her since I got here, so I make a mental note to schedule something more with her soon.

Plopping down in the old rolling office chair, I pull my phone out to see why it's vibrating.

Reminder: Firefly lottery
Today at 4:00

Shit, I would've totally forgotten today's the day. Thankful for the electronic brain in my hand, I open up the shop computer and find the website where we can apply for parking permits to see the synchronous fireflies.

Though they're visible in many areas of the Smokies, parking is very limited, which is what makes seeing them so difficult. It's all the luck of the draw.

Just because Amelia is staying in one place for a while doesn't mean she shouldn't get to keep living out her adventures and checking things off her "Shit to Do" list.

It only takes a few minutes, filling out the form under my own name, putting in my credit card info. Then I do it under Wyatt's, Rory's, Lexi's, my mom's, and Duke's. I consider any of the friends Wyatt and I grew up with who might not mind me using their personal info, consult the address book in my phone, and fill out another half a dozen applications too.

Best case basis, every one of us wins the lotto and my card gets a serious workout that day. But there's nothing else I can do except hope until approval emails go out in a few weeks.

Now we wait.

Looking through the one-way glass out into the shop, bouncing my knee under the desk, I spot my Charger, still in need of some TLC to be road-ready once again.

The one with what better only be scuffs on the trunk and not scratches.

Alone in my brother's garage, the same place he defiled my one and only prized possession, an idea for some sort of revenge forms. Just need to get through some of this workload and when the weekend hits, I'm putting my brand on his precious garage the way he did to my car.

18

Amelia

WESTON
> Meet me at the garage at dark
> Make sure you're hydrated

A bolt of anticipation lights up my nerves, shooting a line straight down from my stomach into my core at the cryptic messages. It doesn't take much to remind my body of what this man does to it.

Maybe it's all the true crime I listen to, but I think I've solved this mystery and my inner muscles clench at the thought of what awaits me.

I haven't seen Weston as much the past couple of days while he's been in charge of the shop. He's been leaving early (yuck) and getting home late covered in grease and sweat, but with a smile on his face that's not just for show.

For two people who "don't do relationships," we've been awfully cozy together lately.

Our nighttime sessions have been shorter than they were our first nights together a couple weeks back. Not that they *all* have to take all night, but it still feels like I haven't quite gotten my fill of him, or hit a point where just once a night is enough for me.

He tells me we might get there eventually, that the couples he knows get plenty of sleep, but I'm not so sure. I've seen the way his brother looks at Rory, the fire in their eyes, the tension that you can almost feel crackling between them, even after however many years they've been together and having a kid.

I wonder if that need ever goes away when you have a love like theirs.

Or a lust like Weston's and mine.

Now that I'm staying with him most of the time, and thanks to some of the earnings I got from painting all those shops with him, I have the means to expand my closet beyond just a small capsule wardrobe that fits in the drawers beneath my bed in Van Gogh. I've splurged on a handful of outfits, including what I'm wearing tonight walking up to the garage.

It's a shirt made for women with pierced nipples, with holes just where you need them to thread the piercing through the material so the metal hangs on the outside of the shirt. It only comes to just below my breasts, revealing my entire abdomen to him. As for the bottoms, I went with fishnet stockings and a pair of dark, fake leather shorts that are so tiny they probably qualify more as underwear, with my favorite black combat boots to top it all off.

I hope he comes in his pants when he sees me and then comes again on me shortly after. This splurge would've been more than worth it.

His texts seemed like he meant business, so also with me is a tote bag full of condoms and lube from his bedside drawer, multiple bottles of Gatorade, some cans of Alani, a few energy bars I stole from his kitchen, and a change of clothes to wear out of here whenever the hell we're done.

I hope we never leave.

When I walk in the only open bay door the overhead lights are off, just a construction-type spotlight on in the middle of the shop, pointed toward the bay doors, shining on the wall in between them, illuminating a large machine with hoses and cords running out of it.

The night air in the mountains is far chillier than the sunny warmth we've had during the days lately, and even if I wasn't already high on anticipation, my nipples would pebble from the temperature alone. Seeing this setup he's put together, the way it looks almost like a stage, spotlight shining there, waiting for a private show, I'm instantly aroused. Intrigue leads me to turn in a circle, dropping the bag down out of the way, and searching for my favorite guy.

Hearing chains rattling behind me, I spin quickly and see him standing where I just came in, lowering the garage door with the chain pulley system they have here. When the door is closed, he latches it in place with a big hook that hangs from the chains to the door to secure it for the night.

"You look good enough to eat," he says in a low, lethal tone, stalking toward me. His eyes, normally a deep, vivid green, look nearly black right now. They soak in my body, the outfit I bought for him. Desire sparks deep in my abdomen and spreads out like wildfire at the appreciation in his gaze.

"Haven't you told me that before?"

Weston's voice is nearly a purr when he replies. "Think I ate you out then too."

"Maybe you need to refresh my memory," I tease, tapping my chin like I can't remember in haunting detail the first time he went down on me. Every single orgasm he wrought from me that night.

"Maybe you need reminding of a few things," he says, close enough now that he circles me, looking me up and down. "Like what the fuck I'll do to you when you look this good."

Weston stops walking, directly behind me, and I feel the warmth of his body against my back as he invades my personal space, but nowhere near as much as I want him to. His fingers trail up my thigh, across the fishnet, teasing the delicate flesh as they travel up until they reach the hem of my tiny shorts. He slips a finger beneath the tight seam, running it over my ass cheek, taking his time to appreciate the outfit.

"Want my tongue beneath these shorts," he growls.

When he pulls his finger out of the fabric it snaps against my skin with a loud noise and I jump at the sudden sound, letting a moan out at this new side of him.

His hands come down on my shoulders, moving down and over my chest from above until he's gripping one breast in each hand. Weston lowers his mouth to my ear and rumbles a deep, throaty noise that I feel straight in my core.

"Want these tits in my face while I fuck you."

He keeps his hands roving, splaying them across my taut stomach and down the bare skin there until he's pushing the tips of his fingers into the top of the waistband of my shorts. He runs them over my fishnet-covered skin teasingly, taunting me. The response in my body is instant. Stomach dipping, core clenching, nipples peaking. I want him in a way I've never wanted anyone else.

"Want these hot little stockings on while I make you come," he whispers, taking the lobe of my ear between his teeth before running his lips down the column of my neck, over my shoulder and across my back, up to my neck once more, burying his face in my hair as chills break out across my flesh.

Moaning, I'm so focused on what his mouth is doing I don't notice how quickly he withdraws his hands from my shorts and snaps up both of my wrists in his grip.

"And I want these hands tied while I do it all," he growls, spinning me around, arms held high over my head.

Weston marches me backward, controlling my movements with his entire body as he takes me to the wall in between the bay doors. All I can see is his strong jawline, the golden skin of his neck leading down to his broad chest, covered in a dark, charcoal tee as he manhandles my arms and hands, something cold colliding with my wrists. When I hear the metallic jangle, I realize it's the chains from the bay door that he's using to wrap around my wrists and secure me in place.

I do my best to keep my breathing steady, knowing we're on the verge of a fantasy I never thought I'd see come to life. One where I give full control to someone else and enjoy every moment.

In moments he has me just where he wants me. Weston steps back to admire his handiwork, pulling gently on my arms to make sure they can't get free from whatever he's done to them. They're pulled tight enough to be held high, secure, but not taking any of my weight off of my legs. They might go numb from the position, but it doesn't hurt, what he's done.

He's like my favorite waking dream brought to life right now, just enough domination in his glare to turn me on without making me scared.

Weston has earned my trust in the six weeks I've known him, and I'm willing to explore the fantasies I've never been able to with anyone else because it's him. Tied up, under his control, it's everything I've let myself dream of, but yet to experience. One major, major, pin on my "Shit to Do" board that he's checking off for me.

"You're going to stay right there," he tells me, voice firm, finger pointed at me, as his other hand unbuttons his jeans to leave room for what's already trying to break free from his fly. "Come when I let you. Swallow my cum when I tell you. And scream when you need to."

My eyes glaze over, lips parting in desire as I watch him like this. If it weren't for that messy blond hair, that glint in the thin ring of green still in his eyes, I almost wouldn't recognize the man he is right now.

"What happened to my Boy Scout?" I ask him, taunting him.

"He's fucking gone for the night, angel. Tonight you're getting the devil who took his place."

I moan, head falling back against the wall and knees knocking together as my pussy floods.

Weston smirks at me, and it's a dangerous look. His eyes flit to the machines next to us, and I realize there are two there but I only recognize one of them. It's got red and black cables running from it, huge clips on the ends that are used to jump car batteries. This beast is an industrial model that you can't get at your local store. It could probably jump start a semi.

As for what it could do to little ol' *me*?

My face heats, a drop of sweat running down the small of my back despite the chill in the air.

That glint in his eyes hardens, sharpening as he walks to the machine, hands running over the cables. He unclips one from where it's hanging on the cart and squeezes the handle a couple of times, showing me the toothy jaws and how much force it takes to hold it open.

My mouth pops open as I imagine him putting those on my nipples, and I can't decide if I love the idea or if it terrifies me. I think it might be both.

Am I soaking wet? Yes.

Do I think I could take it? No.

He's not going to turn that thing on while I'm hooked up to it, is he?

I've heard of electroplay, but I'm not sure I'm ready for that tonight.

Smirking, Weston clips the cable back onto the stand. "Just

warmin' you up, darlin'. We'll save that for another night. I've got other plans for you tonight."

A whimper leaves me. Deliciously cruel of him to tease me with way more than I could take, and now I'm dying to know what he has in store for me tonight.

He takes a step past the cart with the jump starter on it to get to the other machine. The one I don't recognize, with the hoses. He leans down, flicks a switch, and a loud rumbling starts up, so intense I can feel it vibrating through the wall behind me and the chains I'm strung up by.

"Know what this is, darlin'?" he asks me, picking up the thin hose that comes out of that machine and holding it between two fingers so I can watch.

I shake my head at him, clueless. I might know my way around my own van, but I've never worked in an auto shop before. I couldn't tell you what two-thirds of the equipment in here is for, if that.

Weston presses the hose between my legs, against the fabric of my shorts right between my folds, and I gasp at the sudden contact. He must push something that I can't see, because along with a deafening burst of noise, the hose jerks so violently I scream at the contact against my clit, even through the layers of clothes that separate us.

"Look at you, already screaming when you need to. You listen so well, Amelia."

Gasping for breath, my head falls down, system still shocked from the sudden burst of that contact, and I hang, limp, trembling as I try to recover from the jolt of pleasure.

"You keep this up, you're going to do just fine, angel."

Weston removes the hose, humming as he runs his hand along my shorts, right over my pussy, soothing me with his touch. Mewling softly, I feel him pull the material of my shorts to the side and stick his fingers inside, weaving through the openings in the fishnet stockings to check on me.

"Fuck, darlin'. You liked that, didn't you?"

He pulls his fingers out and holds them up in front of my face so I can see what I already know is there.

My desire shines on his fingers, beneath the glare of the spotlight that's pointed right at us.

"My girl likes to get a little freaky, huh? Don't be scared to use your safe word if you need to."

All I do is whimper, fascinated by this version of him.

Weston wipes his fingers on my lips, smearing my arousal on my own mouth roughly, then leans in to kiss it off of me. His tongue presses past my lips, letting me taste what he's doing to me, and my eyes flutter shut, my thighs clamp together, savoring the fresh rush of heat between them.

If he could only see how pebbled my nipples are right now, I know he'd take them in his mouth, and for a moment I curse my choice of outfit. What I wouldn't do to feel his mouth on all of me right now.

He pulls back too soon, and I groan at the lack of contact.

Like he's instructing me, Weston holds the hose up in front of our faces, and says, "This is called an air compressor. Does all sorts of shit in the shop. Tonight, it's got a new job. It's gonna get you off."

Jaw hanging just enough so my lips are parted, I watch this beautiful man transform into an actual beast in front of my eyes.

He presses something on the nozzle end of the hose, and I can *see* the burst of air that comes out of it. The noise alone is so loud it hurts my ears, but the pressure coming out of that thing could probably knock me over if I wasn't strung up.

My eyes feel like they belong on an anime doll they're so damn round, and he must read the uncertainty on my face because he bends over, turning a knob on the machine before standing back up again.

"Don't worry, angel. I'm not going to hurt you."

He pushes the trigger again and it blows out another puff, much less violent than the first ones.

"I know," I tell him softly, licking my lips at the fire in his eyes. The potential of what's in his hands.

"Let's see how many puffs it takes for you to come," he says, mouth twitching up as he drops to his knees in one motion. A scuffing sound against the cement floor makes me realize he's wearing kneepads. This motherfucker planned every bit of this.

Weston kneels between my feet, spreading my legs out to fit his body right where he wants it. I watch, so eager for whatever he has in mind, as he presses one palm against the inside of my thigh, holding me open for him as he lines up the other hand, positioning the nozzle.

Holding it a good six inches or more away from my pussy, still covered by the fishnets and my shorts, Weston touches the trigger so briefly it barely goes off, just a quick blast of air, over in a flash. It's powerful enough that it nearly triggers an orgasm instantly.

I moan loudly, not worrying about trying to keep it in. My stomach flips, tugging with need as molten desire pools, hot and low in my abdomen.

"Fuck that's insane," I tell him, breathless.

"That's one," he counts off. And he presses the trigger again, for longer.

My legs shudder, nipples at full attention, goosebumps all over from the intensity of the pleasure that brings.

"Fuck!" I scream the word, and he smiles at me, a wicked thing.

The orgasm building from this treatment is going to be violent, nothing sweet about it.

"Two," he says, and he presses it again.

I feel my skin flutter beneath the pressure of the air flow, and he jiggles the hose in his hand this time so it feels like I'm being finger fucked by a goddamn ghost of porn star past.

Another curse leaves my lips, and I don't have the breath to scream it this time. I can barely get air, gasping, bent over as much as my restraints allow, watching Weston work on me from below.

"There's three."

Blasts four, five, and six nearly wrench my soul from my body. Each one could make me come in and of itself, but he turns it off so fast every time I'm left panting, on the edge of breaking, going mad from his brand of torture.

"Please!" I cry out. "Give me more."

"More pressure?" he asks, brows up.

"No." I shake my head adamantly. "I'll die with more pressure. Just give me a whole second of it like that."

His head tilts to one side, thinking it over.

"Thing is, I'm kinda having fun watching you shake and tremble for me just like this. I'm not in any hurry here, darlin'. We've got a couple days, at least, before anyone's gonna come looking in the shop."

My knees go weak at the image of being here, at his mercy, strung up in chains for another day or two.

"Far as I can tell, I could keep you here this whole time, never letting you come, just keeping you on the brink until your pussy drips right through those hot little shorts you're wearing and you're so turned on you'll come from a single little breath anywhere near your cunt."

Tears brim my eyes at the picture he paints. "You wouldn't," I gasp.

"Nah," he says, easy smile back on his gorgeous face. "If you wanna come, you're gonna come, angel. How could I not reward you when you're being so good for me?"

He reaches up with the hand that isn't controlling the nozzle and pinches my unpierced nipple, rolling it between his thumb and finger through the shirt. My head falls back, pleasure burning a trail from my nipple to my clit, it's like a hotkey to getting me off. His hand pulls back just before it gives me what I need and I could sob at the loss of his touch.

I get another puff of air, this one a little longer, but still just shy of enough to give me the release I'm aching for.

Weston hears me falling apart, damn near crying at the way he's bringing me to the edge without letting me fall over, time after time.

"What do you want?" he asks me. He always asks me what I want. So fucking thoughtful. Even when he's the one in control and I'm at his mercy, it's all about *me*.

"To come," I tell him, without a second thought.

"Mmm," he groans, pressing the sound into my thigh, lips on my flesh, before biting the skin there gently. "I want that too," he says, admiring the marks he left in my skin.

Weston leans forward, pressing his tongue to the leathery material of my shorts, and licks a trail up my pussy, pushing in with his tongue enough to separate my lips and reach my clit, even through the fabric.

My legs shake around his upper body, and he gives me a filthy grin as he feels it.

So often when we're together it's like he can't even take the time to remove my clothes. He needs me so bad he starts with them still on and in his way. I hope that never changes.

Shoving his fingers beneath the hem, he yanks on the fabric, pulling it to the side so he can watch for himself. "Fuck, you're a mess right now, Amelia."

"So clean me up," I demand, praying he does.

His tongue comes out and I watch as he slowly plunges it into me, through a wide hole in the fishnets, soaking in everything my pussy's been giving him. Those gorgeous green eyes close tight, and the moan he makes rumbles against my pussy in a way that feels like the start of an avalanche. I'm so close, if he gives me just a little more, *anything* more, I'll fall, and it'll just keep going and going. Shit, it might never end, he'll bury me in pleasure and I won't complain.

"Please," I beg him.

He doesn't answer with words, but with his mouth. His tongue licks a path through my pussy and then he presses the flat of it against my clit, hard. My legs jerk, I'm so fucking stimulated and I scissor forward, the chains yanking me back by the wrists, clanking as they do.

His mouth moves back down to my core, spearing my entrance and fucking me with his tongue. Once his eyes shut, slamming closed, it only takes me a second to figure out why. He's let some of the material cover me up again, and with his tongue still buried in me he brings the hose back up and gives the trigger a long, long press.

Air crashes against my clit through the layers as his tongue devours me, and I'm done for. Body tingling, my orgasm crashes into me, coursing through me like a tsunami, barreling me over with pleasure that feels like it takes over every single nerve in my system. There is only one signal going to my brain right now—no dark past I'm running from, no bad memories flickering behind my eyes, not even my pessimist has any critiques on this moment—it's nothing but pleasure, and I never want the moment to end.

I can't help the noises I make as I come, or the fact that I have no control over what's happening to my body, legs jerking, kicking, as he fights to keep me in place while he milks the orgasm from me, forcing me to ride the entire thing out rather than cutting it short by letting off on any of it.

Pretty sure I visit other planets, entirely different solar systems or galaxies as I come back down to earth, dangling from the chains—legs long since given out—Weston rising from between my legs to hold me as I come down from the most insane release of my life.

When my murmuring becomes more coherent once again, he pulls back, pushing some hair behind my ear as he watches me. "For the record, that took eight puffs," he says, an easy, teasing smile gracing his lips. "Good girl for screaming when you needed to, and coming when I let you," he praises me. His words send flutters through me, a tingling warmth that spreads throughout my center at hearing I did well for him.

But as the fuzz in my head clears, I remember that was only two of the three things he wanted me to do.

"When do I get to swallow your cum?" I ask, somehow mustering the strength for words.

"When I tell you to," he says, slapping my ass without enough force to hurt, just enough to jolt me back to the present, out of my hazy, post-orgasmic reverie. "But first, you're going to come again."

His lips close around my nipple through the shirt I'm wearing, teeth tugging on my piercing outside of it, and I know tonight is going to be one for the Pinterest board. An adventure more fun than anything van life has ever offered me.

19
Weston

Christening the garage felt like a rite of passage. The sweetest form of revenge.

It's put a big enough smile on my face that I can even welcome my brother back from New York without wanting to deck him. All I have to do is look at the bit of wall in between the bay doors, his precious equipment for the shop that got some new and creative uses that night—most of the weekend, really—and I feel better, just like magic.

"Hey," Wyatt says, dropping his bag in the office with a *thunk* and stepping back out onto the sawdust-covered concrete of the main floor to meet with me on what happened while he was gone.

At least, in regards to the vehicles I worked on. He doesn't need to know *all* of what went down here.

"When did you start carrying a bag?" I ask him.

He scoffs, as good as an eye roll from him. "My wife got it for me a while back."

"Explains why it's got taste," I say, bouncing my head from side to side.

"Listen, can we fucking talk?" Wyatt goes right into it, and there goes my good mood.

Not the biggest fan of confrontation, but I don't see a way out of this either, so I just nod, shoving my hands in the pockets of my cargo pants.

I lean back on the car behind me, crossing one leg over the other, and he mirrors my position from a few feet away, letting the silence stretch between us for blissful seconds until he breaks it.

"You can't even make it to family dinner on time because you're too busy fucking some girl. How is this any different than high school?"

If Amelia were here, I'm not sure she wouldn't sock him for that, and my stomach drops at the thought.

"I'm into her, man!" I yell the words. "I'm into her! For the first time in my godforsaken life, I actually caught feelings. Okay?"

"Feelings for her mouth, or for her?"

I roll my eyes, crossing my arms over my chest and clenching my fists to stop from socking him with them. "Rich, coming from the guy who almost knocked me out for mentioning his sex life."

"That was for mentioning my *wife*."

"Then you should know not to talk about Amelia like that," I counter, brow furrowed.

"So you *are* into her?" he questions.

"What about that am I not making clear?"

"I dunno, it's just... It's you. You sorta have an MO, Wes."

He uses the nickname he knows I can't stand, his better half not here to jab an elbow into his ribs and make him change course. My eyes narrow on his with more heat than usual. He's trying to get under my skin, like he always does, but this time it might be working.

"Has it occurred to you that I want her to stay too? That I've been working since the first night I found her on the side of the road to make her feel safe here, show her it could be worth sticking around? That she might want to be here with me? I know you only see the fucking worst in me, but sometimes I'm not that bad, okay?"

"I don't think you're *bad*," he hedges, looking everywhere in the garage except for at me, as the uncomfortable tension between us ratchets.

"Well, sorry I can't be perfect like you, Wyatt."

His gaze narrows on mine, fuming now. "Me? You're the perfect one. Fucking golden boy of the family. Everyone's favorite Grady."

I scoff. "Yeah, okay. That why you've hated me for twenty damn years? Because I was more popular?"

"I don't *hate* you." His grumble dies off into a barely audible tone by the end. Even he doesn't believe the words enough to get them out.

"You just hate talking to me, being around me, sharing blood with me, that it?"

I tick each item off on a different finger as I call them out. He doesn't say anything more, so I do.

"When are you going to stop holding it against me? Huh?"

Eyes so similar to my own flash back up to me, a sea of unspoken emotion raging in them. It's time to get it out.

"The divorce, Wyatt, let it out!"

That breaks the dam. My brother goes off. "I busted my ass to get us through that time. All you did was make it harder on Mom."

"What, by loving her? Making her laugh?"

"By being a needy son of a bitch!"

"Is this what you've been holding against me all these years? That I cried when our parents got divorced? That I needed my mother's love? What, you think I'm a pussy because I needed a hug?"

"I was out working, trying to put food on the table for us before Daniel came along. And you made her life harder, not easier, Weston."

Twenty years of space between us because of a grudge over my reaction to the divorce? I know he's always had a low opinion of me, but this might be the first time I actually have one of him.

"I was thirteen, Wyatt! Thirteen! A child. Too young for a job, hadn't developed a sense of responsibility yet. Still had my heart, unlike you. What was I supposed to do? Turn tricks on the corner for money? All I had to offer her was smiles, all I could do was give her a reason not to cry. I'm not going to apologize for having an emotional response to the most devastating thing kids can go through. But I tried too."

Wyatt runs a hand through his dark hair, spilling some over his forehead in the process as he gets out his frustration.

"If you wanted to help, you could've done shit around the house or mowed some fucking lawns or something, West. It's not that hard."

"That's you, Wyatt, that's not me. *You're* the guy who shows up quietly for the people he cares about. I'm the one who lightens the mood. We're not all made from the same mold, and I wish you saw what's good about that, instead of resenting me for it."

His shoulders slump, like my words hit him hard.

"I don't need you to be *me*," he says.

Maybe he hasn't given this as much thought as I have over the years, with him being so preoccupied with losing the love of his life and all, but this is something I've deconstructed in my mind over and over again, and I know what I know.

"Yes, you do," I insist. "You do. You've always held it against me that I'm not you. And here's the kicker." My volume rises, a hit of insanity showing through as my voice cracks on the words.

I fling my arms up in the air and let them fall back down on my thighs with a slap.

"The fucking punchline is that I always wished I *was* you, Wyatt. My big brother, who always had his shit together, who met 'the one' in high school, and always knew what he wanted out of life."

Wyatt's jaw clenches tight, probably to stop from dropping, and he watches me intently.

"It's been the bane of my existence, never being able to find *anyone* out there who made me feel a goddamn thing. Until Amelia, I thought I was broken. I thought I couldn't feel the things you feel. That I didn't have it in me." One fist pounds my chest, causing my words to rumble as I continue. "And the one thing that's been ruining my life all these years is what you've held against me. What you've *used* against me, like ammo. My biggest weakness is your greatest strength. And now I've finally found someone that makes me feel something, and you're determined to keep us apart so that *I* don't fuck it up, because that's all you think I can do."

Wyatt's eyes turn glassy as my emotion leaks through my voice.

"For once in my life, Wyatt, I have someone that *means* something to me. Something worth trying to succeed at. I don't need you making it any harder on me, man."

My brother covers his face with his hands, and I think he might be trying to contain himself. I see his chest shake, inflating with a deep breath or two, and when his arms drop back down, it's regret shining through his eyes.

Breathing heavily, my chest rises and falls, some sort of peace coursing through me at finally airing this out between us.

If he wants to hate me for the rest of our lives because I'm not as good as him, at least now he'll know I wish I were.

"I never knew," he says. He clears his throat, but the words still sound unnatural when he says, "I'm sorry, man."

"Yeah, 'cause you assumed I'm just some fucking idiot you had to share your toys with when we were young," I bite back.

Wyatt shakes his head, and his voice cracks when he speaks. "No, you're my fucking brother, West."

It's more than I thought I'd ever hear from him, a bigger apology than I could've hoped for, and emotion swells in me at the meaning behind the words. I hear what he's not saying.

He pulls me in for an actual hug, not even a bro hug. For once it feels like we really are brothers in every sense.

Pulling back, he turns around to give me a second to wipe my eyes, and I'm thankful for it. After a moment, he clears his throat again and speaks, voice thick. "If you guys are *together* together, maybe you should, like, bring her to family dinner and shit." His booted foot toes the ground, scuffing along the concrete flooring.

"That you saying that, or your better half?" I ask.

"Both."

I'll bet my Charger his wife sent him in today with the order to invite Amelia to family dinners and make shit right with me or he's sleeping in the chicken coop, but still, progress is progress.

"I'll ask her then."

"Good."

"Good," I echo.

Even the caveman in front of me has to feel how awkward this is.

"Thanks for taking care of the shop," he mutters, trying to branch out into using more than one syllable at a time, unfamiliar territory for him.

This is probably about two months' worth of dialogue for him, he might need to go on vocal rest after this.

His affliction must be contagious, because all I say is, "Yeah."

Wyatt takes a few steps, looking around the garage, like a safe conversation topic might be hiding in plain sight. Hands in his pockets, he finally says, "Got a text from Ronnie over the weekend. He's giving up on fixing his old motorbike, I think he was holding out hope I'd be able to help him on the weekends, but with the baby, and Gonzo being gone... Anyway, he wanted to see if I could fit it in here." Wyatt looks around the shop, the vehicles in every direction, holding his hands out, like it speaks for itself. "You got time in your—"

I can practically hear him biting back words that would normally come naturally, something scathing like "busy schedule," to play nice.

"—life to fit that job in for me?" His natural inclination to be a prick must win out, because he tacks on, "Or do you only work on vehicles for people you're fucking?"

My eyes narrow on him in warning, and he holds up his hands. "Below the belt, I'm sorry."

I flip him off. He chuckles, the air lightening instantly, which is new for us so I keep it going.

"If either of us are fucking Ronnie, it's definitely not me. I've heard the man's poetry about your dick," I say, laughing. "And you could do worse in a best friend. He's like your junk's personal hype man."

Now he flips me off. "Dear Lord, don't remind me of his lack of boundaries. I still won't camp with him." Wyatt shakes his head, and his scruff twitches. "Listen, I'll pay you, obviously. But I don't really have time for the job with all this." He waves a hand around the garage at all of the vehicles waiting for service.

I think over the offer, trying not to be persuaded by the

lifting in my chest at the thought of working on bikes again. Before I left town, it's what I thought I'd end up doing with my life. I have a good time with most things I do, but shit, things with small engines are just more fun to work on than anything else that pays legally.

"Besides," he says gruffly, talking to the floor more than me. "You're better at small engines anyway."

"I'm sorry, what?" I say loudly, cupping one hand around my ear. "Think you're gonna need to repeat that, possibly on video."

"I'm not saying it again," he mutters, but I could swear his lips are twitching beneath all that scruff. "Are you gonna take the job or not?"

I put my hand out for his, and he claps his palm into mine.

"Yeah, bro. I'm taking the job."

20
Amelia

Chickens squawk, zipping through an elaborate fenced-in maze among the bright grass of Wyatt and Rory's immense backyard, as I make my way to the picnic table.

"Henrietta, don't get your hopes up," Rory chides, shaking a finger at one of the birds. "Wyatt isn't touching you again tonight, you're in there till the morning, missy."

A ruffle of feathers, the flapping of some wings, and the birds all disappear in what almost sounded like a huff back into their playground of sorts.

"She's such a spoiled thing," Rory tsks. "Obsessed with my husband."

"That so?" Wyatt asks, slinking up behind her, his stubble grazing her cheek as his arms cage around her middle. "That makes three of the ladies in this house then."

Rory rolls her eyes, pats his cheek, and takes off again, leaving him standing there as she leads the way to the wooden table and benches.

It's hard not to gawk at their yard. It's so big it must be measured in acres. Actually, I think this might qualify as a park.

The grassy lawn is obnoxiously green, a patch of wildflowers at the far end lending a sweet aroma to the warm evening air, all hemmed in by the thick woods of their own private forest. I've never seen anything like it back in Minnesota, that's for sure. It's straight out of a storybook.

Makes me wish I could show my mom. Her tulips did come in gorgeous this year, just last week she sent the pictures, but she would lose her mind over the greenery and wildflowers here.

Not to mention the house itself, which is completely dreamy. Even more so when Rory told me the story all about it.

These Grady men are something else.

My very own Grady man (the best one, and it's not even close) comes running up behind me, catching up to me and taking my hand, escorting me to the table. The bucket of ice and beers in his hand *thunks* down onto the wooden planks of the table and he straddles the bench, patting his lap with a cheek-splitting grin in my direction.

"Are you serious?" I whisper through my teeth. "Your whole family is here."

"Not my *whole* family," he says. "My mom, stepdad, dad, and stepmom aren't here. Yet."

My eyes fly open, wider than before, and he laughs. "Just playin' darlin'. They won't be here tonight. Just sit down."

I let him goad me into it, plopping down across his thighs, the sundress Rory brought me back from her trip to New York dusting my upper thighs as I sit. I gasped when I saw the box with my name on it at Weston's the night the brothers made up. It's almost white in color, with small pink flowers, thin straps across the shoulders, and some detail around the bust that is incredibly flattering. If this is the kind of stuff she finds there, I can understand why she goes so often. I love my cozy cropped tees, but this makes me feel a kind of beautiful that's unfamiliar to me. Several levels above being comfortable in my own skin, this outfit demands that I'm celebrated.

Wyatt, Rory, and her stepfather are in and out of the house, setting the table, while Weston and I sit outside, and guilt claws at my insides.

"Should we be helping?"

"Nah," he says, ease radiating from his relaxed pose. "You're a first-timer tonight. That gets you guest status."

The twitch of his lips makes my insides churn for different reasons.

"And you?" I ask.

"I'm showing you the ropes," he says, sliding a hand up my bare thigh, fingertips brushing the inside of my leg and causing an instant reaction just a bit north. Squirming on his lap, his eyes heat in warning.

"Careful, darlin'. You're about to start something you might not want me to finish here at the table."

"Well don't turn me on then," I mutter back to him, as footsteps traipse across the lawn, grass rustling. A dragonfly darts across the yard to stay safe, but I'm stuck right here, seated on a lap I've ridden so many times in the last few weeks, muscle memory alone is threatening to take over for me.

"You're one to talk," he says, eyes trained on my breasts, practically poking him in the eye from this angle. "So fucking hot in this thing I can barely sit here with my hands to myself. Gonna spend this entire meal planning out every single thing I'm gonna do to you when we get ho—"

Weston doesn't get to finish his sentence because I clap a hand over his mouth when Lexi and Rory are within hearing distance.

He mumbles against my hand, and the girls laugh as they approach.

"We have that problem too," Rory says with a knowing look.

Alexis tries to cover up the longing with a roll of her eyes—her go to—but I catch it and feel a twinge of empathy for making her feel lonely with my happiness. It's the way I've felt everywhere I've gone up until now, and I know the unfairness of it well.

You never want to make other people feel bad for finding their joy, but after long enough, every sultry look between lovers becomes a stab in the heart.

If only she knew that my joy is only temporary. That if my secret comes out I'd be run out of town, and forgive me, I'm just trying to enjoy this while I can.

Weston winks at me when I finally pull my hand back before leaning in to press a soft kiss to the side of my throat, on the delicate spot where it joins my shoulder. I try to hide the chills it gives me, but I don't think I get away with it.

Rory just smirks, but Lexi scoffs. "Ugh, this isn't fair. Now everyone around me is loved up and getting laid."

The bench creaks as she plunks down on it. The far end, away from us.

I shoot her puppy dog eyes and hold my hands out to her.

She tosses her head, wild curls tumbling around her with the movement. "I can't be near you two, you're sickening right now."

Weston cackles, hemming me in with an arm around my middle, and grabs a couple beers with his other hand. I try not to focus on the patterns his fingers are tracing on my skin through the delicate fabric of the dress, doing my best to keep my attention on Lexi and our host across from me, trying to stay engaged in their conversation rather than wrapped up in West.

"You're full of it," Rory laughs, waving a hand at Lexi. "You were their biggest cheerleader before they got together."

"You were their second," she retorts, like it's an insult, making a face that one would only pull at a sibling.

"Obviously," Rory says with a catlike smile. "I wanted to poach them both for the Heights. I couldn't be happier at how this is working out."

She winks at me, and I'm reminded again that she's my hero.

I push away the pessimist in me that wonders how long this facade can last. If, when my grant application comes back approved, I'll decide that's enough playing house, it's time to hit the road again.

Luckily, Rory keeps talking, distracting me from the shadows that live within me. "Besides, Lexi, I hear there's fresh meat in town."

Lexi's faces visibly darkens, like clouds rolling in, or maybe lightning struck and that's her hair starting to stand on end.

I'm distracted by the drag of the pads of Weston's fingers across my bare skin, then over the dress again, but I try to focus.

"You *hear* that, do you?" Lexi's teeth are clenched, eyes violent as she has a wordless conversation with her sister that none of the rest of us are privy to. "Could that be because *you* got him here? And stuck him on me? And now I have to work with the most infuriating man-child on the planet, because you gave me no other choice?"

The man beneath me pops the tops on the beers, the bright scent of hops making my mouth water as he places one within reach for me and taking a swig of his own.

Rory sips her white wine, not opting for beer tonight. I wonder if it's because of the new place that just opened downtown, Smoky Sips. We're supposed to do a girls' night there soon, maybe she's prepping her palate.

Me, at a girls' night. With friends.

Pinch me.

She gives Lexi an innocent expression and bats her lashes a couple of times to really sell it. "Whatever do you mean, dear sister? I got you a talented chef, straight from New York. The cafe is going to be so much better off with him behind the line."

"You got me a sandwich maker from a bodega!"

"Wait." Weston perks up beneath me but his fingers don't stop teasing me through my dress, my breaths coming shallow. "*The* sandwich maker? From *the* bodega?"

Clearly I'm missing something because Rory's face turns bright red and Lexi screams a laugh, pointing at her sister in accusation.

"Wilder is *that* man! How did I not put this together sooner?"

I turn to Weston in confusion, and he gives me a subtle shake of his head. "I'll explain later," he whispers in my ear, and the graze of his lips against my skin brings a flutter to my insides and a chill to my flesh, despite the comfortable—okay, hot—temperature.

The girls continue bickering, Rory pleading with Lexi in hushed tones as Wyatt brings out their daughter, just woken up from a late nap and clinging to her father in a way that makes my eyes sting.

It's a mild form of chaos as the men carry the dishes of piping hot food from the house, setting out the family style meal on the table.

I quickly learn that family dinner at the Grady cabin isn't a formal affair. The food was brought back in a cooler with dry ice from New York, and it's delicious too. The conversation is noisy, hilarious, and overly personal. Very little seems to be off the table in terms of subjects up for discussion, and the jibes flying between both sets of siblings makes my head spin trying to volley between them all, like my own personal tennis match. The only person who's more quiet than me at this table tonight is Wyatt, but when he speaks, it counts.

My house was fun once upon a time, but it was never like

this. Love pouring from everyone present, even with the ribbing and some jokes at the other's expense. My brother and I certainly were never close like these four are.

Even the older man keeps up with them, digging into each of them as called for, with lots of *oohs* and *aahs* coming from the witnesses every time he gets one in.

Weston keeps me in his lap while we both eat, and he manages not to get anything on my beautiful new dress. He sneaks in kisses to my shoulders and the nape of my neck every so often, dragging his lips over my skin for a moment longer than necessary each time. I wiggle my butt in his lap just enough so that he gets the point, something hard nudging my ass from beneath me.

"Careful," he whispers in my ear. "You wake the beast, you're the one who's gonna have to tame it."

I turn around and give him a quick kiss, nipping at his lip, and his mouth splits into a wide grin, dimples popping out on either side.

It's easier than I ever thought it would be to have a partner, being with him. His family are so supportive (well, once he screwed Wyatt's head on straight at least), and so welcoming. This is nowhere near as scary as I pictured a milestone like "meeting the family" being.

As long as they don't grill me like the partner's families do in all the rom-coms, we should be fine. All they need to do is not ask where I'm from, what my family does, or anything else that could paint the picture of my past. Easy, right?

Weston's warm breath against my ear distracts me, bringing me back into the moment. "You do realize every time I lean forward to take a bite, I'm just looking down your dress, picturing your tight little nipples begging for my mouth, right?"

The words are so low, so quiet, no chance anyone else hears them, but the bastard has me so turned on I could probably come from readjusting on his leg right now. And he doesn't stop there.

"Nobody here knows your kinky little secrets, do they? You look so innocent in that dress, angel. If only they could see what's beneath it."

Weston slides one calloused hand to the far side of my leg and up my body, away from the eyes of everyone else at the table, only the garden nymphs and maybe Henrietta the Eighth can see what he's doing to me.

Dragging his hand up my ribcage, he lets it wander, teasing the side of my breast as he keeps whispering. "What you look like riding my cock as I pull on that nipple ring and watch your pussy clench."

That's my limit, apparently. I let out something like a chirp and sit up quickly, pulling away from his wandering fingers, his lips, before I fall so deep into his touch I forget where we are and give in to grinding on his leg like I'm in heat. That would be an embarrassment I couldn't come back from.

So I pay attention, I try harder to follow the conversation around us, I laugh at the jokes, I genuinely have a great time with these people. But through it all, my focus keeps shifting to the hardness beneath me, the wetness soaking the new underwear I'm wearing for him tonight. All the ways I want to get payback on him when we're alone.

It's not long before Weston leans forward once again, grabbing a fresh beer from the ice bucket, but now I know it's just an excuse to look down my dress again. Bubbles still fizzle and pop near the surface of his last bottle, for crying out loud, he doesn't need a new one.

His cock rubbing against me, his hips moving with the forward motion to make *sure* I feel it just confirms my theory, and I struggle to sit still through it all, counting down to when I can exact my revenge.

When he's leaned back once more, his lips find my ear again. "Staring at your tits all night has got me so goddamn hard I'm gonna blow the second you touch me. Maybe the second I touch you. I didn't pay enough for this dress."

A soft gasp comes out before I can stop it. "You bought this?" I ask him.

"Did I forget to mention that?" His lips tilt up, and my eyes follow the motion. "Well, I gave Rory some money to bring me back something I'd enjoy," he says, shoulder popping. "She nailed it. I'm going to enjoy the shit out of ripping this thing off of you."

"Lovebirds!" Lexi's harsh bark interrupts us. "You guys can at least keep it to sexting with your phones beneath the table so the rest of us can pretend we don't notice when you detail everything you're going to do to one another later."

She gives Wyatt and Rory both meaningful stares, and Rory's face heats while Wyatt narrows his eyes at her in a scowl. Rory's stepfather looks away, watching the garden and pretending he can't hear this conversation.

My face falls, tucking into Weston's shoulder as everyone else at the table laughs.

"We've all been there," the graying man across from Lexi says knowingly.

"Ew!" Rory and Lexi both shout at once, faces in varying degrees of shock and outrage as they stare at him.

"What? You think your mom and I didn't fuck like rabb—"

"That's enough!" Rory's boss bitch voice comes out, and the table falls silent for just a moment before laughter breaks out across it, including from me.

"This is so unfair," Lexi whines. "Couldn't you get *me* someone too?" she pleads with her sister.

Rory waggles her brows at her suggestively, and Lexi scoffs almost like a child at whatever the inference is.

"No way." She holds her hand up like a 90s girl but then goes back to wheedling. "If you're not going to get me a fuck buddy—"

Rory covers her ears, as does their stepfather, and Rory singsongs loudly over Lexi until she feels it's safe again. Once she drops her hands, Lexi jumps right back in.

"—you could at least approve my request for more flowers!"

"No commission requests at the dining table," Rory says firmly, scooping more salad onto her plate.

"It would look so pretty with more flowers," Lexi wheedles. "Look how pretty your yard is, with the daffodils and the hyacinth."

"We're not spending any more money on flowers downtown. We have two entire city blocks full of trees and flowers. Plant your own in front of the cafe if you want more."

Lexi growls at her. "I already did, but it needs more! Nora's been asking for them, too, you're gonna make me do hers myself? You're such a flower grinch!"

My stomach doesn't nosedive nearly as much as usual at the mention of anything Christmas-related, I'm so invested in their argument. The best entertainment I've had since finishing catching up on past episodes of *Vengeful Vixens*.

The younger of the two sisters isn't buckling under the pressure. "Do *you* want to review the budgets? Be responsible for the purse strings? Why don't you look at exactly how much we've spent so far on landscaping? I'm not giving it another dime!"

Lexi continues arguing. "It's about to be summer! Most of the flowers along Main will be done for the year, and then in fall those maple trees are going dominate downtown, and—"

Rory cuts her off, "We have plants for all seasons, it looks beautiful, NEXT!"

Even Wyatt can't keep from chuckling, leaning over to kiss

his wife on the temple, their daughter in his arms, as the whole table laughs at the antics that never seem to cease in this family.

And I know I can't stay forever, the past will catch up with me eventually, but damn this is a good place to rest and recharge the part of my soul I've been missing before I have to run again.

21
Weston

WYATT
Why is there a tiny ass print on the wall in between the bay doors?

Did you fuck in my shop?

Answer me

I can see you read these

ME
Hey Wyatt, is my Charger buffed out yet?

What, so this is payback?

At least it wasn't on your fucking priceless classic car.

This time.

But combat boots can do some damage.

🖕

Buff my fucking car out.

Heights Bites is in its first week of being open, and the place is *buzzing*. I take the last open table, in the front corner against the expansive plate glass window overlooking the center of downtown, as I finish texting my brother and wait for my date to join me.

The last couple weeks have been some of the best I can remember. Making bank painting by day, fitting in some motorbike repairs at night (I restored Ronnie's and then a few more requests came in that have kept me busy when I can get over there), and then spending the rest of the night buried in Amelia.

She still spends some time with Van Gogh, but she sleeps with me at my place more often than she doesn't. We haven't labeled things between us, and a part of me can't shake the fear that if I sneeze at the wrong time, she'll run, but hell, things are *good* right now. Actually good. Even Sunday night dinners at my brother's have been fun. Amelia's gone on another girls' night with Rory and Lexi too.

The only low point has been the slew of denial emails I got all at once on the lottery for the fireflies. This is the week they're supposed to start, and not one of the dozen applications I filled out got chosen for the parking pass that would let us into the national park to see them.

Lexi flits around the cafe, tennis shoes squeaking, frizzy hair pulled back in a ponytail, eyes frenzied as she runs table to table, taking orders, refilling glasses, and taking people's payments when they're ready.

Only one other server is here helping her, a middle-aged Black woman who was my teacher in elementary school, Ms. Snow. She keeps pointing at her name tag, telling me to call her Wanda now, but I dunno, still feels disrespectful. Ms. Snow taught every damn kid in my generation, Rory, Wyatt, Lexi, and me included.

Wanda (I'm trying out the name) doesn't use a pad and pen

to take orders, she just remembers everyone's special requests and dietary restrictions, which I'm more and more fascinated by the longer I watch the women work.

It takes about ten minutes before Lexi makes it over to me, a large vinyl-laminated menu in hand. "Sorry, West. Didn't realize you were in my section. What can I get you?"

"I dunno, you haven't handed me a menu yet," I tell her with a smile.

She huffs while handing it to me and starts to walk away.

"Hey, I don't wanna ruin your day, but could you bring another? My date will be here soon."

Lexi's mouth pops open. "Amelia's coming?"

I shake my head side to side.

"If you're seeing someone else, God help you, Weston Alexander Grady, I *will* grab a knife from the back and find a new, creative use for it." Her face flushes when she says it, and I hope she's not getting excited about harming me physically.

"No, no!" I decide to go with protecting the nads rather than the element of suspense or a life-threatening surprise. "My mom is meeting me here soon."

"Oh." Lexi's frown relaxes, brows removing themselves from her eye sockets, and a smile comes out instead. "How lovely!" Turning on one sneakered foot, she scoots off to tend to another table.

Looking over the menu, I take in the staple diner dishes, mostly burgers and handheld sandwiches, though with some twists that feel a little more sophisticated than I expected to see. Back when this place was owned and operated by the Weiss girls' father when we were all growing up, it was pretty much nothing but grease on the menu. Roasted red peppers and arugula on a steak sandwich with some fancy sauce definitely wasn't there.

There's also a whole salad section that's not just a handful of lettuce with a couple tomatoes on top, that I have a strong suspicion was Rory's doing.

I'm still marveling over the presence of a candied walnut and strawberry salad when my mom sits down in front of me. The menu is so tall, I didn't even see her approaching over it.

"Mama." Jumping up from the booth seat, I dash around the table to give her a hug.

"Hi, baby boy," she says, eyes crinkling with warmth in the corners. That smile that never fails to come out when she sees me makes an appearance, and I give her one back, loving how her face lights up when I do. I may not be stoic and dependable like Wyatt, but dammit I make my mom happy.

Lexi hustles back to the table, hair messier than it was before somehow, cheeks splotchy and even redder than when I last saw her.

"You good, Lex?" I ask her.

"It's always a great day at Heights Bites," she says, biting the words out.

"I'm not sure if that was supposed to be a joke or a threat," I say.

"Be nice," my mom says, giving Lexi the mom look. "Now, dear, are you getting enough sleep? How about your water intake? Have you had your hormones checked recently?"

"I'm just fabulous, thank you so much, Mrs. Grady."

"Yes, clearly. That's why you forgot that for almost twenty years now, it's Mrs. Suarez."

Lexi stomps a foot, head tipped back to the ceiling as she breathes deeply.

"Of course. Sorry about that. Are we ready to order, Mrs. Suarez?"

"You were going to bring a second menu," I remind her.

A squeal gets strangled in Lexi's throat as she masks a

murderous look with a terrifying smile, and she turns to run off again.

"Actually, never mind," I tell her, calling her back before she can get anywhere and we never see her again, or she spits something poisonous in our food.

My eyes flit to my mom's for a second. "You good with whatever?" I ask her, and she nods.

"Whole menu looks great. We'll take whatever the chef recommends, both of us," I tell Lex, and her nostrils flare out, jaw clenching, but she nods once. "Just no pine nuts for my mom. She's got an allergy," I say as she takes the menu from my outstretched hands, and she's gone.

Good thing this is the only restaurant in town—aka our only choice if we aren't cooking it ourselves—and every customer in here has known Lexi for decades, able to grant her a little grace, because that attitude she's sporting isn't about to win anyone over.

"Well," my mom says, folding her hands on the tabletop. "This place is quite charming. A lot different than I remember it."

Taking in the place, I have to agree. Soft light bounces off of the pale pink walls Amelia and I painted—nearly white, just a hint of color—with a muted tiled floor, a smattering of booths and tables, the tabletops a faux ceramic that gives it a grounded vibe. It's a cute spot.

I'm amazed it's open already. Wilder is the head chef (aka *the* bodega sandwich man) I've heard so much about, and he hasn't been in town very long at all. He must've been busy to get this place going this quickly.

Truthfully, when Lexi is in the back the place is more than pleasant out here. Ms. Snow glides between tables effortlessly, refilling drinks, cracking jokes with patrons, and resetting tables in between guests.

Mostly it's just Lexi's frazzled energy that makes me feel like the roof is going to cave in on us at any second.

Must be stressful for her, having worked in the grocery store since high school, switching careers like this. She'll adapt. I hope.

"They might still be working out some early kinks," I say to Mom, watching as Lexi fumes, heading out of the kitchen with steam billowing behind her. It's not figuratively coming out of her ears, it's literally in a trail behind her as she leaves the doorway to the staff only area and re-enters the dining room. "But it's got promise."

"Nice of you to meet me here for lunch," she says kindly.

"Schedule is lightening up now that I'm almost through the jobs I have lined up for painting," I tell her.

"Are you now?"

She sounds so proud of me, for doing the bare minimum. Does Wyatt get the same favor from her?

"Yeah, downtown is all done now, at least with indoor paint."

I point out a few places to my mom through the window we're sitting by. The facade and window display of each storefront is unique to them, but there's a cohesive energy running between all of downtown that hasn't been there in a decade or more.

"The last couple businesses are all on track to be open in time for the soft opening next week, according to Rory. Then I just have a few more properties off of Main to wrap, but I'm gonna be done here soon," I tell her.

"Does that mean this is goodbye?" she asks.

I reach a hand out across the table and clasp hers in mine, her skin so thin beneath my rougher, calloused fingers. It reminds me that she isn't getting any younger, and I can't bear the comparisons to Rory and Lexi's mom that my mind draws of its own accord.

"I don't think so," I tell her. "Might stick around a while. I've been working on the Charger, and, uh, helping Wyatt out at the garage a bit lately. Working on motorbikes and ATVs and stuff."

You'd think I just told her she won a trip to the Maldives. Her face lights up, eyes bright, and she pats my hand.

"That's wonderful, honey. You two are getting on well, I take it?"

I nod at her in earnest at that. "Yeah, Ma. We actually had a pretty good talk a few weeks ago. I think we're on a good path now."

She gives me a nod of approval, but it didn't come as a surprise to her so I'm guessing she's already heard.

"Did he tell you?" I ask.

"My daughter-in-law did."

"Of course." For someone who hated the town's gossip once upon a time, that girl sure can run her mouth when she wants to. I guess she's a true Smoky Heights native in that way.

"She also told me you're—" my mom leans in, whispering conspiratorially, "—seeing someone."

"Guilty." I hold up one hand, unable to fight my grin.

"Well, that's just wonderful. When do I get to meet her?"

"I'm not sure yet, Mama."

"Well, have you met her parents yet?"

I know things with her mom are complicated. And from what I know, her dad's not in the picture. For the dozenth time, I wonder if that's got anything to do with the little bits she has confided in me, about why she's been on the road all this time. If that's why she feels like she's always a breath away from driving into the horizon and not looking back. And I wonder if I'll ever figure out a way to ask her to open up to me that doesn't spook her.

"Nah, not yet. It's still pretty new."

"Well, you better let me meet her before you meet them. I want dibs on the girl that won my prize of a son over."

She gets another smile from me at that, but our moment is interrupted by Lexi practically dropping our plates on the table. My mom and I pull our hands apart abruptly, and we're lucky we don't get burned.

"Hot plate! HOT PLATE!" Alexis yells as she sets them down gracelessly in front of us.

"And what do we have the honor of trying today, dear?" my mom asks her.

Bless her for asking, because I have a feeling if I tried to Lexi would dump that hot plate in my lap. I'm not sure management should be quite so belligerent with customers, and I make a mental note to ask Rory who the owner is so maybe I can pass on an anonymous message to them that they might want to poke their head in once in a while and make sure their new manager is doing okay.

"This is a house-made five-cheese tortellini with local, farm-to-table pesto," she spouts off from memory. But it's like the memory pisses her off and she spits out every word.

"Wow, that sounds fabulous!" Mom says.

"I don't remember seeing that on the menu," I say, because apparently I am the idiot my brother thinks I am and I forgot how much fun it *isn't* to piss off a Weiss woman.

"Don't. Ask." Lexi turns her back on us and strides off, when I realize we don't even have any silverware.

"I'll grab it," I whisper to Mom, bolting out of my seat to steal two sets from a table in Wanda's section.

"Ms. Snow!" I call out to her, waving them so she sees.

Her head bobs knowingly, already moving to replace the utensils. Tossing one onto the table for her, my mom grabs it and we both dig in.

The noises that come from the other side of the booth are ones a son should *never* have to hear from his own mother.

Then again, I'm enjoying this dish a little more than maybe I should be in public, myself.

One bite in, a shadow falls across our table. A large presence steps close, looming over us, and we both look up. My neck has to tilt farther back than I'd like to take him all in. A giant man in every sense, this guy is tall, broad, muscular, and got a little padding. Not that I'd say that to his face.

He is, as I've heard the girls say, a *big boy*. He's also covered in tattoos, down his arms, across his hands and the backs of his fingers, between the first and second knuckles, but also up his neck, over his throat and even his chin. I'd be willing to bet there's a lot more ink we can't see beneath his chef's jacket too. But with the sleeves pushed up to his elbows, we can see a lot. And there is a *lot* to see with this man.

"You must be Wilder," I say, hand out to shake his.

"Sure am!" His voice booms, deep and rich, for someone who looks even younger than me. I do my best not to flinch from his grip, but I think something crunched that shouldn't have. Flexing my fingers beneath the table after he releases my grip, I try to assess and make sure my hand is still in one piece and I can keep painting as scheduled.

"Wilder Amante, Head Chef. And you are?" Wilder turns to my mother, putting all of his attention on her, and goddammit, I think her eyelids flutter under his charm.

"Virginia Suarez, happily married, thank you for asking." She displays her left hand, wedding ring prominent, and he lets his head fall for show.

"Had to try. I've got a thing for older ladies. Keep this one safe." Looking at me, he jabs a thumb over his shoulder toward my mom with a wide smile.

"Weston Grady," I introduce myself, which gets me a

thump of his oversized palm on my shoulder, jolting my whole body further down into the booth.

I have *zero* idea what to make of this guy.

Looks intimidating as fuck, like a linebacker in an apron, comes off like a giant teddy bear, and hits on my mom all in the span of fifteen seconds.

My brain is confused.

"How are we liking the chef's special?" he asks, arms extended to his sides.

"Oh, it's delectable," my mom says, but I catch her eyes looking at more than the plate of pasta in front of her.

She's literally had one bite and she didn't even try the sauce yet, how does she know?

"Not bad," I tell him, still trying to gauge the town's newest resident and unwilling to go all in on him yet. My primal instincts say he's dangerous, that he's a threat, not to trust the wild smile on his face. Maybe his name suits him.

But my conscience reminds me that Rory knew this guy in New York, at least on a surface level. And she helped get him set up here at the cafe, or maybe it's a diner? There's some sort of background check with the New Heights program, I'm sure she told me something about that, she wouldn't have brought him in if he's the kind of dangerous the alarm in my brain thinks he is.

Urging my instincts toward what my head is telling me, I decide he's good enough to be behind the cooking station at the one and only "real" restaurant the Heights has to offer.

Bottom line is if he stays away from Amelia, I'll have no problems with him, even if some primitive senses deep within me are humming in warning. The man's not my problem.

"So glad you like it," he says, hands on the end of the table now, leaning over to get closer to us, like he's sharing a secret. "That pesto is a family recipe with a secret ingredient, and I grew the basil myself. I convinced the boss to let me start an herb garden, next is gonna be a vegetable garden, if I'm lucky, but she's a tough sell. I gotta keep working on her." He winks at us, and I think my mom *giggles*.

"CHEF!" Lexi's voice could shatter glass and thank God the lunch rush is over and there's few patrons here besides my mother and me at this point.

"Whoops, gotta go," he whispers to us at full volume, and then he lumbers off, back to the kitchen. "Coming, boss!" he hollers out to her as he goes.

Cheeks flushed, my mother looks at me and trills, "Well, he seems interesting."

22
Amelia

"Let's get started," Rory says, stepping around her desk in the New Heights office to take a seat across from me.

I sit in front of her, the optimist in me trying to convince me this is a *good* talk. That her text didn't mean something bad. We're just going over the terms of the grant and what it means.

But if that's the case, why is my stomach sinking further and further down the longer I sit here, her professional façade impenetrable, not the familiar casual elegance I'm used to from her.

"Let's." I try to force my voice to sound chipper, and I hope she doesn't notice the strain in it.

Three family dinners and two girls' nights out might not be enough for her to pick up on things like that from me just yet.

It took Weston less than an hour to learn my tells, but he's clearly one of a kind.

"Your grant paperwork came back with some questions," she says, tone diplomatic and neutral, without a hint of the inviting warmth I've gotten so used to, as she pulls a printout out from somewhere beneath her desk.

My stomach, already hovering somewhere around my

asshole, hollows. I don't think I ever grasped how scary this woman can be. Maybe I still don't.

"What kind of questions?" I ask, my voice even higher pitched than normal.

"Well, one point that needed clarification was your income."

Rory uses a glittering pen to tap at the section I recognize from when she helped me fill out the paperwork. Employer name and wages, and then I had to submit proof of those. That was all factual.

"Mmm?" Words don't seem to be coming to me right now.

"There was concern that your income hasn't been very stable in recent months, that you aren't meeting the minimum threshold to qualify for the grant geared toward remote workers."

"Oh." My voice falls flat.

My work lately has been less than great. That's why Weston let me help him with painting, so he could split his earnings with me and free up his time to work on my engine. But even working with him, it's not like that was exactly a formal job that I can put on the paperwork, and it wouldn't qualify as a remote position, either, so that's no help to me with this.

Unless I want to get a job here more permanently and swap the grant I'm applying for... I guess that was a fun pipe dream while it lasted.

Nope, today's a day the pessimist in me is going to win. The optimist got too long of a run anyway. I should buckle up now before this ride dips any lower because, knowing my luck, it can go a *lot* lower. Like six feet under.

Rory continues, still brusque with me in a way that confirms half of me was right. The shitstorm is just beginning. "That doesn't mean we can't still get you approved for that one. And there are other options. If you decide to take a job locally, or open your own business here, we do have other grants you may qualify for."

Why does she sound so detached? Is this how she always sounds and I've never noticed?

Or are the alarm bells ringing in my head indicative of real danger here? The kind I haven't had to run from in so long I almost let myself get comfortable for a minute.

"Now, I know when you filed this I said you didn't have to make up your mind until the approval was back," she continues, "but I would strongly suggest you not resubmit your application, nor swap to another grant type, without the intention of residing here permanently."

Her brows rise ever so slightly, in challenge.

Does she know?

She knows *something* or she wouldn't be acting so distant from me.

My question now is *what* does she know?

She can't know everything, she hasn't told me to get out of the Heights and never come back.

"These grants are limited in number and intended for those who are serious about contributing to the local community, the society, and economy that exists within Smoky Heights."

"Sure," I tell her, extremities going numb. I think my vision might be blurring, too, if I were to look too closely at it.

"I have to ask you if that's your intention, Avery Flint."

My eyes slam shut, and I rock back in my seat.

"Or is it Amelia Marsh?"

Rory continues down the list of names that I've used over the past nine years, her finger trailing the sheet in front of her, up and down as she reads them off. More than a half dozen in all.

I stop her before she can get to my birth name.

"Please," I say, a shaky whisper.

My nerves should be fraying at the edges, but I think this is where I enter the numb stage.

She peers up from the document in her hand, eyeing me over it.

"Clearly you're hiding some things," she says. "And what they are is none of my business. Your background checks came back clean, so I don't suspect you of some sort of crime ring or anything. The only thing that held up your application all this time was the confusion on the multiple names, because the agency had to continue running those back one by one, and doing a check on each one. And, of course, the question on your income. The fact that you changed your name five times in three years isn't going to lead to a negative outcome on this grant, but it does make me question your intentions here."

My breaths don't come, it's like the air can't reach my lungs, the only thing I'm getting is a sporadic intake of jagged wheezes and gasps.

It must go on for a while because when my vision comes back Rory is in front of me, kneeling with her hands on my cheeks.

"Hey," she says. "You're okay."

She's so strong, so confident, I believe her.

The glass of water she hands me helps, as does taking in my surroundings. The blown up black and white shot of the older woman on the wall. The miniature diorama of the town in the window. Realizing I'm not in that college dorm where my new life fell apart. These people aren't *those* people.

Did I really think I could hide out in this town for long and it wouldn't bite me in the vag? If I were in a horror movie, I'd be the dumb-as-fuck girl who stopped to ask, "Who's there?" rather than running for the hills when the killer got in the house. I would be screaming at me in a theater. It's embarrassing, really. I should've known better.

When my chin stops wobbling, my lungs cooperating once more, I try using my vocal cords. "I'm not lying to you about wanting to be here," I tell her.

One thick, smooth brow of hers ticks up. "Do I want to know what you *are* lying about?"

"I don't want anyone to know," I admit in a small voice. "But it's probably time I told Weston."

"I think so too," she agrees, folding her arms over her chest, leaning back on her desk in front of me.

"And if he wants me to leave, I won't come back," I promise her.

As much as I might want to.

23
Weston

"I need to talk to you," she'd said to me when she got home earlier this evening.

"Me too," I'd told her, practically vibrating with excitement. "And me first."

She didn't put up much of a fight to that, but she also wasn't exactly excited when I loaded her up in my pickup, a lunchbox in the back that she probably hasn't noticed yet. That should've been enough of a warning for me, but I was hyped about my surprise and didn't press that hard.

"What's wrong?" I'd asked her.

She put her hands to her stomach, said she wasn't feeling well, but didn't ask me to stay in tonight or anything, so I'm hoping what I have planned will make her feel better. At least cheer her up. But my stomach is in a state too. I wouldn't call it butterflies, more like some tiny bastards are doing motocross inside my gut. This is excitement on a new level for me.

As we drive, I keep one hand on the wheel, one hand on her thigh where she sits in the passenger seat, thumb running a line back and forth on her bare skin. I steer us through the winding mountain roads, headlights on as we navigate to a hidden area of the Heights, racing twilight to get there before dusk falls.

It took a fair bit of research to work tonight out, but with Duke's help, the romantic geezer, I think we're gonna be golden.

Wish we could've gone in the Charger, but I haven't had much time for it lately and it's not gonna be road-ready for a while yet.

Amelia still hasn't figured it out as I park the truck in a grassy lot, not far from where she parked her van that first night we fucked. What was supposed to be her last night in town.

Racing out of the driver's side, I round the truck to open her door for her and help her down. Grabbing the lunchbox from the back seat, and an extra couple of hoodies I brought for us to sit on (or wear if it gets chilly), I lead her through the wilderness as the last light of the sun blinks out.

We make it to the clearing just in time, and the log I set out earlier today is still there, waiting for us.

"Ta da!"

I wave my arms around, gesturing at the tree trunks on all sides.

"The woods? Is this the surprise? I feel like you've shown me the woods before, Weston." Her voice is tired, drained, not at all what I'm used to hearing from this girl who's so full of life, who finds ways to laugh even in the darkest of situations. That's okay. We all have rough days, but she's about to have one hell of a reason to smile.

I set the hoodies down on the log, then move her over in front of one, pressing on her shoulders to urge her to sit down. She humors me, lowering down and taking a seat.

Joining her, I wave at the trees again, specifically the lower portions of them.

"I don't—"

"Just watch," I interject.

Seconds pass, and then, a glow. And another. Tiny fireflies light up all around us, in synchronized harmony. At least five flashes in a row, and then darkness.

Another series of flashes starts up, this time from the ground.

More darkness when that sequence is over, and then the ones from higher up start again.

Amelia watches, wonder overtaking all the worry in her face, and I watch it hit her, where we are. What we're seeing.

"What? How? I don't—"

"The synchronous fireflies," I whisper.

"But how?" she asks. "I thought we didn't get the passes."

"Turns out we can see them from here." I point with my head to the display all around us, any way we look.

"Clearly," she says, then she gives a soft laugh. "I just... I'd given up on seeing them this year. Maybe ever."

"Well, now you can move it to your "Been There, Seen That" board."

Amelia rushes me, leaning forward to hug me tight, her head buried in my shoulder. I feel her body shaking and it scares me.

"What's going on, darlin'?"

"It's past time I let you in," she says cryptically once she pulls back.

"I think you already did that, though it took some work," I tease, nudging her with an elbow, but her mouth doesn't so much as twitch upward.

"What do you know about the Santa Slayer?" she asks, a scary lack of inflection to her tone.

"This is about true crime?"

"Just answer the question."

I'm not a true crime junkie like she is, but sure I know who the Santa Slayer is. Everyone does. Some whack job who offed a bunch of mall Santas one year before Christmas. I think it was in my senior year of high school. Next Halloween, half the kids we grew up with went as dead Santas of one kind or another.

"Some guy named Artie Sanford went ape shit on some Santas. Knifed 'em up. Is that what you're worried about? Being stabbed randomly by some psycho? Might be too much Vixens if Jynx is getting you scared of something that random and unlikely."

She ignores me and starts talking.

"When I was a kid, I was small. I'm *still* small. But I was a late bloomer, and I was always in the bottom percentile on size and weight. It tended to make people extra protective of me, when that's never what I've wanted. I've spent most of my adult life trying to look less childlike after so many years of insufferable baby talk to my face. Getting the implants, my piercings, the hair, the boots. It's all to help me feel stronger, badder, bigger than I am naturally. I never want to be seen as small again."

I nod, taking her hand in mine and holding it, encouraging her to keep talking.

"Anyway, when I was twelve, my growth spurt hadn't hit yet. Some friends and I were at the mall. I went to the bathroom on my own, and, uh..."

The toe of her white sneaker nudges the ground, trying to find the words. My stomach is a ball of lead and I almost don't want her to keep going, but I need her to all the same.

"There was a man in the bathroom. I think he thought I was a little kid, the way he spoke to me, the way he tried to lure me into a stall with him. But I was twelve, not some first-grader who didn't know better. I stomped on his foot and ran out of the bathroom."

Her breathing turns staggered, and her free hand comes up

to wipe her face angrily. That pit in my stomach grows deeper, and I don't want to know what she's going to say next.

"It should've ended there. My mom could've filed a report with the police, done a sketch, and that would've been that. But no."

Ice runs through my veins, chilling me from the inside out. My asshole can't decide whether to clench like I'm sitting on a glass pineapple, or to let out everything inside me that's turned to liquid. "What happened, angel?"

Her eyes squeeze shut. "She told my dad. My overprotective dad."

I think I know where this is going, but I don't stop her. I wonder when she's ever told someone this story before. *If* she ever has. She probably needs to say it as much as I need to hear it.

"He didn't want a police report. He wanted to handle it himself. By the time I heard the door slam and ran out to the kitchen where they'd been talking, my mom was crying, my dad was gone, and so was the biggest knife from the block on the counter."

The backs of my eyes sting, watching tears drip from hers. Bright teal, even in the darkness, under the moonlight and surrounded by the glow of the synchronous fireflies.

"I never saw him again," she says, sniffling. "Except on the news."

Amelia pulls her hand back from mine, turns to face me, and scoots herself further away.

"Weston, my birth name is Angel Sanford. Artie, my dad, *is* the Santa Slayer. The man from the bathroom...he was a mall Santa. And my dad went to find him. He found the wrong one first. I guess it was a shift change or something, I dunno how that works. By the time he found the 'right' one, others had tried to intervene, tried to stop him, and they got killed too. A security guard, an elf, and a random Good Samaritan who thought they could take him out. He was possessed; nothing could stop him until he got the guy who tried to take his daughter. And then the cops showed up."

Her head falls, shoulders shaking with a couple of sobs, and I can't help myself. I move in closer to her again, wrapping an arm around her shoulders, and taking her hand in my other. Lips pressed against her head, I whisper, "It's okay, you don't have to tell me."

"You deserve to know," she says when she can speak again. "The whole world knows half the story. Only my mom and I know the whole one."

Amelia collects herself, breathing deeply before lifting her head to look me in the eyes as she tells me more.

"I think by that point he realized what he had done. He didn't want to live with himself. He chose suicide by cop rather than face the consequences of his actions. He left *us* to live with them instead."

She hiccups, and I rub her back as I try to take it in. After a minute, she gets her breath back and continues. "My dad charged one of the cops with the knife he'd used to kill five other people in broad daylight, forcing them to fire on him. Coward that he was in the end. Making someone else a killer rather than face justice himself."

The jokes I've heard about the man over the years resurface, playing like a slideshow in my head, a montage of nightly news clips, skits on comedy shows, and even videos online of people pretending to pull an "Artie Sanford." How he hated Christmas so much he took out Santa *and* the elves. It circulates every year. Never once have I heard even a fraction of this side of it.

I can't imagine having to live with the knowledge that someone you were related to, someone you *loved,* committed such a heinous act. But to have it be perpetrated in your name, for your honor? To have those horrible crimes be the one thing you're connected to when anyone hears your name for the rest of your life?

"I am so fucking sorry, Amelia," I tell her.

What do you say to something like this? Southern manners didn't prepare me for trauma like hers. When the worst thing I've ever been through is my parents divorcing, how am I supposed to wrap my head around the tragedy she's experienced?

How quickly my reality has changed should leave me spinning, but I'm so focused on her that somehow I keep it together.

She scoffs. "It's not your fault, Weston."

"That doesn't mean I'm not sorry it happened," I tell her. "I'm not apologizing for it, I'm empathizing with you *because* it happened. You can accept empathy if you want to. Compassion won't make you any less strong of a person."

Nothing could make her anything short of superhuman in my eyes. But I see the shift in her as my meaning sinks in. Her face softens and tears start to form. I have a feeling she's never let anyone lessen her burden before, the way she's so fiercely independent.

My hand cups her face, fingers wiping below one eyelid as I keep talking. "It doesn't make you weak to share your load with someone else. That's what love is. Sharing in the good, the boring, and the unthinkably horrible. It's always better with someone else. You're not alone anymore, darlin'."

"Love?" Her voice is a cracked whisper.

"Yes, love. I love you, Amelia. Regardless of your history, of whatever name you use, I love who you are here and now. How you make me feel when I'm with you. Shit, even when I'm *not* with you, I'm better because of you."

"I tell you my father is one of the most famous killers of our lifetime and you tell me you *love* me?"

"I don't care that your father was a serial killer," I tell her, pushing some hair behind her ear so I can see all of her beautiful face.

"Mass murderer," she corrects me, laughing darkly. "No wonder you didn't make it in the National Association of Serial Killers. You don't even know the standards to qualify as one." She laughs again, sardonic, with a hint of her tears in there. "Dear old dad didn't make the cut."

It makes even more sense now. Her dark humor, her tragic outlook on life. It's all she's had to cope with, on her own, that immense black cloud following her everywhere she goes.

I've heard that trauma victims cope in a variety of ways. Looks like she got the black humor version of healing. I can work with that. At least it's not self-harm, or substance abuse. Fucked up humor, I can do.

"I think we have enough killers in the family," I tell her, gentle smile on my face so she knows I'm kidding and this changes nothing for me.

She's spent years keeping everyone else out because she doesn't want the judgment, the reminders of her past. I want to show her that it's who she is, regardless of what happened to her in the past, that makes me love her.

"If it's okay with you, I'll retire permanently from that option. We'll pick a new career for me together."

She laughs, tears rolling down her face. "You're seriously telling me you're okay with this?"

Okay?

I struggle to control my voice, my volume, as the words shoot out of me, but I focus on assuring her, not scaring her. "Of course I'm not okay with what happened, what you went through. Nothing about that is *okay*. It's going to take time, and probably a lot more talks, for me to really understand what your life has been like as a result of what he did. But it doesn't change the way I feel about you." I scoff before continuing. "Shit, if anything, it makes me love you more, for how strong you've been, the fact that you managed to live anything close to a normal life after going through trauma like that. You're fucking amazing, angel. You managed to let me in after all of it, too, which might be the most amazing part of all."

Her face crumbles and she ducks into my chest, crying harder than before.

It takes minutes, maybe longer, but she calms down eventually. When she gets her breathing back to normal, she tells me the rest of the story.

How the rest of her middle and high school years were hell, complete pariahs, both her and her mother. Her mom couldn't find work that could replace the income they'd lost, and no one would hire her except some asshole who ran a skeevy diner and barely paid her. Amelia's dick of a brother was out of the house by that point, but he held their father's death against both women and was a raging sweaty ball sac to them both.

She tells me how she couldn't wait for college, a fresh start, where people wouldn't know her, wouldn't know her past. And for the first time, once she was there, she was able to have friends, and a boyfriend. Except when she began to trust him and told that motherfucker the connection to her father, he freaked, ruining everything she was trying to build there.

Just a few months to get a taste of what life would've been if she were a normal girl with a normal childhood, and then it was all trashed with one confession. She left school, changed her legal name, and started studying code online.

Amelia explained how there was an insurance payout—back before the law protected insurance companies from suicide by cop—that went to her mom. But she wouldn't touch the money, and put it into a trust for Amelia that she could access once she turned eighteen. While she didn't want the money either,

Amelia eventually caved, using it to buy a used van and convert it for van life. She donated the rest to the victims' families and has been living off of her wages ever since, sending money to her mom regularly to help her make ends meet, and donating the rest to a charity supporting the victims' families when she has anything above what she needs to survive.

Apparently, somewhere along the way, her brother started raiding their mom's mail. Found some correspondence from the insurance company and lost his shit that there was a payout and he didn't see any of it. He started threatening their mom, then Amelia (when he could find ways to get ahold of her), and that's when she got extra creative on keeping on the move, changing up her contact information regularly, and risking no form of connection to any one place or person.

Their mother, though, had nowhere to go, and has been stuck working a shitty diner job for a piece of shit manager ever since. The brother has been using blackmail over Amelia's identity to keep the mother in line all this time, and it's kept her from seeing her mom for nearly a decade.

As bad as all that is, by the time she's finished the entire story, a long time later, it seems like some of the worst parts of it for her are the emotional conflicts it created within her.

"Sometimes," she says, sniffling, head on my shoulder, not meeting my eyes. "Even though I hate him, sometimes I still miss him. And I hate myself for it. How can I miss anything about a monster? But before that day, he was just my dad. Before that day, I had a normal life. A *good* life. And so, so many lives got ruined that day. I don't have the worst of it, I know I don't. I don't have the right to feel sorry for myself when so many others lost their loved ones who were actually innocent. Their lives were shattered and they didn't deserve it. But it's so hard not to think those thoughts, you know?"

Sucking in a breath through my teeth, I consider how to

respond and decide to speak from the heart. "I don't know if there's an easy answer to this, darlin', but I'm gonna tell you how I see it and you can do what you want with that perspective."

She nods against my shoulder and I take it as encouragement to keep going, my hand rubbing her arm as I do.

"The world we live in is full of shades of gray. It's only black and white to the colorblind. The best people can still make awful mistakes. And sometimes there's good in the worst of people. You're not a bad person for feeling something other than hate toward him. Your compassion for the victims and their families makes you a great person, if you're asking me."

The sounds of her sniffling faster tell me she's hearing me, even if she has nothing to say to that, so I go on.

"Emotions are complex, Amelia. The human experience isn't a simple one. Your feelings are valid. You had a childhood of good memories and it culminated in something unbelievably tragic, but that doesn't necessarily change the times you had before that. I'm not telling you how to feel about him, or what you've been through, but you're welcome to talk to me about it if you want to and I'm not judging you for any of it."

She cries harder, and I hold her tight until the sounds soften and her trembles stop.

"I'm a mess," she finally says, sniffing again, wiping her nose with the sleeve of the hoodie she's sitting on.

"You're incredible," I tell her.

"You have every reason to run from me," she says, finally finding my eyes with her own.

The fireflies continue their performance, dancing and glowing in the wooded surroundings.

"You see those?" I ask her, pointing to the fireflies as they light up in harmony, circling us in their greenish yellow glow.

"Yeah," she breathes. "It looks like we're in a fairy tale. There must be thousands of them."

"Every one of those fireflies is a reason I have to love you, Amelia. They stretch out forever, damn near infinite. You are the impossible, darlin'. Too good to be true. The way you care so damn much, how you see the world around you, and the way you make my life worth fucking living despite every reason you have to hate the world. You still choose joy, even after what you've been through. Somehow, against all odds, you are the brightest light glowing in a world of darkness, and there's nothing that could make me run from you."

Her eyes widen, looking between me and the glowing forest around us, eyes rimmed with fresh tears.

"You're too pure," she says, shaking her head, like she's struggling to accept my words.

I let her take her time, making sure she hears them. After a moment, she looks up again, eyes glossy.

"I didn't even think I was capable of love until you, Weston Grady. I didn't think I was *worthy* of love until you. You fixed that. You see only the best in me—"

"—I just see the truth," I cut her off with a smile. She grins, shoving my shoulder with her own.

"You see the best in the world around you, and you make it better just by being you. The world is lucky to have you, but not as lucky as me."

Amelia turns, facing me fully, making sure I don't miss her next words.

"I'm the one who gets to love you every single day."

Reeling from her declaration, I place a soft kiss to her lips, her cheeks, her perfect little nose, and her forehead, keeping my lips pressed to her skin until I collect myself.

"I thought I was broken, I thought I didn't have the capacity to love until you, Amelia. Turns out I just wasn't able to love anyone but you. I don't know if we fixed each other? Or maybe we were never meant to love anyone until we found one another."

Her bleary smile, so genuine, full of heartbreak, healing, and a range of human emotion it might take a lifetime to unpack and understand, it gives me all the assurance I needed that I can be the man she needs me to be. The purpose in life I've been looking for all this time is right here in front of me. Someone to make laugh, share the load on tough days, and give them a reason to smile every single day.

"Although, for such an important moment between us, you forgot to mention how much you love my dick," I tease, swooping in to kiss her. When I pull back, I add, "I mean, I could give you a whole 'nother speech just on your tits. Don't get me started on the rest of you." My eyes flick over her frame and back up to her face, lips pulling up.

"Maybe I wasn't done talking," she says, nose in the air.

"Don't let me stop you," I say, smiling. "Go on, tell me more about why you love me."

"No, I think I'm done now," she says, face turned away from mine to hide her grin.

"Not even gonna give me like one reason per inch? Surely you have close to a dozen." I go into a falsetto to do a terrible impression of her voice. "Oh Weston, I love how your cock is the only one that's ever hit my ribs before, I love that I'll never choke on it because I can't even get it past my teeth, and how I come every time I'm even near it."

We're both laughing by the time I finish my awful impersonation, but she's doubled over, leaning down on my lap, giggling furiously.

"I do not sound like that!" she says.

"Naw," I admit. "You don't."

I let the silence hang for just a moment, long enough for her to think that's it, before I add, "You sound more like, 'Fuck me,

West, no one's ever made me come so many times I passed out, uh!'"

It's so over the top, overdone in such a ridiculous way, that I don't expect her eyes to heat in response, but they do. Warm gold hues popping through those teal rings around the black depths of her pupils, and I'm melting in her scorching gaze.

"I do believe you just gave yourself a new goal, Mr. Grady," she says, all purring seduction.

Amelia stands from the log at my side and drapes a leg over my lap, sliding down to straddle me. Her arms loop behind my neck, mouth pressed to mine, and she whispers, "I love you, West. And now I want you to fuck me and make me come till I pass out."

Who am I to not give my girl what she wants?

So I give the fireflies a show of our own.

24
Amelia

"To girls' night!"

Lexi holds up her glass of wine and Rory, Gracie, and I do the same, joining hers in a clink.

"To girls' night!" we all echo.

Smoky Sips might be referred to as a Suds, but for the ladies. I certainly don't see many men among the patrons here. They're probably across the street, just like all of our men are, playing pool or darts and clinking glass bottles, while we're over here enjoying a refined evening after the soft opening of downtown was a smashing success.

"To good dick!" Lexi cheers even louder than before.

Okay, maybe it's not that refined.

Champagne walls (Weston and I painted them together), with mostly understated decor throughout the cozy space in cream and neutral tones, tied together with ornate crystal chandeliers all make this a decidedly more femme place than Duke could ever hope Suds would be.

Fuzzy pillows line the long bench that serves as seating on one side of the establishment, small circular tables stationed every few feet along the way. The girls and I, however, are stationed at the mirrored bar top in the center.

"What do you know about good dick?" Gracie asks her best friend as Rory and I watch Lexi closely.

Her eyes narrow, scowling playfully, but then Rory leans in. "No, seriously, Lex, when's the last time you got some?"

Lexi's mouth purses, jaw tight, before she comes up with a response. "It's been...a while," she says delicately, avoiding answering. "But you three are all getting it. I'm hoping this is osmosis and now I'm destined to get some, too, if you guys can rub off on me."

"I think you'd prefer a good dick rubs off on you," Rory cracks, and giggles break free from all of us.

"Speaking of," Lexi turns, one arm on the bar so she faces me full on. "Spill. How's it going with you two?"

Six eyes on me, Rory's perfectly made up, Lexi's sharp, and Gracie's softly interested, I buckle under their complete attention.

"It's *really* good," I say, taking a sip of my sparkling white wine.

"Well, we know that," Lexi says, rolling her eyes. "Can see your glow from two towns over. And like that wasn't enough of a giveaway, your limp too. We want details, Amelia."

"Not too many details," Rory corrects. "That's my brother-in-law."

"Like you're not curious." Lexi waves her off, dismissing her.

"I've heard a lot about Wyatt's dick. Well, seen it for myself, actually. I can only imagine Weston is blessed in the same way," Gracie says, eyes wide and round.

"I haven't told you anything about my husband's package," Rory says, mouth agape.

"Didn't say I heard it from you," she giggles.

Gracie and Rory's husbands are best friends somehow. The

guy seems as opposite from Wyatt as you can get, but maybe that's why it works. Two Wyatts? I shudder. That's too terrible to consider. This town only has room for one guy that grumpy. Unless you count Dallas, but he keeps to himself so much it doesn't upset the balance. I don't think I've ever even seen him outside the bar he's always behind.

"So?" Lexi presses me, nudging me with an elbow.

"By far the best I've ever had," I tell them. "There's just one thing..."

All three women lean in closer at once, hanging on my every word.

I lower my volume to a whisper. "It's just, I wish I could blow him. Like, really blow him, not just the tip."

Lexi's jaw drops, Gracie's eyes widen, and Rory just nods, knowingly.

"No. No way." Lexi shakes her head.

"We can't all be born with no gag reflex, Lex," Gracie jokes.

"Sure can't. You're a lucky bitch, Alexis," Rory mumbles under her breath.

"Have you ever seen that meme of the hamster and the banana?" I ask them.

Cackling laughter from all of them warms my heart, which is still learning to let others in, and when I can collect myself, I illustrate my point, opening my mouth as far as it'll go and pointing at it.

Lexi reaches her hand out, circling her fingers against my lips and then holding it up to her face for inspection, mouth still in a disbelieving O as her fingers don't quite touch in the same shape.

Rory doesn't blink twice. "Trust me. I know what you mean. I'm married to a Grady. My jaw deserves a fucking medal."

"I think that rock on your hand *is* the medal," Lexi jokes, pointing at Rory's emerald cut sparkler that's damn near the size of one of the crystals dripping from the nearest chandelier.

Wine flows freely, and the conversation even freer, the four of us oversharing as we're overserved and giggling our way through the night.

I'm glad I told the sisters about my past earlier this week, the day after I told West. Neither of them judged me, just like Weston didn't. Lexi wrapped me up in her arms and squeezed half the life out of me when I was done talking, and Rory just held my hand, eyes shining bright, but it was more than enough. No one else will ever truly understand what I've been through, but for now, being able to share my story with women who want to share my burden was therapeutic beyond words.

West had suggested I ask Rory for help with my brother, finding a way out from under his thumb so we can get my mom moved to town and that nightmare portion of my life can finally be over. Rory offered, too, and we have a meeting scheduled to discuss my brother and mother and possible paths forward.

Truthfully, I'm not sure I'm one hundred percent ready to take my brother on yet. Give me a second to settle, please. These past couple of months have been something I never saw coming.

I'm still adjusting to this world where I have a boyfriend, and friends, and they all know my past and *still* want me in their lives anyway.

The pessimist in me is waiting for the other shoe to drop, for them to come to their senses and realize I don't belong. The darkest parts of me are waiting for the reveal that this is all some joke, they pity me enough they're letting me stick around until they can figure out how to get rid of me. But the optimist in me is trying to believe the best in the situation, and of these people who have given me no reason to doubt them.

Rory probably shared my story with Wyatt by this point, but

I'm not ready to tell Gracie, or stars forbid, let the rest of the town in. My past is something I plan to keep to just the Grady-Weiss family for now, hopefully for good. Just because these few people are good and kind and fair, doesn't mean the rest of the town would be if word got out.

It's not too late for me to be chased out of here with pitchforks.

The smiles I get from the Weiss sisters throughout the night, the knowing looks and hand squeezes, they mean the world to me.

You belong, they say.

It's enough to make my eyes water if I let it. So instead, I don't go there. I stay in the moment, laughing and bonding with the other women like I'm a normal person as they share stories from their jobs, the men in their lives, and life in this small mountain town I'm starting to think of as home.

THE NIGHT FLIES by in a blur of dirty jokes and core memories formed. My third ever girls night in my life, my insides are warm from so much more than the light buzz I still have by the time we're headed for the door.

More pedestrians than usual continue to wander the stretch of Main that makes up Downtown Smoky Heights, probably relics from the soft opening. It wasn't anything like the fancy ordeal Rory is pulling off for the grand opening later this summer, but there was still hoopla, visitors who traveled to see the town that was brought back from the dead, even some press in attendance.

That's why I don't think anything of it when a woman was standing outside the double doors as Lexi pushes one open,

Rory and I walking out linked arm in arm, heads together, still chattering away in the sultry night air.

"Angel?" she asks.

And that's when I see the small microphone in her hand. The person behind her filming the encounter on a handheld video camera.

"Angel Sanford?"

Rory reacts faster than I do, dropping my arm and stepping in front of me. She puts a hand out, blocking the view of the camera, and stands close to the reporter.

"Leave now. Don't come back."

"Eva Ogden with *Snoop Scoop*, we're just trying to get a statement from Angel about the murders her father committed fifteen years ago. We're doing a piece on the families of serial killers, and—"

Lexi launches herself, trying to tackle the reporter to the ground, but Rory's arms catch her before she can do the woman bodily harm. Confused, Gracie wraps an arm around me, piecing together that things aren't exactly great right now, even if she has no clue what's going on.

"You don't know what you're talking about," Lexi hollers at the woman from her sister's grasp, practically rabid.

"No one here has a comment for you. Leave before I call law enforcement and have you banned from the town for good." Rory's voice is ice cold, and I wouldn't dare defy her if I were them.

"And you are?" the woman asks, not fucking off fast enough.

"Aurora Weiss-Grady, of Smith + Colson, her attorney, and commissioner of the Downtown restoration project, which means it's within my jurisdiction to have you removed from the premises if you don't leave now."

As for me, I'm shaking like the leaves on any of the seasonal trees spaced every ten feet or so on either side of the entire downtown stretch.

It feels like I'm outside my body, watching this happen from up the street. I can still hear conversation and laughter all around us, on both sides of the road, but it's faint, and barely makes it past the ringing in my ears.

Rory says some other things that sound scary, but I can't make them out. Lexi frees herself from her sister's hold and turns to put an arm around my shoulder, taking me from Gracie and steering me to the western parking lot at the center of downtown where our designated drivers wait for us.

Poor Gracie watches on, confused, probably horrified at who she's been befriending, but my eyes can't see much of anything right now to put it together. I focus on controlling my breaths, trying to take in my environment, but it's not working the way it usually does.

Because this isn't so different from what happened before. This is going to be on the news, airing abhorrent tragedy to pull views, just like those first days and weeks all that time ago. Except it's just me they'll be showing.

And this time I have something left that matters to me, something I don't want to be collateral damage in the aftermath of what comes next.

A brisk clattering of heels on the sidewalk, then Rory's arm is around me, too, having caught up with us. Her warm, expensive scent grounds me a little, bringing some shred of comfort as the women surround me, escorting me to the waiting pickup where Weston, Wyatt, and Gracie's husband Ronnie are all gathered around the tailgate, still having their own boys' night, an overflow from the bar, I guess. Wilder, the new chef at the restaurant, is there too.

As soon as Weston sees us, when we round the back of the building that houses the cafe and make it to his line of sight in the parking lot, he's sprinting over. He takes over, wrenching me from the grasp of the girls, and wrapping me up in his arms.

"What happened?" he asks me.

I don't have the words to answer him.

"A reporter came," Rory says in a hushed tone, all business. "They are planning a series on the surviving families of famous killers, and they tracked her down and wanted an interview. Some sick gotcha journalism."

"They *what*?" Weston's voice is stony, furious.

"They're gone now," Rory assures him, and I feel her hand on my shoulder. "I'm going to alert the sheriff's office and make sure we don't see them again in the Heights. I'll send a cease and desist letter from any harassment or unwanted contact as your attorney. I'll need to consult some legal codes first, this isn't my usual. Maybe just get some sleep, Amelia."

Weston presses his lips to the top of my head, and it gives me something to focus on in the here and now.

Something other than the fear of my worst secrets, my entire past, and the new identity I've worked so hard to create all being blown wide open and published for the world to use against me, all because I stopped moving and the past caught up to me, wiping out any chance of a future here.

25

Weston

No article has been published in the week following the confrontation after the soft opening. Rory and I check every single morning, preparing for the worst.

I love my sister-in-law for doing what she could to try to get them to back off, but unfortunately their protection as a media organization gives them the right to publish just about anything, including something that doxxes a normal person and runs the risk of ruining her entire life.

Public records are public records apparently.

From what Rory has said, it seems like this particular publication is all about sensationalizing aspects of pop culture to get clicks, and they're not too worried about sticking to the truth. Fortunately, or unfortunately, true crime is having quite the moment in pop culture right now, which is, I guess, what they're after.

Seems kind of ironic that the one place Amelia found comfort and healing from her trauma, true crime, has these bottom feeders living off of the hype generated by those who are giving the industry a good name, like Jynx. That some of these assholes are going to make a mockery of her life rather than bother creating something that takes skill, like a documentary with willing participants, or an exposé on people who actually committed the crimes—not stirring up scandal about those whose lives were ruined because of the evil of others and have been trying to rebuild.

Amelia calls it cosmic karma. I think the only ones who have bad karma in this scenario are the assholes at *Snoop Scoop*. If an asteroid crashes into Earth, it's definitely going to flatten them first. And, you know, killers and other creepy fucks.

Amelia's doing better than I expected, all things considered. She hasn't been up for going out anywhere, hasn't wanted to see anyone, aside from one or two clandestine meetings with Rory. She's sure there's talk in the town after that showdown the night of the soft opening, and she's probably not wrong. So she's mostly been staying holed up, more in her van than my house, but she doesn't object to me spending the nights with her in Van Gogh. I think it's where she feels safest.

My girl's still got her dark, twisted, morbid sense of humor that I love so much about her, and if this hasn't taken that from her yet, I'm considering her a fucking rock star.

There's been nothing to do but wait, help her accept that this is probably coming, and distract her as often as I can, trying to keep her spirits up.

Today is supposed to be one of those distractions, and damn if I'm not gonna do my part.

Last night I finished restoring another motorbike, a Kawasaki Ninja 650 that a guy we grew up with, Diego, wants to sell. Today I wanna take it for a test drive and make sure it's working great once it's on the open road.

Some folks are biased against certain brands or models of motorcycles, but I think they're just like people. Sure, we all have our favorites, but there's something to like about all of 'em. And this bike has a lot to like about it.

This mild June weather makes for the perfect riding climate. Surprisingly warm out, but the breeze will keep us comfortable on our adventure.

Knocking on the door of Van Gogh, I hear the manual hook unlatch and then she opens the door. Sadly, this time she isn't topless, but she still looks close to perfect. A little more light behind those teal eyes would make me happy, and I'm here to do just that for her.

"Hey, darlin'. You ready for me?"

Her smile is out of practice, but she gives me what she can anyway. I grab her hips with both hands and pull myself close to her until our bodies are flush, my jeans to hers. White tee to her dark crop top, and the tempting skin peeking out beneath it.

Amelia doesn't say anything, so I run my fingers along her cheek, moving her hair out of the way so I can lean down to give her a kiss. That, she responds to.

When we pull apart her cheeks have more color, her eyes are brighter, and I slide my hands down her back to nestle themselves in the pockets on her ass.

"You wanna stay here today?" I ask her. "'Cause I'll stay in bed with you forever, Miss Marsh. Say the word and that motorcycle can go fuck itself, and I'll wrap you up like a burrito and cuddle you until I give you a cavity from how sickeningly sweet I'm being."

Head buried in my chest, she laughs, shaking it side to side.

"Please no cavities. It would probably be good for me to get out. Can you treat me like normal for today?"

"I can do that." The words rumble against the top of her head, where my lips are pressed.

"Just promise me we aren't going downtown, where I'll run into a bunch of people that saw the whole thing with that... *woman* the other night."

"Never, angel." I kiss the top of her head, and breathe in her spicy, coconut scent.

"You know," she says, looking up at me. "I think it's crazy how you started calling me that so early on. It's like you knew."

"I just thought you had the tits of an angel," I tease her, squeezing her ass with both hands through the denim.

That earns me a small laugh. "I better, after what I paid for 'em."

Her stark humor gets a chuckle out of me in return, and she pulls back, ready to face the world. Or at least part of it.

"Let's do this, Boy Scout."

She holds her hand out for me and I take it, crouching down so I don't hit my head in here with these boots on, and we walk out the door together. The ride to the garage is mostly quiet, her watching the passing landscape out the window, my hand on her thigh as we drive in a peaceful quiet, some indie music playing on the car stereo.

When we pull up to the garage, I notice the sign has come down. That must've just happened this morning. Maybe the sale went through by now and this place isn't Gonzo's anymore. Or—my morbid little angel must be rubbing off on me—maybe the sign just got struck by lightning?

By the time I get around to her side, Amelia has noticed my brother moving around inside the shop, head under a hood as usual, and she lets out a nervous hum.

"He won't bother you, he's on your side now." He always should've been, but the man's got a hard head and it took a while for some things to get through to him is all. Thankfully Rory can get through to him when common sense can't.

Taking her hand, I help her out of the passenger side. She hops down, gray gravel crunching under her combat boots.

It doesn't take long to get the bike rolled out to where she's waiting, key in the ignition and ready to go. Climbing on, I pat the pillion seat behind me, inviting her up.

Amelia swings a leg over, holding me for balance, and settles herself in behind me. As soon as I feel her small arms wrapped around my middle, we take off. Roaring down the dirt tracks and side streets until we hit the open, deserted mountain roads, I take us deep into the Smoky Mountains. Somewhere she can forget about what's waiting for her back in the Heights and focus on the rise and fall of the peaks, the horizon framing them, and the endless buds and blooms we see along the way. Wind in her hair, man by her side. The important shit in life.

Occasionally, she'll tap my leg, trying to get my attention, pointing at something off to in the distance that I try to take in without making us crash. More often than not, the feel of her hand so close to my dick just makes me want to pull over and bend her over this bike.

Eventually, I even feel her relax a bit, loosening her grip and letting her head fall back, soaking in the thrill of the ride. When I hear her truly laugh for the first time in nearly a week, my chest overflows with strong emotion.

After a while, my hands are going numb from the vibration of the handlebars (it's been too long since I've gone riding), and I take the excuse to turn off on a side road, finding somewhere we can pull over that's secluded and hidden. Bonus points, it's even overlooking the mountains. Not that I need that view when I've got the girl beside me to look at, but still.

She gets off the bike first, stretching her legs, and I follow her lead, birdsong the only sound welcoming us to this pitstop.

"What's out here?" she asks, breathless with exhilaration from the adrenaline.

"Nothing," I tell her. "And no one."

Her face lights up, and I grin.

"Just you, me, and a few much-needed orgasms."

"Just a few?" she asks, pouting.

"As many as you want, angel."

Sex with her is so different than it's ever been for me before. Yeah, there was instant attraction, but the deeper bond we have was built on weeks of friendship, getting to know one another in ways I haven't with other women, one that's only strengthened as things got physical. It laid a foundation strong enough to withstand the firestorm she's about to go through.

The physical connection? That's just the cherry on top to everything else that runs between us. But damn if it isn't everything I wished it would be, having my curse broken. She was worth the wait and more.

I pick her up and she wraps her legs around my waist, letting her arms fall over my shoulders, and brings her face close to mine. "You know, I like it when you call me that. I never thought I'd want to hear that name again. But you gave it new meaning for me."

Spinning her around, I drop my ass back onto the seat of the bike and get one leg over it. She drops her upper body back, splaying over the handlebars, and I groan at the sight of her, so perfect for me.

"You're my dark little angel who fucks like a goddess. It's the perfect nickname for you," I tell her, running my hands up her bare stomach and beneath her cropped shirt.

Finding her bare there, I growl. "No bra?" I ask, surprised I didn't notice when I picked her up, or when she was pressed against me this whole ride. She must've had me distracted by the rest of her for me to miss that detail.

"Didn't want anything in your way," she says, still leaning over the handlebars, back arched and tits pointed straight to the heavens, the lucky bastards.

Leaning forward, I bring my mouth to her exposed skin and trail kisses upward, my nose dragging the fabric up with me as I go. When my mouth hits her full breast, I suck on the skin, playing with the soft underside. She moans, grinding her hips on me as I take my time, enjoying having her all to myself out here, some of the weight of the last week easing in all this open space.

Her hips move slowly, teasing me, rubbing herself in circles over my cock, then switching directions. It drives me mad, but I must be nuts because I love her form of torture.

I could happily drag this out all damn day. Tasting her one square inch at a time, building up the anticipation until both of our blood is boiling, the need enough to make us both snap.

Being patient and understanding is part of this boyfriend thing, and I can do that. But fuck have I missed her like this.

By the time I get her nipple in my mouth, I'm hard enough, needy for her in a way that I might actually blow in my pants if this keeps up.

"Weston," she calls my name, bucking her hips, as my teeth strum her nipple, then the other. Gotta be fair to both here.

"Yeah, darlin'," I whisper around her sensitive flesh.

"I need you," she says, breathy and as desperate as I feel.

"Need you too, angel."

"What are you waiting for?" she asks.

"For you to straddle me and take what you want."

She hops down, shucking her shoes, jeans, underwear and shirt in record time, while I hustle to unbuckle myself, unbuttoning, unzipping, un-everything, so I'm ready for her.

I've got the condom out and open by the time she's climbing back up, and she stops my hand from sheathing myself.

"Can I have you bare?" she asks, bluish-green eyes molten in a way I want to remember forever.

"You can have me any way you want me, darlin'."

I toss the open condom to the side, pretty sure it lands with a soft thunk on the pile of her clothes, but I can't be fucked to watch. Because the girl I love is climbing me, straddling me backward, ass in my face, hands on the handlebars of this gorgeous bike I just fixed up as she seats herself over my cock, legs on either side of mine, making me her custom seat on this bike. I'm about to give her the ride of her damn life.

"Fuck, fuck, *fuck*." I curse on a sharp inhale as the feel of her wet pussy slides over the head of my cock, nothing between us, nothing keeping me from feeling her soaking warmth as she notches me at her entrance and lowers herself.

We're both cursing, panting as she stretches, molding to my girth as she slides down, bit by bit. It's gotten a little easier with time—and a lot of practice—but it still feels like I break her in all over again every time we fuck.

Her head falls back on my shoulder as she gets closer and closer to taking all of me, and I urge her on, lips against her ear, kissing every part of her I can reach as I whisper to her between nips and licks.

"Fuck, look at you, taking me raw." Her moan, loud and completely uninhibited, says more than words would. The way I slip in further does too.

My lips slide down her neck to where it meets her shoulder. "Keep going, angel, you can do it. All of me."

Her pussy clamps down on me, and I fight to keep my hips from bucking up into her, to let her stay in control for now. "More. Take the rest, darlin'," I urge her on.

She moans again and I take her hands in mine, sliding them up her body and placing them on her tits, using two of her fingers to pinch each nipple as I press her against me, her back to my front.

Mouth back on her ear, I grit out, "You're so fucking wet, angel. This for taking me bare? Or is this for how hot you look touching yourself out here in the open?"

I use my fingers to make hers pinch herself, tugging on her

nipples and playing with her piercing, listening to her cries of pleasure as she bottoms out.

"Both," she cries, rocking her hips back to take everything from me.

"Fuck," I groan.

Leaving her to play with herself, I slide one hand down her flat stomach and find her clit, above where she's stuffed full of me, and start rubbing.

She muffles a scream, head tilted so she's biting my shoulder, and I jerk my hips up, making sure she's completely fucking full of my cock before the ride begins. The motion makes her mewl, head rolling on my shoulder, as her fingers work her nipples, and mine work her clit. My other hand is circled around her waist, holding her to me, as I start to bounce her on my lap.

"Whatever you need, angel. Don't be shy with me."

She moans, writhing, lost in the pleasure, living in the moment, letting her body do what it wants. Grinding, bouncing, rocking however she sees fit.

I've never seen something so beautiful. All those years of waiting for her and my imagination never did this justice.

And for what it's worth, the suspension on this bike holds up, and I'm feeling like this thorough of a test should be done on every vehicle I work on from here on out.

Her pussy squeezes me tighter than before, I know she's getting close, but fuck, I don't want this to be over yet. The second she comes, I know I will too. I'm too worked up, too far gone for this girl. I've held out so many times before, but when I feel her shake, knowing my cock is what's pushing her bare pussy over the edge, I'm gonna fill her up with the biggest load she's ever seen.

"So good," she pants, bringing herself so close to the edge, using me just like I told her to.

"Too good," I growl in her ear, and I pick her up, yanking her off of me. She squeals in response, half protest, half shock, I think.

In a blink, I stand and flip us around, splaying her over the seat, positioning her legs wide open on either side of my body, and I hold her up at the right angle so I can get back inside of her with my feet on the ground, get some traction going and show her what it's like to get fucked by the man who loves all of you, even the darkest parts you keep hidden from everyone else.

Bringing my thick head back to her core, I shove myself in with one swift thrust of my hips, and she bows her back, a throaty moan leaving her that's going to get me hard any time I think about it from here on out.

She feels so good I can't take it. In and out, I pound into her, those knees spread around my sides as I support the parts of her that spill over the cushioned seat on the bike, watching her body rock and shake with every thrust. The way her tits bounce always mesmerizes me, but it's her face I can't stop watching right now. That look in her eyes, like she loves me too.

It's more than lust.

It's not just what I'm doing to her body that's making her look at me like that.

Her eyes mirror every single thing I feel about her, and it's entirely new for me.

Something I've only ever had with her.

"Come with me, Amelia," I tell her, pleading. "I want to see the girl I love coming on my dick, no wrapper."

"Fuck!" She slams her eyes shut, face screwed up like her orgasm is within reach, and it pushes me to throw her over the edge.

"I'm gonna fill you," I promise her. "You're gonna feel it all day with how much you're about to get out of me."

She moans louder, nodding her head frantically.

"That what you want? To feel my cum between your legs?" I ask her.

"God, yes." She nods faster, O face on, and it's so fucking hot, the thought that she wants to be glazed by me, my pace turns feral. Hips slamming into hers, my balls slap against her back hole, jeans low on my hips, as I do my best to fuck her into next week. A better time and place, when we're together and the past is in the rearview mirror.

"I love this," I confess, breathless, as I pound into her faster and faster. "It's only like this with you. Only you."

Her eyes open again, watching my face. "I fucking love you," she says, then she's gasping, and I feel it hit her.

Back arching in my hands, I watch as her mouth pops open, blood rushes to her cheeks, her chest, and her body convulses, impaled on my cock as she breaks for me. Clit puffy and swollen, pussy soaked and nearly red in color as she takes my cock, over and over again.

It feels just as good as it looks, pussy throbbing around my dick, squeezing me, and sucking the cum right out of me with that insane pressure.

My balls tighten, spine tingling, every nerve alight, and I blow. We come together, bodies peaking, just like our souls do when it's her and me.

When I pull back, I watch the mess drip out of her, right onto the motorcycle seat. Her release and mine, mixed together.

She lifts her head, watching, as mesmerized as I am.

Scooping and swiping the sticky liquid up with two fingers and a thumb, I shove the cum back inside of her, making her cry out, hips jerking from the sudden contact when she's still so sensitive. I watch as her abs tighten, trying to hold herself up and take what I'm giving her at once.

Her whimpers urge me on, my thumb against her clit, and I massage her, slower and less rough than I was when I fucked her but bringing her to the edge all over again as I watch from above her.

Two fingers inside that perfect pussy, a thumb on her clit, and one hand behind her back, I watch as her legs and upper body shake, breaking for me once more, her eyes on mine in a way that screams this is deeper than sex.

Damn right it is.

I've never cared for anyone the way I do for her. There's nothing that compares to seeing her happy and fulfilled. Getting to see to her needs, emotional, physical, and beyond? It's better than I ever dreamed getting to this place with someone else would be.

Richer, like a sixth layer of perceptions got added to the world, one I never even knew existed, and wouldn't know how to describe to someone who hasn't experienced it. Life before her was bland, no taste, no color, no fragrance. With her, it's complete.

I spent the last fifteen years longing for a connection like this. Now that I have it, I'm not letting anything jeopardize it.

26

Amelia

The ride back to the shop is much different than the one to our little wooded getaway. For one thing, he wasn't all talk. I can still feel his cum dripping out of me, legs spread on the passenger seat of the bike, pussy sore from the way he owned me how he did. Every rumble of the bike sends a reminder straight through my core and into my clit about what just happened.

I'm not complaining, just *very* aware of my current state of *fucked and fucked well by Weston Grady*.

By the time we get back to the garage, to his pickup, I think I might be ready for another round, which is saying something, because when we left I thought I'd need an ice pack and a couple days to recover. But if I haven't said it before, this man is magic in more ways than one.

Weston parks the bike inside the shop, wiping down all the surfaces we...touched.

While he works, Wyatt comes out of the office, face drawn.

"Do you have your phone on you?" he asks me.

"No," I say, shaking my head.

Weston comes over, freshly washed hands on his hips. "What's up, man?"

"Take her home," Wyatt tells Weston. "Rory's been trying to reach you both."

Dread grips my insides, icing my windpipe as it settles throughout my gut.

Weston pats down his jeans, looking for his phone. "I left it in the truck."

Wyatt surprises us all, himself included, when he pulls me in for a hug. "I'm really sorry about everything you've been through. Including what I put you both through." His voice sounds gruff, out of practice, like that was new for him.

I blink away my confusion and whisper, "Um, thanks."

Weston places a hand on my low back and walks me to the truck, opening the passenger door for me to get in, closing it behind me, and then jumping in on his side. He shakes his head as he does. "And to think, just a few weeks ago I felt sorry for me and Wyatt's childhood. That we went through divorce as teens. I think I actually considered it the worst thing a child can experience."

I snort. "Haven't I told you before that trauma is a scale? We all think what we've been through is pretty tough. But the more you go through, the wider your scale gets. Your position on it never really changes, just your perception of how bad the world can get does."

Weston stops backing out of the parking spot and just stares at me.

"What?" I ask.

"You're really fucking smart, you know that?"

"Not smart enough to keep what happened to me as a kid from my dad," I say wistfully.

"You shouldn't have had to, darlin'. Every little girl should be able to trust her dad. That's on him, not on you."

If I had any tears left after this past week, they'd be brimming right now, but between being all cried out and my anxiety reaching a new high after Wyatt's cryptic words, my eyes are dry.

His hand comes down on my leg with a soft noise, thumb swiping a calming rhythm on my thigh as he drives us back to where the van is parked at an overlook not too far off the highway, one that very few people frequent.

Even the gorgeous surroundings and the early summer wind in my hair through the open windows can't keep my stomach from trying to leap out of my throat at not knowing what's going on and how bad things are. The optimist in me is strangely quiet right now. Maybe she finally offed herself and let the pessimist take over for good. I could hardly blame her if so, it was one hell of a tough job.

When we get there, I rush inside, picking my phone up from the countertop where it's laying by my laptop and gasping at the amount of missed calls, texts, and FaceTimes. Mostly from Rory, a few from Lexi, and some from unknown numbers, which is rare.

Weston follows me in the van, the sliders rolling and clicking shut as he closes the door behind us and seats himself on the bed as I dial Rory back.

Her face fills my screen, brow as low as the Botox lets it go, face as serious as I've ever seen it.

"Where are you?" she asks.

"My van."

"I have to tell you something and you're not going to like it. Is Weston there?"

"Yeah, I'm here," he says, standing up to get in the frame of our video call.

"The article came out." Rory drops the bomb, letting us both lose our balance as it gets a direct hit. "I'm not going to bullshit you, it's not great."

Weston's hand comes down on my back, rubbing soothingly, but I'm itchy all over and shake it off.

Resting the phone vertically, leaning against the wall, I free my hands so I can pace the van. Weston tries to back out of my way, but everywhere he goes is exactly where I'm trying to pace, and my irritation flares higher than it should from the mild inconvenience thanks to the anxiety.

"How bad is it?" I ask.

"Imagine all the worst parts of the story you told us, without any of the perspective you shared."

Weston's eyes close, like that's the worst news he could've imagined. Such a sweet man, to not be able to imagine anything worse than that. A good man, pure of heart. Too good for me, the daughter of a monster, who's been outed against her will and whose reputation as damaged goods will now precede her.

"I need to be alone," I say out loud.

"I understand," Rory says.

"Don't hang up," I tell her, pointing to the screen.

A terrible silence hangs for painful seconds, and then, "It's me?" Weston's voice is high, hand to his chest. "*I'm* the one you want to go?"

"I need to be alone," I repeat.

He nods his head, stepping toward the door, uncertainty in his eyes even while he's trying to obey my request.

"Sure, yeah, I can, uh, yeah."

I step closer to him and speak quietly. "Look. I'm good, we're good, I just need to process this alone. It's *my* fallout from *my* shitty life. I'll see you tonight, okay? Just give me this."

He nods, and I see his Adam's apple bob as he backs down the stairs and lets himself out of the van. I don't stay to watch him leave, but I hear the door close as I make it back to the phone, and Rory who's on it.

"Read it to me," I tell her.

"I don't think that's—"

"Read it."

She takes a deep breath and nods, pulling it up on her phone, I'm guessing from the new angle of her on my screen.

"'The Next Generation of Killers,'" Rory reads the title, lips thinned in restrained anger.

Misleading as fuck, but what did I expect?

"'Infamous Santa Slayer, Artie Sanford, murdered five innocent people one snowy December day in Minnesota, fifteen years ago. A loving husband and father, he seemingly snapped over pressure to provide for his family at Christmas, brutally and fatally stabbing two mall Santas, an elf, a security guard, and a newlywed man before being taken out by local police, fourteen minutes after his killing spree began.'"

The usual lies, nothing new there.

Rory's eye twitches, but she keeps going. "'In this installment of *The Next Generation of Killers: Where are They Now*, we at *Snoop Scoop* are finding the people who loved the worst humanity has to offer and explore what they're doing with their lives now. Who's following in their family's footsteps, and who is carving their own path?'"

Loved the worst humanity has to offer? They're making it sound like we're the freaks who wrote love letters to Charles Manson in prison, not children who lost a parent.

Rory's voice wavers, and I see her lip tremble on the screen. She keeps reading anyway.

"'This series examines topics like: is there an inherent societal risk? Does the risk factor stem from a biological trait that can be passed from one person to another through genetics? What is the FBI doing to profile dangerous individuals and stop them ahead of future violent crimes, and do they take genetics into account?'"

These sick fucks. Insinuating that I should be investigated because of my genetics, that I'm destined to follow in my father's past, that I'm a future killer. How is this not libel?

I bite back the nausea and try to focus. The buzzing in my ears makes it hard to catch everything Rory reads, but I try. "'In this installation, we'll explore how do Artie's kids feel about him now? Do they admire him, are they living up to his legacy? Neither of his children, Randall (32), Angel (27), responded to our requests for comment, so let's take a look at their current lives and you can decide for yourself.'"

My vision blurs, everything around me fading in and out as my heart rate soars.

Rory stops talking, and the angle of her camera changes so she's no longer in frame. I hear muffled sounds, and when she comes back into view her eyes are rimmed in red.

I envy her release of emotion. I feel none.

"It goes on to talk about your brother's criminal past, his various arrests and charges, and then they share the name you're using now, where you are, and every single thing they could find about you through official records over the years."

I know she's trying to spare me from the worst of it, but I'm not sure that's helping. For me, the unknown is always the worst part.

Still, I say nothing.

When she speaks again, it's a thick whisper. "Amelia, I'm scared that the way they found you was through the grant application."

My eyelids fall shut and I rock with the realization.

"It went to the state, filed in their records, and I wonder if that gave these people a current trail to follow on you."

I nod, absolutely numb to everything.

I always thought if my world ended, it would be fiery, flaming bits of everything I've ever loved raining down around me.

Turns out, I feel nothing at all.

"I'm so sorry," Rory says, face crumpling as her words break.

"I'm gonna go."

The sound of Rory crying is the last thing I hear before I hang up the phone.

Numbness is weird. I don't know how time works while I'm like this. I'm not sure if I've been sitting, laying, standing, or maybe just floating here.

At some point, I hear my van door try to open itself and that doesn't seem right.

"Angel," says the man's voice on the other side. At least I think it's a man. My ears are still filled with cotton.

I told Weston to leave me alone until tonight. Is it night already? Light streams in through the front windows that I didn't bother covering before we left for our ride what feels like a lifetime ago, so it can't be. Unless it's tomorrow already?

"I told you I don't wanna talk right now, Weston," I say, exasperation leaking through my hollow voice.

Sliding the door open, expecting to see his golden face, I gasp at the face that's waiting for me instead.

Pallid, scarred by acne and a lifetime of bad choices, a patchy moustache and stringy brown hair. Bloodshot, red-rimmed eyes that used to be blue stare back at me. It's my father's face, almost to a T, had my father not known basic hygiene and had a fondness for crystal meth.

Fear shatters the numbness I've been hiding in when I take in that face.

"Randall."

"Angel."

I back up, one foot up the stairs at a time as I reverse into my van, hands fumbling behind me on the countertops, searching, heart pounding a rhythm my veins can only try to keep up with.

Randall lunges for my phone, finding it before I do, and stuffing it in his back pocket. He doesn't realize that's not what I was after.

"I'm just here to talk," he says, hands up, like he hasn't been threatening me since I left home.

I always knew this was a likely outcome for me, and even though I've spent years preparing for the eventuality, it doesn't mean I'm not shaking in my literal boots right now.

It's convenient how loud my breathing is. Hopefully it covers the noises I'm making. My body blocking his view, I feel around in the drawer behind me for one of the six folding knives I keep in the van at different strategic locations in case this day ever came.

Ironic, right? The daughter of the Santa Slayer, crippled by his legacy, yet having so many knives for her own protection?

The nearest can of mace is too far away, but I've got what I need right here.

"We don't need to talk. I have nothing to say to you," I spit at him.

"Then you're going to listen to me. It took me long enough to find you, you sneaky little bitch. Thought you could hide from me forever? I've been working for years to smoke you out."

"You're so clever." My voice drips with disdain. "Letting a reporter do your dirty work for you. Couldn't find me yourself?"

"I *did* find you myself."

"Sure," I nod at him. "It's just coincidence that you show up at my door hours after the article comes out doxxing me."

All he's had to hold over me all these years is the threat of exposing me, and someone beat him to it. Must suck to be him.

Baring his teeth, Randall brings a hand up in front of his face and forms a fist.

The handle of the knife bites into my palm as I grip it harder behind my back, ready for whatever comes next.

Questions pound through my mind, faster than I can answer.

Is he high right now?

Is he going to turn me into a killer, just like our father?

How far away is help when I really need it?

Why oh why did I send Weston away earlier?

My brother clenches his hand, like he's squeezing a can, and leans forward in a threat. Breathing heavily, his grotesque breath curls the hairs in my nostrils, and I fight not to screw my eyes up in disgust and retch. Then he drops his fist.

Seething, his chest rises and falls with his angry breaths. "I found your vehicle registration. Once I had the name you're using now and your plate number, it took me a couple months, but I was able to track you down. I didn't use no damn reporter."

I bolster myself, trying to sound braver than my frantic pulse and shaking knees make me seem. "You mean you stole my registration? Out of mom's mailbox? And then what, you paid off some creep at the DMV like you're in some shitty movie?"

Randall barks a laugh, manic in a way that makes every hair on my arms stand on end. "It's called the dark web, Angel. You can get anything if you know where to look." He snorts. "And Dad always said you were the smart one."

A lifetime of acrid rage and helpless despair pumps through my veins, fueling me. "Don't talk about Dad!"

What our father did was bad enough, no child should ever have to go through that. But for my brother to hold it over my head and refuse to let me move on? He's actively tried to harm me every day of our lives, which in some ways, feels just as evil.

Behind my back, I press the button and the blade springs free. The click is so soft that he probably doesn't hear it above the blood rushing in his ears right now at finally finding me, cornering me, so he can bully me in person after all this time. The prick has probably been fantasizing about this day for as long as I've been dreading it. I wouldn't be surprised if there was foam at the sides of his mouth right now.

"You can't tell me what to say or not say about Dad. It's your fault he's gone."

My response is instantaneous. "It's not my fault he's gone. It's *his* fault he's gone. He was the one who chose to react the way he did."

That's something I'm not sure I fully believed until confiding in Weston, Lexi, and Rory, but saying it out loud, I realize I believe it now. It gives me some extra strength to scare him off.

I just hope it's enough.

"That smart mouth of yours has gotten this family in enough trouble, don't you think? Why don't you shut it, give me what's left of the death benefit, and you can go back to hiding from the world like the useless little brat you are."

He's still so hung up on his fantasy, so delusionally psychotic, that he doesn't believe the money has been gone since before he's even known about it.

Randall has been so fixated on the hope of a free ride that he's never so much as considered there would be nothing for him to take if he ever got this far in his search.

He leans forward again, pressing too close to me, trying intimidation tactics that might've worked on an earlier version of Angel.

Maybe Avery would've cowed under this confrontation.

Amelia is certainly wishing like hell she had the capacity to ask for help when she needs it, because this is the scariest day I've had since *that* day, and someone here in my corner with me might make all the difference. But I'm on my own, just like always, and it's time to get rid of him once and for all.

I just can't stop thinking one thought.

Now he has nothing to hold over me, or Mom, either.

Maybe insanity does run in the family, because I burst out laughing.

"What is this? Why are you laughing?"

The confusion on his face—so similar to our father's in some ways, but so much worse in others—it makes me laugh even harder.

Maybe I can only take so much damage before I break.

Maybe this is where I turn truly insane.

Or maybe the human psyche can only take so much damage before it rejects, instead of accepts, anything new.

Whatever mechanism of self-protection my mind has chosen to employ, the laughter is uncontrollable. A lifetime of trauma spilling over in the weirdest way as tears of laughter stream down my face from how insanely fucked all of this is.

How Randall has tried for more than eight years to track me down, and he finally does on the same day that his one and only threat becomes invalid.

"I can't!" I scream, one arm waving in front of my face as I'm doubled over laughing, and that just throws him even more.

"Angel, stop, you're freaking me out!" He pushes my shoulder, trying to nudge me out of my fit of hysterics, but it doesn't work.

Through the laughter, I manage to speak. "Do you believe in cosmic karma, big brother?"

He just stares at me, absolutely lost. It takes a minute, but I manage to sober up, standing straight, knife still in hand, ready if I need it.

"There hasn't been any money this entire time, Randall. You didn't believe Mom, and you've wasted all these years trying to out me for something I never even had. I donated what was left of it to charity before you ever even *knew* that it existed. That's where Dad's legacy belongs. Doing some good to those who were harmed. Not supporting your habit."

"You're lying," he says through clenched teeth.

"Look around," I offer. "Do you see a stash of money? Designer things I might've bought with it? No. I used part of it on an education, part of it on this van, to get the hell away from where we came from, and then I gave the rest away. I've been supporting Mom with my earnings since I was nineteen, Randall, and living on the change that's leftover. Because you've kept her trapped in the only shitty job she can get back home, and it's not enough to keep the heat on. But now she's free!"

I giggle again and there's fear in his eyes when he realizes there's nothing but truth to what I'm saying. Or that might just be at how absolutely insane I appear.

He pulls back an arm, holding his fist by his head, but he's not gonna hit me. This is him trying one last threat in case I'm really sitting on another 10K he could take as a consolation prize.

I twirl the knife between my fingers behind my back, praying I don't have to use it.

Where is the help I sent out a silent plea for? Come on, universe. Today's the day you can start looking out for me. Any time, now.

With all the menace I can muster, I speak low and slow. "You're going to leave, Randall. I don't care where you go, but you're going to leave and never come back. Don't reach out to me, or to Mom, ever again. Is that clear?"

His face contorts into something even more unattractive than his usual expression. "And what are you going to do about it if I don't?" he asks.

He remembers the tiny, doll-like, fragile girl he grew up

with. Today he's meeting the fierce woman who's spent nearly a decade planning for this moment. Self-defense is only the backup plan. The real goal is to crush the hope he's been holding onto, scare him off for good so Mom and I are both finally free, then turn him over to the law. The closer I get to that finish line, the steadier my breaths are coming, the stronger my stance, and the firmer my voice.

"I'm going to do what Mom should've done years ago. Get law enforcement involved. File charges. You gotta be close to your third strike now, how's life behind bars sound? Scrawny boy like you, you'd make a real nice bottom for some whole cell block to pass around. You don't get lockjaw easy, do you? These country boys out here are hung thick."

One of my forearms swings up to demonstrate. His face drains of the little color it had to start, and I smirk.

"I'll be a good sister just this once and warn you, my attorney is even scarier than the cops *or* your next prison daddy. And if all that's not enough to keep you away..."

My hand comes out from behind my back, four-inch blade glinting in the under-cabinet lighting.

That shit really does go with everything, I'm glad I splurged on it for Van Gogh. Soft lighting that enhances every mood. Including vengeance.

He does a double take, maybe not believing his eyes.

"I'll make sure you never bother anyone again myself." My grin curls up, letting more of my crazy out for him to see.

Randall backs up now, genuine terror on his face.

Knife-Wielding Psycho Carves Up Anyone in the Way.

I wonder if my brother is recalling the same headlines I am, seeing them reimagined in reference to us instead of my father.

I might never actually do it, but he doesn't need to know that.

Stepping forward, pushing him to the door with every

breath, I murmur one last threat. "Don't fuck with me. Don't come near me or Mom ever again, and you can go."

He nods, sallow, pocked cheeks wobbling with the motion.

Snapping my fingers several times rapidly, I point at the counter. "Put my phone back and fuck off."

Randall pulls my cell out of his back pocket and places it on the counter with a muted thud, then high tails it out of my van.

Where he runs directly into Weston and Wyatt.

27
Weston

Just like we knew he would, the guy that I *know* has to be Amelia's brother lumbers out of her van, looking like he's seen a ghost.

Still gaping at what's behind him, he doesn't realize Wyatt and I are about to make his day a lot fucking worse.

He bumps right into my chest, and then he reels back, right into Wyatt's, who's caging him in.

The shitstain is lanky, but not as tall as either of us.

"Hi," I say, menace laced through the word.

"The fuck?" he sputters.

"Are you doing here?" I finish his question.

"We were wondering the same thing," Wyatt says in that terrifying tone of his.

The two of us step closer to him, and he has nowhere to go but for his back to go against the van.

"Who are you?" the guy squeaks out.

"Angel's new family."

"I'm her brother now," Wyatt says with a toothy grin that doesn't suit him *at all*.

"Okay, I'm fucking leaving!"

The fuckwit holds his hands in front of his face, cowering.

"Oh, so it's okay for you to corner someone who's smaller than you, but not for others to do it to you?" I ask him.

Standing outside this van and waiting to hear a sound that would signal I needed to barge in was the hardest thing I've ever done. Harder than leaving her here alone earlier today. Never have I ever had to practice self-restraint like that. Except maybe now, when I want to deck this fucker and possibly take a few of his teeth as a keepsake.

I'm going to have to get Mrs. Dixon, Ernie, and the entire town grapevine a really fucking big thank you basket for tipping us off to her brother's presence in town, letting us figure out where he was headed.

If that article hadn't come out today on Amelia that got all their attention, with Randall's mugshot included in the section on him, they might not have recognized who he was and given us the heads up. Weird how shit works out sometimes.

"It was family business!" he defends, face still screwed up like he thinks we're going to punch him.

I fucking wish.

The adrenaline coursing through my system needs an outlet, but I know my girl and using violence to defend her honor is the *last* thing she would want.

"You have no family here," I tell him.

"And you have no business here," Wyatt adds on.

"All right, I'm going!"

The sound of tires on dirt makes me turn around, and I see four squad cars roll into the overlook. I didn't even know we *had* four squad cars. Lights and sirens off, they came in silently.

"Got an SOS alert," a deputy I know well, Carlos, says, rounding his car, hand on his weapon.

Amelia steps out of the van, head held high, speaking loudly and clearly for all to hear. "This man has been harassing me, stalking me, and blackmailing me for nearly ten years, and today he entered my domicile and tried to extort me. He also used illegal tactics to do all of it. If you search his electronics, you'll find proof of federal crimes across multiple state lines. He has a previous record as a felon, and I have reason to suspect he's under the influence of illegal substances as well."

Her brother starts crying, actually wailing, as the deputies approach him.

That's when I notice the front of his pants is changing colors. The army green cotton turns darker green, and the new shade runs down his leg.

"Oh, you're pissing yourself!" I don't even mean to say it aloud, the thought voices itself, really.

He covers his face with both hands and cries as the deputies read him his rights, place him in cuffs, and argue with one another about whose car he has to head to the station in.

When I turn back around, I notice the puddle of piss on the ground is dangerously close to my shoes, so I jump back, tapping Wyatt so he does the same.

"We're gonna need you to give a statement," Carlos says to Amelia.

"My attorney will be in touch," she replies, matter of factly.

Why do I think I know exactly who that might be?

That speech she gave them had my sister-in-law's name all over it. They must've prepped for this.

The last of the patrol cars heads out, and Wyatt pats me on the back, heading back to his truck, answering a call from what's surely Rory on the way.

"You're unbelievable," Amelia tells me, facing off with me, arms over her chest.

"It's nothin', darlin'."

I'm still riled up from all that adrenaline, having to hold myself back through that entire encounter, but having her in my arms again, getting to breathe her in and know she's still here, she's still mine, will make it better.

"No, you're fucking unbelievable!" It's almost a shriek from her, and I shake my head, trying to catch up.

"Hang on, what?"

"How many times do I have to tell you? I don't need a man to defend me! Did you not hear my story the other night? The last time a man tried to defend me against my will, *people died*. I don't want your fucking protection, Weston!" Her voice rises throughout until she's downright yelling.

I'm damn near just as worked up as she is at this point. "I'm always gonna have your back, Amelia, that's something you need to get used to if you're with me. Somebody comes for you, they come for me too."

Amelia takes several deep breaths, I recognize the signs of her trying to keep herself calm, but she's failing this time. Her voice cracks when she speaks again. "I had everything under control. I had protection and a plan. *I* triggered the emergency alarm. I ran him off for good. Me! I didn't need you and your dumb fucking brother doing my dirty work!"

"You're telling me you'd rather your piece of shit brother think you're all alone and that he can keep coming back for you? That you don't have half our town willing to back you up if you need it?"

Chest heaving, I reach for her, but she pulls back, away from my touch. It stings even worse than it did earlier today, and my jaw tightens. She holds onto one elbow with her other arm, covering her midsection, just out of reach.

"I want to fight my own fucking battles."

"Your battles are my battles too. That's what this means, this relationship thing. We're in this shit together." My hand bounces between us, but she shakes her head.

The fear, the shock, it must be hitting her at once because

she's crying now, and I have no idea what to do to make it better, but I try explaining myself. "I didn't step in, I let you handle it yourself. I was just here for backup, so he knew you had others in your corner!"

I move to step closer to her. I want to pull her in my arms, apologize, tell her I know she's capable of all these things on her own, I didn't mean to trigger anything by it. I just care about her, I want to be there when she faces shit. To be a team with her.

Doesn't she know I wouldn't kill someone? Though, thinking on it a sec, she probably thought she knew her dad pretty well.

And truth be told, if someone crossed a certain line with Amelia, I could do it to protect her. I know I could, judging from the urges that ran through my veins when facing down her brother. But we're a *long* way from that point and I kept my shit together, because I know that's what she would want from me.

But apparently I don't know what Amelia wants at all.

She pushes me away with both arms, and caught off guard, I stagger back, watching as the side door rolls to a shut, my favorite eyes in the world cut off from view.

I hear footsteps in the van and then it turns on, the engine rolling over and right now I wish I hadn't fixed that fucking motor so she can't pull away from me.

But I did, and the independent woman I'm in love with drives out of the lot, leaving my shattered heart behind.

SITTING in my brother's kitchen, he hands me a glass of bourbon and I down it without registering it hitting my tongue.

"Another," he says, pouring me a fresh glass, and I do the same.

After the third, he sits down across from me.

"I'm sorry, man," he says, and he sounds it.

I grunt.

He tries again. "She'll be back."

"You can't know that."

Wyatt looks around his house, the signs of his wife tucked into every nook, and raises his eyebrows at me pointedly.

"That was different."

"Love is love, West. Ours was real, and so is yours. Our stories might look different, but we're both getting our happy endings, man."

I shake my head. "I can't believe you just said that."

He chuckles. "Yeah, you tell anyone, I'll deny it."

I let out a pathetic wail. "I want to go after her but I think that's just gonna make it worse. How did you live through ten years of this?"

He clears his throat. "It was twelve. And she's not going to be gone that long."

"How do you know?"

"The girls are on it. Plus, if she's not back soon you'll go after her before it gets out of hand. You won't fuck it up like I did."

I drop my head in my hands, picturing a future where I'm as miserable of a prick as my brother was for all those years. If I had to be without the love of my life, after knowing what it's like to have her, I would be an asshole too.

Suddenly, I'm judging him a lot fucking less.

Like he can read my thoughts, or maybe we're just more similar than either of us have ever cared to admit, he speaks up again. "I know you said you wanted to be me, but you don't wanna be me, West. You're so much better than I ever was, brother. You found what you want, and you're fighting for it. You're not letting it go." He clears his throat, but his voice is still thick when he speaks again. "I wish I was more like you, man. Back then and now."

"Yeah, well, you're not so bad," I tell him, lifting my head and sniffing. "And if I lose Amelia, I'll be back to being the black sheep of the family anyway."

He flips me off, taking a sip of his bourbon before opening his mouth again. "Not gonna happen, little bro. I should've known from the first night she arrived, when you called me for help. You've never done that in your life. I should've known then this was different. I shouldn't have expected the worst from you. I know you would never have asked me for help with her, especially not so many times, if it wasn't for real. Sorry for being a prick about it."

I shrug, sighing. "Thanks for coming today."

"What are brothers for? Least I could do."

He clears his throat again, and pulls something from his back pocket, slapping it down on the carved wooden table between us.

"What's that?"

"Too lazy to look and find out?"

Grumbling, I swipe it off the table and open it up.

"I don't understand."

"Yeah, honestly, I didn't either. Thank God Rory did. That legal paperwork is confusing as hell."

He picks *now* to develop a sense of humor? I stare at him blankly until he explains.

"It's papers. For a chunk of the land Grandpa left me. The half that should've gone to you. So you always have a home in the Heights."

My eyes burn and I drop the paper so I can pinch the bridge of my nose and stave it off.

"Fuck, Wyatt."

"The second page has the property lines drawn on it. Our land splits right at the spot we always used to camp at. You know the one."

I do know the one. Had to go there not all that long ago.

The stinging gets worse, and I tilt my head back to stare at the light and chase it away.

"Fuck you," I tell him, because this emotional shit isn't what we do between us.

He sniffs and I realize I'm not the only one this is getting to.

"Thought maybe we could still camp out there sometimes. Maybe with our families, you know, if you and Amelia start one."

"I'd like that." It's all I can manage to get out.

"Though," he says, drawing in a breath. "I'm not sure you're gonna have much time off. I hear being partner in a business is kind of a demanding job."

My jaw hangs open as he pulls another paper from his back pocket.

"That is, if you'll go fifty-fifty with me. Grady's Garage. I do have one condition though."

All this time with my brother seems to be affecting me, because all I can do is grunt in question.

"No more fooling around in the garage."

I eye him sharply from across the round table.

"Either of us," he amends.

His gaze swims, lost in memory, as I allow myself to fall into my own. It doesn't take long for us both to shake our heads.

"Yeah, never mind," he says, taking another sip of his bourbon. "Stupid idea. Just make sure I don't find out about it."

The side of my mouth twitches up.

"You gonna buff out my trunk?"

His head falls down in silent laughter.

"Fine, I'll buff out your fucking trunk. So whatd'ya say, West?"

What do I say?

I say I have the best family a guy could ask for.

My palm claps into his loudly, and we shake on it.

Now I just need my girl back.

28
Lexi

It's not hard to find her.

Van Gogh is pretty distinctive, she's the only Sprinter van we've got in the Heights.

Honestly, it's a damn good thing Wyatt tipped Rory off the second Amelia flew out of the parking lot and I could get on her ass right away and catch her before she hit the interstate.

She saw me early on, I know she did. But I followed her for almost an hour before she finally caved, pulling off the pavement somewhere in the northern Smokies, in a deserted parking lot. Took her long enough.

Climbing out of the blue Nissan I've had since high school, I stand by her door, waiting for her to let me in.

When it slides open, two soggy teal eyes staring out at me from in the van, I can't help it. My icy heart cracks for her.

"Big Momma," I say with a pout, holding my arms out.

She steps down out of the van and falls into my hug.

I let her cry, one of the few people I somehow have patience for.

Maybe it's because I see something kindred in her fiery spirit.

Maybe it's because she's been through enough in her short life.

The shit she shared with me and Rory? No one should have to go through that, especially not at twelve years old. To have it all blow up in her face again in one day? Sheesh.

Some compassion might be what she needs right now. And when this wound is starting to heal, maybe then I can bust her tits like I do with my sister. Show her she's one of us now.

She barely comes up to my chin, and she can't be half my width, but I hold her as she cries it out.

"I'm so mad at him," she finally says, hiccupping between the words.

"I know, babe."

"I didn't need his help."

"A badass like you? Hell no you didn't." My tone is light, but I mean the words.

She laughs, hiccupping again.

"Men like him don't know what it's like to have to fend for yourself as an independent woman," I tell her, stroking her hair.

There's something about this girl that brings out the protective side in all of us. Ironically, that's what she hates. The girl could have our whole family wrapped around her little pinky finger and she thinks it's a curse. I'd say it's her gift.

"I've been doing it for eight years," she insists.

"Me for twenty."

"Shit, you're old." She giggles at the scowl on my face.

"Rude."

"How old are you anyway?"

The nerve of this girl. Oh, to be twenty-something again.

"Not old enough to be your mother, and young enough to still have some fucking fun, okay?"

She holds her brows high, eyes challenging me.

"Thirty-eight," I grumble.

"That's not so bad," she sighs.

"Easy for you to say. You're light years away from being as old and cunty as I am."

She laughs again, and the fact that she can recover so quickly from the emotional ordeal she's been through today heals something in me.

"I have hope for you yet, old lady."

"I might be a lost cause, but that's a story for another day." Taking a deep breath, I get back on track. "You won't be gone long, right?"

"I need to refill my tank and empty my gray water," she says, like it's an answer.

"Your what now?"

"My gray water."

My blank stare must inform her that I have no fucking clue what she's talking about.

"The shit water."

My face pulls in disgust. "Oh, that's fucking disgusting."

I step back from the van on instinct, like the shit water is just going to spill out and get on my sneakers. These are the only shoes I have to wear at the restaurant, I don't wanna get them nasty.

Amelia gives a small laugh at my reaction. "I wasn't ready to hit the road. My van wasn't prepped. I can't stay out long, I just had to get some space."

I nod, bouncing my head rapidly. "Sure, yeah, that makes sense. Just, uh, can you keep in mind that Weston is a good guy?"

Her head drops down a bit and she takes a few steps, kicking the dirt.

"I know he is."

"He wanted to make sure you were safe. None of us have been through what you have, I can't even pretend to imagine what it's like to be you. I'll let you make your own conclusions on West, but for what it's worth, I don't think he had any harmful intentions there."

Amelia reaches down to pick up a small branch from the ground and throws it forcefully into the tree line along the edge of the lot.

"I know he didn't."

"It took a lot for him to let you do that on your own. You're supposed to be a team now. Give the guy some credit."

She huffs, maybe not ready for tough love yet. I don't have many other modes, but I shoot my shot with one other path.

"Do you wanna talk about what happened? Any of it? The article? Your brother? Weston?"

She lets out a sigh so heavy her tiny shoulders drop.

"I probably need to take action on some of it, don't I?" she asks me, like she values my input. That's a fucking first for me.

Lucky for all of us, my sister has never not been prepared for what to do a day in her life and thoroughly briefed me on my drive.

"Rory thinks it might not be a bad idea to release your own version of your story at this point. She reached out to the team back at her firm and contacted the publicist they recommend to their clients. She even spoke with her already, and if you're up for it we can call Rory together and she can make a transcript of whatever you want to say. We'll run it through the publicist, get it out there to combat the bullshit these Snoopy fuckers are spreading."

Amelia nods. "Yeah, I can do that. If everyone is already going to know my name, I'd rather they know my story too."

That's my girl.

29
Amelia

"First things first," Rory says sharply.

Squeezing my eyes shut tight, I try to ignore the dip in my stomach. The anxiety at not knowing what's going to come out of her mouth, if it's about Weston or my father, and not knowing which truth would hurt worse right now.

I open one set of eyelids and peer at Lexi, seated next to me in the van, and she gives me a nod for strength.

The icy tone of Rory's voice comes through loud and clear over speakerphone. "You do realize you crushed Weston's heart, right?"

Yep. That definitely hurts worse.

Eyes stinging, I screw them tighter for a second until I can open them both again and blow out a big breath. "Yeah," I croak. "I do."

Lexi folds her lips in, like she's biting them down to keep her mouth shut—something she's not known for doing—but her sister doesn't hold back on me.

"Mmm, I'm not sure you do. That man is like a brother to me, and not just because I married into his family. I love you both, but I need you to know how hard it must've been for him to let you confront your brother all on your own. He stood outside and waited with my husband the entire time, not letting himself jump in to make sure you were safe. And from what Wyatt has told me, there were a *lot* of times they both wanted to. You two are going to need to talk your own shit out, but you're going to need to look at things from his perspective before you do. I can tell you for damn sure, Wyatt couldn't have the kind of restraint Weston did there, the way he respected your wishes against his own instincts like that. West deserves some credit for that."

Breathing through my nose, emotion swarms through my head, dizzying me. "Some credit, sure, but—" My voice cuts off with a hiccupped sob.

Lexi cuts in on my behalf. "Ror, I already talked about this stuff with her. Do we need to do this right now?"

"Yes, we absolutely do, Alexis." Rory's tone could shred paper. My heart gives even less resistance with all it's been through this week. "I'm going to help get your story out there, Amelia, but you did some damage to my family, when all any of us have tried to do is help you."

My head falls to my lap, into my knees, and I hold back a sob. No one in my entire life has helped me as much as Weston, Wyatt, Rory, and Lexi have these past three months.

"He did what he thought you wanted him to do—nearly killed him to do it, by the way—and instead of thanking him, of understanding and appreciating how hard that was for him, you left him in your literal dust."

The visual hits me of Weston standing there, clouds of dust in my wake as I drove off. Did he deserve that? Hearing Rory's take on this cuts me.

Did I overreact? Not hear him out?
Isn't that exactly what my dad did to me?
Should I have stayed when things got tough?

I don't have the mental capacity for this right now.

It feels like I'm breathing through a straw, and Lexi must notice, because she rubs my back in large circles.

"Breathe, Big Momma."

The normalcy she brings with the nickname alone helps ease my airways and my lungs finally expand.

"That's enough, Rory," Lexi says to the speakerphone. "Let's put out the fire before we rebuild the house, yeah?"

"I think that actually made sense," Rory says over the phone, taken aback.

Sitting up now, I can see Lexi's face pinch. "Of course it did, what's that supposed to mean?"

"Phrases aren't your strongest suit, Lex."

"Well, excuse me if I don't want to beat a horse to death, can we just get to the point of this call already?"

Rory stifles her laugh, lucky for me one doesn't threaten to topple out of me right about now though.

"Is he okay?" It's barely more than a whisper, but it's all I can manage.

"He will be when you're back." Rory doesn't mince words. "Which will be soon, right?"

"Please tell him I just need a day." I can't bear the thought of him being as miserable as I am right now, but I need to work through some shit on my own before I go back to him.

"Fine," Rory says. "And one last thing before we dive in, I just want to extend an open invitation to you, Amelia."

I look up, eyes blinking in surprise, but she can't see me. "Yeah?" I whisper.

"If you ever wanna go kickboxing with me, it's a hike to get to the place I like, but it's one hell of a stress relief. Does my anxiety good."

"Hey!" Lexi barks. "How come you never invite me kickboxing?"

"Pfft," Rory scoffs. "Only one kind of cardio you'd say yes to, Lex, and it's on your back."

Lexi sputters, but her sister talks right over her. "Let's do this," Rory says. "Amelia, start from the beginning."

I pack away everything with Weston, lock it down in that airtight space I used to keep my father and brother in, and focus on the task at hand.

WE STAYED up half the night working on the story for the publicist.

I didn't expect very many people to care, to read what I had to say, or to take my word over the online magazine who did the hit piece.

But the girls had me open up a social media account and an email address as part of getting my story out and writing my own narrative, and I woke up this afternoon to *countless* messages, emails, and interactions online.

My stomach bottoms out when one notification in particular pops up on my phone.

@ jynx ✓ followed you

And below it, an email.

> Re: Interview request
> From: Jynx @ Vengeful Vixens
>
> *Amelia, you BADDIE!*
> *I'm Jynx, I host a podcast called Vengeful Vixens where we dive into true crime stories and celebrate vengeance*

against evil and injustice, telling the stories of victims and survivors.

Full disclosure, we had an episode planned for next season on your father, but when I saw your article this morning, I knew we had to change the angle here.

You gave me chills, girl, CHILLS. Your voice is the kind I want to elevate with my platform, and I would be honored if you came on the show and told your story. We have an audience of roughly ten million listeners per episode, and I think it could touch a lot of people to hear what you have to say.

You could come out to the studio in New York, or I could come to you, at your convenience.

Text me anytime.

212-555-4969

XX,
Jynx

I'm practically floating on the ceiling of Van Gogh after the email, and her following me on social.

Did I want to be outed? Fuck no.

Is the optimist in me going to make the most of my new reality, now that I have been?

Obviously.

Looks like she didn't take a bath with her toaster after all.

My brother gone for good. No need to keep running and hiding, the truth is out there now. Rory is already working on a plan to get my mom to the Heights, and she and I had a long, long call a little bit ago. A surprisingly large portion of the world is listening to my story, what I have to say, *and* I have the chance to be on *Vixens* (while I'm still alive).

I could pinch myself to make sure I'm not dreaming.

The one thing that's keeping me from being on cloud nine is this rift in the ether, this fight with Weston.

I have missed texts from him that I haven't brought myself to look at yet. I just needed a day to myself.

Had he not shown up, dick swinging, ready to piss on me in front of my brother to stake his claim, I would've gone to his house last night and we could be together right now.

But no, he had to explicitly disrespect my wishes, showing up to protect me when I didn't need him to.

Did he even stop to think after everything I shared with him why I wouldn't want that?

Does he even realize what it means for me to *trust* him at this point in my life?

Breathing deeply, I take a sip of my Alani and let the memories flood me. All the reasons I have to trust him. The ways he's earned my trust, time and again these past three months.

Rescuing me from the side of the road, offering to help fix Van Gogh when I couldn't afford it, bringing me along on the paint jobs. Everything we shared with one another in our late-night chats, the closeness we developed over weeks of spending day after day together.

And then, the physical aspect. How he knew what I needed—not just what I liked, but intuited what I was comfortable with, and what I wasn't. Sex with him is incomparable to anything I've experienced before. It's just one more way he showed he really knew me, he got me in ways no one else ever has.

Then there was how he went up against his brother for me. Repeatedly.

My stomach swoops at the thought of him working so hard to repair his relationship with his brother but being willing to burn it all down for me.

Without a doubt, my feelings for Weston haven't gone anywhere, which makes this all the more annoying.

There's just this disappointment, this unease bubbling in me at the way he disregarded what I needed and the boundaries I set. But this knot in my stomach is *because* I love him so much. Having this disturbance between us is killing me.

A voice in my head—my conscience can be a real bitch—points out he really hasn't done anything to break my trust, other than to try back me up when I've had an opponent. First Wyatt, then Randall. He went to bat against his own brother for me, then mine too.

Somehow, in the daylight, that seems more sweet than overprotective prick. Or maybe that's just me sleeping on the perspective Rory jammed down my throat.

Am *I* the asshole for the way I've reacted?

The man has been one green flag after another.

It's my own issues that are the problem, isn't it?

I hate when I'm the problem.

I need fresh air.

Locking Van Gogh, I trek through the woods on the side of the lot I'm parked in until I find a spot to sit down on a large, flat boulder.

The air is balmy, even after dusk it's humid. Summer is here. I breathe in through my nose, out through my mouth, appreciating the warmth after the chill of spring.

How long am I going to punish him?

What will it take for me to be able to go back to him, talk out what went down, and work out how to not have this happen again?

I thought time alone would help, and I guess it has in a way. I needed to process, and I have. But I miss him so much it hurts. This emptiness inside me feels wrong after all the ways we've grown so damn close.

But then again, that's why this hurts so bad isn't it?

I *did* finally trust him.

And like my dad, he didn't respect me enough, didn't trust me enough, and had to handle it his own way.

My talk with Lexi comes back to me, along with Rory's harsher words, and I shut my eyes against the truth that's staring me in the face.

I *know* Weston is nothing like my dad in those ways. I've known it since the first night we met.

He's healthy, well-adjusted, comes from a loving family where he's the apple of his parents' eyes. Of course he's going to think he can just show up for me.

That's what his family does, right?

Wyatt, Rory, Lexi. They all show up for one another when they're struggling or in need.

It's me. I'm the asshole who wants to do it all alone, but only because I've had to. It's the only thing I know at this point.

My thoughts are interrupted by a burst of feminine giggles and a voice too low to make out the words, but it doesn't take long for the bodies that go with the sounds to appear on the path coming out of the woods.

A couple are walking together, she's probably around Weston's age, long blonde hair and a curvy body that's noticeably pregnant. The man with her looks to be even quite a bit younger than I am, mussed, slightly curly reddish-brown hair, his heavily tattooed arms wrapped around her and wandering freely as they go. There's gotta be at least ten years between them, but it's clearly not stopping them.

Cheeks flushed, she giggles, leaning harder into him as they walk until her eyes fall on me sitting on the boulder on the side of the path.

Abruptly the woman stands up straight and pushes her partner's hands off of her baby bump, where one hand was going north and one south.

He murmurs something into the curve of her neck, not realizing yet that they aren't alone—or maybe just not caring—and *I* almost blush from the intimacy of it.

"Stop," she giggles. "We're being inappropriate, honey bunny."

"If you want inappropriate, I can show you—"

The woman reaches backward to place one hand over his lips and stops him mid-sentence. With her free hand—can't miss that ring on it, even in the twilight—she points at me.

"Oh," he says, straightening, wrapping his arms around her in a move that looks casual, like touching her every second he gets is just what's normal for them.

"Sorry to interrupt you guys," I whisper, eyes starting to water at how easy and evident their love is.

The curvy blonde giggles again, voice high-pitched, soft and feminine as she speaks again. "No, I'm so sorry. Newlyweds," she gives me a knowing look with a shrug. "He can't keep his hands to himself."

"Never gonna change, Ell." He whispers the words against her temple, but I hear them even over here. "Married a couple months or going on fifty years."

She shushes him again, swatting at him, but that radiant smile on her face doesn't dull for even an instant.

"I'm sorry again, hope you have a good night."

"Don't apologize," I say, waving in their direction. "Please. If you've got a love like that, don't waste a minute of it."

The younger man winks at me before wrapping his arms around his wife even tighter and shuffling back toward the parking lot with her.

"Good advice," I hear him say to her in a low voice, but it's my own words that punch me in the gut as the couple falls out of earshot.

For the first time I have a chance at a love like that. And here I am, wasting precious moments of it.

Staring into the trees, listening to the soft whistle of the wind as it blows between the leaves, now full and deep green, I startle when I see a light.

Yellowish green, so tiny that at first I think I imagine it, but then there's another. And another. In minutes I'm surrounded by fireflies.

A million magical reminders of the love I share with Weston.

And I'm the one that left him when he tried to show me that love by being there for me.

Dropping my head in my hands, I shake with the realization that I'm the one who fucked up. He tried to do this together, I pushed him away and handled it like I always have. On my own.

But I'm not on my own anymore.

Every single firefly lighting up around me is another reason I have to go back and work this out with him, rather than wallow by myself.

Isn't that the point of love after all?

To share in the good, the boring, and the unthinkably horrible?

That things are just that much better when we're together?

"Fuck," I say to the empty clearing.

Sprinting back to my van, I know what I have to do and I send a text I shouldn't have to because I never should've run.

ME

> Meet me at our spot in three hours.

And then I get out my laptop.

IF I WAS MORE PATIENT, maybe I'd have had a better idea on how to show this man what he means to me. How all in on him, and us, I am. Maybe I would've gone and bought some paint for our place together, some other demonstration of the kind of permanence I want with him, our friends, the Heights period.

But now that I've realized where I belong, who I should be with, talking this out with... I did the best I could with the lack of patience I have, then tested the acceleration on the new engine and transmission to get back to him.

When I pull up to the empty field where we made memories to last a lifetime, I grab the extra blanket I keep in one of the wooden drawers and race to the grass to set it up before he arrives.

Placing the laptop on the ground, I prep myself for his arrival, trying to quell the butterflies in my stomach. More than nerves, it's excitement to share with him the things I realized in the thirty or so hours we spent apart.

When I hear another car in the distance, I turn to where I parked, breath held to see if the headlights bounce across the grass lot or pass by. As the beams of light illuminate the field, I run to where he'll stop and park.

Weston makes it before I do, hopping down from his pickup and jogging toward me, stopping to brace himself in the beam of the headlights that silhouette him in the quiet night air.

Those strong arms are open and ready for me. He wraps me in them as I collide into him, enveloping me in his woodsy, masculine scent and that feeling of safety I've never found with anyone else, not since I was twelve. I didn't think I'd ever feel it again, but this man has shown me so much I thought I'd never get to experience.

"I'm so sorry, angel," he whispers into my hair.

"I am too," I murmur into his chest.

Lips pressed to the top of my head, Weston apologizes wordlessly.

"I shouldn't have left," I tell him.

"I'm sorry I made you feel like you needed to."

Shaking my head, I step back, pulling him by the arm to follow me to the blanket where we can overlook the mountain range I've come to associate with a place to call home. Friends that feel more like family. Love.

We sit on the blanket, nestled close to one another but still facing each other.

Taking a deep breath, I go first. "I've been on my own for so long, only worrying about protecting my identity, staying safe. I haven't had to think of anyone else but me in all this time. But I can see now that you do. You always think of me in your actions, Weston. We might handle things differently, and maybe we have some work to do in some areas, but you're the only one I want to do this thing with."

"This?" he asks, waving a hand between us.

"This," I say emphatically, nodding my head. "Life, living, adventures, love, all of it."

His throat bobs with a heavy swallow, and a weight leaves my shoulders.

"I have something to show you." Pulling the laptop in front of us, I wake the display and the screen comes to life on a Pinterest page.

A new board, called "Finally Home."

I hear him suck in a breath as he reads the title, his eyes—the color of the woods all around us—taking in picture after picture I've pinned to the board already.

A converted van that looks a lot like mine.

A close-up of a dirt-streaked masculine hand holding a wrench, working on a car.

Cold cans of beer, condensation dripping down the sides, like we shared that first night we stayed up all hours talking.

Fingers clenching bedsheets, the way he's made mine do, even before we gave in to each other's pull.

Paint rollers, cans of paint, and specific shades that we used as we brought the town back to life. The black and white stripes of the bakery. The pale pink of the cafe. An aqua that shouldn't work in a pizza place, but it does somehow.

A bed that looks a lot like his, the one we shared our first night together, when we weren't allowed to touch.

The Welcome to Downtown Smoky Heights sign that I found a picture of on the New Heights website and saved to my Pinterest.

A tater tot hotdish, so similar to the one I made for us our first night we were together, when we were just a hundred feet from here, over by the wildflowers.

Sunrise over the Smokies, for a morning I'll never forget.

Bowling pins, for the night I never left.

A dark, gritty shot of some chains hanging that makes me blush when I look at it.

The synchronous fireflies.

A motorcycle that looks suspiciously familiar.

Places we both still want to go, like Maine, Rhode Island, and that cute ski town out west he was so interested in.

Dozens of other pictures of adventures we've discussed, plus some things we haven't yet.

A small house out in the woods.

Wedding rings.

Maternity photos.

And a neon sign that says happily ever after.

By the time I stop scrolling, my eyes are so wet I can barely make out the blobs on the screen.

"Fuck, Amelia." His voice breaks, thick with words unsaid, and he dips his head down to pinch the bridge of his nose.

"I'm ready for life with you," I tell him. "Whatever adventures we chase, I want them together from here on out."

"Thank God," he says, relief flooding his voice. "Because you're it for me, Amelia. There's no one else out there for me but you. But I need you to know how much I respect you too. Maybe I need to do better when it comes to your boundaries after what you've been through, but—"

I place a finger over his lips, silencing him.

"I overreacted, and I see that now. I need to learn how to do life *with* you, not all alone."

He nods against my finger, and I drop my hand down into his lap so he can speak again.

"It's not that I think you *can't* do it on your own. It's that you don't have to."

My eyes fill with tears at the trust he has in me, the confidence in me, and the love to be by my side through it all. The permission to share my burden, when I need to. To be stronger together than we are apart.

I don't have the words for what that means to me, but I try anyway. "I love you, Weston. I don't want to do things on my own anymore. I thought being independent was what made me strongest, but I was wrong. I've never been stronger than when I'm with you. Neither of us *needs* each other, but we've chosen each other, and that's more beautiful than I ever knew love could be.

"I *want* to do this with you, together, as a team. It must've been so hard for you yesterday and I'm sorry for the way I reacted. I've had time to think and one thing I realized being away from you is when you have a love like this, you don't waste a minute of it."

One of his thick fingers catches the tear that's escaped my left eye, and I let my face rest in his cupped hand.

"Don't tell my Charger, but Van Gogh is my favorite vehicle I've ever worked on, Amelia, and that's because it led me to you. I'll be thanking the cosmos and the entire damn universe until I die for picking *that* spot out of every highway in the country to have you break down on that night. The way you talk to yourself, your obsession with gory podcasts, your ridiculously morbid sense of humor, the way you're so unbelievably resilient, and let's not forget those magnificent tits. You're all I could ever want and more. Let's do this shit together, darlin'."

I laugh through my tears, resting my forehead against his as he grins at me.

"The good, the boring, and the unthinkably horrible," I reply with a soft smile that feels like it's glowing.

His lips crash down on mine—soft, then passionate—thanking me, teasing me, promising me a lifetime of love.

When we break for air, I bring up my one concern. "Promise me we're not going to become that boring couple who settles down and just stays home with their goldfish. Tell me we'll still have adventures, we'll still be us, no matter what else changes."

"First of all, I've heard goldfish are, like, really hard to keep alive. I don't think I want one either." A smile twists his roguish, handsome features. "But you and I could never be boring, darlin'. Together, you and I are magic. But if you want to settle down and make a home with me, I promise we'll still make it fun."

"Wherever you are is home now, Boy Scout. But if it's okay with you, I'd kind of like it if we stayed here."

His grin is electric and it lights up my insides.

"I was hoping you'd say that. I have just the place in mind for us."

Epilogue
Amelia

Two months later

Transcript of:
Vengeful Vixens
Episode 601
Recorded in June
Released in August

Jynx: Welcome back, Vixens. Season six is going to bring you a whole lot of vengeance, I hope you're ready, babes. We're kicking off the season *strong* here in episode one. I'm here with Amelia Marsh, who as many of you saw in the headlines recently, is the same person as Angel Sanford, daughter of Artie Sanford, also known as the Santa Slayer.

Amelia: Uh, yeah, hey.

Jynx: We had planned to do an episode this season on the Santa Slayer, but when the article came out on you, Amelia, I knew we had to change our angle.

Amelia: Mmm?

Jynx: Rather than focus on the crime and his actions, we wanted to instead bring attention to the people left behind. The effects crimes of passion have on the survivors.

Amelia: Thank you for that.

Jynx: No, babe, thank *you* for being brave enough to come on here and tell your story. After so many years of working so hard to keep your identity a secret and just *move on* with your life, it can't be easy to come out to millions of listeners and get this personal about something so terrible.

Amelia: [laughs uncomfortably] It's not easy for me. I think everyone handles trauma differently. I know a lot of people are able to go on documentaries and rehash it, but for me, I just wanted to keep my past locked away. But with everything that's happened, I think this is the right thing to do now. And for the record, I wouldn't have done this with anyone but you, Jynx. Huge Vixens girl here.

Jynx: [squeals] Are you really?

Amelia: Oh, big time. My partner would rat me out if I didn't tell you myself so I might as well come clean. I think, for a while there, you were kinda my best friend, Jynx.

Jynx: Awwwww.

Amelia: Saying that out loud, it's sounding a little creepy. [laughs] I take it back.

Jynx: No, stop!

Amelia: But, yeah, I listened to you while traveling the country all alone in my van, rooting for the survivors all the way, in every story.

Jynx: A true badass Vixen in front of me, babe.

Amelia: Thanks.

Jynx: Now you've been on the road, living in a van, all this time, alone? Just to escape the stigma and the judgment you got from your local community after your father snapped?

Amelia: More or less. There were more reasons than just that, but, yeah, escaping the reminders of the incident and judgement over it was a big reason. I've finally settled down somewhere though, just recently. I'm done being a nomad for the time being, and my time in hiding is over.

Jynx: And what have you been doing to support yourself all these years? You didn't even have a social media profile until the day you published that article so you're clearly not an influencer living off of income from van life videos.

Amelia: [laughs] Definitely not. I write code, I'm a programmer.

Jynx: We love a baddie in STEM! What kind of programming do you do?

Amelia: Web apps mostly.

Jynx: Say less! Let's talk after the show, I might have a project for you.

Amelia: For sure!

Jynx: So tell me what you're passionate about, Amelia. What is your message for other Vixens?

Amelia: Mostly I'm just trying to do whatever is possible to prevent crimes from taking place, especially ones that change dozens of lives in an instant. Look, do I think bringing awareness to the effects of actions like my dad's is going to actually stop them from happening? Odds are that it won't, but I'm not going to *not* try to do what I can about it after what my family and I have been through.

Jynx: [claps] And there's a charity you're helping gain some time in the spotlight, isn't that right?

Amelia: That's right, the link will be in the podcast description if anyone wants to donate to help the victims' families. I've been donating to it for years, but even fifteen years later countless lives are still affected daily by the tragedy, and many never recover. Even small donations add up.

Jynx: Is it okay with you if I make an announcement?

Amelia: Um, yeah, I mean, it's your show. [nervous chuckle]

Jynx: Because of Amelia's story making waves, how brave she's been coming out and speaking up, changing the lens of how we look at modern true crime, *Vengeful Vixens* is creating a non-profit, Vengeance for Victims, geared toward helping survivors and families of victims who have been affected by tragedies like the ones we discuss on the show. More than just killer entertainment, we want to be a force for good.

Amelia: [gasp] No shit!

```
Jynx: Zero shit, babe. And moving forward,
every sponsor who wants to work with our show
will be making a mandatory, sizeable contribu-
tion as part of their sponsorship. We're also
doing an outreach program to various media
organizations, corporations, and other enti-
ties who profit off of the true crime industry
and shows like ours, encouraging them to make
meaningful donations as well. And listeners,
if you'd like to participate, the link is in
the episode description.

Amelia: [sniffles] I don't know what to say, I
have no words.

Jynx: That doesn't really go over well on a
podcast, babe.

[both women laugh]

Jynx: Tell me about this place you found to
settle down in! What finally got you off the
road for good?

[end of transcript excerpt]
```

It's some sort of cosmic irony that my podcast with Jynx is airing the same day of the grand opening of Downtown Smoky Heights. New beginnings all around, my favorite.

"Mom!" I wave, standing on my tiptoes in the crowd, trying to flag her attention.

Damn these genes she gave me that only let me grow to five feet tall.

"Mom, over here!" I shout.

Through the throngs of people, I see Weston's golden head bobbing through the crowd, guiding my mother toward me. Apparently he has no problem locating me. Like it's a sixth sense of his, he beelines right for me, my mother's arm linked through his.

"Here you are, Billie," he tells my mom, kissing the top of my head. "Delivered you to your daughter, safe and sound"

My mom insisted on him calling her by her first name, and it's beyond adorable how they get along. Hopefully his mom gets here soon and the women can hang out together during the celebration. They've been getting along so well, Mom seems to be adjusting to her new life faster than I did.

"This is quite something, isn't it?" she says, eyes aglow with excitement I can't remember seeing on her since I was a child. "That sister-in-law of yours really put on a heck of a celebration," she says to West, and he smiles at her kindly.

"She sure does."

He shoots me a meaningful wink.

Rory's been working on us, trying to convince us to let her plan our wedding. We're not even engaged, but that's not stopping her from trying to start planning.

With the New Heights project winding down, she'll mostly be practicing corporate law again, with the reduced workload on the commission front. Rory's been very adamant that she will have time for an event of "this magnitude," as she keeps saying.

If he asked, I'd marry him in the woods tomorrow, with just the fireflies and our family as the witnesses, but she says Weston's waited so long to marry me that he deserves an affair to remember.

I argued that he's only known me for five months, he hasn't waited long at all by most people's standards.

She said it's been closer to twenty years he's been waiting and that shut me right up.

Maybe once we're back from our trip to Maine and Rhode Island she'll finally get me. That's if he proposes.

Lexi walks through the crowd near us, and I fail to get her attention too.

"Lex!" West has to yell so loud she can't possibly miss it and her head jerks up.

We wave her over and she shuffles our way, with none of the verve I'm used to from her.

"You ready for the big day?" I ask, nudging her with my arm. "Heights Bites is going to be officially open!" Well, it's been open since May, but this feels pretty epic. "Grandly open!" I amend.

Her face falls, what little color she had in it turning ashen.

I frown, but before I can ask her what's wrong, she's gone again, off through the crowd.

"She'll be okay," my mom says, and I'm inclined to trust her. After all, Lexi's her boss now, and a much better one than she had at her last job.

A bell tolls and the crowd's chatter falls to a hushed whisper.

"Thank you so much for coming to the grand reopening of Downtown Smoky Heights!" Rory's amplified voice reaches us from a podium near the top of downtown, where a giant red ribbon is tied between the sides of the black metal archway that welcomes you to downtown.

The applause is deafening, because every single resident in

this town knows none of this would be happening without Rory Weiss-Grady at the helm.

By her side is the mayor of the town, as well as most of the owners and proprietors of the downtown shops and establishments, almost all faces I recognize at this point.

Giant ropes hang down from each side of the street, connected to banners of green cloth, covering every single sign along both sides of the downtown strip.

Once they cut the ribbon, the representatives of all the downtown businesses will line up on their side of the street and pull, freeing the rope and revealing all the overhead signs at once.

Near Aurora, I spy Wyatt (holding our niece), Duke, even Wilder is up there. I look for Lexi, figuring that's where she ran off to, but being so short I don't have the best view back here. This place is packed.

After the roar of appreciation quiets down, Rory continues her speech about the project, what it means to the town, and to her specifically. Her words move me to tears, but then again, I have been a little bit emotional lately.

Placing a hand on my belly, I stand on my tiptoes, getting as close to Weston's ear as I can. As aware of me as he always is, he leans down to hear what I have to say.

"I'm glad the next generation of Gradys is here for this day."

A heartbeat, then two, and Weston's jaw drops as his eyes travel from my eyes to my stomach, then he scoops me up in his arms and hugs me to him, combat-booted feet dangling in the air.

"When?" he asks, lips to my ear.

"My guess is that day on the motorbike," I tell him.

"My little Ninja baby," he croons.

"We are not naming our baby Ninja."

"No," he says. "I have the perfect name."

Pulling my head back so I can look at him eye to eye, I watch.

"Axle. Axle Billie Grady."

My eyes spring a leak again. "That is kind of perfect," I admit.

He puts me down gently, lowering me until my feet touch the ground, and I bring one of his hands to my stomach, intertwined with mine over my dress.

"You are already so loved, Axle," I whisper to my growing belly. "Your whole family can't wait to meet you."

Weston leans down, and though he speaks quietly, like my ears are tuned to his frequency I catch his words.

"You're going to be our best adventure yet."

A REQUEST FROM THE AUTHOR

Did you enjoy this book? If so, would you be willing to take a few seconds to leave a rating or a review on Amazon and/or Goodreads?

Your word of mouth makes all the difference for new indie authors like me. ♡

Keep reading for a sneak peek of *Playing with Fire*, book 3 in the Smoky Heights series, coming soon to Kindle Unlimited. You can preorder it now on Amazon!

XOXO,
Maddie

PLAYING WITH FIRE
SNEAK PEEK

ONE

WILDER

Pressing on her soft warmth, I watch as juices run out of her thick center.

Damn, I love a juicy girl.

Testing to be sure, because I don't wanna rush and do this before she's good and ready, I push again with two thick fingers, mouth watering as more of that delicious moisture spills out, over and down the thighs.

Perfect. She's ready.

The corner of my lips pops up in a smirk of self-satisfaction.

And to think, I get to do this dozens of times a day, all in a day's work.

"Order up!" I call, tapping the bell on the counter to remind the customer to come back to my corner of the bodega and grab their food that's still sitting there.

I dress a fresh hoagie roll with my special love sauce. Homemade herbed peppercorn aioli, rather than some shit that arrived in a twenty-five gallon drum, "fresh" off a barge where it took two months to ship here.

Nah, my shit's homemade. Full of love. That's why I call it

my love sauce. I even grow the herbs myself, on the roof of my shitty building in Queens.

The bottle squirts out, making a lewd noise that I laugh at, because even though I'm twenty-seven, I'm clearly a child at heart. We're getting low. Gotta fill 'er up with more love when I get the chance.

"Thank you!" The person picks up their sandwich and taps the counter in greeting. Downright *kind* for a New Yorker. Probably a transplant, my guess is from the South, where everyone is sickeningly sweet.

Placing the warm, juicy chicken thighs atop the sauced buns, I spread the rest of the toppings on, then sprinkle on the finishing touches.

Wrapping her up—I'm a stickler for such things—she's ready to go. I turn around, foot long in hand (sandwich, not my sausage), I find the person who ordered it still standing there, waiting impatiently, annoyance all over their face.

I hand over the sandwich. "Your Chicken Love Supreme."

"That just sounds gross," they say, swiping the package from my hand and taking off.

They clearly have somewhere to be that's more important than a thank you.

Yeah, that's what I'm more used to.

I sigh contentedly. This is what it feels like to be home.

Naming the sandwiches I created was my stipulation for taking this job. Ken, the bodega owner, doesn't give two shits what I do back here, as long as it doesn't get him any health code violations or fines. He's raking in a lot of dough with me behind the counter, too. The Chicken Love Supreme is a newer addition to the menu, and it might be my current fave.

It's not the job I dreamed of as a head chef, or even a leg up in the food industry so I can get there one day, but I get to make people food I'm passionate about, fill their mouths with my love day in and day out, and for now, it's gotta be enough.

I do get occasional odd jobs, filling in for a line cook here or there when emergencies happen, but the bougier places I'm interested in working at don't wanna hire a convict who's done hard time. And I don't wanna do dishes at a taco joint just to say I got the experience. So the bodega sandwich counter it is. For now.

Until the day I can open Salt + Spice, *Executive Chef Wilder Amante* at the top of the menu.

Prison took away a lot of options for me, but it also changed my perspective, and it gave me a dream.

I didn't always have this sickeningly cheery outlook, compared to my fellow brethren of the Big Apple.

When you grow up in a family like mine, with a life like mine, your outlook is dark. Shit, your whole past is dark.

But I found a new life seven years ago, when I walked out of the state penitentiary. Fresh air in my lungs, fresh passion for being in the kitchen thanks to my work assignments at the pen, I was ready for a fresh fucking start.

In my family's line of work, that's unheard of.

I did my time and got out. I'm on a new path now. Even got a deal made, so it's official, and that shit never happens.

But I'm Wilder Amante. I carve my own fucking path.

It's been almost eleven years since the day I got thrown in juvie before I was tried as an adult and locked away for four years and seven months over my crimes.

That was the day that changed it all for me.

I haven't been in *the life* since the day I got put in cuffs.

But sometimes I still have nightmares that I never got out.

Even making sandwiches for gruff assholes who don't give me the time of day is better than where I've been, and worse, where I was headed.

Getting started on the next order, I use my favorite knife, a 8.25" Moritaka AS Gyuto, to dice the roast chicken for the sandwich. The same knife peeks back at me in black and white on the mirrored backsplash along my workstation, from among the sea of tattoos covering my arms. They cover my whole body, really, but my entire forearm has a to-scale homage of the knife I can't live without along the outside, and I'd be lying if I said it didn't turn me on in a weird way to see it as I'm chopping the meat for my next customer.

What can I say? I'm a passionate guy. And you know what they say, a chef's best friend is a sharp knife.

With meticulous care, I spread my roasted red pepper jam on the bottom half of the roll, making sure to coat it evenly, and toss the spreader back in the prep container.

The meat gets piled on next, followed by a few dollops of smoked crème fraiche and a dazzle of arugula, and she's good to go.

"Order up!" I call, tapping the bell, and so the day goes on. Just like every other.

The midday lunch rush comes and goes, and I've had the chance in the downtime to restock my station, making sure all of my homemade sauces, spreads, jams, and garnishes are full and good to go for the late afternoon crowd that'll be hitting on their way home from work.

It's a life I'm sure plenty of people would find ways to complain about, but the shit I've seen? Hell, the shit I've *done*? I don't forget where I came from that easily. Can't let myself take for granted that shit could always be worse. A lot worse than making food I love that helps keep the people of this city running.

No risk of getting arrested for doing *this* job.

Probably not even a real risk of being killed while doing it.

Not like my pops.

ONE

The bell on the counter rings, but I didn't press it, so some impatient fucking New Yorker must need their sandwich and need it *now*.

I turn around, ready to give them hell, because *no one* gives me shit once they see me. The 6'5" height on this Italian stallion probably has something to do with it. The giant man who can bench press a couple of correction officers, and has the full body tattoos to prove it, he doesn't get much opposition.

I think it's the neck and finger tattoos that really seal the deal for me. Even the knuckle tat that spells out LOVE across my right hand, it somehow doesn't endear most people to me.

I think it's sweet.

A play on words, my last name means lover, and I put love into everything I make. It was a no brainer. But others think it just adds to the fear factor that I tend to give people, maybe some relic of the shadows of my past that seep through, even when I try to tamp them down.

Could be that the hint of crazy that I had to rely on to keep me alive in prison has never really gone away.

Whatever the case, when people see my face, they don't fucking push me.

But in front of my sandwich counter is a face I haven't seen in an *age*. A woman much, much smaller than me, even at her taller stature in those fancy heels. She wouldn't hesitate to put me in my place, no matter how intimidating I look, and a smile breaks out on my face at the sight of her.

"Aurora!"

My voice booms, no helping it, I've got a thing with volume control. When you're this big, delicate isn't really an option, unless I'm finishing a plate.

Her sophisticated face doesn't give way to much often, but she gives me a big fucking smile today.

"Where ya been, loca?"

The man standing behind her, facing the other way, pulls up straight when he hears my voice. Dark hair, buffalo checked shirt, I can tell even from behind he's not a pretty boy, but I don't know what to make of him yet. I didn't even realize she had anyone with her until I saw his spine straighten.

Turning around, what I'm *not* expecting is to see a baby strapped to his chest, over a Henley, beneath the open button down shirt over it. A little baby girl floats, cooing as she hangs from the carrier strapped to the scruffy man with the grumpy face.

"It's Rory now," he says to me, voice gruff and colder than I'd like. He wraps a possessive arm around Aurora's shoulders, and that's when I notice the boulder sparkling on her hand.

"This where you been?" I ask her, pointing to the man and baby.

She nods, eyes softer than I'm used to seeing them, not seeming to mind that she's got a second asshole attached to her side.

"I moved back home. To Smoky Heights."

"Well doesn't that just sound lovely."

Like something you'd hear in a fairy tale, or maybe see on a postcard.

"*This* is the bodega guy?" Her husband, according to the band on his finger—and that aura of *fuck right off when you look at my wife*—says incredulously, looking between his wife and me.

He doesn't think we hooked up, does he? Maybe it's just the normal threat I tend to pose, no matter how good-natured I am these days. Old habits die hard.

"Aww, you talked about me? How sweet." I flutter my eyelids at her a couple times, and hear a grumble from the guy she's with.

Rory cuts me a look that says not to push this, and I ease up, because after all these years of making her sandwiches, I'm not convinced she wouldn't shove a heel up my ass if I pissed her off.

And considering it's against my ethos to hit a lady, unless it's a nice smack to the ass while I'm hitting it from behind, well... You can see my predicament.

"Name's Wilder. Wilder Amante, nice to meet you, my guy."

"Wyatt Grady."

ACKNOWLEDGMENTS

As a preteen back in the 90s (I'm old, I know), I borrowed a YA series from my local library called *Trash* by Cherie Bennett that gripped me. One of the characters had a secret not unlike Amelia's, and it changed the way I viewed things at a very young age and gave me perspective, making me wonder about the struggles different people face.

Being someone who is enthralled with true crime (as any millennial basic bitch is), once it hit me, Amelia's backstory wouldn't leave me alone until I brought it to life. It was immensely uncomfortable and nuanced, and something I stressed over for the past year. In the end, there were many people who made this book what it is today, who I'd like to thank.

My bitchstie, Kaymie Wuerfel. Is there an echo in here? This is the sixth book I've written acknowledgements for now, and every single one says the same thing, so sorry if you're tired of hearing it by now, but none of them would've been written without you. I don't know how anyone writes a book alone; for me it takes a village, and you are 90% of that village, friend. Thanks for taking my childhood dream, the dream I shelved in my twenties, and making me believe it was still worth going after in my thirties. Getting to bring our imaginary friends to life together is the actual dream. Counting down to the mountain.

The best alpha reader an indie could ever ask for, Dani (_danireads). I can't tell you how much smoother this process of bringing stories into the world has become since you became my alpha reader and biggest hype girl on the planet. I'm not sure how many versions of this book you ended up reading and cheering me on through, but one thing I do know is that Smoky Heights and I would not be the same without your support. Forever thankful for all of your feedback and endless love, your voice notes crying, the infinite giggles, and the way you never stop shouting from the rooftops about my characters.

My beta readers, Maddie, Jenna, August, and most especially, fellow romance author Sophie Hamilton, for helping me take a rough draft and turn it into a finished book. If you ever get sick of me, Sophie, I don't know what I'll do without you. Your keen insights are always so spot-on, and I thank you extra for helping make some of the key scenes in this book that much stronger with your brilliant input.

The beautiful ladies on the content team (the New Heights HQ) who have been helping promote this book and this series, spreading the word about Smoky Heights to all the romance readers who haven't found their way to the Heights just yet. Thank you for your enthusiastic support in every sneak peek, every release, and for helping me with the playlist for this book to boot!

To the ARC readers who gave this book (and me) a chance, thank you for being the first to dive into Weston + Amelia's story, and for telling others who might enjoy them so I can keep following my dream to bring more stories to romance lovers.

All my readers who have taken a chance on me, picked up a book (or five) and especially when you've introduced others to my worlds. Your word of mouth is everything to me and I am so thankful for your support in these early stages of my career.

The cover designer, Sam at Ink and Laurel, for another banger.

My proofreader Juli Burgett, for making me feel easy to

work with even when I probably drive you crazy with my commas and em dashes galore.

My PAs: Paige, you're a literal angel and I adore you. Sarah, I appreciate the blood, sweat, and the tears you put in with me more than you know. Cortney (yes, Cortney from the *What the Smut* podcast), thank you for so many reasons to smile over the last half a year.

Ellie from Love Notes PR for being the sparkliest gem of a human being, and a dream to work with + call a friend.

My fellow gang lords' wives for being amazing friends in all weather and seasons, and making my cheeks hurt from the smiles you bring me every other month when I finally emerge from the writing cave and catch up on our chat.

My best friends in the world, who all have fur and four paws, but can't read this book or the acknowledgements. You make me happier than words can say, and keep my toes toasty while writing, the value of which cannot be overstated. If I were omnipotent, I would mandate you stay by my side, healthy and happy, fur-ever.

And finally, to the most supportive partner on this whole damn spinning rock floating through space, my husband. You've always believed in me, but damn, this one was tough and I made you prove it more than usual. I hope I made you proud with number six. Thanks for always being down to answer my questions about male anatomy or demonstrate how certain *scenes* could work. Being married to a romance author is a lot of work, but you nail it.

BOOKS BY MADISON MYERS

The Syndrome Series

The Roommate Syndrome

The Complacency Syndrome

The Secrecy Syndrome

Smoky Heights

Rekindling the Flame

Strike the Match

Playing with Fire

Standalones

Always My Forever

See all current & upcoming works at madisonmyersauthor.com

ABOUT THE AUTHOR

Madison Myers is an elder millennial best known for writing contemporary romance books with all the feels and all the spice. Her sassy women and the men who are obsessed with them are the perfect escape for other overworked, undersexed hot messes.

Maddie's love for writing romance started in the boy band fanfic days that predate Gmail and MySpace, and while she might be a disaster at TikTok trends and third-person bios, her calling is spice that'll stick with you. She's fueled by dancing to early 2000s music, and snuggling with her pups + the latest book boyfriend—or her real-life husband (a gold medalist at sharing her with fictional men).

Check out her books on her website:
madisonmyersauthor.com

Connect with Maddie on social (she's trying, bless her heart):

- instagram.com/madisonmyersauthor
- tiktok.com/@madisonmyersauthor
- bookbub.com/profile/madison-myers
- facebook.com/madisonmyersauthor

Made in the USA
Columbia, SC
26 April 2025